Out of Madness

Out of Madness

Rithwik Aryan

ink | OCCAM

ISBN: 978-93-6547-778-8

First published in India 2025
This edition published 2025

BluOne Ink Pvt. Ltd
A-76, 2nd Floor, Sector 136, Noida
Uttar Pradesh 201301
www.bluone.ink
publisher@bluone.ink

Printed and bound in India at Nutech Print Services

ink | OCCAM

To my mom, Ritu Kumar, who became Ritu Jaiswal and
taught me the true meaning of hard work,
dedication, and persistence

Prologue

It's prom night.

I'm four years away from faking my death. Five years away from pleading guilty to three counts of slave trading; three counts of human trafficking; two counts of making child pornography; two counts of distributing child pornography among public institutions, including our local middle schools and even the Parliament; three counts of sodomy; and one count of harbouring a fugitive terrorist in the basement of our mansion.

While the going is good, I'm six years away from faking insanity, seven years away from ending up inside Clemency's Mental Asylum, and eight years away from facing the embarrassment of having to explain my misdeeds over the last seven years to my future wife, Ms Staci (the most talented starlet actress and the heartthrob of our nation).

'Say,' you might be thinking, 'what's the need to offer any sort of explanation about anything to your wife, Moron ji? Who does that anymore? Don't you live in a free country?'

Well, comrade, as you will see, it would become imperative that I offer her an explanation. And it better be a good one, for if she doesn't buy it, then we would both surely die the next day (I mean, my wife and I).

Or, in the very worst case, she would survive, but I sure as hell would be dead. And I would die a virgin. Despite all those erratic convictions, despite being married to another horrible woman at one point in my life, and despite dating an actress of such fine acclaim, I would die a damned virgin.

It's like how my dearest friend Zahed used to sing back in college: 'I have lived a virgin. I'll die a virgin. But if I ever fuck, I sure as hell will fuck a virgin.'

Didn't quite work out for me very well, if you want to know the absolute truth.

Anyway, it's prom night. I've let myself out of the backdoor, unhinged, into the frigid streets of Boston. My face radiating as usual with the same drunkenness from Jägermeister and a few too many LITs, with extra helpings of Grey Goose vodka. A sharp expulsion of coldness from my mouth—a shriek—and then sight: it's late evening. The usual silent seaplanes are settling into the dockyard of Boston Harbor. The Boston skyline shimmers with its glimmering red tower lights. There's a sudden, distant gunshot somewhere, followed by blaring sirens rushing to the crime scene. But here, my sweet, virgin Tania has only just relieved the sergeant of the greatest erection he claims to have ever received. And my sweet, little childhood love, Tania, has done her service. I couldn't have stayed inside that horrible ballroom to hear their great climax.

Over time, I've trained myself to walk in a straight line, no matter how drunk or hungover I am. I've ended up vomiting all over myself a few times in the past because of excessive drinking. No doubt, I have. But mostly, alcohol brings me an unknown solace. Say, if I wake up in the morning after a night of debauched drunkenness, usually my face radiates rather than losing its charisma. Say, if

I've been developing horrible acne on my face over the last few days, with enough alcohol in my veins, it simply disappears.

I begin walking homewards, wary of the many pickpockets who might try to rob me at this silent hour of the evening. And then, I suddenly catch a glimpse of myself in the excellent glass panel of the American Express towers and skyscraper. I'm wearing a white crewneck T-shirt and a pair of black denim jeans. My reflection is inspecting my real self with a glint of amused laughter. I greet myself with a drunken 'Hah!'

If you want to know the truth, I look a lot like my father. A lot. I have the same beautifully carved, innocent Indian face. The same broad forehead. The same perfection when it comes to my beard. No receding hairline and no expected hair loss in the upcoming decades. Phew! I look altogether very charismatic now. With my slender athletic features—my arms, which used to be scrawny throughout my childhood, are now around eighteen inches. My chest, which used to be an assembly line of too many disgusting ribcages, is now packed with solid chest muscles that stretch all the way to my deltoids.

Until now, however, my looks have barely rendered me anything of significance. For instance, I have never been able to assemble three distant, walking Latin fairies at my doorstep in broad daylight just by simply passing by. I have never had an obsessive, psychologically disturbed blonde girl stalk me from my high school to home. I have never been taken upstairs to an empty room during a roaring house party by some crazy, cock-thirsty, five-foot-six-inch, black skirt-wearing brunette whose sole purpose of existence for the past few weeks had been to consume me—raw. I have never had a girl tie my hands to the bed. I have never been blindfolded into absolute surrender by a pair of giggling twin sisters who looked at me naughtily, then at each other, and wondered, 'How do we fuck this evil man into unconsciousness?'

My looks never really worked for me until a few years later when I got back to India. After one failed marriage, one faked death, and one faked insanity later, I goddammit vouched for my own handsomeness by seducing the most renowned, most worshipped, and the most daydreamed-of actresses of our generation—inside a lunatic asylum. But let me not get too ahead of myself. I tend to blabber a lot when I'm drunk. Not because my senses aren't intact but because of the sudden excitement about life that comes when some sweet, expensive alcohol is circulating through my veins.

Anyway, most of the crimes I will be convicted of committing in the near future might end up being psychoanalyzed as various imbalances of libido. A lost identity? A helpless Indian boy getting his afternoon course of beatings on the rushing street of a Boston square? A classic case of juvenile delinquency owing to a person–environment misfit? A failed member of Tajfel's—both the ingroup and the outgroup. Though I have come to learn somewhere that, probably, it was because I looked a little too much like my father.

Here is how it goes.

So when my father brought my mother to Boston—newly married and completely new to the United States of America—and then, a week later, was caught sleeping with some crazy underaged neighbourhood hoe, my mother, too traumatized to accept that her marriage was practically ruined, chose instead to forgive him and maintained her composure as if she were a Buddhist monk. In fact, seeing her incredible composure, I believe my father became so frightened that he decided to mend his ways forever, swearing he would never as much as touch another young, budding chick from our neighbourhood—no matter how drunk she was, no matter if the dirt-ridden ranch of the famous polygamist John Green was only a night's drive away from our house, no matter how badly she begged him to fuck her, or even if he were Kevin Spacey from *American Beauty*.

A few months later, when the minor incident was altogether forgotten and I was still a very recent addition to my family, while I was suckling at my mother's breast one languid evening, she saw a reflection of her husband in my one-year-old face and became so worked up that she ended up unloading her repressed hostility on me. She thrashed me cruelly and restlessly, a fine blue bathroom slipper here, two vengeful claws there, while I cried and wailed, having defecated in my diapers. The whole scene was such that every damned developmental psychologist on this planet would have flocked around my house to examine my case in detail—if it had been sighted or reported by some unsuspecting housewife from our neighbourhood.

I think that would sum up the reasons why I was going to commit such outrageous crimes against humanity in the future—just this one incident. The shock I experienced when I was beaten by my mother while too small to even know my own name. All that brief horse manure of Sigmund Freud about criminals acting out based on their repressed urges. No defined motive. No motivation.

That human being's lack of self-regulation and free will. So I, as an uncivil criminal, acted out of my subconscious motivations. But then there's a more elaborate reason why I committed such atrocities, if you really want to get to the crux of it.

We lived in a closed Boston suburban neighbourhood that primarily comprised Indian communities—mostly professors and academicians of Indian origin who had moved to the States for its excellent remuneration packages and the recognition that folks from the States tended to show for their line of work. Our Indian neighbourhood was only a mile away from the great Harvard Square behind the now-shut McLean Psychiatric Facility. I remember spending my childhood in wild fascination with Harvard, the asylum next door, or the great MIT.

At two years of age, I caught a glimpse of them from the window of our family wagon one afternoon while my father was driving me to the dentist's clinic. I saw three undergrad Californian girls exiting the Beer Café on Downtown Street. Picture this: my nose practically squashed against the closed window of the rear seat, my eyes widened as if they had caught the most dazzling sight human eye can achieve to catch—of these three extremely fine, barely legal college freshers emerging into the afternoon sun from a café in short denim shorts and matching white crop tops, so cropped that had I not been a two-year-old toddler at the time, I would have chased them barefoot—made me utter my very first word: 'Mommy'.

And upon hearing this, my mother turned back, her eyes almost teary, rejoicing that her son's first word was 'Mommy'! But when she noticed that my eyes were not seeing what my mouth had just uttered, she became so furious that she swore I would never be allowed to visit the Boston Square again. My mother feared that if I were caught ogling and potentially molesting the upcoming blonde future of the United States, my father's visa might get cancelled, and we might be forced to return to India forever. Instead, I was promised that the avenues of Boston would open to me on the day I either got into Harvard or MIT. Until then, I had the rest of Boston for my growing up.

Most of my memories from before my preschool are now only accessible to me in the form of comforting, rapid, and almost dreamlike montages that appear and disappear before I can assemble them into any sort of coherence. The earliest memories of my existence are somewhat intact, especially from one summer afternoon after I had turned six years old. My face at that time was beautifully carved, like that of a Gandhara idol of an Indian god—my nose pointy, my eyes as innocent as the eyes of the sleeping Buddha. I'm standing at the very edge of the town, past the Boston Metallurgical Plant, in the company of a few arrogant foreign crappies who live in the same suburban neighbourhood as me but have barely made the effort to even learn my name.

There's a loud blaring from an industrial locomotive nearby, a horn bellowing from a train that is at a standstill on the adjacent railway tracks. Meanwhile, a baseball game is in progress—it's rules I barely understand. That day, I'm fielding at the outer edge of the boundary. With the laws of segregation still governing my childhood, I've never been allowed to bat. I'm standing at the very periphery of the match, almost as distant as the edge of daylight itself.

A few moments ago, there had been a faint disagreement among the two arrogant teams about who should admit me into their group. When the disagreement escalated to a point where it couldn't be settled, the teams decided to simply position me at the very edge of the field—delegating me the task of finding the ball if someone hit a really retarded homerun.

And it's not just that segregation I was wary of. If it had been the only problem of my innocent childhood, I would have raved and rambled and probably started a small protest in my neighbourhood. A small act of non-cooperation, a hunger strike near my community school—to draw the community's attention to the post-modern racial discrimination happening right in our own backyard, gentlemen!

I remember being afraid of simple things. That was the general order of my life. Say, on an evening when we were a troop of children bicycling down an untrodden path, I would usually be the last in the tribe. Pedalling my bicycle and struggling to keep up with the procession, I would be torn between wondering whether I should have joined this expedition in the first place or if it was too late to turn back now. And when our troop would encounter a small yet challenging hillock or a stretch of forest with bushes that were a little too tall and mysterious, I would stop in terror. Unnoticed by the ignorant army, which would continue babbling and cycling forward, I would be left all by myself, unable even to remember how I had managed to get there in the first place.

One evening, while we were exploring the wasteland behind the Boston Water Treatment Facility, I managed to get left behind and was lost so brilliantly that dusk had turned to night before I could decide whether to go back home or keep chasing my troop. Scary sycamores surrounded me, and loud crows began retreating home. A feral dog came to sleep in its usual spot only a few feet away from me. And even before I could come to a decision, my eyes were met with a million silent, dazzling stars in the darkened Boston sky, and I almost knew that I was going to starve and die in that desert within the next few days. And while I prepared for my impending death stoically, a strange man revved towards me on his scooter out of nowhere and enquired jovially, 'Are you lost? Do you want me to drop you home?' It turned out that this Indian man knew my father through an indirect association and was rather happy to drop me at my doorstep.

Till today, I sometimes sit on my front porch and wonder that had it not been for that blessed Indian gentleman that day, but instead had been some child molester (as child molesters were making quite a few rounds in the neighbourhood in those days), and instead of my doorstep, had he taken me to some unidentified doorstep of some unidentified house on some unnamed road, then my organs would surely have been trafficked to the prized international market.

After the horrors of that expedition, I decided that I was better off in my own little suburban neighbourhood. So, I began staying at home, relieving the dullness of my days by playing in my backyard. I experimented with the arrangement of logs and stones, spending endless hours trying to construct small and strategical rain bridges or imaginary war-grade weapons. But then I would grow impatient by the evening, dismantle and ruin my labour, and run inside to have dinner with my father, who would have just returned from his office.

In fact, I discovered that the simple act of lying around and daydreaming was far safer and more enjoyable than actually labouring in such dreadful forests and ending up with a scratched elbow or knee. Sometimes, I would take my baseball bat and a rotting leather ball to the nearby park, and among bored pregnant housewives and a few impatient lovers in sight (who were sniffing for a private spot for their own private playtime), I would play baseball solo. Hitting the ball against a wall, letting it bounce back, and then hitting it again into a home run. An imaginary crowd cheering me—Moron! Moron!—a louder cheer and sataaak! A banger home run.

One might believe that by growing up in such loneliness, I would have become a totally harmless, almost saintly member of society who would go on to produce and raise a dozen moral and harmless children. However, I developed a strange sense of curiosity from such solitudinous expeditions. The sort of curiosity that began putting me in unpredictable troubles—the kind of troubles that couldn't even be managed by a team of, well, just one person.

For instance, on the day of my uncle's wedding ceremony, while my family and guests were packed inside the ceremonial tent, I was busy in a completely different corner of the celebration, experimenting with a giant firecracker (which had been bought for the occasion and had refused to go off despite multiple attempts from multiple people and had been therefore discarded in a corner). When I stumbled across that object of disaster, I began ripping its wrapping until I could see the small fuse of the cracker. Not anticipating that it would actually go off, I set a burning matchstick to the fuse, and that horrible device began going off. It let off bright sky shots into the air, which struck me with awe. However, a few of those sky shots didn't really end up in the sky but simply ripped across the white tent where my uncle's wedding ceremony was happening. Before I could flee, the tent was set ablaze, and people started fleeing. My uncle's new bride had a very narrow escape from being barbecued before he could lay his virgin hands on her huge, round breasts.

A year later, I went to a salon in the downtown market for a nice haircut. The hairdresser had to momentarily step out, leaving his enterprise under my protection. Out of curiosity, I opened his drawer and simply walked off with 500 dollars before he could return. I didn't even need that money. It's not like I was dying under the burden of some international multi-million dollar loan. I just got some unexplainable kick out of it. However, I returned a few days later to that same barber, this time asking him to give me a nice head massage. He recognized me instantly but remained calm as a saint until he finished serving me. And then, just as I was about to leave, he blocked my way to the exit and exclaimed, 'Where the fuck do you think you are going, son?!' He locked the door of the salon and called the cops on me. That bastard even had a CCTV footage of me from my previous visit. It turned out that he had run that footage on the local news for weeks without my knowledge whatsoever. That evening, my poor father had to drive down to the local courthouse bail me out, and there the judge asked him 'to ensure that the little fellow of his mends his ways'. I'm still sometimes plagued by the image of my father crying and sulking in the driver's seat of our wagon as we drove back home. I looked at his face and resolved once and for all to never put him through such anguish again, only to end up robbing a local dentist as soon as I turned thirteen. This time, I was not captured by any CCTV camera or by the victim.

A year later, I shifted my interest to a totally different enterprise—printing forged dollar bills. For this, I partnered with a masturbating school friend of mine, Mukesh. His father had an expensive laser printer in his office, and he would let Mukesh use it because he wanted him to become a digital artist. And a digital artist that rascal became, supplying me with hundreds of fake dollar bills (each printed on one side of an A4 sheet of paper). I had to sit in my room during the evenings for endless hours at a stretch. With a pair of scissors and a glue stick in hand, I would sit and paste those dollar bills. I thought that I would end up making billions from that enterprise until one evening when my mother walked in on me while I was in the middle of my business. On seeing the freshly pasted dollar bills, a look of pure horror crept upon her face. I tried to haggle with her, making excuses and expressions of pure surprise. *Oh hell, Mommy! They belong to a friend of mine. Very rich fellow, I must say. Oh dang, Mommy! I thought it was real money, but what the hell? I think I discovered a chest of fake currency in our very own backyard, haha!* But my mother saw through my bullshit and unleashed such fierce anger on me that evening—whipping me with my brand-new school belt, calling me a traitor, and a Mother India-hating anti-national bastard—that I couldn't stand up the next day. My enterprise ended quite melodramatically—with my mother standing at the edge of the kitchen, a leaking gas cylinder on one side (she had detached the pipe of the cylinder from the stove so that all the LPG was leaking), with a matchbox in her hand. She threatened that she would not only kill herself but also reduce the family to ashes. She said, 'I am done with your father. That rascal sleeping around with underage neighbourhood girls. And his son is trying to commit outrageous crimes right inside his bedroom.' She ultimately didn't set that match on fire, and we all thankfully survived.

Such disastrous affairs in my life continued for an almost endless spiral of time until one Saturday afternoon, near the end of middle school, when I was sitting alone in my veranda, waddling my legs, when a small transport truck idled up to the house right opposite mine and out stepped a white thick-necked Russian carpenter along with what looked like his pregnant wife. Finally, a third person stepped out. It was the first time I saw Tania. She was the same age as me. For many days, we didn't meet or speak, even though we used to go to the same middle school. We were barely thirteen then. With a girl like Tania, I could almost guarantee that with her golden auburn hair, an extremely fair face (which used to practically sparkle in the sun), and her curious grey eyes, she would have grown up into a perfect Russian mistress one day. And, therefore, because of such great perfection on her part, my limited senses altogether failed to register her presence. So, during the course of my childhood, she was as good as the sun or the moon to me. She was always there, but only a madman would want to possess her someday.

Then we encountered each other one spring afternoon. She was squatting on the edge of my front lawn. It looked like she was trying to cremate a dead millipede in the soil. At first, when I went to stand near her, she seemed unaware of my presence. But when my curiosity got the better of me, and I went good-naturedly to peep at her ritual up close, my shadow fell over her, and she got up, startled. I was immediately drawn by her curious, ferociously white, and evidently confused face. She had twisted her head to one side of her torso and was surveying my face for any malicious intent I might be harbouring toward her. After the perceived threat had diminished, she pointed her small fingers towards the deceased insect, as if inviting me to participate with her in its last rites.

That is at least how I have stored our encounter in my heart. But as per an observer's version, it probably would have gone down like this: my princely Indian skin reflected against her white glossy skin. She was startled, but only by my unusually curvaceous, hairy face—my long nose, my expressive eyes—and, abandoning the dead insect right there, she screamed and ran back home (poor girl, holding onto her dear life). A few seconds later, she came out with her mother, who examined me from a distance and explained to her daughter in broken English that I was not a detestable, unsociable monster but rather a human being.

I thought I would be all done with her after that. But later that evening, her mother—probably fearing a wild neighbourhood protestation of 'BOYCOTT ALL WHO BOYCOTT INDIANS' and possible ostracization from our society, in which the majority were Indians—rang our doorbell, greeted my mother with a freshly baked plum cake, and made her daughter apologize to me. We shook hands to commemorate our friendship, which we cherished for a very long time.

The rosy visions I have saved from our last summer of middle school are of the two of us bicycling through the idle summer streets of our neighbourhood with maddening intensity, appearing and disappearing from the front doors of various neighbourhood houses like thunderbolt lightning. Round and round and round. And then, more dangerously, racing like madmen down the Boston City Main Road. Me, speeding on my Indian bike and clearly winning by a record margin, while she pedalled and chased me on her cycle, with her back bent and her small legs rotating like a tiny speed fan. Later, when she started catching up to me, I would skid my bike impressively to outdo her, sometimes leaving twenty feet long tire marks on the street.

One silent afternoon, while our mothers were napping, we had ridden our bicycles a little too far into the bustling township. Past the rushing traffic, cautiously crossing the 43A freeway, and then across town to the 'GO to 24/7 Shopping Centre', where among curious toys and daily household supplies, she bought me an orange Slurpee and a pink lemonade ice-spice.

With Tania, I could become more of a man than I ever thought I had in myself. One evening before Halloween, I courageously took her to a deserted wasteland—the same old, grim forest of which I have saved the most horrible memories—where I had lost my way as a kid and had since refused to leave my neighbourhood. I was leading the way, and Tania was following me dutifully.

When we reached the overgrowth of those tall bushes, she stopped her bicycle, and the look of the same fearful disgust crept upon her face, the one that had once paralyzed me as a kid.

'It's fine, Tania. It's fine. I'm here with you. Come on,' I said cheerily. She did, and we crossed those bushes of uncertainty, only to be met by a nice, gleaming lake on the other side. Though it was also somewhat scary—those news reports of the many dead bodies being discovered on different lakesides in the city by the Boston PD made me a bit anxious. However, there we sat side by side, her Russian reflection mixing into my darkened childhood. She leaned her head onto my shoulder, said something in Slavic, and kissed my neck.

'What is it? Why'd you do that?' I asked, all alert.

But she remained silent.

It's not that she had gotten all helpless and scared at that abandoned lakeside, clutching to me as if her life depended on it. I think she kissed me that day because she felt proud of me for some reason.

Apart from that one isolated incident, though, during the usual school days, it was she who used to protect me from the malice of my childhood. She was my wild Russian protector, often shielding me on rough afternoons from the unruly gang of high school seniors who would corner me in some ghosted alley and ask if my foreskin had been removed successfully—or if not, then I must go and eat pig skin that very afternoon.

'Isn't blowjob haram in your Muslim household, Moron boy?'

'I'm sure your mother's ass would be as tight as yours. All unfucked and all, ha?'

While I would struggle to defend myself, Tania would appear majestically out of nowhere (as if I had signalled her telepathically about the threat to my life), hurling stones and abusing those bastards in Russian. Once they were gone, we would hold hands, and she would buy me an ice cream from her own pocket money in consolation.

As time flew by, Tania grew taller and rounder. Our Human Biology class became more interesting during those days, as Ms Serene would tell us about the myriad of bodily changes occurring among adolescent boys and girls. *Don't be startled when you see such new changes. Your body is just adapting. Girls hit puberty before boys. Girls will notice the broadening of their hips and an enlargement of their breasts. They may also experience their first menstruation.* And broader her hips became. Her breasts were scaling to the perfection of human imagination. Her facial features turned out to be supremely inspired by an artist's creation. Inevitably, she soon joined the school cheerleading team. She started staying back after classes to practise with her girl troop, wearing a short blue skirt and a blue varsity crop top, her legs pubescent and shining brighter than my future. Pompom in both hands, one leg up, and 'Heaah!' Another leg up and 'Heaah!' And then the pompom went left and right and left and 'Varsityyyyy!' And as avid sufferers of American literature would predict, over the course of eleventh grade, she began daydreaming of letting the embarrassing changes of her body be explored and appreciated and enjoyed by the captain of our baseball team—the white drill master Sergeant (who was named Sergeant for his crew cut and a bravado that would belong to an army sergeant)—while I had taken the back seat, being demoted to a social cause that needed her volunteering rather than a psychopathic madman who deserved her friendship.

My puberty didn't hit me. It trampled on me. I had the moustache of an Indian street dog, and as if my skin tone was not already bad, there was a supreme outburst of acne. The situation was so bad that on a drunken night, one could count the stars in the sky more easily than the number of pimples on my face. Such outrageous disasters in my youth made me stick to my many … uh … Indian brothers. We were the usual lot then—the masturbating Dinesh, who was preparing for that year's Math Olympiad and would solve algebra, naked, horny, and drunk; the Bharatnatyam-learning Mukesh, who, if you caught sight of during Thursday's after-school practices—in black spandex tights and an oversized T-shirt—would make you want to commit a mass genocide on Indians; and the Puja sisters, who barely got out of their father's Mercedes S-Class and spent most of their time with their foreign aunties or on expensive vacations to Ibiza and Croatia with their respective boyfriends.

As far as Tania was concerned, with the growing high school years, her prevailing attitude towards me changed. I believe it was her mother who had explained something to her about growing up and all—some real-life wisdom about who she was and where she was meant to be. Something along the lines of: 'Stay away from that boy, Moron. He is going to ruin you. We have worked so hard, so damn hard—your daddy cutting wood all day long, grooming you to date a Russian spy and all. And here you are, showing your titties to the guy who could possibly crash a mighty plane into our neighbourhood someday. He already once tried killing his family and relatives at his uncle's wedding.' And then Tania went all Ms Havisham on me. She greeted me when we met—that she did—but we stopped having our endless conversations. She began taking the bus to school instead of the usual bicycle. Fuck, even in our small classroom, she started sitting in the other corner. She would be warm and cordial when I approached her but would no longer be the first to greet me.

That summer, my mother died during childbirth. That was the exact reason. I'm not mistaken! A damned childbirth while I was about to graduate high school. It had something to do with some disastrous complication during the C-section. That's exactly how I recall it. She had been taken to the hospital for her delivery. The doctors noticed an anomaly and told my father, 'We will be performing a quick surgery on her. If we can get your signature here and here, then we can get going.'

And then she was gone.

Maybe I would have had a permanent Tania in my life if my sister had been born. Maybe I would have seen the world for all its beauty if she had begun irritating me as she grew up. Maybe she would have helped me find a beautiful love. What a brilliant wingman she would have been. But my mother died, altogether exempting me from the cruel effects of a set of vocabulary I soon became deserving of—'motherfucker'.

After her death, my father retreated into solitude, from which he barely emerged until his own death a few years later. Not that he was drinking every night, passing out in his own urine and vomit. Nor did he go on a crazy hooker rampage—fucking every hooker in town. He didn't hit on his students or ask them to spend a weekend getaway with him for a few extra marks. If anything, he took the opposite path. He started sleeping through those long, endless summer days in the strange quietness of his bedroom. The door of his room was usually ajar, and whenever I stood at the door, he would wake up smiling to see me. My father began eating simpler food, lost an enormous amount of weight, and became very lonely.

As far as I'm concerned, I still sometimes sit on my front porch and wonder what had really hit me after my mother's death. The morning after her body was cremated on the banks of the Pacific, I somehow neglected the entire experience of the past few weeks with Tania as if it existed only between the lines of a nightmare and an actual occurrence. The next morning, before school, a restless fluttering settled in my heart. After lunch, I decided that I was in love with Tania. That I had been in love with her ever since we were kids. That love had burgeoned beautifully over the course of a decade, and now it was only a matter of me declaring my passionate la amour for her, and she would lean in and kiss me fervently after hearing my confession.

After school, I desperately hunted for her. When I finally saw her, she was standing near her bus with a friend. I signalled to her from afar. She saw me and gave her friend a look that said, 'I dunno what it is.'

I pulled her to the curb side and told her, 'Listen, Tania, I love you. I have loved you ever since we were kids. Would you want to be my girlfriend?'

And girlfriend she became. Her face acquired a disgusted, horrified expression that I had never seen before. I believe she was going to say something really nasty to me in Slavic. But her rage was only momentary. Then she softened upon seeing my anxious, horrified, motherless face. I believe she still respected the remnants of our childhood friendship and felt sympathetic, given that my mother's death had occurred only a day ago.

So instead of asking me to politely fuck off, she said that she was just glad to be friends with me. She said that she didn't quite feel that way about me at all. And I stood there and took her rejection like a champion. But that, too, was only momentary.

'Very well, Tania,' I said. 'Very well. Okay! How about a few years down the line?' I said, almost breaking into an episode of manic sobbing. 'How about a few years from now? When I might prove my worth to you? Maybe you can become my girlfriend then?'

'Well, we'll see about that,' she said, sighing thoughtfully.

'I mean, what if we are meant to be?' I asked, breaking into a loud, frustrated cry.

'Oh yes! Then we can't do anything about it. All in due time. Please take care of yourself and your papa!' she said, trying to push my insistence by a few years.

The next day, I showed up at her window again. She was sitting at her study chair, busy with some project, when I energetically knocked on her window and rattled it.

She looked at me, startled, and drew the window open.

Standing at the edge of a drainage pipe, I proposed to her again, using the exact same words as the last time—verbatim! As if a second proposal would have knocked some sense into her. *Ah! Yeah, Moron boy. Absolutely. How could I not? Please just climb through that window and fuck me on my bed right away!*

This time, she said that, if I must know, she wasn't attracted to me at all. Not even a cent. And that I should forget about endearing her even five or six years down the line and probably find another girl for myself. She mentioned that she had come across an orphanage down the street with some of the most dazzling Indian girls in need of rescue, and I ought to try that place out.

I didn't.

The next day at school, I cautiously crept up to her and handed her a letter that I had written the previous night.

Dear Tania,

I have come to love you with a madman's desire. You make me want to become a better man for myself.

She was nice enough not to throw that heartfelt letter in the bin. However, around recess, Sergeant came up to me on the playground and said, 'Hey, Moron boy. Stop bothering her, man. She's scared of you now. Plus, everybody knows we're kinda together. Like, I'm ramming her every evening, boy. Why would you want to chase her when she's getting all drilled by the drill master sarge, huh?'

'I'm sorry, Sarge. I'm sure I misunderstood,' I said, promising him that, as an esteemed gentleman of the community, I would honour the code and back off and stop harassing the missus.

Thereafter, I began telephoning her house at random hours, waiting for her to answer. Sometimes her mother would pick up, and sometimes Tania would answer the phone. Whenever I heard her voice, I would get all nervous and immediately hang up, slamming the telephone and running outside, pretending to look for my bicycle, though inwardly hoping to catch a glimpse of her again.

In the month of February (exactly one month before we were to enter the final year of high school), I proposed to her a total of twenty-six times, presenting every damned logic for why she should choose me as a suitable mate. She rejected my proposal all twenty-six times. I believe somewhere in that hallucinatory month, I even told her that I would be absolutely fine being her cuckold for the rest of my life, but all I cared about was being something to her. And then finally, on the twenty-seventh day, she said, 'But why should I be your girlfriend? I mean, who are you? If I do end up dating you, everybody will be like, "Oh, why is Tania dating that guy? Who the fuck is he? A damned nobody!"'

I remained silent.

'No, really, Moron.' (I think it was probably the first time I had heard her use my name in a long time.) She continued, 'Why should I date you? I'll just end up embarrassing myself. Also, I suggest you consult an experienced dermatologist quickly. Oh God, that disgusting acne on your face is leaking. Yuck!' She said this with evident disgust and then walked away.

With these many proposals in line, I think her attitude towards me had changed again—from maintaining a safe friendship with me (because I was motherless, lonely, and her long-time neighbour) to distance, then anger, and finally hatred. After that day, she would become furious as soon as she saw me. Say, if it were lunchtime and I was walking in the corridor of our science block (not even planning to propose to her until school ended) and she unexpectedly saw me, she would get all worked up.

'Can't you please absolutely leave me alone? Oh God. Fuck off. Geez,' she would say.

'But, but…' I would attempt to feebly protest.

'I think I will have to report you to the headmistress.'

'I wasn't even planning to propose to you right now.'

'Yeah, Moron. Just lay it down. Get over with today's anxiety. Why wait until evening? Just do it.' She would mock me and leave with disgust.

And then came the dreaded day of the baseball finals, the grand occasion on which she was to perform and cheer for her captain, the drill master Sergeant. We were also only a week away from our eleventh-grade prom night. From what I presumed, this would be my final attempt of the many final attempts I had made to declare my love for Tania. In preparation, I had gone to the downtown grocery store the previous day and bought her the most expensive chocolate I could afford with my savings. I kept the present neatly tucked in my schoolbag, and then on the day of the finals, when I saw her (in black spandex tights and a black T-shirt) rehearsing near the basketball court with her team, I moved towards her, the chocolate clutched in my hand. She hadn't seen me; she was busy scolding her group and trying out a particular manoeuvre (a fish arrangement) for the evening's performance. I walked up to her and presented her with the chocolate in front of the entire cheerleading team. She looked at me in horror and then at my 10-dollar chocolate. She took that chocolate in her hand, gave it a long patient look, and then flung it on the concrete floor so hard that the poor thing almost ripped itself open.

Words would never suffice to describe the monstrous wrath she unleashed on me that day. Screaming and abusing me in a mixture of English and Russian, her features contorted in fierce disgust, her mouth stinking from days of starvation and dieting, I caught a glimpse of a Tania who was no longer Tania. In that moment of heat, I resolved then and there—I would never love a girl again.

After the horrors of that day, I had a moronic idea of doing something dangerous before prom night. Something that would really push me to the edge. Something whose outcome might even cost me my damned life. She had a point, after all. *Who the fuck was I?* Which depraved girl would want to graduate high school and enter college with the dubious accomplishment of having lost her virginity to Mason Moron? When I look back, even I feel bad for that girl who might have accidentally lost her virginity to me back in high school. Though things are very different now, but still.

So over the weekend, I invited my old ally from my money-minting enterprise—my Indian friend Mukesh—for an exchange of Hardy Boys magazines. One case of Thomas Hardy being exchanged for another. During our meeting, I shared my lonely desire with Mukesh, who had abandoned a future in digital design and was now studying to become a mathematician. Upon hearing about my horrible tragedy with the Russian princess Tania, Mukesh suddenly announced, 'Crack cocaine is the future, boy. No amphetamines. No Adderall. None of that super genius bullshit. Boston needs crack cocaine.'

'What are you talking about, Mukesh?' I asked him, fearing he had probably lost his sanity. 'I want to talk about Tania, Mukesh. Not narcotics.'

But Mukesh, who had read a little too many reports about extremely rich Indian doctors being caught by police for writing illicit prescriptions of morphine and other opioid-based painkillers to celebrities, and having seen newspaper articles about hundreds of top-grade sports cars being uncovered from their overseas vacation homes—all from the filthy money they made off selling morphine—had ended up meticulously applying the same idea among the folks of academia.

He elaborated: 'A primary research study I conducted last month in the basement of my very own house led me to discover that a mathematician can solve a linear equation three and a half times faster after snorting three grams of crack cocaine with a blunt Marlboro cigarette. We are talking about the real deal here, boy. None of that money-printing crap.'

'Well, what has that got to do with Tania, man?' I asked. 'You want me to make her a crack addict so that she starts sleeping with me to fulfil her dependency on drugs?'

'No. That won't be necessary, Moron bhai.'

'Then?'

'You kick a little ass. Fight a few cops. Escape arrest. Be kickass. Like that Sergeant. And she'll be at your knees, my brother. But join me on my adventure.'

'Of?'

'Of running the crack business.'

'And how will I do that?'

'You know how to drive, right?'

'Yes,' I nodded.

I knew how to drive because, with my mother gone and my father being a lifelong devout user of public transport, our family wagon had been left unattended. So, now family-less and unsupervised, it drew me towards itself—demanding to be driven. And I learnt to drive it on my own.

'Well, I know the business,' Mukesh continued, 'and you know how to drive a car. How about we drive to Los Angeles? I have my contacts there, of course. We just drive down to LA and pick up a courier from there. Then, we drive back to Boston and deliver the courier here. Right in Boston Square. And I'll pay you $8,500 for your services.'

'How the fuck did you get into all this, Mukesh? Weren't you studying to become a mathematician?' I asked.

Mukesh chuckled. 'Hush, hush. I'm afraid I can't share all that.'

'You want to make a drug run with me?' I asked.

'Yes. Once-in-a-lifetime offer, Moron boy.'

'What if we get caught?'

'You ever been caught carrying a packet of Burger King in your car? Come on, dude, we're Indians. As long as there are no genuine bomb threats around, they won't stop us. And the shipment is smaller than a package of Burger King, if you must know.'

'But how will all this benefit my purpose?' I asked, failing to see the connection between securing Tania's love and becoming a small-time drug peddler.

'The same way it would benefit you,' he said. 'If you were in the army or a dreaded gangster, boy, she would respect you.'

It seemed alright to me. LA was a three-night drive from Boston. Plus, $8,500 could go a long way. I could take a few pit stops at some good roadside hotels with big chandeliers and some nice Russian ass.

However, on the day we were supposed to embark on our mission, Mukesh called to inform me that he couldn't stop going to the latrine. He said he had eaten too many pickles at once and that his bowels wouldn't allow him to go on such a long expedition. He added that if I could bear the strain, he would pay me $8,500 upfront, and another 4,000 upon return if I were willing to drive there all alone.

Had it not been for Tania and the prospect of earning $12,500, I would have never agreed to this preposterous idea. But unfortunately, both of those aspects were involved.

'12,000 upfront and 5,000 upon return,' I haggled with Mukesh.

'9,000 and a Russian hooker upfront, and 4,000 upon return.'

'Hell, boy. I will be damned. Why are you bringing in the angle of a Russian hooker?' I asked.

'These are only a few of the many things you don't understand. I'm not talking about any Russian hooker. I'm talking about *the* Russian hooker. You have to outperform Sergeant if you wish to win over Tania. It's like when you go inside her, she should know that it's not an ordinary penis that has hit her. You understand, Moron ji?'

'Hell. I never thought about it that way,' I said, growing thoughtful.

'Well, go on then. The hooker awaits you in LA.'

For when you are afraid, it's bliss. Every sacred moment of reality, every trickle of water down the slanting roof, every paper boat left to explore the water pits, every ship that sailed through the Boston sea. Every moment of my mortality closing in, every heartbeat I wasted finding Solace.

The Tania I was so deeply in love with had outgrown her childhood. Though I was still stuck in that ageless, bottomless stage in which fear and sadness dulled my days. I hadn't cried over my mother's death. Well, I had, but I had never felt the grief that event should have inspired in the first place. Maybe I was running away from this reality so fast that somehow I outran myself.

That weekend, I drove to LA solo, my black family wagon cruising and blending into the darkening sky. I would cruise haphazardly, mixing the R&B with EDM over the radio, disappearing into red sunsets and then reappearing in the lit entrances of dingy diners that smelt of stale vegetable oil, where bikers and escaped convicts would raise their heads from their meals and look quizzically towards me—my skinny Indian shade stirring their interest—and they would ask me, 'Are you the Buddha?'

'I don't know, dear sir. Would Buddha have known he was Buddha while he was travelling as Buddha?'

And then, at a robust intersection across the LA freeway, I was greeted by Mukesh's promised Russian. An old, overworked hag who seemed as though she had been forced to leave her supreme country for some evil reasons.

'Hey, boy,' the old Russian said in a manly voice.

'Hey yourself,' I offered her my scared greeting.

'What hotel are you up in, baby?'

'Oh well, I'm really sorry to break it to you, but only now has Daddy figured that I have gone a little too far from home. And at this very moment, I have to rush back to him to calm his furious anger. I hope you will forgive me, Madame,' I said in a horrible European accent.

She shook her head in disapproval, which I could see was not a new feeling for her. She had been tossed around a lot. She demanded her usual fifty and a cab fare to LAX. I happily gave her a hundred-dollar bill, after which she sauntered to a waiting car with a sad-looking mafia gangster sitting in the driver's seat.

Having altogether abandoned the idea of courting that Russian missus, I found myself with an even deeper longing for Tania. Oh, Tania! The light of my darkened childhood. Wasn't it only destiny that we were to court each other, mate and sleep, and raise a troop of Russian kids who would abuse in Hindi and drink in Russian?

Having saved a fortune of 500 dollars, I checked into the scenic Beverly Hills Hotel, with fresh palm trees reflected in the blue, post-meridian pool. The hotel was known for its notorious Hollywood scandals. In fact, I was informed by a handsome waiter (also the stunt double in three of my Hollywood movies) that Ms Marilyn Monroe's death suite was only a floor above me.

'Worry not, sir, if you see Ms Monroe in your bathtub this evening.'

'Haha, waiter ji.'

I changed into my evening gown and settled by the pool right in the midst of the sprawling valley of Hollywood. My legs stretched out into the red sunset. I waited patiently for the dealer to call for me from the reception. When he didn't, and it was past 7:30, I ordered a few Piña Coladas. When the poolside DJ began playing his sundowner EDM and a few of the Hollywood Harlow were twisting their blonde heads and dancing to his beats, I started my rounds with the LITs. A raise of my hand, a waiter summoned to my side, 'One LIT please, Coke base.'

'Righto, sir.'

I gulped down LITs with magnificent thirst, enjoying a helping of nice crispy cheese balls here, a Californian burrito there. I believe, while I was in the midst of my feast, a young American child actress came up to me and asked if I was the famous Indian actor Shah Rukh Khan or if I knew him through an indirect association. I told her that he was expected to be in my suite this evening for a private dinner. Then she was abruptly dragged away by her mother.

I must have passed out because eventually, a sad-looking waiter woke me up and informed me that my father was looking for me at the entrance of the hotel. I wondered why, of all the relations one could have lied about, Mukesh had asked the dealer to pretend to be my father. A burly African-American man greeted me at the doorstep, gave me my parcel of Burger King, and drove away in his McLaren, leaving me to my own vices—with another 8,500 dollars and a stash of crystal meth, which could have resulted into another 200 dramatic bathtub murders had I mixed that amazing bag of sugar-like crystal candies into the hotel's water supply.

I didn't, of course.

I came back to the absolute silence of my suite, which overlooked the Hollywood sign. It was depressing and lonely—my life without Tania. I tried to call my father, but the call went unanswered. So, I browsed through the TV channels, and an hour later, I called him again.

'Hey, Daddy.'

'Hello! Are you all good?'

'Yes, Daddy. We just reached Professor Kamath's house. He and his wife are downstairs cooking chicken tikka.'

I had told my father that Mukesh and I were driving to LA to meet a renowned Indian psychologist who had agreed to help us with our application for Harvard next year.

'Work hard. You already are. That's a good thing. I just pray to God that you get what you are seeking,' he said.

'Did you eat, Daddy? How was class?' I asked.

'Yeah, it went well. Yeah.'

'Alright, Daddy. Got to go now. Got to submit my application for Harvard tonight,' I said, and we disconnected the call after two seconds of silence.

That night, I drove madly towards Boston and Tania.

The next day, before driving home, I made a pit stop at the Boston City Mall, an upscale marketplace that half our high school lied about visiting over the weekends for reckless shopping sprees. Inside, there were mostly old couples and a few weary mistresses who looked tired and distressed about recovering their daddy's hidden will. I tried on a few bomber jackets at Diesel & Co. and then a few shirts at the Valentino boutique. I hated them all and ended up spending all my money on a nice white Versace T-shirt and a pair of jeans and Nike J5 sneakers, which cost me the entire 8,500 I had earned and an additional 4,500 I pulled from poor Mukesh's share.

Mukesh was a good friend, and had I told him that his money went towards the greater purpose of me being able to seduce Tania, he would have closed his eyes, nodded in understanding, and asked me to make him proud.

When I reached home in the evening, I saw my father reading the day's newspaper. He looked up when I walked in. 'How'd it go?'

'Amazing. They absolutely loved it. In fact, I was paid for my reports. Here,' I said, tossing a few hundred-dollar bills onto the table. I don't quite know what it was with my father. No matter how impatient or anxious I was about the world outside, I would feel a sense of calm wash over me in his presence. I would always sit and ask him if he had eaten. Is he sleeping well?

'I have been promised a scholarship in LA if my reports get the final approval, you know,' I said.

'That would be great, wouldn't it? Absolutely. I just want to see you all settled, my son. Taking care of your life. You know how things have been lately.'

'Yes, Daddy. But I must run now. There is this prom I have to attend.'

Then I drove to our mad prom in my black station wagon and white Versace T-shirt. Half the high school stood and stared at me in amusement. I felt I had finally acquired the look of a criminal—a dreadful, threatening madman who would shoot you on the spot if you dared to raise a crooked finger at me, you son of a bitch. I was met by my dear friend Mukesh right at the entrance.

'How's your stomach, Mukesh? How are you feeling now?' I asked.

'It's alright. But look at you, all gangsta, Moron boy!' he said.

'Where is Tania?' I asked, not even looking at Mukesh or the awestruck crowd anymore.

When I finally saw her, it felt like a year had passed, not a week, since I had last seen her. She seemed unrecognizable. She was chatting animatedly with Sergeant, whispering something into his ears. When our eyes met, she held her gaze for a brief five seconds. 'Who the fuck are you?'

'I'm Mason Moron, Tania. Shove it in your daddy's face'.

We danced the night away—Mukesh, Dinesh, and I—chugging neat vodka and Piña Coladas. Before the night ended, I had one last haunting glimpse of my sweet Tania—of her leading Sergeant to the end of the party. A sharp turn into a deserted bathroom, a soft thud of the door, and then my lifelong fantasy began to materialize behind those closed doors of the men's washroom.

Right after they left, the music stopped. People looked around in confusion, and then a few eyes scanned me in aghast horror. When I walked up to the closed door of that restroom, I could hear the frantic announcements of Tania's amour. I discovered at that moment that one of Tania's kinks was that she referred to herself in the third person when she was not in control of her emotions. 'Oh, Tania needs to be absolutely fucked, Sergeant! Oh yeah, spread her butt, you like Tania's ass?' She was moaning, and her voice escaped from behind the closed door of that restroom. Sergeant, altogether scared of her demanding passion, was muffling an audible, 'Oh yeah! Oh yeah, Tania. My goodness, what a nice ass.'

I had never anticipated facing such a public humiliation in high school as the one I faced that day. I thought I might end up committing suicide. That I would just go off and drown myself in the sea while wearing my white Versace T-shirt and Nike J5 sneakers. I ran outdoors onto the frigid streets of Boston, looking for a cab or a speeding car that might have the honour of trampling me to instant death. My eyes were met with a monochrome black-and-white poster of Ms Staci's Onyx eau de toilette perfume ad. Ms Staci, the global sensation and absolute heartthrob of our nation, seemed to be looking straight at me. There was this poster on one side, the horrible image of Tania getting drilled by Seargent on the other, and then there was me, still breathing and sobbing in the middle of the road.

Though, I had my revenge with Tania over the course of the next year. Apparently, the afternoon after prom, she snuck out of her house while her mother was asleep and hit the road with Sergeant in his broken trailer, abandoning her home and family forever. Over the next few months (I tracked her movements through her social media updates), they travelled like old roadside hippies. She posted her skinny semi-nude pictures from a deserted diner or a freeway and a clear picture of her small breasts from a discreet red-light motel. For the remainder of the high school year, she posted twice about the joyous news of her pregnancy and then the equally heartbreaking news of the abortion. As she said, 'America was too capitalist for them to raise a kid into normal childhood.' After that, they travelled from Massachusetts to New York, where they moved into a dismal one-bedroom apartment in Brooklyn with a broken spring mattress and a rotting fridge. The last piece of information I had was from an advertisement she posted—she and Sergeant were offering a 5-dollar spiritual healing session to troubled couples and tormented roadside artists. From what I could gather, they we re selling themselves on the side as the proud, open-minded voyeurs they had always been, offering threesomes and orgies in exchange for a good meal.

A few months later, a friend of ours showed us a clip of Tania and Sergeant being arrested by the NYPD after they had started a small cult in Brooklyn. They were brainwashing and recruiting pretty-looking suburban teenagers to vandalize and break into the houses of the affluent and famous, claiming to liberate America from capitalism. I'm sure those bastards thought they were going to end up running for President and First Lady of the United States, only to be busted and arrested later.

I, on the other hand, surrendered myself to the typical rules of an Indian heartbreak, studied relentlessly for days, and was accepted into Harvard that year.

The memories of Harvard now come to me only in dreamlike montages—of the energetic slapping of the River Charles by the shiny iron oars of our Harvard Rowing Team. A team of young, athletic men hunching in their canoes, wearing blue spandex shorts and vests, rowing and grunting, practising every morning against the backdrop of a red sunrise. The palatial arches and ivory-golden roof of the Elkins Widener Memorial library—which was accessible round the clock—where I found unexpected solace in browsing first-edition, leather-bound hardcover copies of books by William James (The Father of American psychology and a Harvard graduate himself) and J.B. Watson. I spent sleepless nights flipping through the endless pages of *A Brief History of Psychology, An Extensive Look into the Etiology of Bipolar Affective Disorder, A Complete Walkthrough Guide for Substance Abuse and Deaddiction,* and other profound literature of this kind.

Not very long ago, there had been rumours about two mind-control experiments having happened in the basement of our college. Call it delusion, but I convinced myself that I could conduct a successful experiment on this. What else, hmm? So back at Harvard, my hunt for pussy was replaced with a more meaningful hunt—the hunt for fame and recognition in modern psychiatry. During those long, studious nights, dreams of Tania and my dead mother plagued me. One might assume that under such a torturous regimen, my scholarly expeditions would wear me out. Though what I did end up getting weary of was not the expeditions I was venturing into over my weekdays but the ones I undertook on the weekends.

Every weekend, there used to be a party at the Four Seasons, where our dorm would gather after spending the evening in the many pubs and nightclubs of Boston. There was a girl in the room next to mine, Andrea, whose father owned a few premium resorts in East Asia. She was a sweet, petite, long-haired, and small-breasted girl who wore expensive kimono gowns at night and cute floral dresses by day. Any sensible sleepwalking man on our campus would have gone to crazy lengths to sleep with her. However, I didn't have the energy or desire to sleep with anybody after my traumatic experience with Tania. Andrea was just a good weekend companion who would take me to nice, expensive house parties and then the exclusive, hard-to-get-into 'afterparties'. There, I drank and danced and forged superb, one-night-lasting friendships with a lot of shallow townsfolk.

The Four Seasons at Boston Harbor was usually considered a pleasant spot for late-night debauchery. So, after a roaring afterparty, when the alcohol was full in me and I could sense the world with drunken clarity, I sauntered through the various adjoining rooms of the grand presidential suite of the Four Seasons, witnessing the deplorable deeds people commit in the darkness of the night. Long after the DJ had passed out on his console, when most of the people who had been expensively dressed, cocky, condescending assholes only a few hours ago were now helplessly drooling and sleeping and collapsing over each other. When the night was at its darkest and the skyline outside at its brightest, I would witness the girls sneaking into the bathroom with the boy they were not supposed to be going in with. A cold splash of the shower, a shriek, and then her boyfriend's best friend is deep inside her, her wet hair being caressed, she getting all the love she thought she deserved while the boyfriend, all worked up, is hunting for his lover in the lobby downstairs.

On one of my drunken patrols, I remember accidentally crossing paths with the fierce-looking, big-breasted Sasha. This big-breasted Sasha had been in my business management class throughout, but me being me, I could never muster the strength to strike up a conversation with her. But on this beautiful night, Sasha was all sad and teary. She had just broken up with her boyfriend, but my presence seemed to have filled her with some great hope. She was all teary. She was crying and drooling, and when I consoled her, she began telling me what an amazing person I was.

'How do you recognize me?' I asked her.

'You are Mason Moron. We go to the same college,' she said.

She told me how it was only a matter of the saddest of shocks that I didn't happen to be in possession of a girlfriend. And then she was all teary again.

'Where is he?' I asked. 'Your boyfriend?'

'I don't know. He just left.' I sensed an evil idea creep into my head. She was so damn teary and sad that, if I could have accepted my Indian skin in that foreign land, I would have fucked her into paralysis or happiness or both. She had begun beating her breasts out of sadness. She was beating them so damn hard that one of her breasts had popped out of her dress. But I found myself helpless.

'Please attend to your breasts, dear,' I said and began walking away, my eyes still helplessly fixed on the first pair of titties they had seen.

As I was walking away, she started wishing me all the very best. She said that next Sunday in church she would pray to the Almighty that I achieve all my dreams.

By the final year of college, even Andrea had run away with her boyfriend. Only this time, my successor was Dutch and not American.

By the time I was set to graduate, apart from the tumultuous ambitions of owning a mid-sized bank in some golden European isle under my own name, I had figured that I was going to spend most of my life in that same deserted loneliness. I would grow up resentful of people and their corrupt existence, and it would be only a matter of a few days before one fine morning I would end up buying a fully functional matte-black light machine gun and setting it off in some crowded evening market before committing suicide.

Though this trajectory changed somehow midway one summer evening a week or so before my convocation ceremony after I had returned home from college, when I accidentally encountered another Muslim boy, equal to me in age, sitting in my bedroom and eating from my big bag of fried potato chips. It was not that I had suddenly become schizophrenic. A few bad bitches to the ashes and ka-boom! Here I am y'all, inventing imaginary friends for myself. Apparently, in my absence, my father had done a favour for an old Indian friend of his and had readily accommodated his son in our Boston household while the boy was on his spring break and visiting the States for the very first time. So there he was: Zahed, this erratic first-time USA-visiting Muslim boy who had come to the States right after the 9/11 apocalypse had made waves. His father was a very close associate of my father. So much so that after my mother's death, if there was anybody whom my father would still call in the middle of the night to talk to, it would be Zahed's father, Professor Saeed Mirza. Together, they would talk and brainstorm about the most challenging and unsettling subjects that concerned their lives and the course of their sons' futures.

Professor Mirza was residing back in India and serving as the dean of Nalanda University, an ancient, some 2,200-year-old university that was once completely burnt to ashes by a depraved conqueror. It served as an archaeological site for a few centuries. Then, a few years ago, it was resurrected to fuel the political agenda of the ruling party of the state of Bihar.

As far as Zahed and I were concerned, apart from two dead mothers, two lonely Muslim fathers, the realization of eternal loneliness, and the same appetite for sex, we shared the same bedroom and even the same bathroom slippers for the course of that summer. Our friendship, therefore, was inevitable.

And he really was a famished bastard. What a terrific guy, really. He appealed to me from the very start.

On the very third day of his visit, I offered to take him to see the Boston Museum of the great martyrs and veterans. He got dressed in a brand-new white T-shirt and a pair of black denims, trying his best to look all American. When we stepped out of my house, he paused for a moment, looked at me, and asked if there happened to be a cheap American whorehouse in the vicinity.

I thought he was outright mad for a minute. But then, after seeing that same mischievous smirk creep onto his face (which I had sensed creeping onto mine a lot of times as well), I told him that practically the entire world was a cheap whorehouse if one considered the current state of affairs. He laughed and asked, 'If the hoes back at Harvard had really, after all these years, learnt to only appreciate diversity, or had they started fucking it as well? And if so, then he would love to be introduced to some of the prettier, big-breasted, wonderful girl classmates of mine.'

'I don't think they would talk to us with that much interest. Until you can offer them your class notes or help them finish their assignments while they are outside partying,' I said.

'Who says I want to talk? I just want to creep around their homes and take their pictures while they are in the shower or some shit.'

'Why? What purpose would it serve?'

'A person is most vulnerable when they are bathing or taking a shit. Imagine what brilliant artwork it would make!'

'What would you do with such artwork?'

'I'll sell those pictures online. For a lot of money.'

'You will get arrested for saying such things out loud, boy,' I said.

Though he didn't really mean any of what he said, nor did I, for that matter—whorehouses, for instance, or photographing unsuspecting nude college undergrads in their most vulnerable situations. We both knew it was just a joke, one of the few lively things about our dying youth. We weren't supposed to act on such immoral urges; we were simply supposed to say them out loud and get a heck of an entertainment by saying such outrageous things.

However, I remember one night when we almost turned that mindless blabber of ours into reality. Our combined fortune and savings had exceeded a thousand US dollars, and our appetite to really ram some depraved and promising American blonde had reached the brim of our boyhood, so much so that we would have sold our damn houses if we could have found a girl who would warrant great lifelong sex with us in return for a small mid-sized suburban duplex.

That night, we ended up wiring some $500 to a Russian pimp we had come across online. He had sent us a few photographs of some of the most fairy-tale-like mistresses a man could ever come across. These were pictures of amazing, tall, brunette Russians and Ukrainians who looked like Hollywood actresses, except they came with an attached rate card. We settled on the most premium of the prostitutes, who came at a cost of a solid $500.

'Would she do a threesome?' I asked our pimp over the phone.

'She doesn't. But for you and your friend, I can make an exception,' the pimp said.

So, then what? An immediate wire transfer of $500 was made to a shady-looking Russian bank account. With our room cleaned, scented candles lit, room freshener sprayed, pubic hair shaved, and some expensive manly hard rock cologne applied, we waited for the pimp to arrive with the girl.

'Damn, if only I had known that ordering a dream wife is like ordering a pizza delivery these days,' Zahed said, stretching his pelvic muscles and warming up for his self-proclaimed 'stellar performance of the night'. And an hour later, when the pimp hadn't shown up at our doorstep, we started getting restless. We began calling him like retards, and he kept pushing us around, making excuses, telling us names of random places in Boston where the traffic was too heavy, and saying he would be right there.

'Are you with the missus?' I enquired.

'Yes, absolutely. I'm with her,' he said.

'Make us speak to her,' I demanded.

'Oh, she ain't ready to talk. Only excited to fuck.'

'Hell dammit! I, as a customer, demand to speak to the missus. Right now. Vamos!' I said, anxiously mixing my Spanish with my Russian.

And then, much to our bafflement, that rascal of a pimp immediately changed his voice and pretended to be the Russian prostitute himself.

'Oh, I no prostitute. I do you both for two thousand. Either pay in advance or go to hell.'

After being scammed in that late hour while we were at the peak of our manhood, we decided to fix the damn problem right then by going on a prostitute hunt in the middle of the night.

'Too many beautiful streetwalkers around, Zahed boy. There are tons of them, I'm sure. Let's go to the city and come back with the merchandise ourselves. Fuck the delivery. Let's go on a pickup,' I said.

We then ended up taking my father's station wagon in search of a whorehouse. We drove cautiously through the deathlike silence of the Boston streets. After an hour, we crossed into the rumoured red-light district of Boston. However, there were no escort services in the advertisements—just a few strip clubs with some sad-looking, old-aged grannies for strippers.

'Don't just look near the neon signs, boy. I've heard that some of the most exemplary whores don't advertise themselves. They just tend to a few limited customers in a few giant mansions.'

'How do you suggest we go knocking on every damn mansion at this hour and enquire if there happens to be a whore inside?' I asked.

'Just drive on,' he said.

And so I drove. More furious, more hungry. Past the endless city lights. Past the Boston Metallurgical Plant. We were now in the industrial town side of Boston, which had factories that would operate the whole night, churning out black fumes as the underpaid labourers slogged inside till their doom. We stopped at a red light, rolled down our window, and asked a very tired-looking underpaid labourer if he knew where we could find the prostitutes the town was widely known for.

'Down the parallel road, sir. Just go straight and take a right onto the very next lane. Or don't,' he said. 'I suggest you don't. I've heard it's a vile place. You're at risk of getting robbed or raped or both.'

'To hell with it,' we said and drove on.

But as soon as we entered the lane, very surprisingly, our car broke down. A total dead stop. I tried igniting the engine a few times, manically twisting the keys, but the car wouldn't make a sound. It was dead as the despair of that night. Fortunately, we were not robbed or violated that night, as there was barely a soul walking around at that hour. But we had to push that doomed station wagon all the way back home in the middle of the night so that it would be parked in our garage spot before my depressed, lonely father woke up.

Often, before going to sleep, Zahed would borrow my cell phone to make a long-distance call to some girlfriend of his back in India. I did not tell him that my bill was nearing a hundred dollars every damn night (5 cents per minute, 100 dollars for a night) for every long trunk international call he was making to that unnamed lover of his in Nalanda. The irony was that he barely even spoke to her while she was on that call with him. Half the time, when I would eavesdrop on him, he would be saying something nasty like, 'Call me daddy, baby. Not abba.'

'Don't say Christ. Say Allah,' he would say in a soft muffled tone, and the remainder of the time, he would stare at the floor of our bedroom with an expression of shame and sorrow as that unnamed girl from Nalanda asked him to mend his ways and become a better man.

'Why don't you ever talk to her nicely, Zahed boy? Why don't you just have sex with her once you are back home?

It will save us the sweat,' I asked him one night at a silent pub that served some foul-smelling onion rings along with free cheese dips.

'Talk about what?'

'About life. Career. Things of that sort.'

'I can't. Not with her.'

'Why is that?'

'I'm brainwashing her into polygamy. For that, it's imperative we don't discuss life and career. Just unhappiness and the truth of everybody getting just one life to live and fuck.'

'What does she do? When she's not scolding you over calls?'

'Well, if you really want to know, her name happens to be Phoebe. She's a year younger than me.'

'What does she do?'

'Same shit as what I do.'

'Look for Russian whores?'

'No, you dumbass. We are in the same class back in Nalanda.'

Hell, I didn't even know what he was studying back in Nalanda. Or if I had asked him someday, I would not have remembered for shit.

'Still?'

'Medicine. MBBS. She's trying to specialize in neuroscience. I'm trying to become a gynaecologist myself.'

'I think you should exchange courses. Life is not something to be joked around with. I don't know if you will ever be employed if you study gynaecology. Just ask her to study that. You go for the neurosciences.' And quite surprisingly, he did a year later.

'Why do you love her, Zahed?'

'She's the daughter of this very powerful minister of human resources in Bihar. The most diaphanous of beauty. Apparently, it is rumoured that she's a hybridization of two of the most beautiful and renowned actresses of our nation, Ms Staci and Ms Anamika. Her father has announced plans to attend our convocation as the chief guest. It is said that he is choosing three of the most brilliant minds from our class to invite them to the state gala dinner.'

'Oh, hell. Why not continue fucking her then?'

'We haven't fucked yet.'

'Why?'

'She ain't ready.'

'So what do you plan to do? Just convince her.'

'In due time,' he said, still smirking, 'you will see. The day that minister plans on eating dinner with the three most gifted men on our campus...' Zahed stopped for dramatic effect.

'Yes?'

'I plan on eating his daisy fresh of a daughter, Moron boy.'

Wednesday nights at Boston Square used to be overly crowded with ladies as there was always some ladies' night happening in one of those fancy clubs. 'Free drinks for girls. Free pretty drinks for pretty girls. Body shots on the house.' There we struggled to get entry into the nicer clubs, waiting in long, endless queues, being pushed around and squashed among huge, horny, protein-fed bodybuilders or pathetic-looking girls who wore makeup as if it were the most essential element for their survival.

And what did we do once we got inside? You wonder.

We stood at the corner of the dance floor, staring at the dancing crowd with shame and helplessness. Zahed would be holding onto a glass of almost-finished whisky, pretending to be damn busy or depressed—or both—about something. I would be ordering some or the other fancy LIT (Coke base, please? Strawberry base, please? More dash of vodka, please?) or straight-up Jägerbombs from the bar.

At random instances, Zahed would disappear from my sight, and I would suddenly wonder, 'Oh hell! He did finally get pulled inside the ladies' room with one of those Latinas he was eying, ha!' I would dash to the men's room myself to fix my hair and wipe the sweat off my face. And I would end up encountering that bastard right there. I would always end up meeting Zahed (sans Latina, sans fellatio) right in the men's room, standing in front of a giant, greasy mirror. Without a word, I would go and stand right next to him, and we would stand together, in front of the mirror, applying wet napkins to our faces and drenching our hair in tap water so that it never lost its shine.

'Imma drown a bitch in my hairpiece one night, boy, you will see,' he would say. But I would remain quiet.

We would end up staying late sometimes—until the club was totally shut and the bouncers would empty out the sad, drunken, sleepy crowd into the night. And sometimes, even after that, instead of immediately going home, we would just walk to a nearby eatery on the lookout for more bitches. There would, of course, be a few girls from my class itself. The usual partying lot, getting crazier and fatter by the night, always driving around in a Porsche or a Range Rover with a gangster boyfriend.

For instance, on one particular night, if I recall correctly, the fair, big-breasted Dia Purdon was standing by the kebab grill of a steakhouse, and the scrawny yet beautiful Saum Bharton was by the cheesecake display of an outlet of The Cheesecake Factory, standing with Yams Potpourri from my Business class and Simiara Paddox from English. Fuck, it's crazy how I still remember their surnames, though we never had a conversation even once.

And there would even be the broke hippies (Trash of Hum Bio, who did horse riding and had hairy feet, or Anoushka from Business, who was super sweet but used that virtue to compensate for her unfuckable looks), waiting impatiently for a taxi or a cock (in whatever order it might come, but finding neither). Even they didn't seem to recognize me in that pristine marketplace, so we were left to suffer and walk back home.

With the prospects of sacrificing our virginity to some angelic Russian diminishing day by day, one would have wondered if we would soon abandon the dreaded bitch hunt. But from what it seemed, we were really starting to believe that this hunt would continue for a lifetime, even after the purpose of the hunt has been met.

However, as the days of our summer came to an end, we dropped our standards dramatically. I recall one such gallant drop—the lowest point of our enterprise—with utter shame when we began attending those afternoon techno parties that played EDM and had these busty, sunglass-wearing bitches dancing and raving in a mechanical, almost robotic sort of dance. And hoe and behold, we found ourselves ready, in fact desperate, to fuck them as well. We would look at them in horror and wonder, 'Damn, how jobless has our Boston become! How the fuck did this happen? Which famished bastard parties in the afternoon?' But that crowd didn't pay any attention to us either.

Also, as one might have noticed, my indifferent vocabulary towards my better female counterparts, particularly my sorry habit of referring to them as 'bitches' every now and then, had quite significantly ruined my chances of sleeping with a girl on those sunnier occasions when, by a stroke of luck, I had managed to strike up a conversation with some poor-looking, dancing techno girl.

'Hey, what's your name?'

'What?' she would say with irritation in her voice.

'Your name? Name?'

'I don't have one.'

'What?'

'I don't have one. You can call me AB, as in Abe.'

'Ah. So, you visit here often?'

'First time!'

'I see!' I would say.

'Do you visit here often? How do you like this place?'

'It's nice. Yeah, the drinks are nice. Too many nice people. And the bitches are super nice. Too many of them around.'

And that poor dancing girl would widen her eyes in shock and worry and without stopping her dance, would slowly retreat to a distance.

The thing is, I didn't refer to them as bitches out of disrespect. I said it mostly accidentally because I would end up getting all intimidated and shy. Suppose whenever a nice, approachable girl would actually start indulging in a conversation—one that 'I' had initiated. Imagine my torment when her white, glossy features would begin speaking 'actual words' to me. Her faint human scent brushing right up my nostrils. Say, when I would be so damn close to her that I could look into her real human eyes, see her real eyelashes, and the fake mascara that she had spent a considerable amount of time applying. And now, she is speaking to me. To Mason Moron, a virgin and a scholar.

'Oh yeah, really nice bitches around.'

Anyway, that tired, hopeless night, Zahed and I walked back home, groaning and abandoning any leftover faith we might have had in humanity.

'I think I'm gonna pop an artery in my penis if I think of sex anymore,' Zahed said. 'I have been erect for so long that I have begun to feel that I'm developing a disease.'

I added to our weariness. 'I think I'll descend into lunacy if I try to imagine a woman naked anymore.'

With that dead end of our civilization, we had decided that in order to have sex now, we must either kidnap a girl from the neighbourhood or marry one right off from a matrimonial website. Though this might sound outright bizarre in the western end of civilization, this was often the common way of life in the eastern frontier of the world—in the distant land of Bihar.

On the night after my convocation, Zahed and I left the ceremony early for he had to pack his bags and recheck his papers. He was flying back to India the next day. It was our last night of togetherness, and we walked side by side—me in my tartan black robe and a fresh $125,000 Harvard degree in hand, while he had flung somebody's black robe from the ceremony, which he said complemented his black leather shoes. We tiptoed in the snow. It was late at night, and we were like two black fairies floating over the three-foot-thick sheet of snow in the town of Boston. There was nobody a mile ahead of us and nobody a mile behind. All there were were traces of our marching footsteps. Zahed said suddenly, 'Do you think we can skid on the snow and it would look like we are flying?'

'I don't know, man. You can try,' I said.

But my friend had already started sprinting. One, two, three, four. With energetic footsteps and a flawless swoosh, he flew off. 'Son of a bitch!' he said. 'Look, I'm flying. Come. Come on, Moron, don't be scared.'

I ran, skidded, and covered a solid twenty feet of the Boston snowscape. I roared, 'Hell, Zahed. Let's go faster.' And faster we ran, skidding and balancing our bodies with the wings of our two hands. If somebody were to look at us from a distance, it would have appeared as if we were two witches floating on the ghosted streets of Boston instead of two drunk virgins toppling back home.

'You want to see magic? Ha, boy?' he asked suddenly.

'Sure. Sure, go ahead,' I said, laughing.

And he ran again, skidded again, and before he could come to a stop, he gripped an electric pole with both his hands and flung his body around so that his skinny frame began twisting itself around the pole, making him look like a wizard performing a pole dance.

'Get down, boy. You will get electrocuted,' I said.

He landed on his two swift legs.

'Fine. Let's race home. A full thousand dollars. Bet?' he screamed.

And we ran and raced homewards, skidding and floating through the streets of Boston. All the miseries of the past behind. All the fantasies of the future ahead.

Back home, my father had been sitting and sulking under the dim golden light of the dining table. He had just gotten off the phone with Professor Saeed Mirza.

'Oh! Moron, boy. My son. A graduate. Finally!' he said, a glint of pride in his eyes.

'You bet, Dad,' I said.

And before I could go ahead and rave and ramble about the course of my future, his face dropped again.

'What is it, Dad? Everything alright?'

'Yes, yes,' he said, his eyes fixed on the wooden top of the dining table.

'You can tell me, Dad,' I said, sitting opposite him. Zahed, following my lead, sat right next to me. 'What is it, Dad? What is wrong? Tell me now.'

'It's nothing. I just got off the call with Zahed's father. We were talking about you two. What great pride I feel today, son.'

'No, Daddy. Please. What is it?'

'It's just that I have waited for this day for so long. And finally, it's here. I can die in peace now,' he said.

'Are you ill, Daddy? Do you have a hole in your valve?'

'Ah, no. No,' he said. 'I just miss your mother. I miss her so badly. She would have been so proud of you today.'

'And what else, Dad?'

'Well, I don't see the point of staying in the States anymore. It gets lonely. I mean, if you want to stay, then by all means, I will be happy to stay. Now that you are going to have a job and all, probably you can take care of me along with your own family. You are a grown man now. Very soon, you will have your own wife and kids.'

'What nonsense, Dad. I'm still a kid myself. Why would I want to produce another?' I said incredulously. 'Will you please tell me what has happened?'

My father stopped, surveyed my face for a while, and said, 'It's just that I was on a call with Saeed Mirza, and he, out of the blue, started speaking about your mother. About how I met her in Nalanda. You know, she had come to intern at Nalanda University when I was just starting with my professorship.'

'Yes, I know, Dad. You met her at the university.'

'Yeah, just that. Saeed Mirza says there is an opening for a job. One for me. One for you. Back at Nalanda University. I also have this large piece of land I bought in Nalanda. Quite a fortune it has become. I mean, no pressure, son. I don't even know why I am saying all this to you. Maybe I'm going mad.'

That was the thing with my father. He had been so selfless and caring towards me, loving me with an intensity that fathers usually aren't capable of showing. But here he was, having spent the last five years of his life in a ten-by-ten room so that I could grow up to become something.

'It's alright, Dad. What were you saying about Nalanda? I didn't know we had property back there.'

'Oh, it's humongous,' he said. 'I remember how your mother fought with me for a week because I had taken a loan of Rs 15 lakh from the bank to buy that piece of land. It's all paid off now. Worry not, son. It's just...'

And we have a job awaiting us?' I asked my father.

'The job is amazing, and the pay is ... ah...'

The next morning, we took the Virgin Atlantic eastbound to India. The decision was so hasty but so prudent in the long run that my father had to commission a lawyer friend to sell our house in the States while we continued to build our new house in Nalanda. So we flew, leaving behind Boston and the Boston Metallurgical Plant, Tania and her Sergeant, Mukesh, and Harvard—like the dreamlike traces of a past that, to be quite honest, I didn't want to revisit anyway.

'Fuck load of virgins in Bihar, Moron. Loads,' Zahed kept telling me on the flight. 'In fact, if you must know, there are only two places where a man can find an honest, virgin girl for himself. I'm not bullshitting. I swear on my head. It would either be among some very selective tribes in Africa or the state of Bihar in India.'

'Hell, boy,' I said.

'Yeah. And mind you, you won't find them all over India. Just in Bihar,' he reassured me.

'And why is that?' I asked, clearly not convinced.

'I dunno. Something to do with the British colonization and Western influence. In the places they colonized the most, which include India and Africa, and especially in the epicentres of these countries from where the revolutions started, you would find the maximum number of virgins.'

'Where did you read that stuff, Zahed?' I asked incredulously.

'I made that theory myself,' he said a little too proudly.

'So you say we can find a girl like this in Bihar?' I said, snapping my fingers. 'Like this?'

'Yeah,' he said. 'You remember my girlfriend Phoebe?'

'Yes, yes. I do.'

'I can introduce you to a bunch of Phoebe's friends. They are quite a catch! All fairy-like sporty virgins, boy. None of that Russian Tania criminal shit,' Zahed chuckled, clearly congratulating himself on hatching a plan to get his friend laid.

1

Five Years Later

I'm inside The Clemency's Mental Asylum. Tomorrow morning, if I make it out alive, it will be exactly five years since I was brought here—to the ward of the criminally insane, alongside the most notorious and most talented A-class director of pornography, Bahubali. I've been admitted here for an indefinite period of time.

Much unlike the excellent McLean Psychiatric Hospital in Boston, Clemency's isn't advertised in fancy newspapers or talked about with fascination on celebrity talk shows. Very few people are aware of its existence—mostly scholars or family members of patients who had to be brought to Clemency's because they posed an imminent threat to themselves or others. It might sound mythical altogether, but it's just a sad place. The nights are starless and silent. The evenings are haunted by crying crows and resting vultures. Clemency's is surrounded by a sprawling forest with trees of pine and juniper. Tall and dominating, these trees sometimes reach over 200 feet. There is a Dutch church down the gravel path, where a few madmen play badminton and volleyball in the evenings, and a small library designated for the patients' recreation.

Clemency's is spread over an expanse of 220 acres. This excellent facility was built in 1857 by the British Crown to imprison the most revolutionary freedom fighters of our country who were fighting against the British Raj and who, quite frankly, began posing a real threat to the succession of the British Crown. All the British offered them in return was a diagnosis of madness and a lifelong exile to Clemency's Mental Asylum. Though now it's ancient history, Clemency's is now used as a place of disappearance for people like myself or for those who have gained more international fame and notoriety than even I have.

Inside this regal madhouse, we are an unusual lot. There is Harrison Brown, a boy five years my junior who wears Velcro Oxford sandals and knee-length shorts. He has been brought here because he knifed his own mother to death on his birthday. There is the charming Ms Prerna—a fascinating and affable lady with a beautiful hairdo who is always anxious about being a really good mother to her daughter and a really charming wife to her husband. Her desire to be the most dutiful wife to her husband and the most loving mother to her five-year-old daughter is so strong that it has gotten her all neurotic only. She spends most of her time in her room—fully dressed, makeup intact, and hair combed with a foldable comb—and awaits eagerly for the weekend to come. That is when her husband and her daughter are due to visit. Only the husband and the daughter never visit her, for they don't exist in the real world. They are but a figment of her mad imagination.

We also have with us a former banker of the Reserve Bank of India, a madman whose tale of insanity is reserved for some other time. But this is the one man that I envy, for he is solely responsible for putting Bahubali in Ward A (a ward which is allocated for only the most severe cases). And lastly, there is my master, Bahubali. A man of fine greatness who doesn't stay in the same ward as me anymore, even though we were brought here together. His madness had become so disturbing that he had to be shifted very recently to that ward.

Anyway.

I'm standing at the edge of a window, holding in my hands an obituary that I had written about myself after I had faked my death. This appeared in the *Hindustan Herald*'s Nalanda Edition four years ago.

Mason Moron, a renowned research scholar and professor, the only living child of the great researcher Moron Senior and his wife, both now dead, has died in a fatal car accident. He is survived by his widowed wife, Noel.

Survived, my ass. What a sister-fucking, pig-skin-eating lie. If Noel did anything after I staged my death and disappeared, it was to sleep around more shamelessly. More passionately. As if her childhood dream of becoming the most notorious prostitute of three surrounding districts was now only a few fuckings away. Anyway, I will tell you about her very soon. But what a fantastic cunt, really!

Five Years Ago

After a fourteen-hour flight from the US, Zahed, my father, and I finally landed in India, in the capital city of New Delhi. From there, a connecting low-budget airline took us to Bihar. And Bihar was a strange, famished land—so strange that modern literature simply can't describe the strange things that were happening in the city.

A day after reaching Nalanda, Zahed drove me to the city on the lookout for the promised virgin—one of the many virgins he had warranted Bihar was full of. For this special purpose, he had taken down a hunting rifle from what appeared to be a brass showpiece hung on the wall of his living room.

'Boy, this looks like a fake rifle. Does it even fire?' I asked him.

'They won't know it's fake. Sure as fuck they won't, as long as we act all tough.'

Then, tying a rope to the two ends of that rifle, he hung the weapon around his neck, pulled out his Royal Enfield bike out of the garage, and asked me to hop on the back. So, I rode pillion towards the mad city with his fake hunting rifle between us.

With the horrors of Boston fading behind me and the fresh air of Nalanda slapping against my forehead, I closed my eyes and opened them again to survey the giant peepal and sheesham trees passing overhead. And then a feeling of ultimate happiness took over me. After all, there was an angelic virgin waiting for me in some unattended room of an unknown hotel.

We crossed a railway barricade and a few police Gypsies, and after leaving the city behind, we were on the state highway. Hardly a few minutes had passed when Zahed suddenly stopped his bike at a small tea stall. A poor-looking tea seller was boiling tea over a wooden pyre, and a bunch of shabby, street-side gangsters were hunched around in a circle, chewing betel leaves and talking about how magnificent their neighbour's daughter's pussy was. From what I could overhear, they were talking about abducting a girl from the neighbourhood. Abductions, about which I will brief you shortly, were a routine thing in Bihar back then.

'A tea stall like this is an ideal place for people who are about to commit a crime or are taking a break after just having committed one. It's a perfect stop for gangsters when they are in the middle of committing a crime but need to catch their breath! Ha!' Zahed tried to explain after noticing the inquisitiveness with which I was staring at those gangster brothers.

But hell! I wasn't even concerned about the abductions anymore. That was, quite frankly, their business, not mine. I was concerned about a more serious issue.

'What is it, Moron boy? Don't look at them like that! Have they hypnotized you?'

'Is this where we are supposed to find the virgin?' I almost screamed at him in frustration. A few shabby boys broke off their meditations to look at me.

'No. Not here. Here, we have come to drink tea. The best in town.'

'You think the tea will go down my throat? In this heat?' I shouted again.

'Relax, Moron boy. Ramesh ji,' he said, looking at the old tea seller, 'my friend has come from the US. Serve him the best tea.'

'Where is the virgin, Zahed? Where is the virgin?' I asked my companion, feeling hopeless now.

'You gotta relax, Moron boy. That's your problem. You are so desperate to fuck a virgin that you tend to ignore the happiness in small things,' my companion said, straightening the hunting rifle hung around his neck.

The situation at hand was preposterous. The heat was unbearable, for one. And then I had been foolish enough to believe that if anybody was a true virgin around me at that point in time—apart from the promised invisible girl—it was Zahed. How could he have gotten me access to a bunch of virgins when he himself hadn't fucked one until now?

So I stood there on that sunny afternoon, absorbing Bihar. Absorbing the streetside gangsters. Absorbing the true crisis of youth. When suddenly, on that ghostly afternoon, emerged from a distant corner of my eyesight, a black SUV with tinted windows and alloy wheels. It sped past us so fast that if somebody had been crossing the street at that moment, they would have surely been hurled to an instant demise by that mad SUV.

'Geez, boy! They think they flying a darn aeroplane,' I swore as I jumped aside.

Suddenly, all the pity gangsters who had been huddled in the corner of the stall stood up and bowed their heads to the empty road—for a few brief seconds.

And then a police escort sped past the humble tea stall. Then another black-armoured SUV. And then another.

By the time my tea had started going cold in my hand, a total of forty-two black SUVs had sped past us. One behind the other, leaving a trail of roaring dust on the ghostly streets. Once they were gone, there was a huge commotion on the streets—people cheering and whistling.

'Woah!' I said to Zahed, forgetting about the virgin now, 'Is the President visiting Nalanda? What an entourage, boy!'

'Nah. It's just Bahubali,' Zahed said.

'But I'm sure he is more powerful than the President,' one of the gangsters piped in.

'Bahubali? Who is that?' I asked.

Zahed, a little cautious now, pulled me to a corner and said, 'If you must know, boy, his name is Anand Thakur, alias Bahubali. He is not the President, but he is a very powerful politician for sure. The most dreaded gangster and also an A-class filmmaker.'

'What films does he make?' I asked as I too was a savant admirer and critic of Indian cinema back in my days.

'The best kind,' Zahed said, closing his eyes and shaking his head in exhilaration. 'If you must know, he makes porn—cheap, third-grade pornography. He lives in a guarded compound that nobody has ever accessed until today. Only cameramen and crew and top A-class prostitutes of the adjoining districts are allowed inside. You are a lucky bastard to have seen his entourage today. He barely leaves his mansion, boy—once in ten years or something.'

'Why haven't they arrested him?' I asked, 'I'm sure it's a hell of an illegal thing to do. Making pornography and all.'

'The police station moves with him. The policemen guard him. And it's not even illegal to make porn in India. People hardly care,' Zahed said.

'Oh, hell,' I said.

'They did, I think,' Zahed said suddenly after being silent for a minute. 'They did try to arrest him once. When the ruling party in Bihar was in the Opposition. Those folks got an entire file on him. Rooms and rooms of evidence against Anand Thakur. Evidence of mass corruption. Illicit money made from arms deals and illegal taxation. However, a day before his court hearing was scheduled, the record room of the secretariat caught a massive fire. Poor records section! All the evidence, along with the accusations against Bahubali, was reduced to ashes. It was after that people started calling him Bahubali—the great warrior. For everybody knew that it was Anand Thakur, alias Bahubali, who had managed to set the state secretariat building on fire.'

Upon hearing this, I shivered a little, and my heart swelled with pride and awe. That was my first encounter with Bihar and Bahubali.

It may seem like I was an outsider. Somebody on the periphery of such bizarre occurrences. But my father's estate sat right in the heart of the town of Nalanda. Right on the warden road. This meant that people around would have probably figured that the masters were back in town or something. It made me feel that I probably was not much of an outsider after all. Our incomplete estate was a giant affair with an overgrowth of tall green grasses and wild trees on either side of the site where our new house was being built. We had peepal and jackfruit trees all the way from the entrance to the back of our compound. There was also a giant banyan tree in the middle of the front lawn. For lawns, we had eleven full-sized gardens with separate fencings. The house garage (an old-time construction) was adorned with bougainvillaea and dandelions. A broad road led visitors from Warden Road to the inside of the premises. A few narrow roads (which were built inside the premises) led to the back of the compound, which had four servant quarters and a few stables. By the time my doctorate at the university started, the house was halfway built.

During the initial days, while our house was being built, we lived with Professor Mirza at his house. And what a charming host he was, really! My father and Professor Mirza used to drive to the university together and drive back together. They would cook dinner together. And after Zahed and I were led to the university library for our evening study hours, they would sit and chat until late evening, after which both would get busy with their own academia. The late-night dinners at his house were silent and meditative, with everyone sitting encircled around his giant dining table. We mostly kept to ourselves, but there was an overall shared emotion of happiness and even optimism among the four of us. Even though my life will notably be overshadowed by the weight of unbearable crimes—infinite cases of human trafficking, pimping, and even grooming a renowned actress into fornication—the times I spent at Saeed Mirza's house bring a strange comfort to me. I believe, quite strangely, that was the only time when I was truly happy.

I like the warm effervescence of fire slapping across my face and the heavy incense it engenders. If you want to consume the world, breathe it in. My father, too afraid to choose burial (which had been the principal way of bidding goodbye to the world as per our customary Muslim ways), had chosen cremation as his way of exit.

However, a day after his death, I ended up burying his corpse in the backyard of our incomplete mansion instead of cremating it at the banks of the River Ganga. It's not like I had something against cremation. In fact, after his death was announced at the excellent RML Hospital (the sad old cardiac arrest), I had gone to inspect the banks of the River Ganga at the Manikarnika Ghat in the nearby township of Varanasi as the probable spot for his cremation. The nation of India cremates over 300 corpses of their loved ones every day on the banks of Manikarnika Ghat in Varanasi.

So we travelled—Zahed and I—having secured a last-minute reservation in a third-class compartment of a train from Nalanda to Varanasi. My father's body was being preserved in the mortuary at the RML Hospital.

It must have been midnight by the time we reached Varanasi Junction. A rickshaw took us to the township of Manikarnika Ghat, dropping us at the edge of the township near the police barricades, from where we had to walk on foot.

I remember marching through an impossibly narrow alley in Varanasi, with a few random, ghostly houses and a few faithful street dogs spread-eagled on our path. Shadows of closely packed minarets and small temples hovered overhead. Tears made it tough for me to see clearly, but I remember vividly that even before I reached the banks of the Holy Ganges, my nostrils were flaring with the dizzying smell of holy camphor and sandalwood. I wanted to run away. Not because I was terrorized by the loneliness of those long-abandoned streets of Varanasi but because the smell was so damn nauseating that I knew for a fact that tomorrow I wouldn't be able to carry my dead father all the way to this riverbank.

And then, upon reaching Manikarnika Ghat, the mere sight of so much human carcass—a half-burnt leg stemming out of a pyre and a human skull suddenly popping from another pyre, some five feet into the air before exploding like a tiny firecracker—horrified me so much that I joined my arms in a respectful composure, bowed my teary head so that my chin fit right between my chest, and resolved once and for all that if there was anything worse that could happen to my father after death, it would be this final, incinerating barbeque of his body.

So, instead of complying with his dying wish of a liberating cremation, I chose a more optimistic farewell and took his lifeless body from the hospital to our incomplete mansion, where I buried him in the backyard.

After that, my house came to be known as the Cemetery House. That's what the neighbourhood housewives began calling it, shivering in terror as soon as the name of the roofless mansion was mentioned out loud on tombola nights or during ladies' get-togethers. In the evening, people tried to stay away from the house. Children were pulled and rushed past my front porch, prams hastened, bikers sped by, and even pets stayed aloof. The Cemetery House.

Mason Moron's Cemetery House.

After my father's death, Saeed Mirza feared that the devastation of such a loss might push me into a state of lunacy and therefore, offered me a place in the university's dorm alongside Zahed.

'Stay with him. After all, he is like your elder brother,' Dr Saeed Mirza told me when I was still crying, and the world appeared to me through my foggy eyes as a dusky, crippled affair rather than a boon full of hope.

Having nowhere else to go, I agreed. That night, I was moved permanently to Nalanda University. I remember the deep reverberating sound of the tyre sticking against the road as I lay in the backseat of Saeed Mirza's car with my ears pressed against the Styrofoam seats. Zahed was sitting in the front seat with his eyes fixed on the road. Shadows of ginormous trees passed over my head, and bereaved as I was, I couldn't even register the road taking me to my new home. All I could think about was my father.

'Really, if it makes you sad, then don't think about it,' Zahed said.

I felt like getting up and slapping that rascal across his face but couldn't muster the energy to do so.

'Okay,' I said.

'Good boy,' he said. But I think he realized the stupidity of his insolence because after that, he remained silent and kept his attention on the road ahead.

Once I had moved into the dorm, I found myself slipping into an endless spiral of despair. The situation was quite funny, if you must know. Most of the time, I missed my father. More than sadness, sometimes it was just this heart-wrenching screaming impulse I would get when I desperately wanted a chance to talk to him one last time.

Even though my father and I never sat down to talk and discuss life as much as I would have liked, now that he was gone, I felt that maybe I should have. I should have told him that he was the greatest, most hardworking man on earth and other things of that sort. But in his absence, I was consumed by this impulse, this huge compulsion, to have one last conversation with him. Even though I was able to suppress it during the day, it was really at night, while sleeping, that I was plagued by strange, overwhelming dreams. In my dreams, I would be walking in a random crowded market, and then I would spot an affable-looking man at a distance who would turn out to be my father himself. Only this version of him was younger and full of life. I would be so happy and excited that as soon as I ran further to see his face clearly, I would wake up to find Zahed sitting at his study desk in one corner of the room. He would be under a table lamp with the *Encyclopaedia on Human Anatomy II* and *Liver Toxicology Series I* piled up in front of his clueless and horrified eyes.

'Want to go for a run, Young Moron?' he would turn his head towards me and ask energetically.

'What time is it?' I would ask, scratching my eyes.

'Time to get laid, darling,' he would say, mimicking some lame actress from a cheap serial. 'It's 4:45, boy. Come, let's go for a run.'

'Why the fuck would you want to go for a run at four in the morning, Zahed?'

'Hell, boy. It's Phoebe's house party next month. It's about time I get in shape. I've read in some literature that a session of early morning empty-stomach cardio burns more fat than any athletic pursuit,' he would say.

Hell! It was Phoebe's party next month. Phoebe, if you must remember, was his girlfriend during our time in Boston. The girl he would talk to with his mouth muffled into the cell phone. That sweet, virgin daughter of a very powerful minister. And she was throwing a house party next month. The magnificent occasion for which Zahed had been running and working on his stamina like a mad Olympian. That was the promised night on which he planned on losing his virginity.

In fact, this early morning jogging became a routine practice after that day. Somehow, I believe he was trying to make me outrun my grief.

So, after waking up, we would pinch our noses and grunt, walking shamefully through the narrow alley of the university dorm. Passing the smell of cheap talcum and urine from the half-sleepy boys of Nalanda University. And then we would exit the campus and enter the narrow state highway (which was mostly deserted at that early hour of the day) to begin our loathsome jog.

A few minutes into the mournful jog, I would realize that I had not properly finished my sleep from the night before and that it was a horrible idea to have woken up from a nightmare and decided to go for a run in the cold mist and dew.

But life has its own way of moving forward, and really, what was left on that bed apart from horrible loneliness? So I would begin running and chasing my companion, who would have left me a few hundred feet behind by then.

A few moments later, we would be jogging side by side against the backdrop of an early sunrise. We passed the vanishing university dorms and the sound of a humming maulvi escaping from a nearby mosque. And at some point, having escaped the grievous memory of my dead father, we would enter Champasari Street, where sleepy milkmen and vegetable hawkers would be setting up their stalls in the early morning hours. There, we would be tantalized—not by the serenity of the early morning but by a powerful advertisement of Ms Staci's Black and Silver Onyx eau de toilette poster. It was a giant forty by thirty poster of Ms Staci that overlooked the Nalanda market up close and the university campus from a distance.

'You know, Moron,' Zahed would say, looking at the tantalizing picture of the great Ms Staci, 'if one day she comes and sits on your lap, she will make you forget your own name. Let alone your dead papa.'

'You mean my wife? Staci Moron? That's what she would be called after I end up marrying her one day,' I would tell Zahed.

'Ha, boy! You think she would marry you only to be called a Moron? What an honorary surname for an actress. Moron!'

'Hell! I will change my name into anything but Moron if she were to announce her favourite name. I would change my surname for her,' I would say.

'Ha, boy, then all these boys here would be called Zahed.'

'Fuck off.'

No, really, Ms Staci, with her ongoing onyx eau de toilette ad and a few others—one for some exotic mango juice brand and another for a travel agency—at one point her stardom was so magnificent that she had become a brand ambassador for an entire country. And then, apart from that, with over three films of hers hitting the cinemas in that prophetic year, she really was a miraculous, lustful, beautiful dream housewife that every man in the nation would want. At that time, there were over 120 crore people in our nation. This particular poster of hers gleamed and overlooked the campus. A presence so dense and delightful that even the windowpane of a random apartment in her background could possess and draw a man into a magical fantasy. With that poster, she was always there but never really there.

Anyway, for a few weeks, the memories of my dead father continued to haunt me. The fact was that I was now an orphan. I had thought that with grief of such magnitude, I would be reduced permanently to a sad, unenergetic, and pliant man who wouldn't want trouble with anybody anymore. I had started accepting that ill fate for myself. Professor Saeed Mirza feared that the pain of such a loss might hamper my mental growth. So he arranged for an appointment with a renowned psychotherapist friend of his. This old, friendly man would make me sit inside his psychotherapy chamber and explain the five stages of grief to me. The importance of resilience. Things of that sort. When nothing seemed to work, he finally gave me a piece of his personal philosophy before abandoning my treatment completely. 'Don't be plagued by the memories of his existence. He had to die anyway. If anything, celebrate that he existed. Your father can be a source of great pain or great enthusiasm for you. It's all up to you. Young Moron. All up to you.' This was some advice that took years for me to decipher.

And then there were other mild attempts made by Zahed towards my recovery. A friendly conversation he arranged between me and a friend of Phoebe's. An unsuspecting, outstandingly hot batchmate of Phoebe accosting me under the shade of a giant peepal tree during lunch—trying to act like my girlfriend, suggesting that I take her out for coffee. Though inwardly, I would know that she had been bribed by my dear friend, and she would think of me as a wild pervert even if I were to take an interest in her.

Apart from that, there were routine instances of Zahed suggesting I visit the local whorehouse. He looked at my orphanhood as a door into a brand new world where I was allowed to do anything and everything since there was nobody to stop me from doing anything.

That part about being allowed to do anything and everything was true. With my father's death, I had complete ownership of Cemetery House. A day after I buried him, I had to inspect the locker in his bedroom before I could vacate the house and shift to the university. Inside his locker, I came across bundles of 1,000-rupee notes. A sum totalling over Rs 20 lakh, which initially made me feel quite guilty upon discovering them. It was as if I were a thief trying to rob my own dead father. But later I figured that, with him gone, it anyway belonged to me. I mean, I was deserving of that money. My father would have wanted me to keep it.

Apart from that, it was getting quite difficult to hold onto my grief for a very long time inside the comical environment of the boys' hostel at Nalanda University.

The boys at the hostel discussed the endless possibilities the world holds. The boys discussed the strange possibilities of fucking war-famished girls in distant war-famished lands. The boys dreamed of becoming prison guards so they could take advantage of men and women in equal proportions. Mindless blabber of this sort. But really! There were so many wrong, horrible, detestable things happening all over the world. Somewhere in a distant land, a generation of gorgeous, long-legged, big-breasted Ukrainian women were being murdered by the bastard Russians in the Russian–Ukraine war. The Russians were plundering their villages and bombing their homes. In fact, there were countless pictures of beautiful, recently orphaned Ukrainian women surfacing all over the internet. Distraught homeless people just like myself, sitting in front of their shelled houses, crying and waiting for somebody to save them. And, funnily there was not even a single sensible man alive who could traverse to Ukraine, climb over the remnants of a destroyed civilization, rebuild the nation, and proclaim princedom and lordship over those distraught yet totally desirable fairy-like girls. Maybe I could have if I had sold my house and collected the leftover money according to my father's will. However, when I thought about it, I felt guilty and undeserving of spending any of that money. You see, there was this strange grip of morality that afflicted me as soon as I became an orphan. Grief does strange things to a person. Maybe I was becoming manically depressed.

I'm not telling you all this to hint that I had gone all insane after my father's death. It's just that, against the backdrop of such events—such tragic lapses in history in which every Ukrainian girl was in dire need of a dick—how could my grief outlast my lifelong hunger for sex?

My penis, though it could have not stopped that sad war, might have altered the course of a civilization. Only what I didn't realize then was how badly I had misjudged the entire situation, as I misinterpreted my loneliness for horniness.

Then, the day of Phoebe's house party arrived.

Zahed and I drove into the upscale urban complex of Palm Meadows, where she lived. It was a gated community of mostly foreign expatriates, diplomats, and international award-winning artists who lived in giant, golden-lit duplexes. Expensive houses with lines of fresh palm trees and high-school girls jogging around with their mothers in spandex tights and sports bralettes. I remember all those houses exuded a scent of such richness that I thought it would have been a burglar's dream to have broken into one of these houses and devoured whatever fortune there was left inside.

Phoebe greeted us at the entrance. She looked as usual like a fairy in a white, halter-neck bodycon dress with her brown hair done into a high ponytail. Inside Phoebe's party, there was a civilization of teenagers bristling and brooding with the long-repressed sentiment of sexual release ever smiting their conscience.

They had bottles of Grey Groose and Jäger—my ever favourites! There was this clear-skinned, annoying-looking Castro on the DJ console hitting remixes of golden-age EDM with hip hop. With a glass of Jäger and Red Bull in one hand and pineapple juice and Grey Goose in the other, I pushed myself into the crowd, made my way to the sofa, and began drinking to my heart's fulfilment. Zahed signalled me from afar, indicating that he was going upstairs with Phoebe for a very important assignment. So I sat there alone, drinking and watching the French DJ hit the bass. His Pioneer EC 18 DJ set was setting things in commotion. In a drunken haze, I saw the music escape from his boom box speakers, the giant exonerating wave of music hitting against the young, athletic thighs of some fifteen underaged college girls. I let them dance and unveil the pleasant gift of their youth, their mass offerings to be ravished upon. I also observed a bunch of semi-random, formally dressed, stuck-up, neurotic boys who clearly didn't have the grace or strength to muster upon and devour the juvenile offerings of these carefree girls. Meanwhile, Zahed was working his magic on Phoebe upstairs.

Around two in the morning, when the party had dispersed, I was called upstairs by my fair companion, who had me sit in Phoebe's bedroom while he and Phoebe were in the adjoining bathroom, trying to fix the jacuzzi, it seemed. So I sat in the silent oblivion of Phoebe's dimly lit bedroom. The leaves outside the window were crisp with the cold, dry winds blowing from all sides. I sat on her soft, white rug and noticed Phoebe's black padded bra lying right in front of me. I examined it from a distance and thought, 'What a sexy-looking piece of work. Really grand!' And then my old friend Zahed zoomed in and asked me playfully to leave them alone for a while. I waited outside in the lobby, looking intently at the sparkly floor. I heard the sound of their shrieks escaping from the bedroom. The sound of my friend's skin slapping against his girlfriend's thighs. The sound of Phoebe and Zahed losing their virginity. This was the materialization of a dream of a lifetime.

It was three in the morning when I was summoned again; this time not into the bedroom but into the bathroom. To keep company with my two grown-up friends. After the heat of their passion had subsided, Zahed and Phoebe were sitting in the bubbling jacuzzi, looking at each other with eyes still haunted by desire. Phoebe's hair was all messed up, as it often is after sex. Her eyeliner was still impressively intact, not smudged by their passionate lovemaking. I knew they were both naked—that was quite obvious. The bubbling water reached the edges, covering Phoebe's breasts and Zahed's cock. And as I looked at his recently ravished girlfriend, I announced my sudden epiphany.

'I think I'm manic-depressed, and I need to blow off some steam. I need to have sex.'

And Zahed, having only recently acquired his seniority and therefore his right to school me about the principles of fucking a girl, told me gallantly, 'Of course. Of course. To become a man, you must fuck. Must have sex. It had only now been discovered by me, Moron boy, the brain chemistry tends to change a lot after an organism copulates. You were a boy, crying about his father's death. Now, it's about time you fuck and become a man and celebrate life. From now on, there is just one resolution—that you sleep with the very next girl you come across. Not this girl, for this girl happens to be my wife and your sister-in-law,' he said. 'But the very next! Let me be your sherpa towards sexual enlightenment!'

A few weeks had passed since that incident, and the freshness of such great resolve was still reverberating in my veins. I had, in fact, ended up gaining the superpowers of a dreadful pimp, who has the keenest sight for a woman who might not look eternally great but could give a man pleasure immense enough to accelerate a murderous war. Breaking away from my sad reveries about my dead father, I surveyed the campus of Nalanda University this time, not with the eyes of a grieving orphan Moron, but with the thirst of a sex-starved maniac who had only now broken free of a maximum-security penitentiary and would fuck anything of significance. There were mythical, extremely well-toned creatures hovering around the campus, who could provide me with the pleasures that Zahed had promised would put me out of my grief.

From the haze of my pain, I would spot a fine, big-breasted girl walking from the academic block towards the library in cute spandex tights, a pile of books held against her chest. This would stir up my manhood, and I would go like, 'Hell! Boston ain't got shit on this.' But by the time the girl came near me, she would have lost her charm mid-journey. So, no matter how fairylike she looked from a distance, up close what would be presented to my eyes would be a a poor-looking kid with a compromised future and a set of teeth so misaligned that I would feel like funding her dental work at the local dentist's from my own humble salary.

In the class I was teaching, there was a fair share of beautiful girls around my age, appearing and disappearing in rapid montages. But then their seductive charms were not enough to make me feel all romantic—as if I desired to father their children. Nor was the risk of getting rusticated because of the scandal of sleeping with an underaged student worth taking in those days of my orphanhood.

I had therefore theorized that the girl I could really fall in love with must either be half my age or double it. This meant either I had to resort to an infant or a woman who happened to be raising one. In despair of such broad spectrum, it was finally in Dr Saeed Mirza's office one morning that the person of significance was marketed to me indirectly. The dean had called me in and informed me that a young missus of a saleswoman was coming to town from Delhi that afternoon to give a one-day seminar at the college. He said that such travelling women of the corporate breed couldn't be trusted or left alone with just any student from the university. In the past, there had been incidents involving corporate folks scheming and trying to seduce the innocent and intellectual post-doctoral lot of our college.

'The intellectual nerd seems to be the most promising future husband material in the market, with his great salary package and a six-month fully sponsored trip to some foreign university,' Saeed Mirza told me with a hint of pride in his voice. He said that since Zahed was very busy with his papers and also quite a fool when it came to women, as his elder, more responsible, and most favourite son, he would very much like me to go and pick her up from the airport and look after her while she was in the town of Nalanda.

And I remember Santos, Saeed Mirza's loyal manservant, and I driving to the nearby Gaya Airport that day. I stood waiting for her arrival in front of the oriental Bodh Gaya airport, standing by the university's Sumo car and watching the unusually large aeroplanes that sometimes flew in from tropical countries like Tokyo and Laos. Long-extinct airlines, including Nippon and Hong Kong Airlines, still operated at that specific airport, with massive Airbus 320s touching down, dropping off Buddhist monks (who visited Nalanda on pilgrimage), and then immediately taxiing to the runway and taking off for their connecting destinations.

Outside, in the otherwise scanty spread of that urban airport complex, we waited for an hour or so among a few horse-pulled tonga carts and a few giant black Mercedes buses, packed with orange-robed monks, sitting and staring at the happenings of the world outside with clueless eyes.

When the flight from Delhi arrived and passengers began exiting the air-conditioned terminal, there was a sudden burst of confusion in the parking lot. A lot of mix-ups. Taxi drivers rushed to negotiate fares. Bus conductors slapped their buses, signalling the drivers to move. Santos raised his hands a little higher, holding up the Nalanda University placard so our visitor could identify us. When she still didn't appear, I started to get anxious. And then I saw her for the very first time.

Noel.

She stood gleaming in the midday shade. Her face freckled, her skin glowing and radiant, her hair a cosmos of various shades of brown and gold. She was a sight to behold, and I thought, Noel or no Noel, this woman was the most stunning creature I had ever encountered. And then, very suddenly, this young man (someone who had accompanied her unannounced!) emerged from behind her, placing his hands on her shoulder and glancing at us with side-eyes, as if to exhibit from a distance that the promising merchandise of a beauty belonged to him.

But anyways, she was an exotic creature in the hinterland of Bihar, revealing here and there such amusing embarrassment about herself. A string of her black bra peeked out from under her crop top when she raised her hand to greet us. And then, a pair of small black moles on her motherly cleavage became visible when she bent down to pick up her luggage.

As she came closer, Noel squinted her eyes, trying to figure out if we had come to pick her up.

'Are you Ms Noel?' I screamed anxiously.

'Yes. Hi. I'm Noel. How do you do?' she said. 'I'm sorry to keep you all waiting. I hope you have been drinking water all this while. Oh God! This sun is going to burn us alive.' She was now standing with me in the shadow of our Sumo that was parked, her companion following her. She had a very understanding presence about her, with a habit of curiously looking into my eyes as she spoke, as if she had known me for a very long time. That was when I lost my game. That was when I knew my hunt for the mistress was over.

'Yes, Ms Noel, absolutely,' I said, smiling. I tried to ignore her companion until that bastard interrupted us, dropping his luggage on my foot and saying, 'Here, young man. Just put it in the trunk, please!'

As the two of them settled in the backseat, and she adjusted her head on her companion's chest, her athletic thighs almost brushed against my elbow once, igniting in me an altogether supreme passion. 'I hope your journey was fine?' I asked nervously, but my voice was left to float in the air. Unattended. Unanswered.

The driver looked at me blankly.

The voyeurs had begun snuffling and cuddling in the backseat as if they were on their honeymoon. They were completely oblivious to our presence as if we were some third-grade taxi drivers habituated to the general sight of intimacy between young travelling couples who couldn't restrain their passion while on vacation.

Suddenly, Noel said, 'What was it you were saying, sir?'

'I hope you had a fine journey?' I said, as if I could have done anything if their journey hadn't gone well.

'Oh, yes. Terrific! Absolutely terrific!' Her companion said, still gazing deeply into her eyes.

The remainder of our journey was mildly unsettling, as Santos drove recklessly, as if we were being chased by violent Maoists. During the ride, Noel caught me staring at her a few times in the rear-view mirror. When our initial awkwardness had faded, she asked whether it was safe to stop for some water in the gangster land of Bihar.

You see, I was their designated concierge and security, and even though I was recently orphaned, their safety at that point in time depended entirely on me. How thrilling it would have been if I had abducted the two travellers, torturing and fondling one and hurtling the other from the speeding car!

Santos pulled up at a gas station. I got out to fetch a bottle of water for her, and then she said that she wanted to urinate. I mean she said that she wanted to use the ladies' room, and because her companion was busy on his cell phone, I was commissioned to walk her to the public restroom. There I stood, guarding the sanctuary of the ladies' toilet at some random pay-and-use toilet in the middle of nowhere while she peed.

But altogether, she was a supreme creature, I must say.

During the rest of the ride, the couple bombarded me with questions about the historical sites that studded the Nalanda Airport Freeway, and I entertained them with exciting tales of the oriental East.

Say, when an ancient-looking white cubical structure passed by, she would get all excited and ask, 'Oh! What about that building, I wonder?' Hey eyes would widen with curiosity.

'That's the only surviving Dutch godown in town, miss. They used to store opium and morphine inside this building during the Dutch invasion of India,' I said.

'Godown to store morphine? I thought it was illegal,' she said, and then, turning towards her lover, she cooed, 'Isn't it, baby? Isn't storing morphine illegal?'

'Not at that time, miss. Not then,' I said.

After a while, when we finally approached the endless, semi-burnt red walls of our university, Noel asked, 'Woah! What about this one? What building is this?'

'These are the old ruins of Nalanda University, miss. Approximately 2,000 years old,' I said, as if they were 2,000 years old because I had made them so.

'You seem to know your history quite well,' Noel remarked. 'How do you know so much about the opium trades and the passage of Dutch tradesmen from the early 19th century? What do you do, Moron ji?'

'I am … well … ma'am,' I stumbled over my words, 'a scholar researching the various effects of morphine on curing sadness. I am also the assistant professor of psychology here at the university.' This perhaps changed her perception of me, as she suddenly shifted away from Herman to the edge of her seat. She remarked coyly, 'You look a little too young to be a professor!'

To this, I responded with silence.

'Your parents must be so proud, so proud, Moron ji!' she said.

And then, to reveal the horror of my ultimate despair, I informed her, 'They're all dead now. My father died only last month. I'm still mourning him.'

'Oh dear!' she said. 'I remember losing mine when I was in high school. It gets better with time, Moron ji. I hope you have somebody looking after you.'

I felt the air shifting between us—from me being a singular object of pity, we were now two orphans travelling through the streets of Nalanda on that dull afternoon.

For the remainder of our journey, I supplied her with a brief summary of my dissertation, probably to imply that I too could be a desirable mate for her if her boyfriend ended up accidentally abandoning her in this terrific land of Nalanda. She was enamoured with my scholarship. I think at some point she had accepted me as a favourable companion for the rest of their journey, for briefly after my introduction, Noel and her companion were all laughter. Noel asked me about the opium godown in greater detail and then about the history of the university campus. She said that she had heard news and seen a documentary which informed her that our university was 'resurrected from the ashes only a few years ago?'

I kept amusing her with stories—some real, some fictional—which she lapped up with great enthusiasm until we reached the guest house where the two were supposed to stay.

It's very interesting how time flies when a beautiful chick with pretty brunette hair is actually interested in listening to what I have got to say.

After seeing them off, I walked to my dormitory and spent a sleepless night. Zahed had abandoned me altogether in this quest since he was busy spending his days 'inside Phoebe', as he described it. Tossing and dreaming restlessly that night, I realized that it was quite possible for me to heal and overcome the grief of my father's death in this living world because now, instead of being plagued by the anxiety of lifelong loneliness, I was being haunted by dreams of Noel.

How fantastically her brown hair parted and fell over her face, the terrific smell of her breath when she laughed and exhaled near my ears (accidentally), her black nail paint glistening in the rear view while she caressed her companion's chest, and the softness of her thighs when she brushed them three or four times against my orphaned elbows.

The next morning, I reckoned, she would have been awfully tired after having spent a sleepless night of an uninterrupted saturnalia with her beloved companion. When I went to wake them up for the seminar, Herman outrightly refused to step out of the room. He complained of a pain in his lower back, which I presumed was a result of too much humping and jerking from the night before. Noel stepped out alone and greeted me shyly. She was wearing a plain white shirt and a pair of black office trousers.

Noel was here to advertise American Express's line of student-friendly credit cards with almost zero interest on student loans. She conducted her seminar in the mostly vacant auditorium of the university. Her presentation was attended by a motley group of ten or fifteen boys, who had probably come in search of some free coffee and vanilla muffins.

After her seminar, I took her out for lunch to a nearby motel. There, we sat and ate under a depressingly ghostly shed among vacant tables, with another deserted car in sight and a depressing waiter at our service.

This is probably that one moment in my life when I have her all to myself. I stared at her wonderfully pedicured feet while she was scanning the menu for desserts. *If there were to exist any hypothetical lapse in time that might permit me to work my magic upon her and allow me to fuck her goddamn brains out, it was right now!*

'How are you liking Nalanda, Ms Noel?' I asked.

'Oh, quite good. Quite good, Moron ji,' she said.

'Would you like me to take you to some of the more interesting and historical places of Nalanda?' I asked, praying that she wouldn't excuse herself for being tired.

'Can we go to the most monumental place of Nalanda after this?' she asked. 'Like the Nalanda place?'

'Do you like lakes, miss?'

'Oh yeah, I won't mind,' she said, though looking a bit deflated.

'Would you want to go right now?' I asked, an excitable rush building in my heart, because if she said yes ...

'Sure, why not.'

Hell, I would get to spend a solid afternoon with her—all alone.

I took her to the palatial Venu Vana, a Japanese monastery with a huge stretch of forest and a giant pond in the centre, where a few large Japanese fish swam. There in Venu Vana, we accidentally caught each other's reflection in the pond. She smiled and opened her heart to mine.

'So how is life in Nalanda, Professor Moron?' she laughed, playfully emphasizing on the word 'professor'.

'It's quite terrific, miss. It's quite crazy,' I said.

'Do the students here party a lot?' she asked mischievously, having somewhere shed her previous motherly know-it-all sentiment.

'You see, it's like a rave, Ms Noel. We party so much. Every weekend. I mean, the job pays well. But it's the opportunities here. So many of these young bastards running wild. It's just like Boston. But only super cheap.'

'Oh, you have been to Boston also?' she asked.

'I used to live there, miss. Me and my parents.'

'Oh, for how long?'

'Until I graduated, miss.'

'Where did you graduate from?'

I believe that was the longest conversation I had had with a woman since Tania walked out of my life for good.

I remained silent for a moment as if the answer was altogether too obvious.

'Harvard, miss.' I believe I saw her pupils dilate when the name of the great institution was mentioned.

'Well, of course, you did,' she said, suitably impressed. Then, 'You got nice clubs here?'

'Crazy places here, miss. Absolutely crazy clubs around the town,' I said. I would have pounced right away on the opportunity if she had asked me to take her to a nightclub that night before she could return to her office in Delhi.

'Miss, the alcohol is super cheap. There is this Blue Frog Club. And then you have a club that has this real classy jazz music. I can't recall the name, but it's brilliant. There are just far too many clubs here in Nalanda. You toss a newborn baby from a car, and he is sure to end up on the dance floor of a crowded nightclub. Anyway, what's your favourite drink, miss?'

I could see her blanking out for a second, and then she said very fancily, 'Martinis?'

'Oh, Ms Noel, you should try the Jäger in Blue Frog. It's crazy.' It was not. It was just that a few shots of the mighty Jäger with the mightiest 93 per cent alcohol concentration would have knocked her unconscious that night. Or probably would have gotten her super aroused and steamed up. And with nobody to unleash her passion upon, she would have probably dragged me to a cheap motel room in the middle of the night and committed such outrageous deeds that Professor Saeed Mirza would have been scandalized even to imagine them. Oh boy! The way I would have ravished her if she had wanted to try Jäger.

But then she just paused and said very sincerely, 'I'm so glad you are recovering from your grief so well, Moron ji. It's nice to see you smiling.' She held my gaze for a while and then got up to say that we should explore the city more.

We explored the swinging mountain cable cars of Nalanda that took us to the hillock of Shanti Stupa, where a few sad, meditating monks were seated. Suddenly, Noel put her arm around my shoulder and told me that she was awfully tired and needed to urinate again.

'Say, Mr Herman isn't going to join us anytime soon?' I asked.

'He might,' she said. 'Wait, let me call him.'

Even now I sometimes wonder why the fuck I was such a supreme retard then, acting all shy and asking her to remember her sugar daddy when I should have been using that time to work up my own magic on her.

She called Herman a few times, but there was no signal on the top of the hillock. After a minute hiccup, I was again the subject of her attention.

'So where are you from, Ms Noel?' I asked.

'I'm from Nepal. South Sikkim, actually.'

'You don't look Sikkimese, miss.'

The aboriginal tribal Sikkimese are characterized by their Asiatic slanted eyes and their jovial nature. Their extremely depraved socio-economic conditions, if we consider the general situation. I immediately regretted saying it. But she was busy calling her lover again. No signal yet.

'Oh, yeah. That's because my father was not Sikkimese. I guess that's why.' Then she turned her pretty face towards me and asked, 'How did you end up in Nalanda, Moron ji?'

'It's a long story, Ms Noel. After my mother's death, my father began missing home. And then he left the States and came back to India. And he just died here.'

She seemed all motherly again.

Regardless of my suffering through those depressing parties at Nalanda University, at that moment, if someone from my university had seen me with her, they would have considered this nothing but a clandestine romance I was having with the visiting woman from Delhi.

In the evening, Herman called to inform her that he had healed himself from his horrible backache and that he would be joining us for the remainder of the expedition. And all of a sudden, the great sense of confidence I had woven around our newly found romance collapsed.

She was altogether so responsible and loving towards her Herman that, the moment he joined us that evening, took a rickshaw, and met us at the foothills of the Swarna Bhandar Cave, she immediately abandoned me like a public urinal and attached herself to her mighty lover again. They charmingly walked uphill to the Swarna Bhandar Cave while I trailed them, bearing the bottle of water I had bought for them in one hand and a chocolate I had secretly bought for her in the other.

Up at the Swarna Bhandar, I was asked by my travelling voyeurs to take a few snapshots of them against the backdrop of a red romantic sunset.

Herman handed me his Polaroid camera and ran towards Noel. He lifted her in his arms and began kissing her passionately. Apparently, they were trying to align their lips with the backdrop so that, in the photo, the setting sun would appear to be right between their kissing lips.

'Did the photo come out nice, guide brother?' Herman asked and then kissed Noel lightly on her lips.

'I guess so,' I said nervously.

'Well, then take more photos. Don't stop!'

During our return drive, dusk was beginning to settle over the ginormous monasteries of Nalanda. I was sitting in the front seat, suffering the horror and angst of a heartbroken maniac. In the backseat, Noel was all fidgety and juvenile, playing with Herman's hair, fixing his shirt. To add to my misery, this was followed by the sound of slurpy kisses. I would be sitting and focussing on the smooth-sailing west-bound street ahead of us, and then suddenly there would be a loud kissing sound in the back, followed by a few hushed 'sshhs'.

I have always been so fond of such sad and heartbroken expressions as the one I had acquired that day in the Sumo. I remember being all teary and bearing a deathlike silence. Such a disturbing silence that the travelling lovers of Delhi had to stop their foreplay and check whether I was alright. I said dully that I was missing my dead father when the fact was that my existence had been trampled by the traversing Nepali, and the dreams I had dreamt on top of the Peace Pagoda had been crushed and thrown into a public toilet. Noel could have been my future wife, but here she was, nestling into her boss' arm in the backseat of the Sumo. And if that were not enough, tomorrow they were to fly back to Delhi on the 2:00 p.m. The Tokyo Airlines flight and the flames of a romance ignited that afternoon in Herman's absence would continue to consume me for the entirety of that golden summer.

I think somewhere I was feeling manically depressed, and with that earliest episode, we had started to see the distant signpost of our university's guest house. I realized that not tomorrow, but probably right now, I was spending time with Noel for one last time. Tomorrow, I wouldn't be her Moron but a simple concierge who would be dropping them off at the airport. All I would have for myself tomorrow is that they would greet me and thank me with rapid handshakes, and then I would be left all alone.

Suddenly, a war erupted in the backseat. Noel had murmured something, and I believe Herman had blurted something nonsensical, causing Noel to slap her forehead in aghast horror. She began muttering like a madwoman, revealing her authentic Nepali accent which she had been concealing all this while. It was something to do with Herman's wife (weren't he and Noel supposed to get married? This fall?), to which Noel responded with a verbal 'How could I? I'm just your mistress? Just a haram? I can't show my face anywhere anymore.'

'What the fuck?' I announced and looked behind.

Noel suddenly demanded that the car be stopped. She said she would like to catch a bus to Nepal instead of going to the campus, while her boss instructed the driver not to do any such thing.

'What happened, Ms Noel?' I turned around and asked.

'You ask him what has happened! Why would you consult a prostitute like myself on such worldly matters?' Noel said as she raged.

It really upset me to see her like that. Calling herself a prostitute and all. She was such a pure, innocent girl after all. And really, what was her fault? She hadn't broken my heart like that horrible Tania had. We didn't have an arrangement set up in the first place. I was such a fool to believe that she would behave like my rightful wife as soon as we had met.

'No, Ms Noel, please be mum. It's quite alright. Whatever it is, I'm sure we can handle it.' I placed my hand on her thigh and coaxed her right in front of that bastard Herman, and surprisingly, Herman didn't seem to mind at all. So what if he had protested against me brushing my hand against his girlfriend's bare thigh? In a matter of such great distress, I would have called up my many brothers and had him buried right in the middle of that street.

Noel shed her tears on my wrist and said that her redemption was upon her. She said she was deathly afraid of Herman's wife, that her ruin was closing in.

'Then don't go to Delhi, Ms Noel. I mean, figure things out first,' I said, having altogether promoted myself to be the director of her life.

She replied that she was awfully scared and wanted me to escort her to the guest room and then help her catch a train to Sikkim.

'I can very well escort you to your house, miss, if you want me to. But don't cry like this, madam. There is absolutely no need to worry when young Moron is here,' I said.

Her worry materialized as soon as our car reached the front of our guest house—in a white salwar kameez. A five-foot-one angry dwarf who was apparently pregnant and had been married to Herman for three years now.

'Oh no, no, no!' Noel began screaming, pulling herself against the leather foam seat of the Sumo. 'She is here. She is here. Herman's wife is here!'

'She won't eat you, Ms Noel. I can assure you she seems deprived of any carnal properties. Besides, look! She is pregnant,' I said, growing nervous myself.

I still sometimes wonder how that woman managed to track her traitor husband to the university and enter the campus that day.

With her pregnant belly, Herman's wife roared and screamed at the sight of our Sumo approaching and hurled a heavy potted plant at the windshield of our vehicle. She then began chasing us on foot, swearing revenge that would result in the demise of all those who had brought her shame. Poor Santos pulled the wagon back, and Herman jumped out of the vehicle, throwing himself onto the road. To avoid trampling him, we had no option but to stop the car then and there.

Such was the wrath of the betrayed wife that when she did catch Herman by his collar, we feared she would turn herself into a widow. She thrashed and beat her husband, screaming at him for being a fraud and a cheater who was sleeping with his employee. Herman defended his head from the punches and his scrotum from the kicks while also attempting to calm his wife, who seemed as though she was either going to have a miscarriage or become a lifelong widow.

When she was done with her husband, Mrs Herman's gaze fell on our lamented goat—Noel. Stupidly enough, Noel got out of the car and ran. Seeing my beloved under threat, I screamed, 'Aihhh!' in anger. But wait—I pulled out my cell phone to call Zahed. There was a wild commotion on the campus. Curious students and even the engaged scholars broke away from their meditative spell to witness the wrath Herman's wife was about to unleash on her husband's kept woman.

'Aihh, you stupid bitch!' I screamed and ran after them, but Noel sprinted hastily like a winged fugitive. She ran and ran to the very end of the sunset, and when she got exhausted, she collapsed on the ground, joining her hands and begging the pregnant wife for forgiveness. Noel was dragged back to the Sumo by her hair, sweeping a good hundred feet of the dust-laden street of Nalanda University. Before I could run back and save her from the crazed monster, Herman's wife began hunting in the car for a weapon of destruction. By the time I reached them, she had found a screwdriver I had the habit of toying with during my ADHD episodes, and she stabbed Noel in the belly, right in front of my horrified eyes.

'Oh my God! Oh my God!' Herman screamed, sounding like a ravaged Russian tourist being molested on the streets of South Africa. As Noel lay bleeding on the ground,

Herman was dragged away by his wife into a private taxi, which was waiting for her in the driveway.

'I won't let anything happen to you,' I announced passionately, holding Noel's head and placing it on my lap. Her eyes were still open, and she was still perspiring. 'Don't worry, Noel. You will be absolutely fine,' I said, kissing her forehead as she began to faint.

I picked up my phone like a nice suitor and called my dear Zahed. When he picked up after a couple of rings, I said, 'Listen, boy! Listen, you medico fool! It's time to change shit up.'

'Change shit up?'

'Yes. Noel has been mortally stabbed!'

'What the fuck? Hold on a sec.' There were murmurs and ECG beeping tones of dying patients in the ICU in the background. 'Mortally stabbed?' he asked.

'Yes.'

'Ha ha! Boy! With your dick, ha? Finally, you fucked her?'

'No, brother. She was stabbed by Herman's wife.'

'Oh hell! Wasn't he the boss?'

'Yes. He was the boss. And he was fucking her, and he was also married. His wife caught them and stabbed her. She is bleeding to death. I can't take her to the hospital. Your father will figure it out. And then he will distance me from the whole matter. He is a nitwit. I am bringing her to our room. We must save her.'

You see, I couldn't have left her alone to the vices of those bystanders. I had to bring her body to my dorm room. Had I just deserted her to that crowd that evening, they would have transported her to our local hospital, where she would have made a nice recovery. And then what? Then her old friends from Delhi would have flown in and snatched her away from my desiring arms.

Actually, more than the love I had developed for her, it was my undying hatred for those untouchable corporate bastards from Delhi that prevented me from taking her to a hospital. Her colleagues from the corporate world—guys with nicely groomed moustaches and freshly ironed shirts—probably used to loom around her back in Delhi, trying to get a chance to sleep with her. And to be quite frank, even this clueless phony bitch would've hung around them, hugged them jokingly, and they would have hugged her tighter. Together, they would've clicked pictures and smiled and cuddled and be dazzled in the fool's paradise of lifelong friendship.

This disturbing flash of an image haunted me—how, upon hearing that she had been abandoned by her boss, her many prospective lovers would rush down to Nalanda to save their concubine's life and declare ownership. How they would take her back to Delhi, tease her and humiliate her, then hug her. And once she had recovered, they would have fucked her some twelve times on twelve different drunken occasions. All the while, the reality was that after everything we had been through—if there was someone who had the right to fuck Noel, it was me. Now, you tell me? After everything that had happened between us since morning, how could I have let her go?

I didn't.

Instead, Noel's body was dragged that evening into my dorm room at the boy's hostel (which was mostly dark and vacant at the time, as there was a Chinese festival down at the common grounds).

Witnessing Noel being stabbed had driven me into a state of outright madness. While she fought for her dear life in my room and Zahed was trying to save her, I ran downstairs and hauled Santos up, practically blaming him for everything that had led to this. I told him that he was hereby dismissed from the job. That, I, Mason Moron, was firing him with authority.

Poor Santos stared at me in stunned silence. Then he said suddenly, 'You just need a pussy no, Sir Mr Moron?'

'What?' I snapped, my eyes all confused and agitated. 'What the fuck is wrong with you, Santos? A person is fighting for their life, and this is what you say? You think it's funny, you brainless bastard?'

'Oh, tell me, dear sir! Oh, boy!' he said, tears rolling down his cheeks. 'You just need a pussy only, no! I will get it for you, sir ji. You go and fuck a nice prostitute in Chaturbhuj, and I will pay from my own humble salary. But don't fire a loyal manservant like me. As you must know, Chaturbhuj is the largest red-light district in our land of Bihar. Second largest in the nation. Please go on, sir ...'

He was so damn heartbroken that even I felt bad for him for a moment. Really. I felt his pain as if it were my own. But my Noel was passed out in my room. That was a greater pain. So, abandoning the plans of firing him, I scratched my head in confusion, turned back, and ran to my dorm. The same dorm room that I would soon be abandoning, leaving Zahed and even Noel forever.

So weak had been that pregnant lady's passion (more of helplessness) during the attack that, thankfully! (oh dear lord, I cried as if she were the mother of my child) the screwdriver had only penetrated a few inches away from her liver (the soft tissues of the human body are cushioned and protected on all sides by fat deposits and soft bone structures).

'She will live on,' announced the proud doctor while our Phoebe sat on the window ledge and comforted me.

I am not sure if I remember it correctly, but I believe I took out a bundle of 500-rupee notes from my dead father's suitcase and stuffed them into Zahed's blood-stained hands. Three months later, on my wedding day, he returned those same blood-stained banknotes to me as my wedding present, along with an assortment of chocolates.

2

We feared that during the course of her hiding, a scrawny-looking, nondescript detective might be dispatched form the commissionaire's office in Delhi (probably after a complaint about a disappearing lady had been reported by her office) in search of a half-convulsed, middle-aged Noel, who was actually being secretly revived in our dormitory. I sat by her feet and nursed her scandalous body, often shielding the remnants of her honour by covering her bare torso with a white feather sheet whenever it would accidentally slip off, and then sometimes rejoicing and nourishing myself on the sight of her breasts when Zahed was gone for his third-year end-of-semester classes. On my Noel, he administered ointments and painkillers, and also a heavy dose of expensive antibiotics. For three days, Noel lay unconscious. This mighty mysterious lady with such an infinite sex appeal made me surmise that it was nothing but fate that had made her end up in my dormitory even before I could have gotten to know her surname.

'Why do you sit here all day, Moron? Are you in love with her?' Zahed asked me one afternoon after I had finished changing her clothes.

'I'm afraid so,' I declared, acting more like her lawful husband than her suspected abductor and kidnapper.

'Then we must wait for her to gain consciousness. Assuming she had become amnesiac due to the shock of the attack, I'm sure we can get her to believe that she loved you deeply before she was mauled.'

I looked at him in surprise. 'You mean if she has lost her memory, we would tell her that she and I used to be lovers?'

'Why not!' said the stupid doctor. 'And then she might get all confused and let you play out your heart's desire with her. You might lose your virginity with her rhapsodic self right in your bed. Oh boy! I had to go out on so many nights to get laid. But look at you. You had this lady fall right into your bed where you used to masturbate, Moron Boy.'

The truth was that nobody came looking for her even after a week of the incident. Her cell phone never buzzed. No policeman came knocking on the campus. She had no friends or family calling her. And I realized one fine full-moon night that, just like me, Noel too was all alone in this world.

And then one afternoon, when Zahed was gone (as usual), Noel woke up. Hell dammit. She woke up. Mildly sedated. She let out a soft 'Akh' as she held her abdomen. And then her eyes met mine.

I stood up all of a sudden, so quickly that the stool on which I was sitting fell on the floor. But I kept standing.

'Ms Noel,' I said, more like her guide and partner in misery.

'Hey, you,' she said, her eyes still half-closed.

I was glad that she hadn't had a panic attack upon finding herself in some unnamed dorm of some unnamed boys' hostel with a man she didn't know well, who had been her tour guide until the last week.

'Do you remember what happened, Ms Noel?' I asked, worried that maybe she had gained consciousness a few days ago and had been eavesdropping on my conversation with Zahed.

'A little bit, I guess,' she said, still calm. Still fine being inside my dormitory. And then she asked, 'Where is that mad bitch?'

'You mean Herman's wife?'

'Yeah.'

'Oh, miss. She is gone. She took her Herman back. She stabbed you. That mad bitch.'

'Yeah, I realize that,' Noel said, now looking at me as if she were in love with me or something. Or maybe the situation was so damn frightening and uncertain that I was hallucinating. Who knows.

Anyway, things seemed fine altogether.

In the evening, Zahed came with Phoebe and, after running a preliminary check on Noel, asked me to get her some fruit juice.

I did. And while I was handing her the juice, this bastard said, 'You know, Ms Noel, he has been sitting here ever since we brought you here. He hasn't slept. Hasn't eaten properly. Poor guy just kept sitting here.'

I giggled in confusion.

'That's not true…' I said.

After she had gained consciousness and a few days had passed, I was plagued by a more practical matter—how long would she stay like this? I simply dreaded that it was only a matter of a few rosy afternoons before one day she would make me sit down, look at me, and ask me to kindly send her back to the hills by the 5:20 evening train. That would be the end of my rosy dreamland. Just a nice, fantastic wet dream she would have become—Noel. Coming to me in the night and disappearing before I could wake up.

Though after that brief conversation, Noel barely spoke a word for the next few days. She spent most of her days staring out of the window, scanning the vast and strange expanse of Nalanda. She sat and sulked and refused to eat while I stuck around her—bringing her all sorts of nourishment: mutton soup, veg farmhouse pizza from the farmer's market, chocolate brownies.

She would look at me with gratitude, eat her share, and then when she couldn't finish her brownies, I would feed her with my own hands.

Though she was mildly catatonic and confused for a brief period after she had 'gotten a second life', she seemed to have accepted me as her nurse and companion. She made an effort to strike up a conversation here and there when an anxious quietness on my part made her uncomfortable. She would tell me stories with a light-hearted friendliness. She even enquired about my favourite movies and novels, and as time passed, I extinguished my fears of abandonment by simply but most fervently suggesting that she must stay for a few days until she made a solid recovery.

'Oh no, no!' she said. 'That would be too much. Too much burden on you, Moron ji. I can't do that. I would prefer going home.'

'No, really,' I said. 'There is no question of that. You must stay until that wound is dried up. I have read in a very informative book that such deep wounds can be subjected to the worst bacterial attacks. Even gangrene. You might rot and die. The thought of you travelling like this is totally out of the question.'

And then, a day later, she told me that she was missing her mother and wanted to go home. This time I saw an expression of fear clouding her face when I absolutely refused her request to leave my bedroom.

'No way, Noel. I suggest you stop irritating me with that suggestion.'

Her face began to twitch in fear. Then, 'Oh fine, miss,' I said, finally pretending to have fallen for her cries. 'Let me arrange an air ambulance for you. This will take you directly to your hill house. But please, you must not travel by road or train.'

Noel's eyes widened in disbelief. 'Are you mad, professor? Oh no. No need for that. Fine! I'll stay. Oh my God, this professor is all crazy.'

'No, no, Noel. I must,' I said. I pulled out my cell phone and began dialling some random number, when she almost got up from that blessed bed and said, 'Oh no. Please don't. I will stay. I will stay as long as you wish to keep me here, professor.'

With that I was able to secure my 'possession' for another few weeks, which I believed was enough time for me to ignite something in her that would stop her from leaving me at all. A kiss, probably? Since intercourse was plain out of the question. Her wound was worse than a fresh Caesarean delivery. Had I tried anything fancy with her, I was absolutely certain that she would bleed to death right then. So I figured that if I somehow managed to kiss her in the next few days, then at least I would have had that. After all, which orphan can't use a kiss to blackmail somebody into cohabitation?

So after a few more weeks of those light-hearted conversations between us:

'I miss my father,' I would say.

'Oh, me too,' she would say.

'I have a giant house, miss, the roof of which is incomplete. I dream of building it one day myself,' I would say.

'You will make such a terrific husband, Moron ji. Taking such good care of me. I'm sure half of Nalanda would be dying to sleep with you.'

And then, one rainy afternoon, when she began walking—completing the journey from my bed to the attached bathroom without my assistance—I asked her if she would like to visit my incomplete mansion, where I had buried my father.

'Absolutely. Oh yes,' she said, starry-eyed, that same motherly presentiment making its way back into her countenance.

In fact, while we were being driven to the Cemetery House, she asked Santos to stop at a florist, from whom she bought a pair of fresh lily and orchid.

'I'll put these on his grave,' she said as if she had known my father for years.

'Lilies are my favourite. And his too when he was alive,' I said.

'Here,' she said, handing me a lily from her bunch and looking at me practically with teary eyes.

So, from what used to be Santos driving his old Sumo with me sulking in the front seat while Herman and she nestled into each other in the backseat a few weeks ago, it had now changed to me sitting next to her. I was staring at her thighs, still the same glossy youthful thighs that had driven me mad with desire a few weeks ago. Noel was still somehow the same girl who had made me forget my father's death. This time, I placed my hands on her thighs, and she, with her eyes still fixed on the outside, placed her soft hands over mine.

As we sat near my father's grave, I whispered something inaudible into her ear. She turned towards me, surveyed my face, and asked, 'What?' Then I planted a sudden, anxious kiss on her lips. She paused and looked at me with sorrow and concern and told me that she didn't have much time left.

'Are you going to die, Noel?' I asked sorrowfully.

'No,' she said. 'I just don't have much time left. You see, my mother must be looking for a suitable boy for me. I am jobless. I don't have a future. I don't have a future unless I have a husband who would fight for my honour and save me from the catastrophes of this world, like you have been doing all along.'

'Would you like to marry me?' I asked. I suddenly sank to my knees and came up with a sudden proposal. 'Oh dear Noel! You are the most beautiful women a man can ever come across. I love you. Will you marry me?'

'Don't be a fool. Think. You are a boy. You are just a boy. I think we should not take this anywhere.'

'But I am rather fond of you. Listen, Noel,' I said. 'It was not a coincidence. You coming to Nalanda. Getting stabbed. Ending up in my bed. I swear on this grave. (Oh, bastard me, swearing on my dead father!) I really believe that there is much of destiny's will in putting us together. We are lone voyagers. We must be there for each other.

I have learnt from a book that it's true love when two broken people heal each other.'

And without needing either consent or any counsel, I held her in my arms and kissed her again—this time with such force—that she relaxed. She pulled my head closer to hers and kissed me even tighter as a forlorn sparrow chirped somewhere and a dog was trampled by a speeding car at a distance.

The very next day, I put Noel up at a nearby hotel. After this, the matter of her romance with me was totally out of the university's jurisdiction.

I met Zahed that afternoon after weeks. He came down to our dorm with Phoebe. There, I informed them about my great accomplishment of the week.

'You stupid son of a bitch! Are you fucking stupid, Moron?' Zahed exclaimed. 'You were supposed to fuck her, boy. You retard! You weren't supposed to marry her. What a fool, oh geez!'

But Phoebe immediately came to my rescue. 'Wow! That's how you think, huh? That a girl is born only to be fucked by your majestic dick?'

'Oh shit, no! No way, oh God!' Zahed said, looking at me in helplessness. 'She is going to eat him alive. You don't understand. Only last week she had been stabbed because she was prostituting herself to her boss. How could you let him marry that rascal?'

'It's been three weeks,' I said. 'That's a long time.'

'Listen here, you Moron boy. Don't be ridiculous, okay? You either fuck her or you don't. But you've got to take some time, boy. I know the fire that has erupted now is unstoppable. But you must stop it. Preserve sanity. At least explore a little! Get to know other girls. I'm sure Phoebe has friends she can set you with, just like this,' he, said snapping his fingers, 'just like this.'

Phoebe butted in. 'You think I supply women during my free time? That I'm a pimp?'

'Oh no, baby,' Zahed said, ' I don't think that at all. It's just that this doomed rascal is planning to marry her because he is lonely and desperate. He thinks he won't get a nice pussy to fuck. So he is reserving one for a lifetime. Oh, you all don't get it. He must take some time.'

'Zahed,' I said, 'the fire you are talking about, not only has it already erupted, but it's unstoppable now. It has already consumed me. I'm hers. I'm all hers. I will run away with her if need be, but I won't leave that poor girl alone.'

'I will kill myself if you do such a thing, Moron. I will hang myself from this ceiling fan,' Zahed said, almost reaching the point of breakdown.

'Don't be stupid. You don't understand. She is as lonely as I am. We both need each other. Tell me, how much harm can she mean? What is the threat you are so scared of?'

Though there was some logic to it. Only three weeks ago, she was being ravished by Herman. She was waggling her tiny tail around him, feeding him, getting all nasty with him behind the closed doors of our guest house, fully aware that he was a married man. And not just any married man—he had a wife who was six or seven months pregnant. Which famished bitch would want to fuck a man who has a pregnant wife?

And what have I gotten from her? A damned kiss? How much does a kiss cost? In return for all those expensive antibiotics and food that I had been buying for her with my dead father's money? Will Daddy be proud knowing that of all the girls in the world, I was in love with a thirty-year-old (excuse my vocabulary or the lack of it) 'corporate slut'? How could I have possibly returned to her hotel room that night? Knowing that these were the questionable affairs of her life?

I didn't.

Instead, I went back to Cemetery House and sat by my father's grave, cleaning his tombstone with one hand. Funny how he had spent all those tireless years in the curse of such eternal loneliness. The same curse which I couldn't even bear to survive for a day. And with that, my passion for Noel began to die.

But within a few lonely hours, my passion for her started rising again. Fine! To hell with it if she was fucking Herman! I saved her life. At least I deserved to fuck her once, right?

And after all, she was such a delightful, playful companion to me. During the course of our various fancy dates and mid-summer lunches at expensive roadside cafes, we used to kiss and make out in the back of the cab like madmen, she exhaling her warm breath on my neck, making me all worked up; me forcing my tongue into her mouth and tasting the peanut buttery essence of her mouth.

Though, when I would try to take our foreplay a few steps ahead—say, by trying to grab her crotch with my impatient hand—she would just stop me by slapping my wrist while continuing to kiss me with her lips. She informed me with the most sorrowful eyes, deeply locked into my impatient gaze, that she would only like to think about having sex now once she was married.

Though I can't really recall, I'm sure she sold that sorry idea of abstinence to me with the expertise of a great saleswoman from her past life. She assured me that If I kept my patience and sanity intact and waited to have sex with her after marriage, I would be gifted with the most surprising, most enlightening sexual experience. Something that only a few mortals are destined to experience in their youth. A sort of enlightenment that only comes in the form of wisdom once an impatient man holds his newborn daughter in his hands or, otherwise, when he makes love to his wife for the first time since nature had decided for the girl to be his wife. Such nonsense, combined with the promise of a rosebud-like, A-class, night-long sex, a possible sweaty intercourse in some distant European hotel room during the course of our honeymoon with closed doors and flying curtains, made me wonder, 'What was the haste really?' She succeeded in convincing me to wait until we were married.

You see, I was not like her Herman—dragging her along only to let her die at the end of the journey in a distant, unnamed land.

'So be it!' I announced. 'We will fuck when you become my wife.'

I had also been informed by movies that as far as sex is concerned, such prudence goes a long way in running a successful marriage. A little sacrifice on my part, and she would probably have been so impressed that she would have vowed to be my soulmate. I would have been able to revive in her the innocent girl she used to be while growing up—before she had slept with Herman or any of the many strangers she had sadly slept with—and was only dreaming of a husband who was 'manufactured for her and only her'.

Apart from that, I really waited because, at great intervals of time, I was blessed with unknown, unfathomable delights. Say, while I would be sitting on a chaise lounge in our tiny hotel room, she would suddenly appear and sit on my lap while I was busy working on my dissertation, which was due in the fall. And sometimes, during dinner, I would be so engrossed in my scholarly expeditions that I would suddenly notice Noel loitering in my vicinity, playing and fidgeting with the night lamp as if she were a restless schoolgirl. And to calm her, I would place my hands on her round buttocks while she wore a semi-white skirt, revealing the most pleasing sight of her pelvis.

Not that I wasn't in love with her. I had found myself deeply, agonizingly, and madly in love with Noel. I wrote her poems, composed pastiches, and hired live singers at our sunset dinners to perform her favourite songs. I was spending my money on her like a crazed madman. Buying one nice pair of sweatshirts here, a gold nose ring there (she had lost the previous one when her head had collided with the cement floor on the day of her stabbing). I even bought a damned scooter she wished for so I could take her on evening rides. Say, if I was sitting on my bed and she was browsing my computer, her eyes would light up upon seeing some expensive lingerie on the internet (40% Flash Sale!). That lingerie would then be found lying on her bed the very next day, all laced up with fresh orchids and roses.

I also enjoyed the bouncing of her ponytail. I'm not sure why I feel the sudden need to mention her ponytail in a separate narrative, but there was something magical about it. That golden auburn hair, which I had marvelled at one fine afternoon at Bodh Gaya Airport. And now I was going to own her and her hair in just a few more evenings. I had indeed fallen deeply in love with her.

One day, when we grew tired of spending our endless nights in that small hotel room, I asked her to move in with me at Cemetery House.

'Move in and do what? Maybe I should go to Delhi and look for a job again?' she said. 'I can't be a burden on you for the rest of our lives.'

'You are not a burden, Noel! Don't say that! As I have told you several times, I want to marry you. I want to be your husband. And a mighty husband, no doubt! A protector. I have planned everything out.'

'Don't rush like this. Marriage is a whole different world. Don't you want to take some time?' she asked.

Horrified by the possibility of losing her to the third-grade corporate world if she were to go to Delhi, I said, 'I have it all planned out, Noel.'

I assured her that with my scholarship money, I would be able to provide for her. The remuneration the university was giving me was a small but steady fortune that could help us complete the roof of my house and also repair her own broken house in the hills. With my grant money, I could afford her vacations and cold-cut meats. The prospect of living in the college town of Nalanda was an inviting prospect. It was quaint, and with my growing reputation, if her secrets remained hidden, there wouldn't be a house in this township that would not invite us for evening soirees and wine-and-cheese tastings.

I told her that she could go hand in hand with me on long evening walks, dressed in a navy green strip frock and a complementary navy green sandals—one day (I said wondrously) with a pregnant belly. We could raise supreme and moral children in this neighbourhood, where their grandfather was raised not long ago.

And then I said we could absolutely wait for her to see this town and my love in the coming spring before deciding whether she wanted to marry me. There was no hurry. 'No hurry at all, Noel.' When I finally finished my heartfelt monologue, she had tears in her eyes. In fact, her head was bowed down in front of me. I could see an eternal golden light of acceptance descending upon her. With that, she accepted my invitation to my home.

I believe that rather than the horrors she had faced due to her past, she decided to stay with me because of my childlike impatience. Besides the offer of good food and a place to live, she saw no harm in my proposal. And so, the next day, we moved into my Cemetery House.

With the advent of spring, as rosemary bloomed and cicadas whirred, her passion for me blossomed magically and naturally. Over time, we settled into an old-world, predictable routine. Say, when I was at the office, she would call and ask me to fetch groceries. And then later, she would consult me about what I desired for dinner.

'Would Moron want some momos and hot, hot mutton soup?' she would say, referring to me in third person. I could hear her wet, impatient lips rubbing against the phone.

'Oh, you want me to come and help you with so many chores, Noel?' I would say.

'No, not really. Finish your work. Just come soon. Your Noel is lonely,' she would say.

When I returned home, I would find her standing by the kitchen counter, cooking thick mutton soup and momos.

Back home, against the backdrop of faint sunlight, we made out with tender passion. I put my mouth inside hers, delicately fondling her breasts (caution had to be practised because her wound was still fresh), and afterwards, she coached me fantastically on matters of kissing and caressing a woman until she would gasp and moan in ecstatic delight.

In the night, her fair thighs rested on mine as she slept, snoring peacefully, and the horror of eternal loneliness was replaced with Noel.

What enamoured me about her, though, was that despite my futile fear of being abandoned someday (I barely knew anything about her, if you want to know the truth)—that she might just someday decide to walk out of our arrangement and stay with somebody else—she seemed to be repelled by strange men altogether. Say, if we were crossing a busy marketplace or were at a crazy house party, and a stranger approached her with a doglike smile, she would adopt a look of reproach and disgust towards him.

Her phone seldom buzzed. When it did, it was usually her mother, and the mother–daughter duo would babble endlessly in Nepali. She had informed her family that she had found a new job at the university and was planning to pursue academia now. That she wanted to earn a doctorate in psychology.

Oh, she was an avid learner. She consumed my lectures with impressive rapidity. She read novels by Anna Freud and Carl Rogers, and in the night, she told me to take it easy when I refused to sleep without sucking her breasts and playing with my penis.

In a matter of a few months, in a distant, undiscovered stretch of civilization at a ceremony ground whose name I don't recall anymore—though it had something to do with rosy beaches and a giant sand dune—I married Noel under a beautiful sunset. In her bridal attire, she looked awfully different from how I had imagined her to be—not a girl with new menstruation cycles and strong inquisitiveness that drives them to do unimaginable things in bed. But she looked like a grown woman—as old as wisdom itself—in her white, heavy dress, golden anklets, and an expensive necklace. She was her voluble self, missing her dead father, shedding tears of joy in a bride's gloom, for fate had eclipsed, and our togetherness was as undeniable as my love for her.

During our ceremony, a few underfed, sad-looking Nepali men sat on the edge of their seats, their pants pulled high enough to reveal tucked-up socks and dried, flaky, hairy feet. Every time I passed by them, they would say something in Nepali, and when I narrowed my eyes and said, 'Hein?', they would break into laughter.

There were, no doubt, a few estranged lovers from her past in attendance as well. Two Nepali boys with glossy skin and sharp haircuts sat together through most of the procession, trying to mimic an intense heartbreak, as Bollywood often depicts. I asked my DJ to cue a few sad, heartfelt songs for them as that would no doubt have been a treat to their sadistic hearts.

Noel's mother—my mother-in-law—whom I was meeting for the first time, was a different breed altogether. Very sincere. She was not too glamorous or good-looking but was definitely a gentle lady. The truth is, if anyone had already accepted me into their Nepali heritage, it was her mother. During half the procession, mother and daughter sat around my dead father's grave, whispering to each other. Then they would laugh, hug, and keep talking, as mothers and daughters so often do when the daughter is getting married.

'So what's all the hush-hush about?' I asked as I approached them from the altar while they were in the middle of their conversation.

'Oh, Moron ji! What a sweetheart. Looking so smart, so handsome,' her mother said, taking my hands into her dark, wrinkled hands and surveying my face with sad curiosity.

Had my own mother been present that day, I wonder what would have become of us.

When her mother left us, the new husband–wife, to our own devices, Noel suggested that she might go back to her home with her family once the ceremony was complete. She said she missed her home terribly and that, more than anything, her mother was missing her like a madwoman. So much so that her health seemed to be deteriorating. Meanwhile, she suggested that I could judiciously use this idle time to finish my obligations with the university.

'Idle time? How much time are we talking about, wife?'

'I don't know. Umm, you can always visit,' she said. 'I would just like to be at home for a while.'

There was a sudden twitch on my face. The last girl in my life whom I had trusted enough to let sleep all alone back in her own home at her own vices was my Russian Tania (not that I had any other choice, but still, I would have liked for Tania to stay with me. But then, it could not be materialized). And look what became of her. All rotting in jail and all. And a sudden, terrible realization dawned on me—this was the girl I had been staying with all these months. This was the girl cooking delicious mutton momos for me in the evenings and coaxing me to sleep at night. And here she was, ready to abandon me and run back to her mommy as soon as she had legally become my wife? The rightful heiress of Cemetery House? The future mother of our children?

I could feel an instant bitterness slowly creeping into our marriage. However, this was only one of the many dreadful and truly sad incidents that were to follow.

There was also the matter of our unfulfilled intercourse. If it did not happen soon enough, I knew I was going to turn into a madman.

'So what about our honeymoon?' I asked her.

'We will have a lot of time for that, honey.'

'I'll come with you!' I said, my face all sad and teary. Hell! The truth was that I had been waiting for so long, holding my monstrous—almost inhuman—urges to finally fuck her. And here she was, suggesting that she would be leaving on the very night of our wedding. A time reserved for the stellar intercourse of a lifetime? What a bitch.

'Why would you come with me? I'd be glad if you stayed back,' she said all worked up. 'You must have so much work that has been left unattended because I dropped in like this! So many research projects to conduct. Classes to teach,' she said, sounding worried. 'You might lose your job like this. Hell, what will we eat after that?'

'I don't know. I just will. I'm thinking of quitting my professorship anyway so that I can give this time to our family.'

'And the money?' she said. 'What about your salary?'

'Well, you tend to undermine my degree, wife. I received this degree only last year from the most prestigious institution, supported by an excellent scholarship. You think I'll let you die of poverty and misery and hunger?'

'No, honey. I just worry about money sometimes. Maybe I'll take up work after we go to the hills.'

'Oh, there won't be a need for that, Noel. Do you think your Moron would let you wash dishes in some café in the hills?'

'Oh no. It's just that I don't want my family to be a burden. You are so young. A kid! Still a kid! How could I let this happen? Oh God!'

'Let what happen, Noel?'

'How could I really?' she said, tears rolling down her face.

She said that she had a brother whose diploma fees were yet to be paid in the fall. There was also an insurance policy that she was planning to buy for her mother. She mentioned something about another cousin she had been looking after, after his parents had died in a bus accident. She said that this cousin had a terrible drug problem, and had she still had her job in Delhi, she could have sent him to an excellent rehab with her good salary.

I held her hands, trying to calm her down. 'I'm here for all that,' I said. 'I know this marriage isn't like a usual marriage. However, come what may, I will look after your family. What else is a husband for?'

'But how much money do you have?'

'Oh,' I groaned, 'I have loads of money, Noel. Loads. Some fifty lakh are still intact from my father's inheritance. We could, of course, use that. And I can always take up any job in any place we might want to live in in the future. But right now, if you want to go to Namchi, then we go to Namchi,' I said, suddenly picturing the studious, courtly life I would be spending in the magnificent hills of Nepal. She had told me once that one could see Mount Kanchenjunga (the second highest mountain peak in the world) on a bright, sunny day from her window. I imagined myself sitting on a swing chair, surveying the distant snowy mountains as well as my wife as the cold night descended upon the hills. That way, I would always be around to keep an eye on her. If only I could successfully extricate myself from all the stupid obligations with the university.

As for Noel's friends, nobody from Delhi or Sikkim came to attend her sombre wedding. When I asked her, she said that she had cut ties with most of them and didn't intend to maintain relationships with them anymore. A remark I appreciated so much that soon after that, I was able to get into the dazzling groove of a groom who was grandly marrying the girl of his wildest dreams in his father's mansion.

From my own side, there was Zahed and Phoebe and a few friends of Phoebe's. Looking at her friends, I realized that all of them looked far better and more desirable than my present wife. Phoebe's friends were so kind; they helped me get dressed, showered me with flower petals, pulled my cheeks, and even struck up a conversation with the communists from Nepal. They were genuinely sweet and kind people, and it broke my heart that just as I had gotten to know them, I would have to part ways with them as soon as the ceremony ended. Noel's family suggested that they should leave for the hills of Namchi that very night, a decision they made because the family neither had a hotel to stay in nor the money to afford one. In fact her entire tribe had hastily gotten ready for the ceremonies in my own spare bedroom. Imagine that!

While departing Nalanda, pale shadows of crimson and sandalwood trees hovered in anticipation of the unmitigated disaster I had made beds with. At the railway station, the train whistled and started dragging itself onto the dismal land of Nepal. Or was it Sikkim? I didn't bother asking. How did it matter? In some darkly unmentionable way, it was all going to turn out to be the same thing later. I stood in the narrow alley, inspecting the new count of that Nepali tribe, which spoke in a unknown language, and also Noel, who after getting rid of her bridal wear was now transformed back into the girl I had endeared. Having changed into her track pants and a T-shirt, though, I believe I sat and stared at her in repulsive confusion—her voluminous hips and the widening of her stomach into absolute obesity. And from more than my wife—this short, toadlike, energetic girl I used to breastfeed from and desired with aplomb—she began looking like a rented mother I always needed.

120 Days before I Fake My Death

One might have sensed my growing contempt towards Noel. The bitterness creeping into my tone. You might be wondering why I have suddenly, out of nowhere, started hating her. I think we both are very close to the answers now.

The next afternoon, a worn-out shared taxi took us uphill from the city of New Jalpaiguri—a township famous for its black magic and witches dressed as regular housewives—to the hilltop of Namchi. It was a tortuous five-hour journey I completed with my new Nepali family. The green waters of the Teesta River flowed on one side of the valley, a giant grey hillock on the other. There were no fewer than twenty-five occasions when I had to cling to dear life on that drive uphill. Despite the unpredictable turns, the driver was driving recklessly, passionately humming some Nepali song, and there were other Nepalis blabbering in the car. I was resting on my wife's lap, and she was scratching my face with her pointy nails; I would be kissing her belly while she herself burst out laughing at some funny Nepali joke, and then bam, the driver would dash his brakes and I would pounce up to embrace my ultimate calling, but the Nepali blabber would continue, and so would the journey uphill.

She lived in a small, two-storey wooden house perched on top of an unnamed hillock, inaccessible by road.

As a result, we were required to trek uphill from the Namchi market. Short-legged Nepali men and women with narrowly slanted eyes sped by, appearing and disappearing in their cheaply manufactured leather jackets or elaborately warm fur coats with mufflers wound around their invisible necks. They paced faster than we could, appearing at the top of one hillock one moment and at the bottom of another the next. I trekked, following my group on that hilly terrain, hopping from stone to stone, placing my feet with meticulous caution. If I were to slip even slightly, my body would topple down the hill, and I would crash to my death even before anyone could turn to check if the newlywed husband was still following. Uphill, there was a noisy stream running right behind Noel's house, which, upon closer inspection, turned out to be a foul-smelling sewer.

Her modest, shoebox-sized house was dimly lit from the inside. It was barely ten feet in height, though in the past it had been described to me as a 'royal two-storey mansion on a hillside'. The arrangement was so poor and the house so tiny that, once inside, I realized that if I just raised my hand and punched the ceiling with enough strength, the entire structure would come crashing down. The restless footsteps of the people upstairs could be heard downstairs as if the commotion were happening on the same floor.

In fact, the entire family had devised such a helpless yet innovative way of communication. For example, if her mother screamed something from the kitchen on the ground floor, ordering the elder son on the first floor to sacrifice the pet pig for the celebratory feast, the brother just had to scream 'Huss! Hass!' and the mother would clearly understand that the pig would be sacrificed right away.

I am not telling you all this to degrade my wife or her humble abode. It's not that I had not sensed all these things before. I had figured out her humble dwelling right from the time of our cohabitation. But I am telling you all this because it had me wondering, 'How the hell am I supposed to fuck my wife amidst such tight security?'

Once we had settled into our bedroom, I said, 'Noel, where is the restroom?'

'Right there,' she said, pointing towards a small cabin that was covered not by a door but with a curtain.

'Say, Noel, I am wondering,' I said, giggling and trying to hide my ultimate anxiety, 'where are we to consummate our wedding?'

And Noel, a little too embarrassed to get into the details, said, 'I don't think that's a possibility right now, honey. The wound is still fresh. Not tonight, husband,' she said.

'Then when, Noel? I think my groin is swelling. I need to have sex,' I said.

'Don't worry. That will be taken care of on the honeymoon,' she said, and before I could descend into madness, she disappeared into the kitchen to help her mother cook for the celebratory feast of the night.

In the night, while her family was downstairs roasting the dead pig, Noel entered the bedroom silently, shutting the door behind her. I might have passed out from the intense nausea I had gotten from our taxi ride, for when I woke up, I saw the shadow of a naked Noel walking towards me with the excitement and arousal of a newlywed bride. Her long hair was parted in the middle and falling down her back. Her round, pointy breasts caught the glint of light that escaped from the window of our bedroom.

'Noel,' I muttered, more like an impatient child who has been waiting for his mother than a rightful husband who has been waiting for his wife.

But she had already walked up to the bedside and was leaning her head forward for a passionate kiss. She held my head with her hands and kissed me with such passion that, after the mayhem of all those defeated years, I figured the time for my redemption had come. I raised my hand and tried to grab her by her titties, but she slapped my hand away. She said playfully that she 'didn't want to be disturbed at such sensitive hours and that I should lay back and relax'. And then, instead of continuing with the foreplay, she slid her hands into my trousers and began playing with my giant, homeless penis. After a while, she took my penis into the warmth of her mouth and simultaneously held my face against the mattress of the bed on which I had been sleeping. I tilted my face to the side to gasp for air, and my eyes were met with the view of the outside world.

In the silence of the night, a hundred million stars illuminated the sky with their constant brimming and blipping. The glorious view of the outside world from Noel's window could be described in the following poetic notion: because it was dark (pitch dark) and the mountains were giant and distant from each other, they prevented the moonlight from entering the valleys. Thus, the twinkle of billions of stars in the sky seemed to illuminate seamlessly and merge with the darkened floor of the mountain which then faded into the valley. There were also a thousand houses on the other mountains and a cluster of homes in the valley. Small patches of star-like white light escaped from the windows and rooftops of those houses, and because of the pitch darkness of the night, the stars in the sky seemed to merge with those star-like houses on the ground. The familiar dimensions of time and space faded so that all around me were a gazillion celestial stars. The starry brimming of the house lights with the infinite glory of the midnight sky made the outside world look like heaven—from Noel's window, it seemed like the indefinite promise of tomorrow.

When I came, she retreated to her normal self, put on her bra, and asked me to come downstairs. Downstairs, her communal tribe was roasting a giant pig on a barbecue stick. The scent of burnt, charred meat filled the air, while one of her brothers brought chopped wood from a nearby forest. Noel's face radiated the red light of the bonfire. Her beautiful hair fell across her face. This was my delicate wife. The sight of her filled me with an altogether supreme passion once again.

For a few minutes, I felt content. As if I were the rightful husband and captain of that hillbilly tribe. I felt a sense of ease. But because greed has a tendency to overpower contentment, I went near her, sat down, and hugged her. Right in front of her family. Noel looked at me in surprise, retreated playfully, got up, and sat next to her mother, who was sitting opposite me.

All this while, she smiled and looked at me teasingly, and I stared at her profile in admiration. *Holy fucking shit,* I thought staring at her glossy legs, *this is my wife. The woman I can fuck for the rest of my life. Holy fucking shit.*

And more than contempt, I got this mad desire to fuck her finally. Why settle for less, right? I mean, she had probably fucked that Herman a hundred times? Didn't I deserve that much? As her lawful husband? She had given me a celestial fellatio only minutes ago. But still ...

I mean, she did her best. She did all she could. But then, that was all she had ever done. I mean, the fellatio.

For the next few days, my thirst for fornicating with her was on a constant rise. After marriage, my life had been practically divided between staring blankly at those mountains for hours and contemplating the most feverish of wet dreams in wakefulness. Things I would have done with my wife if she hadn't been stabbed for sleeping with a married man. And then the remaining half of my time was spent taking elaborate trips to the Namchi market with Noel's mother or a brother. I bought unusually expensive mountain vegetables and kilos of meat from the market with my duffle bag money (I had hastily stored all my father's leftover money in a brown cargo duffle bag before leaving the Cemetery House on the night of our marriage). I also stood at the edge of her broken roof, supervising its repair by a bunch of hired repairmen who were again being paid with my father's money.

I tried my level best to please her and her family. And they seemed grateful for the things I did for them. It was not a challenging task to get her family to fall in love with me. Oh, what a great sponsor I was. Funding her brother's college tuition, buying him and our tribe a Honda two-seater scooter, and even a damn washing machine so that her mother would not need to wash clothes with cold, freezing water on that cold mountain. I did all I could to win over her family. And my plan was working like a charm! But as for matters of sex and the consummation of our marriage, of all the schemes that could be achieved on earth, this seemed to be the most distant of fantasies.

Let alone sex, the husband and wife couldn't find any time for sacred privacy in that household. Her house was always so full of strangers. The usual drop-ins included the loud-mouthed hillbilly wife who lived next door with her truck driver husband (who had a drinking problem and unleashed almost all his anguish upon his wife with a leather belt). This monstrous state of affairs was recounted to me by my wife, who was sorrowful after the woman had dropped in to see us following our wedding. She would drop by now and then in search of a particular kitchen spice or vessel, which my mother-in-law kept in the safety of our bedroom. And, there were the usual running-ins with her brothers. Say, I would be sitting on my bed (which really wasn't mine), famished and imagining my wife naked, when her cousin would come in, spread a mattress on the floor, and begin his afternoon nap. If I were to go on the roof of her house (which was broken until I had it rebuilt with my father's money), her mother would be sitting in the sun, looking up, and humming a Nepali song.

Apart from that, something really hilarious happened after about a week or so, once Noel's course of medication was over. I thought it was a good time to bring up the topic of sex again. And I started doing so by suggesting it to her again. Sometimes directly. Sometimes even indirectly. I would stand near the almirah in our bedroom while she lay on the bed reading a magazine. I would groan and say, 'Oh! Oh damn,' and she would be like, 'Oh hell! Whattsit?!' I would reply, 'Nothing. There is just an ache in my groin. It hurts so bad.' She would ask, 'Oh, why is that, honey?' I would tell her, without complaining and crying, that I was suffering because my penis wasn't getting the ultimate relief that it sought. And she would idiotically roll her eyes, raise her eyebrows, and return to the article she had been distracted from.

Sometimes, I would jokingly mention the increasing divorce rates in our country, all due to the drop in sexual adventures that occur so frequently between a husband and wife once the routine monotony of marriage sets in. I would indirectly threaten her with a divorce, saying things like, 'Oh, I wish my sex life could be as happening and as celebratory as that.' I would say this if we were watching a movie and she was spooned in my arms while the actor on screen was having the time of his life with the actress. But during this sad episode of our marriage, things were working in a contradictory way. Instead of a fair share of disappointment on my part and an apology on hers, our marriage turned into a mini battleground for ideologies concerning sex. On the one hand, I argued that, as a husband, I deserved my wife's offerings. And she, on the other hand, contended that a husband should not feel entitled to such things. While the wife may be physically ready, sex is more of a mental journey than a mere physical release of bodily fluids. Initially, these playful disputes seemed amusing, but when the issue of Herman was brought in—the fact that Herman had fucked her on countless occasions while I, as her protector and provider, had to haggle for even one such chance—the entire situation became quite horrible.

A few days later, I was screaming into my phone at Zahed. 'She won't let me fuck her, boy. She complains of a pain that she can't quite describe. In fact, I am planning to confront that stupid bitch straight up. I'm going to walk up to her and tell her that I know Herman had fucked her multiple times before I came into her life. How am I any different?'

'And then she would let you fuck her, huh?' Zahed retorted. 'She would be like, "Oh, so sorry, my twenty-fourth lover. I totally forgot that I was a routine fucker before getting stitched up. I was fucking my former love in broad daylight and the dying days. Sometimes he would just be sitting on our bedside table, sipping tea, and the next moment he would be fucking me. Oh, I totally forgot that I was not a virgin. Oh yes, of course, please fuck me now."'

I shook my head in silence.

Zahed continued, 'You don't barge your way into a pussy like that, my young fakir. You don't force it. The more you struggle, the tighter it closes, which, as you may notice, will make your passage even tougher.'

'Then?' I asked.

'You've got to scheme your way into it. Work on her. The passage to the pussycat is not a one-time run. The pussy must welcome you. The pussy must long for you.'

'How the fuck am I supposed to do that, Zahed?'

'Here is how you will achieve your wife's pussy: you go around playing with her. Let her do her usual. Let her grip your dick. Let her shake it. Work your way around her groin, as you have successfully done on various occasions.

By the way, congrats for achieving at least that. Very many congratulations, my orphaned brother.'

Zahed continued, 'And then, when she begins to retreat, this is what you are going to say. You are going to say, with your fingers pinching and your eyes all narrowed, "Just the tip, please." Beg her, "Just the tip. Let me, please. I'm dying for it. I promise it will be just the tip." And then you will see that she herself will stop her ordeal and think for a bit. She might even retreat her hand and tap the side of her head with her fingers, like "hmm", and then you keep begging. "Just the tip, please. Noel, my wife, I really must." And she will then make you promise that it will be nothing but the tip. Do a pinky promise. And then, with those spells of pure, unbeatable magic, she will put some spit on her dried-up, worked-up pussy. She will make some minor adjustments. She will shift and nudge a little.'

I was completely silent, listening to every word of my friend.

'Hello, are you dead, brother?' Zahed asked.

'No, no. Please. You must go on, Dr Zahed.'

'And then you insert the tip. And you insert it again. But boy, listen. Listen very carefully. You must be lying completely over her while you are doing the deed. Cover her, and keep inserting the tip. And then there will come a time when she will get all worked up. She will get worked up because she doesn't trust you for shit. I mean, look at you. You can't trust the promises of a man any more that you can trust the instincts of a child with their wild passion and dizzying inquisitiveness. So she will go all like, "Okay! That's it." But you start moaning, Moron boy. You start moaning your sonorous, helpless moans. And then, before the blink of an eye, just shove that dick inside your wife's unwelcoming pussy. Shove it and fuck her. You will see that, contrary to what she is saying, her thighs will still be open. And, instead, she will help you fuck her nicely.'

And, before I could say anything, he said, 'Of course, once you are done, she will retreat in silence. She won't talk to you for a day or two. Probably she won't cook either. But don't worry, oh brother. I can always get the food delivered to your doorstep.'

'And what do I explain to her?'

'Explain to her that you couldn't help it. You couldn't help it because her pussy was so nice. So tight and nice, indeed, that you wonder if Herman had an organ as great as yours. Get all teary. And then it will only be a matter of a few dingy afternoons before she visits your study again. All skirted up, no pants, and then she will ask you to fuck her again.'

Zahed's plan was a work of primitive genius. Baboons have been known to bribe female baboons with bananas and shiny, sparkly things to mate with them. I reviewed his scheme and resolved that, in due course, that is how I would achieve the impossible.

The next day, when miraculously we were all alone in that communal house—her brother had gone for a band practice while her mother had set up a stall at the local market—I decided to put Zahed's advice into action. I remember I was lying on our bed, my elbow tucked deep into the mattress, while she was on the same bed, reading a magazine.

'I love you,' I said to her with a tone of divine finality. *There, I said it. Kaput!* 'I love you, Noel.' And then I advanced to hug her, secretly planning to slip my hands into her pants, but she, with her worldly wisdom, retreated (not physically) and continued reading her lame magazine with her fake glasses and cooed, 'Love you too,' in a fake fanciful tone. She was totally unbothered and stared at the horrible magazine in such a manner that had I pulled out my cock at that precise time, she would not have even raised an eyebrow at my grand gesture.

This led me to figure out that Zahed's whizz of a genius plan was workable on a girl of nineteen but not on a woman of thirty-one.

As for her romance with magazines, it was a clear indication of how old and tiresome Noel was, in contrast to the image I had built of her in my mind. In fact, I had noticed this most unusual habit of hers ever since she had given me that fellatio, as if she had given me her everything. She would sit for hours with some useless fashion magazine in front of her, not talking to me or fidgeting with me. Instead, she would be sincerely and silently reading some horrible literature, with the back of her neck protruding into a fat hump. She had devised her own ways of recreation, which were quite dissimilar to mine. I would have used two or three different cocktails of drugs to pass the day. I would have engaged in the most scandalous and passionate intercourse with my wife six or seven times a day as a means of daytime recreation. Exploring the true feel of intercourse in every damned corner of the house. But not her. She seemed too full of dicks. As if her past courses of intercourse had been enough to make her avoid falling prey to my longing claws anymore. Hell, while I might sound desperate for sex, dear reader, had I been able to consummate my marriage, perhaps I too would have been one of the more peaceful and pacified husbands. Probably

I would have sat by the ledge of my window as a senior scholar and researcher, penning my dissertation on the myriad effects of morphine on a grieving brain. But being desperate to feel my first pussy, I couldn't help but loiter around Noel all day, scheming and struggling to get even once chance to fuck her.

I think, more than the mere principle of gaining pleasure from it, I wanted to have sex with my wife because it would have helped me trust her completely. Her offering me her whole body would have been a gesture of absolute reassurance. A wife offers herself to her husband as a sign of devotion. And here I was, reminiscing about the scars of her misfortune, aching and grieving even though she was right there in front of me. Even in marital relationships, it's not practically possible to be around your beloved wife at all times. On a brief Sunday afternoon, for instance, a gentleman of a husband might fuck his wife a good two or three times, and then, after his passion was extinguished, he might take a nice shower and relax on a lounging chair in the afternoon sun with fresh talcum and black wool for chest hair. Meanwhile, the wife might choose to bid him goodbye and go to a Sunday church service or get some fresh vegetables from the weekend super sale market. That's the normal, healthy rhythm of a marriage. Absence creates longing. But not mine! I had to find an excuse to be with her at all times. If she was getting dressed for an evening out, I would poke my nose around the corner of the room. I would scamper around her like a wayward child and ask, 'Where are you going?' just casually, and she would tell me the most unbelievable, unfathomable stories.

One evening, she said, 'Well, my friend Puja is coming from Gangtok to see me, so I'm going to get a few drinks with her.'

'Do I know Puja? Have I met her?'

She didn't respond. She was too busy fixing her fake eyelashes.

'Baby?'

'No. She teaches at a school in Gangtok. She couldn't come to the wedding.'

I didn't believe it for shit. Noel was not the kind of person whom people would travel miles to meet. And with a horrible suspicion vibrating through my veins, I made up a nonsensical excuse so that I could join her. 'Oh! Why don't I come with you, and we can prank her? I will observe from a distance, acting like a stranger while you and your friend are drinking. Then, right in the middle, I will come and ask Puja for her phone number. I will tell her that she is pretty and charming and that I want her number. Since she hasn't met me, she will think I'm a random guy. Only after she has given me her number will I come and sit right next to you. I will start kissing you, and we can enjoy the look of shock on her face, ha!'

I know it sounds ridiculous, but then that was how my life was turning out to be anyway.

By devising schemes like this, I was always able to accompany her on her expeditions. Say, if she was going to the market to get some turnips and carrots (while I would be sitting in my study), as soon as I heard the unlatching of the lock, I would scream, 'Honey! Can you also please get some white chocolate ganache?'

'White what?' She would scream in confusion.

'White chocolate ganache?'

'I don't know what that is. Just come and get it yourself.'

And I would hop, dance, and go with her to the Namchi market.

Such disastrous affairs in my married life continued for half of that spring. Half of my existence was consumed as I struggled to seduce the woman I had married, while the remainder of my time was spent struggling to find some solitude in that tribal communal house. The peaceful married life I had hoped to buy with some good amount of money was instead being spent to fund the dreams of the many strangers who dwelt in her hill house.

At the end of the summer, I suggested we take a trip to Bali. I told her that I was getting a fatherly urge to raise a kid. And if that was not the case, then probably it was time for our much-anticipated honeymoon.

I pictured her turning into a carefree wife with dedicated intentions of pleasing her wonderful husband as soon as our plane touched down at Nusa Dua Airport in Bali. I pictured the warm, crystalline beaches, washed and rewashed by blue and white ocean waves, cleansing the many nasty sins that had happened on that turf. And an adults-only resort reserved for married men and billionaire playboys with Russian mistresses, who came there to enjoy the desolated carelessness of the place. Where Russian mistresses and even my Noel could go on topless surfing trips or snorkel in protected reefs with me, allowing me to feast my eyes upon them. And then what? It would have been only a matter of a full moon, a windy, lonely night before my wife might accidentally forget the shame she had brought upon herself and pounce upon me with her bare thighs. I would have probably lost my virginity in the most inspirational and cinematic fashion, while half our college was still fucking in the privacy of a wooden standalone loo.

But then something funny happened.

I have always been a man who needs reassurance about most matters concerning life. I explore and consult my fellow, wise human beings. It was probably the need for the same reassurance from her that led me to enquire about her sexual predicament. I wanted to know whether her health would allow her to have sex with me in Bali (I asked her normally every time she added some disgustingly expensive white netted bralette or even a damned Swarovski crystal necklace to her shopping cart). And one day, she just paused, looking awfully tired, and asked me if I intended to take her to Bali merely for my sexual recreation. And if that was the case, then I was free to use the services of various renowned prostitutes in Bali and Phuket while she happily stayed home, repairing the broken roof of her house, and I could go and enjoy my honeymoon alone.

It was a horrible situation, really.

Though in the end, the trip didn't happen because my wife didn't have a passport. She didn't have a damned passport after prostituting herself in Delhi for decades. Ha!

'Couldn't it be made now, Noel?' I asked her as I was about to book the flights for the trip.

'I don't think so. No. Not now,' she said , growing all nervous and paranoid.

A week after our voyage had to be cancelled, by some disastrous miracle, she decided to become an artist. A painter. Monet, Van Gogh, and Picasso, she said, with her heavy bosoms and corrupted face, that she must really 'possess her art before it possesses her'. Then, one evening, she transformed herself to look more artistic. She was dressed in navy green shorts, which exhibited her glamorous thighs, and an off-blue T-shirt with flowers and butterflies. My wife set up her canvas, a canvas sheet, and a full-blown, overflowing palette of oil colours, ready to paint her first of many million-dollar fetching paintings.

For shit! I thought, *For absolute snow-crackling shit.*

She stayed up the entire night, and by morning had produced a poor-looking rendition of Mount Kanchenjunga with her house at its foot. That still could have gone for a hundred, because, after all, her legs were so damn beautiful. But she had altruistically put her dead father in that painting—not as a man but as an angel. As Mount Kanchenjunga itself. A protector, always looking over his sweet, prostituted daughter.

What hurt me the most was that she didn't even ask for my opinion on her production. She just became even less loving. Dismissive. This time, not because her senses had been captivated by some buff, clean-shaven Delhi guy but because she was an artist.

The next day, she added rimmed spectacles to her get-up. And then a few really annoying, comical sunglasses. She started staying up late, sitting and reminiscing on the roof of her wooden hut. Then one night, she woke me up from my deep, deadly sleep and told me that she had somehow forged a spiritual connection with me. That she loved me.

As a brave man, I remained calm, and then she came and sat on my lap. She started kissing me violently. I sensed tears rolling from her eyes. Her face (though rough) was warm, and she was weeping. And I began weeping. I presume we both began crying violently because we shared a pain that belonged to her as much as it belonged to me.

Muffled in her breath, I began kissing her, and she didn't resist. I kept shaking and then immediately placed my hands inside her knickers. But she stopped me right away. It must be reported that to my aghast horror, she was not crying anymore. In fact, she had not been crying at all. I had just mistaken her for it. And there, in the silence of that midnight, with rippling fresh sewers and a few mountain foxes crying in the distance, I proved myself to be the stupidest person to have ever landed in a marriage.

10 Days before I Fake My Death

The horrible affairs of my marital life continued in an endless spiral, and I feared they would never come to an end. Until one fine afternoon, Noel announced that she had to go to Delhi to look for a job again.

'Are we relocating to Delhi? Oh God! How long will you be there for?'

That horrible witch hadn't even asked me beforehand for permission. Imagine, in the pre-Independence era, a woman would ask her husband for permission even if she went next door to chat with her friend over a cup of tea. And here was my exemplary Noel, such a little bitch that she didn't even feel it right to tell me she was ashamed of her unemployment and was on the lookout for a job—only when I had left mine to spend my life with her tribe.

'What time are you leaving? Will you be safe? Should I come?'

'No,' she said. 'Not this time. I have to find a job for myself by myself. And you need not worry. My old friend Rose is coming to pick me up at the railway station.'

'What will I do here all alone, wife?'

'Well, there are some obligations that have to be fulfilled. Kanka's diploma fee, for instance. I would be grateful if you could go and pay that to his college tomorrow.'

'Oh yeah, sure. Are you in the midst of a breakdown, wife? Are you only worried about his fees? Is that why you are looking for a job so desperately? I can pay that off and many more,' I said, feeling an insurmountable ache building in my penis.

'No. It won't do. I must go to Delhi. I have to be with Rose. There are a few old friend entanglements that need to be resolved. Please let me go.'

'When are you leaving?'

'Right now.'

I had tears in my eyes.

'Look, don't worry,' she said. 'It's just a matter of one day. Can't you look after the household for just a day while I get my affairs sorted with my payments and my new job?'

'Just a day?'

'Yes. I'll be back by the day after tomorrow.'

'Will you be safe?'

'Of course. I lived alone for years before you came. I survived alright, right?'

'Yes. Absolutely,' I said, nodding my head in dismal approval.

She was off by the 2:00 p.m. SNT cab to the New Jalpaiguri Railway Station, from where she had to catch a train to Delhi that very night.

With her gone, I was left with her rowdy brothers, who were laughing and joking in the kitchen. I felt so damn abandoned that I can't even describe the anxiety I got after she had left. I had not felt this abandoned since my own dear father's death. I retreated to my marital bed and drank some bland rice soup with the weakness of a geriatric old rogue and passed out in hopelessness and despair.

The next morning, she telephoned me from her hotel and sounded altogether distraught in that lonely town. She asked me if I had gone to pay her brother's fees.

'Not yet. I will go now.'

'Okay,' she said.

'How have you been? You reached? Oh my God, I miss you so terribly,' I said.

There was utter silence over the phone.

'Hmm. Yeah, all good. Got to go now,' she said.

I said energetically, 'When will you call again? Any more jobs lined up over there?'

'Yeah. I'm meeting Rose right now.'

'Why are you sounding so depressed, Noel? Should I come?'

But she had already hung up the phone, and once again, there was absolute silence in the hills.

In the afternoon, I took out my duffle bag, pulled out a bundle of some fifty thousand rupees, and went downhill to the Namchi market in search of her weed-smoking, wrist-cutting, semi-depressed, and totally jobless brother Kanka. Down in the market, they were playing some Nepali songs on a boombox. I saw these happy, celebrating Nepali faces—girls better looking than Noel—laughing, dancing, and singing. The hill people were celebrating some Nepali festival about which they were totally pumped.

I met Kanka in a darkened alley and handed him his bundle of cash. Kanka invited me to a Nepali house, which had a dark teal green minaret with a narrow staircase leading to a room where some boys were smoking cheap hillbilly pot from a plastic bottle. The aroma of some cheap garlicky Nepali noodles filled the room. A Nepali girl cheerfully offered me a bottle of HIT beer. In that sheer moment of abashment, I could've either recoiled and drunk from the beer this fat, utterly happy Nepali girl was offering me, or I could have gone down to buy a semi-automatic gun from the Gorkha Market and opened fire in the celebrating marketplace, creating one of the most gruesome massacres recorded in modern history. I chose the former—I took the beer with both hands, thanked the girl by bowing, drank and drank, and dragged myself home to urinate and pass out again in my deserted bed.

At night, I bravely called Noel again, but the call went unanswered. Then, consumed by some ferocious zeal, I trudged into her room and, taking advantage of her absence, began inspecting her cupboard with a rash curiosity. I examined her old clothes, which smelled of history. Her small bralette, a wristwatch (which she had inherited from her father), a photo of her with Andrew (her first love, whom she had met when she was twelve years old and I was not even born yet), and a few more papers. A bank document from last year revealed a fortune of a few thousand rupees.

I remember standing in that empty bedroom of hers, indulging in her past, when suddenly I realized that no matter how much I scrutinized her life or the fact that the last few months had been all about Noel, she was a complete person in her own right—none of that 'oh, only your love can make me complete' bullshit. I realized that Noel could be my domestic lifelong partner or a complete stranger without a moment's notice. There was nothing in between.

The next day, which was to be the day of her return, she called me (I suppose from the terminal of the Delhi airport) and informed me in a distraught, almost sickened voice that she had only now discovered that 'we must separate and break our marriage right now'.

Now, I tend to be neurotic and hyperactive in my normal state. I can't remember having one calm day in the last decade. But when Noel said this out of the blue, I felt as if my absolute death was certain. I somehow embraced it like the learned gentleman I have been all along.

'Why do you want to separate, Noel? Must I not know the reasons for this sudden decision? Tell me.' I had read in an article from Harvard's Annals of Modern Psychiatry about the role of empathy and the willingness to listen to better your life with your partner. Such calmness has done the trick to save the most disastrous and violent marriages. What was I, compared to the feats that literature had promised?

'Tell me, wife. You can tell me whatever it is. But at least tell me,' I coaxed.

She said that she had discovered she was suffering from a disease that would kill her in a few days and that it would be altogether a good idea if I never saw her again.

Now, I'm an anxious man. I know, for instance, how I can curl up and get all nauseous and blind when a panic attack hits. But I remained calm in that particular situation.

'Oh, that's ridiculous, Noel. My wife. Are you mad? We will spend the last of your days together. We will get you treated. We can sell my house. But don't worry. I won't let anything happen to you.'

She complained of tuberculosis, a disease that was too prevalent among rickshaw pullers and streetside beggars in Namchi.

'Tuberculosis can be healed, Noel. With a special diet and a good lifestyle.'

She fell silent on the phone.

'Just come back here, wife. Okay? You want me to come and get you?'

'No,' she said. 'I have booked a flight for this afternoon. Come to the airport around 2:00 p.m. Or, I guess, just don't. I will take a cab.'

'I will be there, wife. Just like I was there when we met for the first time at Nalanda. I will be there at all costs,' I promised.

'Okay.'

I got up from that strange bed, unbrushed and uncombed. I put on my mountain boots over my nightdress and caught the next cab to the airport.

On the way to the airport, I kept thinking about her possible death. Now, usually these are pathetic words for a husband to hear about his wife's imminent death. I should have lost my composure and screamed, cried, and wailed like a madman. But instead, I simply told myself, 'She won't die. I saved her life once. I will save it again. And if she does die, then I too will die. I will commit suicide right when her death is announced to me. Immediate, instant suicide.'

And just as I had once waited for her at an old airport in an old town, I stood there waiting for her again. Growing impatient and nervous again. That same old hunger to understand her mysterious mind again. The same old dream of losing my virginity to her. And from within an old, uncivilized crowd, my sad-looking Noel reappeared in my life. But this time, she was mine. Totally and absolutely mine!

She remained silent all the way back home. She did not look at me but kept her eyes fixed on the valley. I took her hands in mine, and she smiled with her teary eyes.

After all, such are the private affairs of a husband and wife. Even after death, doesn't the husband spend his lonely sunsets by his wife's grave, telling her things only death teaches?

'You know,' I said suddenly, 'by the end of the day, we will have 1.5 crore rupees in my bank account.' I, her saviour, informed her that the fortune had been arranged so that my precious wife could be saved from the curse of the dreadful disease she had contracted.

'How so?' she asked, chuckling as if I were a kid.

'Cemetery House is on the market for sale.'

I briefly explained that another call could be made to the bank to arrange another 1.5 crore against my excellent salary if necessary. I was absolutely prepared to sell this entire world to protect her at all costs. But she kept looking out of the window.

I know, Noel, that the prospect of death can intimidate anyone into silence. But we are going to go through these hopeless times together. As I mulled over this, the car took a turn and an old colonial church loomed into view. As I looked at the cross in the sky, I turned to kiss my wife on her forehead.

Noel looked at me in silence for a few seconds. Then she announced, 'I slept with Herman. Last night.'

And in that grey valley of death, I saw an instant shadow of my dead father and Zahed. His words echoing in my head. *Only last week, she had been stabbed because she was prostituting herself to her boss. And you want to marry her?*

'What?' I exclaimed. One can see this reaction in movies when the husband hears that his wife has fucked somebody else. He says, 'What???'

But she had her lips pursed. And then I went into a crazy quiz rampage.

'Did that bastard cum inside you?' I demanded, like a madman.

'He is not a bastard,' she said, growing all anxious and sad.

I slapped my head in mock horror. 'What?'

'I said he is not a bastard. It was my fault.'

Was she actually saying that?

For a moment, I felt like raising my hand and crushing her jaws, but then, by some miraculous flash, I suddenly had a vision of myself rotting and crying while she fled back to her lover, shivering in his arms and probably lodging an FIR against me. The matter at hand was simple. She had let that man fuck her, feet tossed in the air, all hail to the Almighty, while not letting me have sex with her even once. I wondered feverishly how she would have groaned and moaned as he polluted her while crazily and maliciously whispering into her ears the possible names of my mistaken children.

'Did he cum inside you?'

'Why are you asking that?'

'Did he cum at all?'

'Of course, they never stop before they cum.'

'They?'

'Men.'

'Did he wear a condom?'

'Please forgive me. Darling, please forgive me. It didn't mean anything at all.'

'Without a condom, then?'

I don't recall what the ordeal was after that, but at some point during mid-confrontation, the cab had dropped us off at the Namchi market, from where we had to trek all the way up to her home. Before the realization of the time and place could hit me, we were already in our bedroom. She was sitting on our virgin bed with her polluted buttocks. I was standing against the excellent support of the wall for I was not able to stand straight.

'Without a condom, then? Noel?'

My dear fellow sufferer, she nodded her head in deep sorrow, closed her eyes, and then opened them to look at the wall I was leaning against, as if words were too few to describe the horrible ways in which Herman had ravished my wife.

'If you must know, I'm allergic to condoms. Have been since birth.'

'What?'

As the deplorable night wore on, I had the unpleasant pleasure of hearing the deep sounds of her crying and sobbing. Whenever I walked up to her and asked, 'Why, Noel?', she would begin crying and croaking, and her once-sparkling face would turn all red.

During the course of that night, there were instances when she would try to place her head on my shoulder, seeking reassurance about whether I was planning to abandon her. And somehow, the sight of her small, bobbing head apologizing did ignite in my heart a desire to wipe her tears, take her face, and kiss it. Kiss her parting, sobbing, spitting, and drooling lips. She would have hugged me and clenched my back, and in the moment of regretful horror, I might have very well fucked her like some depraved, sex-deprived bastard making love to a wild, homeless woman. But instead, I just got up and left her crying in that miserable room.

That was the general rhythm of the household for the next few days. I figured that if she continued to cry and wail like this, she would dehydrate herself to death. I would get worried sometimes. I would ask her to drink a glass of water or some stale sherbet, but then, mid-consolation, I would just look at her blankly and mutter, 'Why, Noel?' and she would start crying all over again.

After a week, she seemed to have outgrown her pain. Maybe it was because I hadn't abandoned her yet. I was still sleeping in the adjoining room. Though I wasn't talking to her anymore, I was still talking to her mother and her brothers. All I had for my aggression was a simple 'Why, Noel?' Maybe she figured that I was still a child who was too helpless to leave her. Then one afternoon, when I saw her in the backyard of our house, I failed to recognize her as my own wife. She looked like an absolute stranger whom I had never met. When I approached that scary lady in the sun, she was digging a hole in the ground with a plough (she was trying to plant a rose), and her hair bounced over her face and concealed her eyes completely.

'Are you really sorry, Noel?' I asked.

There was utter silence.

'Are you really sorry, Noel?' I asked again, but my own voice was croaking to an inaudible mutter.

'What?' she asked, more confused than annoyed.

'Are you really sorry for what you did?'

She raised her head and looked at me as if I were speaking to her in Portuguese. Then, that mad bitch just flung the damn plough onto the ground and stormed off in anger.

What a stupid thing to ask really!

In the evening, I walked around the Namchi market, trying to figure out if there was some way I could get her to feel the same guilt that I had managed to make her feel only a week ago. When at last all imagination failed and it was dark, I returned to find her fat voluminous self sitting on the floor. This time, she was packing her suitcase.

'Where are you going, Noel?'

'Nowhere that concerns you,' she said, her face all swollen from crying.

And losing all composure, I leapt forward to slap her. Hell, I almost raised my fist to strike her jabbering jaw as that seemed to be the only possible way to force her into submission.

And then something strange happened. I stopped midway.

You see, even though admittedly I have been a retard, a moron, and an extremely sex-deprived pervert with wild, unfulfilled fantasies, I was not a fool. The moment she saw me raise my hand, she gave me a look of pure sinister. And I don't mean some moral sinister. I am hereby making a faint reference to the paranormal sinister. If I had landed a much-deserved punch on her face, she would have gone insane. She would have either murdered me or walked out of that room at that hour, screaming and waking up half the sleeping hill station of Namchi. She would have gone door to door, knocking at orphanages and even homeless shelters, and would have fucked every living man in that hill station. And not just that, she would have crafted a story about how I was an absolutely impotent husband. That how I lasted in bed for only about five seconds, and when she expressed her dissatisfaction, I knocked out her poor face with my impotent fist. She would have lit a study lamp, dragged a chair, wetted a feather with blue ink, and written a letter to my beloved childhood love, Tania, from the third grade, about how big of a rascal and impoverished fool I was. She would have vehemently congratulated her for not giving me a chance back when I proposed to her in high school over twenty-seven times. Hell, she would have gone on national media. If she didn't have enough money to book a slot on the national news, she would have sold my house, gone to the national media, and announced that from now on, she was a prostitute without charge. Free gratis, and anybody and everybody who desired to fuck an A-class woman could absolutely fuck her for free. She would have hung herself in Namchi market, butt naked, and screamed out loud, 'Hey y'all, I'm Mason Moron's wife, and today I stand before you all to reveal my unfulfilled pussy.' And then what? That would have been the tragic end of all the honour I had managed to collect in my tiny little life.

So, in the same systematic order in which I had raised my fist, I brought it down, and she pretended not to notice my foolishness. I stormed off again, out of the house, past her foolish brothers, and past the horrible, noisy waterfall, this time clambering uphill until I reached the very top of the mountain, where a feral monkey scared me off. I realized on that hill that I had absolutely nowhere to go. I was also quite anxious about her packing. I wondered if she was going back to her lover to stay with him forever.

So when the mountains started freezing and the air became unbearably cold, I returned to find her sitting on the floor. She was eating some wet rice with dal she had cooked, while she should have been dressed up in some hoe-inspired Halloween costume, all Bugs Bunnies, to try to cheer up our married life. But she sat there with her dry, balding scalp and ate, and I knew at that moment that it was time for me to bid goodbye to her and disappear once and for ever. There was no point in living with her anymore. To get Noel to mend her ways, it was time for me to vanish from her life entirely and reappear a year later as a brand new man whom she would respect and be loyal to. Or otherwise never appear again. Probably start a brand new life with some brand new Russian Tania back in Boston.

But disappearing was a tough job. Say, wouldn't I be sighted as a heartbroken maniac dwindling and racing through that hillside in the middle of the night? And wouldn't someone report my disappearance to the police? But the truth about the hills was that such occurrences were common in the state of Sikkim. So much so that even if Noel's family had gone to the police to report her missing husband, the Nepali policeman might have chuckled and instead concerned himself with Noel's breasts.

'Let him disappear, young bride,' he might have said, 'For I have appeared now.'

The sadder part was: who, apart from Noel, would have bothered looking for me in that dismal and altogether strange land?

So instead, I decided it was time to go back to Nalanda. To Zahed. It was time to abandon this scary marriage right there in the hills and return to normalcy.

The next morning, I took a cab homewards. But the descent from that hill turned out to be a frightening horror show in itself. I sat in a speeding taxi, squeezed between two fat Nepali women who laughed and coughed throughout the journey. And the diesel fumes from the taxi ahead made me nauseous and my heart ache more intensely. I felt sad, pukish, and, worst of all, hopeless. All of a sudden, the world seemed so big and lonely without her breasts.

At the sedated NJP Railway Station, I sat in a clueless haze against the bright summertime sun and waited for the NJP Nalanda Capital Express. I had secured a last-minute reservation in the First Class cabin, so at least I was sure that I could sleep comfortably through the rest of my journey towards Nalanda. But as the train whistled forward, sleep came and went in lapses of dreams about Noel and the possible horror of lifelong loneliness.

I think I might have forgotten my slippers in despair because when I showed up at Phoebe's doorstep in Nalanda at three in the morning, I was barefoot.

A horse trotted outside Phoebe's house. Her duplex shimmered in golden light. Inside, from what I could see through the window, she and dear Zahed were laughing and baking a pie. I stepped onto their porch and screamed for Zahed instead of using the doorbell.

'Sans slipper and sans sex, boy!' he said, opening the door. He was wearing loungewear and had grown a good stubble, which suited his face. I stared at him with such tumultuous torrential rage that he quickly became sensitive and sombre about my return.

'Has Noel called you already?'

'Yeah, she has.'

'Did she seem worried?'

'Heartbroken, you mean?'

'Yeah.'

'Not really.'

'What did you tell her?'

'I broke her heart, alright. I asked her how much suffering a man can really tolerate. The death of your father and then having to see your wife fuck somebody else in the same lifetime … Don't tell her I'm here,' I added.

'She knows already. She knows you too well, boy. That's your problem,' he said, fixing his robe. 'I think she might already be on her way to this town, where you have come to hide yourself.'

'What can I do, Zahed? I'm fucked.'

'You can come inside, please, for starters. Hell! That's what she said, boy. You can come inside, Herman!' He said, dancing like a mad retard.

When I went inside, Phoebe appeared in a white see-through dress and, without the customary greeting, made me sit on a couch that also functioned as a temporary bed. She then brought me a slice of pie, while Zahed disappeared into the kitchen, leaving me under the watchful eyes of Phoebe.

'Is it alright if I sleep here tonight, Phoebe?' I asked.

'Yeah, of course. Where else did you think you were going to sleep? Of course,' she said with a smile.

'Can I sleep right now, Phoebe? I think I might commit suicide if I don't get some rest,' I said with a sigh.

'Yeah,' she said, growing a little anxious. 'It's all ready. I have made your bed. There is an extra comforter in the attic if you feel cold.'

'I feel stone cold, Phoebe,' I said as I lay down, feeling as distraught as a cuckold could be.

As Phoebe went to the kitchen, Zahed reappeared.

'He fucked her without a condom, if you must know,' I said without looking at Zahed.

'You saw the video?'

'There's a video?' I exclaimed.

'There is always a video with you, boy. That Tania and her Sergeant had a video back in Boston. So how bad would it be if there were a video now too?'

'No, no video. I just asked her.'

'When?'

'When she confessed.'

'Why?' he asked, confused. 'What were you trying to get out of it?'

'I don't know. I would have always wondered if I hadn't asked.'

'Hell, boy! It's like your wife confessed, and you started a damn interview with her, son. What are you, a reporter from Cuck News?'

'I don't know, man. I just need that witch to come crawling to Nalanda on her damn knees. All crying and begging me to sodomize her.'

'Hell, boy. Some fantasy, huh!' he said. 'So what are we to do about that?'

'I just wish I could do it all over again. Meeting her. Getting to know her. Ensuring every now and then that she remembers her place. I wish I could redo everything, apart from my father's death, of course. What retard would want to witness that again?!'

'Are you talking about a philosophical rebirth?'

'No, you lame fuck. I'm talking about an entire rebirth. I'm talking about faking my death,' I said with finality.

'Is that why you have come here, to Nalanda? What will you get out of that?'

'For Unos, she would miss me. For Dos, she would kneel in front of my photo and beg for forgiveness. And for the finale, when I reappear on this planet, she would love me like a mad poetess, and then the entire matter of "fucking" her would only be a small part of the many advantages I would get out of our wedlock.'

Zahed looked at me as if I were a total madman. As if I hadn't entirely recovered from the news of Herman fucking my only wife without a single condom.

'She will run away with your house and your money if you die or disappear. So not only would you lose a wife, but also a giant fucking mansion. Hell, you would end up losing your father's grave to that Nepali witch, boy.'

But the idea of a dramatic rebirth had pumped a new form of life inside me. The prospects of returning to my life as a changed Moron. And apart from that, this was something I really wanted to experience. I wanted to get as close to death as I could while possibly being alive. Maybe it was just to resolve my own fear against death. An answer to the philosophical question what happens after we die? I knew I could have divorced her ass very well. But then I wasn't sure that it would really fix anything in me. Will divorcing her make me capable enough to endear Tania or any other girl of my choice within a second of my eyes falling on her? Not really. To be quite honest, I think it was not even about Noel that much. Still, I told Zahed, 'Zahed, not many men of my age or academic acumen have witnessed their own deaths. But then, not many men of my age or academic acumen have been denied the soft thrill of their wives' pussy.'

'What the fuck,' Zahed said.

'Let me be frank and explain it as some loudmouthed hilbilly of lady with a narrow frame and annoyingly loud voice in a cheap onion-ring-serving café would say it (breasts being beaten).'

'Sure, sure, Moron ji,' Zahed said.

'After her cunt had been uncurled.'

'Ooh!' Zahed had come to sit by my feet.

'After the mighty barbarians had schemed her into offering herself as a cheap two-dollar souvenir present.'

'Two-dollar souvenir. Waah! Not a dollar but two,' Zahed said.

'The shrewd, silent man made his way between her comforting, welcoming thighs. The last drain of the stranger's semen coated her cunt and swam in it. But she stood and walked. A woman of principle. A woman who chose her mates with liberty and ferocious empowerment. A revolutionary with nothing to revolutionize, actually.'

'Sir Mr Moron, now that you are bedridden and suffering, what may we do to comfort you?' Zahed asked, kneeling and acting like my sidekick.

'Warm ginger ale and her pussy, please.'

'Is that how you absolutely repair a cuckold back to his manliness?'

'The cuckold must be eliminated,' I said, 'The burning desire for revenge was extinguished.' Otherwise, as the cuckold complained to his dear friend, he found himself capable (magically) of creating mass havoc. 'Of plundering small villages in Nepal, burning huts, and torturing prisoners in Cambodia.'

And then the doctor, who had only a few days ago stitched my wife for me, breathed into my mouth. 'Be calm, dear friend. Stay put for now. Hush. Remember the lullaby your mother used to sing while you were in your pram, and be composed. The ocean engulfs and plunders, but it also remains silent under the dazzling stars.'

I believe I blabbered and cried into the night, and after an hour or so, I saw a sleepy Phoebe descend from the stairs.

'Sorry I slept off,' she said, sitting near my legs. 'It will be okay, Moron boy. Just forget about her. I should have listened to this bastard that day. I should have gotten you somebody else,' she said, looking at Zahed.

'Oh hell, I knew it. I always knew it. Yeah, you get him laid tomorrow, darling. The first thing you have to do tomorrow is get him laid with one of your friends,' Zahed said. Phoebe looked at him in distaste.

'It will take time. But rest assured, I will get you someone. How about some beauty sleep, Moron? Tomorrow is another day. And the night is always darkest right before ... well, you know when.'

Then they left, tucking me into my blanket.

'Don't kill yourself, Moron,' Zahed said as he walked upstairs, Phoebe following him like a loyal kitten.

I lay still on Phoebe's wonderful chaise couch. The clock showed 4:00 a.m., though it was still dark outside. And then suddenly, in response to some distant disaster, just participate with me—seeing Zahed and Phoebe disappear upstairs as a singular unit put another haunting thought in my head.

No matter what doorstep I banged on or what bell I rang, no matter among whom I sat, to Phoebe, Zahed, or anybody, for that matter, I would only ever be a lodger. A guest, an intruder, and nothing more. They might embrace me now, but they wouldn't embrace me forever. And in the face of those dire realizations, I was overcome by extreme sorrow and involuntarily reminded of another lonely creature—another person living her life for the first time, just like myself. Someone who failed to be understood. Someone as lonely as me. Noel. I wondered what she would be doing. Crying? Fucking her Herman again? Contemplating suicide? Planning to jump from those hills? Imagining this, I was filled with an unexplainable terror. So, I cleared my throat, wiped my hands, and decided I would take a train back home as soon as I woke up.

But when I woke up, the sunlight slapping across my sleepy, cuckolded eyes, I was met with the figure of Noel zooming closer towards me.

Zahed and Phoebe were sitting on a couch, looking agitated by her visit.

'I'm sorry,' Noel said. 'I really am, honey. I have come to take you home.'

'Take me home?' I said, rubbing my eyes. One part of me was terrified by her presence, and another was comforted—she was alive, after all. Hell, I was so sleepy that the vision of Noel was all blurry to me.

'Honey! Come, let's go home,' she said as she stretched her hand towards me.

'I don't have a home,' I said, getting up. 'Somebody else has fucked my home, oh God. Can somebody please get her out of here? Please. Zahed!'

But Zahed was himself too stunned to say anything. He simply sat and stared at Noel.

'And why are your feet so dirty, honey? Where are your slippers? Did you get robbed?' Noel asked.

'You have robbed me,' I said to Noel and then added more dramatically, 'You robbed me of love. Then, you robbed me of my peace. Oh! Of the house. And now you've robbed me of my honour.'

'But this town has not yet heard of my mistake. How will they dishonour us if they don't know?' she asked.

'Just like before?'

She remained silent.

'You think Herman won't go around telling on you?'

'No. We are all grown-up people here, Moron. We will handle it maturely.'

That's one hell of a degrading vocabulary I have come to hate in recent years. I was asked to act mature and all because I ended up marrying a lady as old as ancient history.

'What's so mature about fucking somebody else, Noel? There is a difference between prostituting yourself and acting mature.'

Hearing this, Noel looked at me silently for a few seconds, left the hall, and returned gallantly, bearing a meat knife from the kitchen.

'There, finish me once and for all. Finish your disgrace, and throw my chopped pieces into a sewer. But you must forgive me right away. Pronto! You forgive me or else I will commit suicide,' she started weeping.

'Suicide, my ass. Murder yourself, you tribal bitch,' Zahed cheered for my wife from behind.

'Ay, don't say that,' I said, getting anxious. 'You don't know Nepali women, boy. They have a fetish for knives. She will do it. She has been dreaming of doing it.'

'My ass. I will stitch her up again. Do it!'

'See, you are making a laughing stock of our marriage,' Noel said as she dropped the cold steel knife on the floor and cried miserably. 'You really are. I came here to talk to you.'

I was taken aback by a ferocious burst of disgust, horror, and sadness. Somewhere deep down, I guess I still loved her. I was starting to get all teary myself.

'Okay, I will handle it. Zahed! Leave us alone,' I said, but Zahed wouldn't leave. 'I demand we be left alone! Please!' I said, looking at Zahed and Phoebe, but they wouldn't move an inch.

'Please,' I think I began to squeal. 'Pleaaaase.'

'Fine.' Zahed raised his hand in defeat and walked away.

My wife sat near my legs and stared at my dirty feet, and then she took them in her hands and began crying even more violently. More loudly. She put her head right between my dirty, hairy feet and kept whimpering. The cries of her apology jingled sonorously in my ears, and she wept and wept, shedding warm tears of regret.

I leaned forward and lifted her face. It was flushed and hot, and she was drooling from one side of her mouth. This was the body of a woman I had married only three months ago. Polluted, no doubt, but here she was, at my feet. I derived some sadistic solace from torturing her for a bit.

'Absolutely no way, Noel. I mean, how could you?' I said, acting like her rightful husband once again.

She cried and begged.

'If you wanted sex that badly, you could have just consulted me. I would have fucked you, alright? But see what you did.'

'I will,' she said, 'I will. You own me now. You own every inch of my body. Every moment of my existence. I am yours truly and totally. Just please forgive me right now. I ...' she gasped for air, 'am not able to breathe.'

'It's not a question of forgiveness, Noel. My heart has already forgiven you. But I don't know if I will ever be alright again.'

'Oh yes, baby. You will be. I will make you alright.'

'Hmm,' I said, and then asked her to let me have a quick talk with Zahed. 'It will be quick,' I said and left.

Then there followed another round of negotiations with Zahed. Just like we had a few months ago in my dorm when I told Zahed that I wanted to marry her.

'No, you dumb fool. How could you forgive her? Oh God. She will never respect you,' Zahed said, getting all worked up again.

'She was at my feet, boy! She was wiping dirt off them. She says I will own her from now on. Imagine that, you sick bastard! Own her!'

'You forgive her now, and she will fuck you, and then she will go to Delhi by another train and fuck that man again.'

'What do you suggest we do, boy? I can divorce her whenever. Of course. But I can't fuck her after the divorce, can I?'

'Oh my God,' he said, realizing something in grotesque horror. 'Are you sure he only fucked her once? What if, while you were here crying and lamenting, she fucked that guy again? You never know. One phone call after your disappearance, and she could have called her Herman to Namchi, and he would have shown up at her doorstep and fucked her on your marital bed in your absence. What if,' he said, widening his eyes and whispering, 'What if she has not come here to apologize on her own? What if she has been sent by Herman? You see, she sleeps with you once, spends a few days with you, lets you fuck her a couple of times just for the heck of it, and then she divorces your ass and runs away with half of whatever you possess?'

'Holy hell,' I said, sweating and feeling my forehead. 'I reckon I have a fever, boy. I'm going to die. I'm going to die right now.'

'Oh geez, Moron boy! You are burning up,' Zahed said, feeling my forehead like a doctor. He then took out a stethoscope from a nearby drawer, placed it on my chest, and asked me to breathe deeply.

'It's too much for him to take. Let him go. He must go and sleep more. Let him go with her if need be,' Phoebe suggested, becoming mildly scared of my situation.

'He shall. But there is one small task that needs to be attended to immediately before he can be set free,' Zahed replied.

'What is it?' I asked.

'We need to hire a detective, boy. He will go and collect all evidence of the great infidelity your wife has committed in Delhi.'

'Why will we do this at this point in time, Zahed?' I asked, baffled.

'Because, unlike you, I tend to use my brain to think. Your father was a great, great man. He loved you dearly. He loved you so much that he left you an entire mansion and enough money to last a lifetime. But the thing is, you are a damned fool. I have heard rumours that you have put your house up for sale.'

'That was a mistake. I didn't sell it though.'

'Of course you didn't. But with that Nepali around you, it will only be a matter of days before she takes the house, takes half of your duffle bag money, and runs off to Delhi. She will fuck you, no doubt. But she will fuck you nicely, boy! She will damn nearly rob you of everything while simultaneously fucking you.'

'So why do we need to hire a damn detective?'

'So that he can collect enough evidence against your wife. If she goes crazy after getting your cock and runs to some courthouse, claiming that you have domestically raped her, then at least we will have enough evidence to save you and your fortune.'

'When the fuck did you start thinking so logically, boy?' I asked.

'The great advice comes from my father. It must be followed,' Zahed said.

'Your father knows about all this?'

'He says he saw it coming months ago.'

'Then why didn't he save me, Zahed?'

'Well, you didn't want to be saved. You don't want to be saved even now, boy. Do you?' Zahed said.

The situation at hand was preposterous. I couldn't leave Noel right now. Not at all. I would have starved myself to death.

'Not right now, Zahed,' I said, 'but eventually.'

With that, Phoebe was left to keep a vigil over Noel while Zahed, our poor Santos, and I drove to the city in search of a detective agency that could trace my nemesis in Delhi and recover evidence of the great deed my wife had committed there.

Overall, the prospects were hopeless. A forty-three-year-old detective with a polished moustache and hat offered his services but said it would only be possible to render them in December, as he was currently busy hiring and pimping girls for a renowned filmmaker who went by the name of Bahubali. Of course, we knew Bahubali.

'There must be other detectives around, Santos. Drive fast,' Zahed said, growing restless.

'Detectives are quite outdated, sir, if you must know. My father always wanted me to drive a car for the police. That is much like a detective's job in itself, if you would like to know the absolute truth. Maybe you can just send me to

Delhi. I can get it done like this,' Santos said, snapping his fingers again. 'Like this.'

'Fuck off, Santos. Just drive,' Zahed retorted.

We drove on in absolute silence.

'Oh boy!' I said, suddenly hit by another wave of insane anger. 'If only I knew where that bastard Herman lives in Delhi. I would have murdered him myself. Can I maul my predecessor with my bare claws? I can do that. But only you can tell me if it would ever fix the past. If it would make my wife unfucked. If it would raise her morals. And if, at all, it would fetch me true love. Only blood, oh brother! Cold, sprinkling blood can give me some solace.'

'Also, Delhi is quite far, you see,' Zahed said. 'And I'm sure they have some jurisdiction that is distinct from ours. In our society, it's absolutely normal to shred a man to pieces just because, say, you didn't like the colour of his hair. Or he teased and abused your sister. But Delhi is the capital. It's not like Bihar; Delhi is governed. There are laws and shit.'

'Shut the fuck up, Zahed! Boy! Absolutely! Pronto!'

Zahed did shut up. But the silence was deadlier than the noise. The truth was more horrible than the lies. The pain was greater than the anger. And, therefore, with another setting sun, we concluded that Herman's life would be left in peace.

With that useless toil of ours almost coming to an end, I sat and faintly mused that even if all things in this world could be fixed, there is one truth that absolutely can't be fixed—that Herman had fucked my wife. That Herman had fucked my wife even before she let me fuck her.

'I really wish to murder that man, boy! I think I won't survive a day if I don't murder him with my bare hands,' I said. Zahed, however, was thoughtfully gazing out of the window. With his attention diverted, I stared at Santos in the rear-view mirror. Santos smirked in the driver's seat, and our eyes crossed in the mirror—a glance exchanged with a promise of lifelong loyalty and a flash of sudden genius. Abruptly, I ended up nominating him to eliminate Herman and to gather intel about how he had managed to fuck my wife after all these days.

'Santos,' I said, pulling out a bundle of 500-rupee notes from my jacket.

'What the fuck are you doing, Moron? Oh geez,' Zahed said, breaking off from his reveries.

'I'm going home to my wife,' I announced. 'But you are going to Delhi tonight. Here, take this fifty thousand rupees. It's all yours. Just don't come back until you have all the news about Herman.'

3 Days before I Fake My Death

Noel and I left Phoebe's house and reached Cemetery House that night. I don't remember seeing much of it because it was dark by the time we reached home. But in our depressingly lit living room, I remember I was still not talking to Noel. She kept breaking into random bursts of crying. I remember taking her hands into mine to assure her that somehow we might still be able to work it out. What I had observed was that despite her infidelity, Noel could be a really docile housewife. I think immediately upon our arrival, even before I could settle my luggage into my old bedroom, she went to the kitchen to make dinner. I thought of going and standing next to her as I used to back in Namchi, but instead, I lay on the bed, and by the time she could have ignited the stove, I was already in deep sleep.

The next afternoon, I met Zahed again. There was a new British pub right down Warden Street. Zahed and I ventured alone, leaving Noel to her vices. By that time, I was sure that she had dismissed all plans of committing suicide. She was in the kitchen when I left the house, probably baking a vanilla cake of all the cakes that can be baked by an unfaithful lover. So with Noel back in Cemetery House, we sat in the early evening hours, drinking clear vodka and tropical LITs. Zahed was at ease. He raised his head, closed his eyes, and let the cool air from the standing fan breeze through his hair. He was at such great ease that it seemed like he had finally derived his liberation. By means of getting me to have sex with Noel, he had hereby retired from his earthly duties.

'I haven't fucked her yet, though,' I said.

'Take it easy now. Don't rush. Breathe. Look at our Nalanda sunset. Loosen up a little. Tiptoe back home, and be the man who finally gets to fuck his begging woman.'

So tiptoe I did. The evening was redder than usual, and I was filled with unbinding optimism because, all along the way, I could see the russet of the giant crimson and peepal trees falling on the street. Long-forgotten neighbours greeted me passionately, and I even stopped and hugged a child who had come to me with a broken rose.

When I went inside my house, Noel greeted me from the washroom. When I went to the washroom, I found her standing, wearing only my old white T-shirt and no pants. 'Can you get me my period pants?' she asked, a little embarrassed. But being the drunkard I was, I fetched her pants and even made her wear them while she still stood almost naked, holding me by my shoulders. One leg up-tip. And then another leg up-toe. Then she excitedly asked me to go to the kitchen and start dinner, saying that she would be right there!

There in the kitchen, over a polished tabletop, she had left a cake and a letter.

In that letter, she had written in very horrible handwriting that, over the course of a night, she had forged a spiritual connection with me. I was her ruler and her emperor. She said that she had been a fool. She had failed to see that I was, in fact, the incarnation of her dead father and that she had now committed her life to serving me and being my caretaker. She promised to be my companion through the tough situations of life. But what stood out from all of her heartfelt eloquence was that she had also written that since last night she had been dreaming of rearing our babies. 'There is absolutely no haste. Take your time. But whenever you deem it fair and possible,' she wrote, 'I shall be the proud and fortunate bearer of your prince.'

I read that letter over and over again, a few times, and then, after chuckling and tossing it in the bin, I went to stand by my father's grave. Dusk had turned to night by the time I had come to my bedroom. I fixated myself on our bed right next to her.

She was still sobbing and crying her melancholic, shameful cry. But, I believe, after reading her elaborate letter, I became somewhat sympathetic. As if, after reading her letter, I had somehow bought into the idea that I was, in fact, the reincarnation of her dead father. Noel was only a few centimetres away from me. I began massaging her back to provide her with some relief from her period cramps. It felt more like meshing hard dough. A few minutes or so must have passed when Noel turned towards me and told me shamefully that she loved me dearly. I kissed her forehead, and she closed her eyes and held on to it as if it were something she was going to cherish until the day of her death.

I then got up in an excited rush and announced that we must take a vacation to some subtropical island and feast on a sunset, eating crabs and drinking champagne. I still don't quite know how such outrageous ideas end up in my head at the most outrageous of times, but I guess that my lunacy can only be explained in one manner—when the wife is open with her warm domestic offerings, the husband is stirred into excitement. Not to mention there was a duffle bag full of money right beneath our marital bed. Noel turned towards me sleepily and murmured, 'Do you remember that my younger sister from the valley is visiting us tomorrow morning?'

Oh hell, I did. I did remember. It was her sister's wedding in a few weeks. And even though the idea of having to attend another Nepali wedding seemed downright miserable, this sister she spoke of had a big mole and a childlike innocence. She was traversing down the hills to lodge with Noel for a few days, just to spend some nice, contemplative sisterly time before she could probably go around and ruin some man's life.

'I think you should ask her to cancel the visit. I don't want people around now, Noel,' I said.

'Neither do I,' she said. 'Neither do I, baby. I don't know. I'm such a fool. I totally forgot about her visit until she called me from the station. Fuck. I think I should just kill myself.' And then she began crying.

'Nah. It's fine. We will see what can be done. Let her come,' I said, drawing my unreliable wife closer to my chest.

You see, the reason I didn't want that little sister in our household was that I feared this visitor of ours might end up drawing my mouse away from my thirsty claws. Say by always keeping Noel busy in something or the other. An afternoon shopping trip? A sunset gala gossip round? A sisterly sleepover in pink matching pyjamas and socks while the elderly husband is left to suffer in his own bedroom? I feared that with that stranger in my house, I would need to stop acting all stuck-up and pissed off and instead pretend to love Noel with such ferocity that the little sister would only go back home and report to her Nepali family what a great lover and husband I was to Noel. Until now, even though it was me throwing all the tantrums and acting all distant, it would now be my lovely wife throwing a tantrum along with her younger sister, and I would have to sweetly comply.

Though in the end, I ended up letting her invite her younger, less prostituted self to our broken domicile with the dreams of probably getting to sleep with both of them. Or to derive some kick one night, say, from fucking the elder one too loud with the door of our bedroom wide open so that the younger one could hear the wild slaps of my thighs against her elder sister's pelvis and get all aroused. And thereafter, she might walk in upon us, sleepy-eyed, and might end up joining our superlative performance of two.

However, that night, I was plagued by the most sensible and inevitable of nightmares. I realized that the wild imagination of an upcoming threesome was a giant miscalculation on my part. Instead, I was haunted by visions of Noel sleeping with Herman on my bed while her little sister stood guarding their locked gate. And then I had another nightmare in which I saw Noel crying, beating her breasts, and telling her little sister of all the tortures I had inflicted on her instead of all the tortures she had subjected me to.

And the very next morning, pretty little Neonika showed up at my house. It was such an early morning hour—when good-natured sleep had only just begun blessing me with its depth—that there was a gentle rattling of the door.

We woke up together and walked to the entrance of our bedroom, and we found our little comrade standing in the living room.

Upon seeing us, Neonika dropped her two very heavy purple suitcases on the floor and sighed a heavy, relieved 'Phew!'

On seeing her younger sister, Noel suddenly transformed—broken free of all guilt and torture. She thundered over to that hillbilly cousin of hers and hugged her tightly for a solid five minutes. Then, letting her loose, she exclaimed something in loud Nepali, which roughly translated to: 'We are going to fuck this town of Nalanda, oh my little one! Now that you are here!'

I was still standing at the entrance of my bedroom in my torn white vest and a pair of white boxers, rubbing my eyes. I remember being very sleepy when the elder sister led her younger comrade into the adjoining guest room. Midway through, Neonika turned her tiny features towards me, smiled, and said, 'I am so damn excited to see you after all these months.'

'Oh yeah. Oh yeah,' I groaned.

With her cousin in my residence, there was a constant babble of Nepali in the household. Loud noises of the two sisters excitedly and impatiently gossiping about some affair or other back home. I decided that it was good for my sanity to busy myself in academia and stay away if I wanted to terrorize Noel into utter submission. So for the remainder of the day, I sat in my bedroom, twisting the pages of a very heavy encyclopaedia of recent breakthroughs in neuroimaging. Amidst that clatter, I kept raising my head in wonderment as to why Noel was taking so much time to leave her sister in the guest room and come back to me. It was about time that she dropped that sisterly love, showed up at my feet, and began acting like the absolute mistress she had promised she would be.

I believe an hour or so must have passed before she finally dashed into my room (looking for a T-shirt for the younger comrade), and I asked her to sit down on the bed. She sat. Immediately and dutifully.

'What's there for breakfast, Noel? I'm hungry. Why have you abandoned me like this?

'Oh no, no!' she said. 'No way, honey. I thought you were still sleeping.'

'I'm not.'

'Are we disturbing you, honey? Are you really busy with some deadlines?'

'Well, yeah. But you can't just leave me like this. Can you? Is this how you plan on reinventing our marriage?'

'Come lie down with me, babe,' she said, lying on the bed and opening her arms.

Should I fuck her right there? Right then, be done with the inquisitiveness.

'Wait, let me shut the door,' I said and got up to close the bedroom door.

'Oh, that would be so disrespectful to our guest. How can we do that? You must understand the situation.'

My ass I would understand the situation. How disrespectful would it be if I slapped you to death while your tiny sister was busy unpacking her bags?

'For how long will she be here, Noel?' I asked.

'I don't know! Oh God! Don't say that, babe. She likes you so much,' she said, and then, abandoning her plans of embracing me on the bed, she got up, put on her slippers, and told me, 'Brush your teeth, and come sit with us for breakfast, honey. Or would you like me to serve it right here?'

'Serve it right here.'

'In a whizz, honey. I'll be right there.'

Though I appreciated her sincerity in serving me and tending to my appetite with such dedication, on the whole, I still resented that comical fool for not understanding the very basis of making me happy.

No lunch would fulfil me, Noel. Only your tiny, polluted offerings would do.

After she was gone, I saw our poor little Neonika walk to the washroom, towel in one hand, clothes in the other, her skinny, scrawny features innocently approaching the bathroom door. I got the urge to run to her and deliver a thunderous kick to her small torso so that she would die at that very moment. But when she shut the bathroom door and the pitter-patter of the shower began, the thought was replaced with the fantasy of peeping at the bathing little sister through a hole in the door while the big sister was busy cooking in the kitchen.

I leapt out of bed. Barefoot. Still in my boxers. Through a tiny hole in the door, I struggled to see the younger sister's beauty. Hardly had I seen her eternal form when I heard a sudden thud in the kitchen followed by Noel screaming for me.

'What is it, honey?'

'Would you like some cold-pressed juice? Or do you prefer warm milk?' she asked.

'Sure. Anything works,' I said and went back to my study.

A few minutes later, Noel walked into the bedroom, holding a bowl of steaming oriental soup. I made her sit on my lap and told her to get naked.

'Right now?' she exclaimed, widening her eyes.

'Yeah.'

'Oh God, you are crazy. She's going to come out any minute. You want to get caught?'

'I don't mind.'

'Haha! Disgusting, you,' she said, playfully pushing me away by my shoulders and walking off, laughing.

The thing this bitch doesn't understand is the seriousness of the matter. Or if she does, she's acting all too damn smart about playing innocent.

While gulping down spoonfuls of the soup, an outrageous idea came to my head: What if I don't fuck Noel? What if I threaten her with an ugly divorce? And once she is scared and coiled up, I tell her, 'Okay, Noel! You might be forgiven. But as you know, you slept with

Herman, right? So it's imperative that we become equals. I would like to sleep with your sister. You can be present, of course. And I can take turns. Don't I deserve that? And don't you deserve to sit and watch? You dumb fool?'

A few minutes later, Noel walked in again to clear my plates. Ah! What a dutiful wife! She was also carrying a tray of cashews and dates in one hand and a glass of cold milk in the other.

'I'm sorry, I keep disturbing you again and again,' she said.

I grunted.

She stared at my face for a few seconds and then muttered, embarrassed, 'We are going to the market. I mean, if I'm not interrupting, would you mind dropping us there?'

And before I could get up, slap that heavy encyclopaedia on the floor, and pin Noel by her collar against the wall of our bedroom, her little sister walked in.

'Is this really where you both live, Moron ji? Oh my God, what a giant library you have!

Suddenly breaking away from the most violent of urges, I said to Neonika, 'Oh, you like it?'

'Yeah. Such a cosy space,' Neonika said. 'I wish I could sleep nestled between you two in this room. I'm sure it must get so dark in here.'

'Yeah, too much chitter-chatter, Neo. Go get ready. I'll be right there,' said Noel.

'How long is she going to stay, Noel?'

'I don't know. A few days. I suggest you eat quickly, please. We need to reach before sunset.'

And with that, one part of me was startled by the image of Noel, Neonika, and me sleeping entwined on our marital bed. I wondered how many gifts the night would have unfolded upon me. An accidental rub against one sleeping sister here, another accidental brush of the breasts there.

I figured that I had probably gotten the idea of Neonika all wrong. Maybe she was not even my nemesis but an eternal present. An unmarried present meant to have the most carefree and scandalous romance with her brother-in-law before she could be married. Maybe I was her husband.

And so I drove them to the evening market. My Neonika and my Noel settled in the back seat, chirping endlessly into the sunset while I drove crazily.

After their shopping spree—where I ended up losing a fortune of 12,000 rupees so that the elder sister could buy an after-wedding dress for the younger sister—I chased them, bearing their shopping bags in my hands, while they sped through the maddening crowd of the Nalanda market. We stopped at a roadside eatery where they had a few plastic chairs and a plastic table with an umbrella spread right on the roadside, a little too close to the speeding trucks and cars.

Noel was a crazy consumer of streetside food. She could eat anything that was spicy and oily. She always devoured roadside chowmein and momos with ferocious attention and then wheezed and inhaled cold air from her open mouth to calm the spiciness that tortured her tongue.

At the eatery, I grabbed a vacant table for four and sat on one side, expecting my dutiful wife to come and sit right next to me. Instead, she sat on the opposite side with her sister.

'What should we eat?' asked Neonika.

'I'm not hungry,' I announced. Noel looked at me with sadness.

'What about you, cha?'

'Anything. Anything works,' Noel replied.

We both ate nothing that evening while the little sister sipped a slushie and tried to keep up a conversation amidst our deathlike silence. With her seated right opposite me, I saw a flash of guilt creep into her face again. Though it disappeared before I could rejoice for she was soon drawn into some old, flavourful, spicy Nepali gossip with her sister instead of indulging in our tasteless marriage.

During the night, I was impatiently hoping for the younger sister to act on her desire from the afternoon (I really hoped that she did desire me) and show up in my bedroom to sleep on the very same bed as Noel and me. Though the fantasy of a gruesome threesome seemed impossible. Through the ajar door, I could hear the two sisters conversing and unpacking their shopping bags, and it seemed that the longing for that magic would last a lifetime. Though there was something stellar that did occur in the middle of my routine tortures. Apparently, the little sister was trying on her wedding dress in the adjoining room with the door still ajar.

I cautiously approached the room and peeked in. Neonika was in a black bralette, her small, pretty breasts dangling, while the big sister who had her back towards me, was changing from her jeans to her nighty, which revealed her perfect buttocks to my starved eyes.

I figured that if I didn't fuck any of these two women that night, I would go mad. But how would I get to the final deed?

At bedtime, the two sisters came to my room. As soon as I heard their footsteps, I began pretending to be asleep. Noel sat down on her rightful side of the bed and asked the little one to sit comfortably and chit chat for a while.

Figuring that the old brother-in-law had slept, they resumed their sisterly babble.

The little sister was getting all anxious about her marriage.

'Cha, you think I should shave down there? How would he like it? I'm so nervous.'

'Ambo, yeah, obviously. Use my razor tomorrow.'

'What if I cut myself by mistake?'

'There is nothing to be cut.'

They gossiped and babbled while sitting on my very own bed. The little sister sat right across her big sister while I lay motionless, shrouded in a white bedsheet in between them. I was feigning sleep while they laughed and teased each other. At one point, amidst their girlish giggles, Noel screamed something in Nepali and slapped her little comrade's breast with a loud sataak! And then suddenly, they stood up on the bed and began running around. With my wife trying to escape the return slap her little comrade was struggling to plant on her breasts. At one point, somebody's foot barely missed stamping on my helpless sleeping balls, and upon hearing their commotion, I pretended to wake up.

When there was peace again, the two sisters again sat across from each other while I sat up in startled confusion and stared at them in cluelessness.

Now, I don't know what it is with the entire malleability of time and things of that sort, but it was right after this very incident that my life was suddenly subverted from the prospects of a nice night-long threesome, the most rhapsodical of fantasies, to the most bitter and dreadful of nightmares.

At some point mid-conversation, the little sister looked at me and Noel and said to her elder sister, 'Oh, cha, big sister. You need to also school me on the various tricks of pleasing my man.' Then she broke into embarrassed laughter. 'Moron ji, you must be so lucky. Having all the fun all alone with my elder sister in this very room, ha?!'

I looked at my wife's clueless face, bearing signs of second-hand embarrassment. Then even she broke into laughter. 'You will do well. Oh girly, you will!'

'No, really,' the little sister said, 'but how many times is good? And for how long? How long do you last, Moron ji?'

I looked at my wife again, this time feeling really threatened by the little girl's advances. I was like an infant looking at his mother for consolation. But all I got from her was another roar of laughter. 'Oh, we haven't had sex yet.'

A sudden silence filled the air. The sister looked at me in fierce confusion. And then there was awkwardness.

'Why is that? Is there a problem? Hell, dammit, something personal?' Neonika asked.

'Oh no! Nothing like that,' Noel said, exhaling the last of the laughter from her chest. 'He still has to prove himself to be worthy material.'

Words fall short to describe the fierce anger that roared inside me. I felt like getting up and thrashing the two girls until dawn. I believe I even got up to unleash my powerful wrath on my wife, but by the time I could do so, the two of them had gotten up and left the room, whispering something cruel in Nepali.

After midnight, Noel came and lay right next to me with her face turned away from me. I was barely reining in my fury, crippled by an intense desire to deliver an astounding kick to her spine. Then, turning towards me and holding me by my nightshirt, Noel said, 'That little brat just chirps on and on, oh God. She will be gone the day after tomorrow, though. I can't wait to be all alone with you.'

I remained silent for a second. And then I told Noel, 'Well, you sort of deserve to commit suicide, Noel. Were you lying like this on the day he fucked you? I thought it was missionary,' I said, with my heart twisting and clenching in fear and amazement.

Did I actually say that? Verbatim? I did. And she began crying again. Trembling and shaking.

'What is it with you communal whores? I need to prove my worth to sleep with you? That's what you have been telling bitches around the colony?'

But she kept crying and crying. Like a damned madwoman on death row. I let her stay like that for a few minutes. I thought of taking a cab to Zahed's house at that very moment and divorcing her ass right before her little sister could even think of marriage.

But a few minutes later, I felt guilty, so I put my hands on her shivering back and began to console her.

'I'm sorry Noel. I didn't mean it,' I said, but she cried and cried. I kept caressing her back. Slowly. Staring at the blankness of the ceiling. Wishing that I could disappear at once and come back into her life later, years later, either as a man she could not help but love and worship or as a maniac who she and her sister couldn't resist having a threesome with.

I can't remember when sleep took over, but when I woke up in the middle of the night, I found Noel missing from my side.

I sprang to my feet and began surveying the house. *Has she run away?*

It turned out that while I had passed out, she had gone and slept on the couch.

'Noel,' I said, struggling to see her in the darkness. There was no movement. 'Noel.' I held her feet. 'I'm sorry. Can you come and sleep with me?' But Noel lay motionless.

Fuck, has she committed suicide at last?

'Noel,' I said, shaking her shoulders. 'Noel, are you okay?'

'I didn't sleep with Herman, if you must know,' she said in the darkness.

'What the fuck? What?'

'I said I didn't have sex with Herman. You think in the course of one night I just went to Delhi, met him, fucked him, and came back running to you?'

'Then?'

'I lied. Of course I lied.'

It didn't seem to be the most convincing explanation one could offer, but it was an explanation that promised such relief that I would have believed it for the rest of my life, even if it were a lie.

'Swear on your mother? You didn't?'

'I can't swear. I just didn't.'

'Swear it.'

'I won't.'

'But why would you lie, Noel? What have I done to you for you to make me go through all this hell every day?' I said, my voice quivering into near-cries.

'Do you sometimes ask yourself what wrong you have done to yourself that you put yourself through all this hell every day?'

'What is this? Some tongue twisters? Are you on some psychedelic stuff, wife?' I asked her.

'You are not happy with me. You were never happy with me. This is an unhappy marriage,' Noel announced. 'This has always been an unhappy marriage. I just wanted it to work. I try every day to make it work. But you never give me any time. You didn't give me time after I was stabbed. You didn't give me time when I asked you to let me get my head straight before we could live together. You didn't give me time when I asked you to let me go to Namchi and think over our marriage. I just needed time to think and clear my head. But you would never give it to me.'

'So?'

'So I took it by telling you that I slept with Herman. At least you left me alone for a day after I confessed. That time was enough for me to see all the good you have done for me. All those times you put me above yourself. All those times you worshipped me even when those bastards in Delhi were laughing at my tragedy. That's why I came back.'

'Hell,' I said. 'Please forgive me, Noel. Shit. I deserve to die. Oh shit, honey.'

'I think we should just get a divorce and be done with it. We are too different. We are so damn different.'

'Can you please just come and sleep with me? We can talk through this tomorrow, Noel. Or after your sister is gone,' I pleaded.

'Whatever,' she said—my loving soulmate of a wife. 'Also,' she said, 'as far as sex is concerned, you know now that Herman hasn't polluted me. Let's have sex tomorrow. First thing. And then we can plan a divorce?'

'I will kill myself if you try to divorce me, wife.'

And all of a sudden, all the bitterness of the marriage evaporated along with those tears we had shed in those last few months of tragedy and unhappiness.

'If you don't mind, Noel, can I just go and take a walk in the garden for a while?'

'It's three in the morning.'

'I just need to walk, honey!'

I went out to the drawing room, ran to our telephone, and called Zahed some seventeen times before he picked up.

'My ass, she hasn't slept with Herman,' Zahed said over the phone. 'If there is even a grain of truth to that bullshit, boy, I would let you fuck Phoebe herself. I knew it. I knew what that bitch was cooking up in her head.'

'How can you be so sure, Zahed? You don't know her. You weren't ever married to her. How can you tell?'

'I have seen bitches more horrible than her, boy. Tell that bitch she ain't nothing. Tell her that if I find her, I will bury her alive in your house.'

'What's wrong with you? Why are you so mad?'

'Listen, Moron, boy! Sex or no sex, threesome or no threesome, but she absolutely slept with Herman that night. Poor Santos is in Delhi. And he has heard things so nasty and grotesque that he refuses to eat.'

'What is he saying?' I asked anxiously.

'He's not saying anything. That's what. I got a call from Delhi. It was his brother. He said that poor Santos is so unsettled he can't speak, man. Some problems he has had since he was a kid. Let it be. Let him come. He will be here tomorrow. Let's see what the deal is.'

'What do I do until then?'

'What you have been doing ever since you married her. Keep begging for sex. Now is a golden opportunity. Tell her that in order to prove her love, she must, as a wife, let you fuck her now.'

The next day, I had to go to the university to borrow a few books from the library. There was also the matter of some outdated cheques I had received for my monthly grant that needed to be exchanged for updated ones. Apart from that, I figured it was in my best interest to simply stay away from those two witches during the day so that Noel would be forced to wonder about my absence. Otherwise, with me always looming around her, I was beginning to feel that I was giving her all the opportunities to reduce me to the status of a whining child once again, instead of the saintly, forgiving cuckolded husband I had become.

1 Day before I Fake My Death

The next morning, I woke up to find Noel missing from my bedside yet again. I walked to the living room and found her sitting idly at the dining table, eating heartily the breakfast she had cooked for herself.

'Oh, there you are. I thought—'

'What?' she said, raising her face disinterestedly from her coffee and then going back to drinking it.

'Uhmm, nothing.'

'I think you should go and get ready. You are getting late for the university.'

'You want to scoot me way, huh? You want me gone, wife?' I asked Noel playfully.

But she ate and ate, shrugging her shoulder once in reply. 'Early go, early come, I guess. I will be waiting for you.'

I laughed, patted her head, and kissed her cheek. She smiled and kept eating, so I resigned myself to go to the washroom. I went past her sleeping sister, who had one leg flung out from the blanket. Her bare, shiny thighs and the arch of her buttocks were right there for my early morning inspiration. Though the concern was secondary for now.

Inside the bathroom, I stood naked under the running shower. I was groaning and laughing at the same time for I figured that Noel was slipping from my grip again. She was as careless and carefree as she had been earlier. After all, she hadn't done anything wrong to me now. 'A pure wife,' that's what she was according to her. As pure as the clearest of morning skies.

After getting ready, as I walked to the door with my briefcase, I could hear her in the kitchen. She was humming a Nepali song while washing the breakfast dishes. I banged the door a little too loudly, expecting her to rush and kiss me goodbye. But despite the eternal thud at the door, her song continued, and so did her satanic existence.

However, when I reached the main entrance of the house, Noel appeared at our door from a distance and waved goodbye, her eyes staring satanically at me.

'Goodbye,' I said from afar, stepping into the sunlight, hungry and thirsty for food and love.

While at the university, I kept checking the clock on the wall of my office, and as soon as two hours had passed, I telephoned home to check if things were alright between us and to see if Noel was going to get some lunch for me. But she didn't answer.

Is she dead? I thought. *Who knows? Maybe poor her slipped and banged her head on the tile. Or maybe she did it herself.* It was possible. Maybe she was not growing distant but was instead depressed. Perhaps she found her existence altogether meaningless.

Was I too harsh on her? I mean, I know I can sometimes be too intense with people.

So I called her a few more times. After each unsuccessful attempt, all my senses told me not to play the fool again. What if she was just in the shower and the little sister was sleeping? I'd end up frightening both of them enough to make them run back home.

Fine! I would just come up with something urgent. Maybe, let's assume that if she is alive and sees so many phone calls, she will get all puzzled and worked up. I'll just tell her that it's something urgent.

I can ask her to look for my father's death certificate.

And then again, when she didn't answer, I wondered: What if she were sleeping with somebody? What if, while I—Mason Moron—was sitting in my office in my crimson shirt and black flannel pants in anticipation of my honeymoon, Herman was in my bedroom, on my bed, fucking my wife, her hands tied to the bed?

I mean, from what I knew of Noel, it was possible that maybe it wasn't even Herman she would wait for to get a nice afternoon fucking session. She was so superbly nonchalant about morality that she could have just seduced a delivery man to commit the deed.

In that restless neurosis, I remember sprinting out of my office and running all the way to the main road. With no taxi in sight, I ended up hitching a ride with a cyclist. It must have been another one of those Tuesdays; after all, the days after my cuckolding were so disorienting that I had to stick to the directions of the sun and wind to keep track of time. The cyclist paced smoothly down Warden Road, a loud cry of a child here and two dogs chasing each other there. After almost missing a fatal accident with a speeding truck, I jumped off the cycle when I reached my house, thanked the cyclist, opened the latch of my mansion, and rushed inside to hunt for my unreliable wife.

I braced myself for whatever gnarly shit I might encounter as soon as I entered—only to end up walking into the aftermath of a mad party the two sisters were having in my absence. Picture this: a silver shimmery pom pom lying unattended in the front lawn along with a few disposable glasses which smell of whiskey and coke. A half dead speaker still playing some Nepali music. An instant flash of the two sisters dancing and playing on the lawn with loud, maddening music blasting from the boombox. Apparently, Noel and her sister had gotten so drunk in my absence (having emptied all the expensive scotch from my father's minibar) that when I marched in, I found the little comrade Neonika lying on the floor of my veranda, her head slumped into a plastic bucket in which she had puked her guts out due to the excess alcohol. *No wonder these bitches couldn't hear the telephone,* I thought.

My wife appeared from our bedroom—also drunk—and before I could say anything, she quickly pulled me inside and began kissing me violently.

'Here, take a shot,' she said, handing me a bottle of Chateau XIV Double Malt Whiskey (an expensive liquor with 110 years of distillation). *Oh hell!*

'Take a shot,' she said, acting like a domesticated cow.

I chugged more than half of the bottle as she looked on with amusement.

'What else?' I asked.

'Nothing. Oh! You look like you could ruin me today, lover. So damn energetic. I want you to fuck me. Right now.'

'Right now?'

'Ah, never mind. How about you hop into the shower really quick? The geyser is already on. I will set up the environment in the meantime.'

And suddenly, I was pushed into the sanctum of my bathroom. What a beautiful golden light illuminating my life. With the hot droplets of water trickling down my spine, I felt as if her drunkenness had seeped into me as well. I stood there, wondering if there was any need for me to chug that bottle of whisky. I started getting anxious that I might ruin my performance of a lifetime if I drank more. But then suddenly, I caught a glimpse of the younger sister's lingerie—blue netted underwear and a magnificent velvety bra lying rumpled on the floor—and the sight filled me with supreme inspiration.

With the warm water descending on my head, as if it were some heavenly blessing, I ended up with a massive erection. My penis was so damn erect that I felt as if I could have just rammed the wall of the bathroom and the entire household would have collapsed. I picked up her underwear from the floor and examined it with my drunken eyes. I rubbed my cock with my sister-in-law's underwear and, thereafter, in pursuit of the real action, marched out of the shower with an open robe. My giant penis poked out of the robe as if it had a life of its own.

The door to our bedroom was still ajar when my wife came up to me, fully clothed, rubbing herself against my naked body. I could feel her tight breasts pressing against my back. She kissed me and hugged me. And I resolved to fuck her right away. I was going to dart straight towards our marital bed, and there was absolutely no need to go a few extra steps to shut the door. In fact, I would have rejoiced if the little comrade had walked in on us. I wanted her to catch us in action and accidentally witness my stellar performance.

I figured there was no time to waste. No time at all for that foreplay tomfoolery. So instead, I pushed Noel onto our bed and stripped her to stark nudity before she could realize what was happening. The door was ajar, and the half-dead drunk sister was still somewhere outside. As soon as I spread her thighs with my hands and my eyes sought the greatest reward of her offerings, she started to get a little nervous.

'Are you ready, Noel?' I asked. Realizing that there was no going back, Noel became a little sober.

'Umm hmm. I am,' she nodded.

And I shoved my head right next to hers, letting my nose inhale the scent of her hair. My face was pressed into the bed while hers was facing the ceiling. I believe in that impatient missionary stance, the alcohol had so thoroughly mingled with my rising manhood that I would have committed a damn murder if somebody had interrupted. Instead, I surveyed the texture of her skin and the creases of her neck while simultaneously operating the magic of my hands around her groin. With her thighs flung open and my own rump protruding towards the open door, I could feel the outside air slapping me right across my asshole, and then, when it was time, I remembered my dead father, my dead mother, and my sweet Tania, and descended to shove my mighty weapon inside for the great intercourse. And as mighty virgins like myself would agree, I failed miserably to locate the exact entrance of her vagina. In fact, I had to sit back and inspect the vagina up close, but even then, I was not able to find the exact spot of heaven on the first try.

'I can't find it, Noel. Can you please assist me?' I asked, surveying my wife's face with enthusiasm.

But it seemed that Noel has suddenly turned into a wincing, begging human carcass, frightened by my rapid and energetic advances.

I remember that back in Namchi, she would still get excited and extract my semen into uselessness. It was no wonder she had been a loyal, apologetic soldier all this while, crying and bleeding and baking cakes for me and things of that sort—perhaps also convincing herself that it was finally her time to yield.

But, at the time of my stellar performance, she got so frightened and disgusted by my advances that as soon as I began rubbing my penis against her open thighs again, she shrieked and closed her eyes and took a deep breath with a comic effect. My penis sought what it had been longing for in the annals of mankind's history. I ignored her frightened recoiling body and lurched forward and pushed as she unwillingly directed my penis towards the entrance of her pulsating vagina. I remember feeling, in broad daylight, that soft, warm pulsating organ almost a shove away from my eager penis. I was on the verge of moaning ecstatically and helplessly, about to enter the enchanted only-claimed heaven on Earth, when she suddenly placed her firm hands against my thighs, stopping my descent, and announced, 'I'm doing this just for you. Just for you. You better be grateful for this for the rest of your life.'

'What do you mean? Noel. Not now.' I begged, getting emotional. But she wouldn't remove her hand.

'Noel? You wanted it, right?' I said, trying to thrust again with a mightier force, but with my hands taking all the weight of my bent-over torso and my knees supporting my raised-up rump, I was in a wrestle-like deadlock with her until she removed her hands from my thighs.

'I mean,' she said, looking unaffected by my avalanching passion, 'that I'm doing this for us. So that our marriage can work.' She added that I must, from this point on, forget all the horse manure she had spouted a few days ago about my owning her for the rest of my life and all that nonsense.

'So you don't want it, Noel? You aren't as impatient as I am to have sex with me?'

'Nah,' she said.

She told me that by fucking me, she was doing a giant favour for our marriage and that she deserved to see some form of gratitude for her heroic deed.

And when I didn't offer any consolation, 'Stop this blabbering bullshit. Pretending to be a fourteen-year-old virgin! It's not the first time you are doing it. Not even the hundredth time. Just let's talk about this in the evening. Not now. I think I'm going to burst an artery in my penis if you stop me now,' I said.

Immediately, the heavenly cavity was drawn away from me, and she surveyed my raging face with her rebellious eyes. And as the plans for that delightful afternoon were already unfolding contrary to my expectations, her sister also suddenly marched in. Right then, while my wide gaping bottom was still facing the outside, my face was shoved somewhere near Noel's face, and my terrorized penis was waggling like a trampled snake, our mighty little comrade exclaimed, 'Mr Herman, please be careful with my sister. At least close the door, oh God!'

'But I'm not Herman,' I announced to both sisters, my face talking to one and my asshole talking to another, 'I ain't no Herman. I'm Mason Moron.'

Why that drunken little child mistook me for Herman is a mystery I thought I would never solve. But right after that mishap, my wife sat up, covered her face with her pillow, and began screaming.

'Feed on pig excrement, you dubious pie dog!' she shouted and accused me of committing marital rape on her. She said I was unattractive and hairy. And though I was startled into absolute madness, I quickly tied my robe while Noel continued to hurl horrible and deplorable accusations at me.

'He is a mad rapist, Neonika. He kidnapped me when I came to Nalanda to deliver a seminar with my boyfriend. He is a psychopath kidnapper. Please call the police. Oh, please, call the police!' Noel screamed, and her sister—half her size—immediately came between us, coaxing Noel on one side and comforting me on the other. 'It's just the alcohol, Moron ji. Just the alcohol speaking. I suggest you put your erect penis back inside the robe. There's absolutely nothing that can be done about it right now. Also, I believe it's somewhat indecent.'

I looked at her in complete confusion.

'What did I do wrong? I was just trying to have sex with my rightful wife. And it was she who suggested it in the first place,' I stammered, trying to explain.

Neonika waved her hand, trying to diffuse the situation. 'Oh, nothing, Moron ji. Just leave her alone for a while. It will be okay. She is very drunk right now. I will look after her.'

Thereafter, I was forced to retreat to the bathroom, teary-eyed, frightened, and disturbed by my wife's reaction, startled also upon being mistaken for Herman, while simultaneously battling one of the greatest erections any man had ever had.

In the evening of that fateful day, as I sat sobbing near my father's grave, little Neonika approached me and sat beside me. They must have had a fight, apparently. The little comrade and her horrible sister. Neonika was evidently crying and sobbing, and cursing her elder sister.

'She accused me of trying to ruin her marriage with you,' she said.

'If anybody is ruining the marriage, it's Noel. Why would she blame you?' I said, trying to console her.

'I don't know. She says that I was attracted to you. That's why I walked into the room while you were trying to have sex with her. That's why I called you Herman. So that you would divorce her and instead sleep with me. It's not true, Moron ji,' she said, 'it's absolutely not true.'

'Oh, absolutely no chance. I can't agree more,' I said, trying to calm my little friend.

'She's a horrible person,' Neonika said, 'I called you Herman because I was too drunk to judge. Also, while you were gone and she was drunk, she was blabbering about how badly she wanted Herman to fuck her. I can't help thinking—why don't you just divorce her?'

'I will. Of course, I will. But what's the deal with her? I just need to hear the truth. Out loud.'

Suddenly, an expression of fierce anger appeared on Neonika's face.

That blessed evening, that distraught little girl went ahead and told me the absolute truth—Noel was just a miserable woman. Herman was not her only mistake. I heard news of her great infidelity, that when I, distraught, had left her and come to Nalanda, Noel had fucked a few more men here and there.

'How do you know all this?' I demanded.

'She told me. Out loud while you were in the office this morning,' Neonika recounted. 'In fact, as soon as she had descended to the valley that day after you disappeared, she accidentally encountered another of her estranged lovers from high school, Kuldeep. She told me she kissed him while they were waiting for her train to Nalanda. In fact, she promised marriage to him as well, while, I believe' she said, 'she was giving him a blowjob in the unsanitary washroom of the railway station.'

As I looked at her, absolutely speechless, Neonika told me very solemnly that 'after marrying her, I had entered into something that half of Namchi could see, but I was so blinded by my passion that nobody could dare warn me.' Neonika told me that 'apparently, half the hilltop of Namchi had slept with Noel while she was growing up, and the remaining half just stayed aloof from her entire cursed family'.

When I look back, this wasn't a bolt of thunder that came out of nowhere. In fact, I think I had known the truth all along.

'Hell,' Neonika told me, 'Noel is a professional adulteress who is being researched for her corrupt morals in three different privately funded universities in Nepal.'

For bearing the flag of her household, I too had been an outcast in the hills. And honestly, I don't know if this had any authenticity, but she sure as hell left me with a piece of information that would help me finally and freely fake my death and disappear.

She said that Noel was not even a citizen of India. Her mother had fled with her father from Nepal under mysterious circumstances. Her father had been involved in various small, pitiful businesses in Namchi, selling wood, bootlegged alcohol, and stolen shoes. But on the whole, their wooden house had appeared on the hills as suddenly as they had themselves. Neonika mentioned that Noel had to sleep with many eminent people to land a job in Delhi in the first place. Neonika said that she had had a knack for sleeping with her bosses during her corporate days. More than just an employee, she was their rightful mistress, merely making ends meet.

Neonika said that the marriage I had with her was as illegitimate as the children we would have produced one day, and on that account, she had absolutely no right over my Cemetery House because, apparently, she didn't have the documents—no identification, no passport—nothing to claim her legal ownership over the mansion or even her marriage for she wasn't even a legal citizen of our country.

Anyway, keeping the geopolitical differences aside, after all, these matters concern the government and not a cuckold. After that incident, I abruptly left my house and shifted (more like rehabilitated myself) into the comfort and certainty of my old dorm room with Zahed. I lay on my soft, welcoming mattress and stared outside our university window, where endless stars glowed palely. Sometimes, from the depths of my sadness, I would suddenly get an uncanny glimpse into the gazillion shining stars, the purple and blue, and the infinite miraculous burning gases of our solar system. I relied heavily on sleep, and such were the mighty miracles of nature that unravelled and unfolded before my grieving eyes.

Even though I had not expected such delight, a safe distance from that witch brought me more comfort and solace, and I felt happy that I would be living the rest of my life far away from her. But Dr Zahed said, 'You are hallucinating, Moron boy. Yes! You are. You must drink water. Must maintain a good sodium–potassium balance. I have learnt from books that the old and bereaved tend to hallucinate a lot before death has the final blow on them.'

He said, 'Women, or widows, have been known to go to crazy lengths to reminisce about their dead husbands. Only yesterday, a magazine narrated the extremely sad, heartbreaking news of a woman who would call her dead husband's cell phone over a hundred times every day just to listen to the ringtone.'

'To hell with it, boy. Let her rot. I'm just worried about my house. Actually, it's not even the house. She can stay in it with her tribe. Or we will just get it demolished. I'm worried about the estate in general. About my father's grave. How will I visit that anymore? If I'm to fake my death?'

'My ass, she will stay there. Right after we help you fake your death, I will request that my papa send a damn bulldozer to that house so those whores can be vacated immediately.'

The next afternoon, there was a soft knock on the door, and poor Santos marched in, his face flushed and his mouth sealed.

'What is it, Santos? Welcome back, old gangsta!' Zahed said.

But Santos wouldn't speak.

'To hell with it, Santos. Have you summoned a fucking ghost?'

Suddenly, Santos said, 'All I can summon is that he walked past that door fiercely determined.'

'What door, you fool? Determined about what? Have you gone mad?'

'The door of her hotel room. Herman, sir,' Santos said, thereby clarifying that, without playing around, he had plunged straight into the matter. 'I have investigated the matter thoroughly,' Santos said. 'The evening shift staff members of the hotel recall that evening in particular. They say that in the entire course of running that hotel behind the New Delhi station, they had never seen a man so determined. He dashed right into the hotel, more like kicked the door of that woman's room wide open, and of course, there were thuds and a lot of rattling, so everybody saw. They say they had never seen a man so determined about something.'

'Determined about what?'

'Determined about enjoying every drop of that girl's married existence. And when he walked out, a solid two or three hours later, it seemed that he was relieved. As if he had met his resolve.'

'Do you have any evidence, Santos?'

'I, of course, have all the evidences right here,' Santos said, presenting a page he had apparently filched from the check-in register of some hotel in Delhi.

And there it was. On a paper stolen from the Hotel Royal Deluxe Inn of New Delhi. My wife's name, scribbled in her hasty handwriting, along with her cell phone number and her beautiful signature, which I absolutely couldn't fail to recognize at once. There had also been a visitor check-in at 11:35 p.m.

'It could have been any visitor, Santos. How can you tell it was Herman?' I asked.

'Well, if you let me finish, Moron ji. I know it's painful, but my report must be finished. Right after leaving the hotel, I went to the American Express building in Gurgaon (the place where your wife used to work, of course) and befriended an amazing guard and a cab driver who drives for the Amex people. I fed them good hot tea and breakfast for three solid days, and on the fourth day, they spilled the ongoing office rumours. You know how it is. People discuss all the shit either in cabs or right outside the office buildings, totally ignoring us poor guards and drivers as ill-read rascals.'

'True, Santos. Very true. Fuck, even I tend to do that,' I said.

'Here,' he said, presenting a photograph of himself along with a poor-looking guard taken right outside the luminous Amex building. 'You see, I don't spew shit like your wife. This guard is my good friend now. His name is Firoz. He tells me all the rumours about the great corporation of Amex now. He recalls the rumours about this Noel madam quite precisely.'

'What's the rumour, Santos?'

'Now, Sir Master Moron, the real tragedy is—again, this is only a rumour (you know how these rumours work and transpire, very unreliable),' he said, slashing his hands, 'but what is circulating in these offices right now is that your wife had ringed him a day before meeting him. Yes, their encounter was not incidental. She had called Herman and told him that she hadn't fucked you yet. She said she had gone out of her way to ensure that no Moron could pollute her Herman's lady love. And therefore, if he still harboured feelings for her, he might consider divorcing his pathetic wife while also enjoying the warmth of her offerings without any disgust. In fact, sir, I believe your wife offered Herman the chance to alternate between fucking his own wife and then also fucking her, just like lunch and dinner.'

'How the hell would a doorman know all this, you fool?'

'I'm not sure. I have a tendency to fill in the gaps with my own vivid imagination. But I'm sure even you would know this if you were a sensible, well-read, scholarly man. Your wife was capable of doing this, wasn't she?'

And putting an end to the gibbering, he said, 'I hope that finally I have brought you some relief.'

And oh, my brothers! My fellow sufferers! I was in such angst, not because the rumour had surfaced, but because I could clearly picture my Noel—how helpless she became whenever Herman popped up on her cell phone, how she would shake and get all helpless—that indeed, she would have rung him and helplessly informed him something as poetic as, 'Not that the universe had other plans for us, but your Noel is still unpolluted.' And pollute her he did, damn right.

'Now, this predator we are talking about, sir,' Santos said again, 'we have learnt about this from a reliable source. Actually, from the cab driver who overheard a friend of Herman discussing the tragic affairs of that night with another of Herman's friends while he was on his nightly duty, that Herman was not even that adamant about fucking your wife. He was, in fact, dreadfully anxious at the time of the deed. While he was doing his usual rounds with the lady, he was extremely paranoid. During the act, he raised his head twice when a distant noise reached his ear, just to inspect the landscape around. But then your wife drew his surveilling face to herself, so he instead surveyed the landscape of your wife.'

'If we are to leave out all the poetry and romanticism,' I said, growing impatient, 'then what are you trying to imply, driver ji?'

'That it was not he who fucked her. It was she who made him fuck her.'

Hearing this horrible, heartbreaking but meticulous account, I didn't know whether this bastard even went to Delhi in the first place to really inspect the matter. Or if he did, he might have merely strolled through Connaught Place, drank to his heart's content, and then on his way back home, he just picked up a cheap, third-grade magazine, something like 'The Infamous Infidel Wife' or something from a roadside shop, and was now just describing to me in his famous vocabulary the things he had learnt from the magazine.

Still, his description did have the desired effect on me. And therefore, I resolved to embark on my quest, walking slowly and solemnly towards the door through which Santos had entered, with Zahed and poor Santos staring at me in pale confusion.

'But where will you go, Moron? At this dark hour?' asked Zahed.

'Towards light. I will go towards the light.'

'Where is he going, Zahed ji?' Santos asked anxiously.

'He's going to fake his death and disappear.'

'How will he do that, sir?'

And I was so nonchalantly still approaching the door that I overheard Zahed for the very last time.

'It's imperative he goes. We must help him. We will make up some shit,' Zahed was telling Santos. 'Some narrative about how, after hearing the detailed account of his wife's misdeeds from her sister that very evening, the distraught husband lost his sanity. He began walking around the streets of Nalanda and then ended up wandering to a different district, where he was starving and begging. The next roaring afternoon, he got trampled by a speeding truck and died on the spot.'

'What about the body? Zahed ji? Do you think they would believe this shit for even a second if they don't see Moron ji's corpse? Wouldn't the police investigate? And what would you tell your father?'

'As far as the police are concerned, they already did the investigation. Only today, I performed an autopsy on an unidentified obese male who had been run over by a truck. The police are waiting for me to confirm his identity to the best of my ability. I just need to call and tell them that it's my dearest friend Moron whose body has been incidentally brought to my table.'

'But whose body is it, Zahed ji? Does his face match Moron ji's?'

'Ah! That corpse is all disfigured, boy. You think getting run over by a truck is a joke? The face is all squashed. Even the penis is all squashed. The full torso. It was sad. Took me hours just to identify the organs. It doesn't matter whose body it used to be. Might have been some poor homeless man. But now, as we are to witness, even our Moron is homeless. So, from now on, that poor unidentified run-over body that I dissected today will be called Moron!'

'Alright. But what about the cremation? Say, while we are carrying that body, what if that mad bitch shows up, all sad, and demands to take a look at the body of her cuckolded husband one last time? Wouldn't she immediately know that it's not Moron ji but some poor homeless man as soon as she takes a look at that trampled corpse?'

'Hmm,' Zahed paused for a moment and then suddenly said, 'Don't worry, boy. I will put that mad whore in the guilt of a lifetime. There is no hiding. We will cremate the body right at the Cemetery House. Right in front of that brand-new widow.'

'But what if she demands to see the corpse? Are you sure she won't recognize it?'

'Yeah, it's quite bad, Santos. It's the perfect corpse. I can guarantee it. Plus, we can take some additional precautions. The trick is, while we are cremating the body, we must get a few ladies to keep that mad, distorted bitch away until the body is half-burned.'

'Or better yet. Let's knock her unconscious,' Santos suggested.

'That's not practical, Santos,' Zahed said.

'Okay, how about we just tell her some mad lie. Tell her that Moron ji had written a will long ago naming her as the legal heiress of his estate. And that while the corpse is being cremated, we need her to sign some papers to establish his death immediately. We tell her that she must ignore the corpse and sign a few documents right away. Just to ensure that the property is passed smoothly to the deserved heiress. Of course she would. That bitch would be so excited she won't bother checking the corpse.'

'Oh yeah, we can do that as well. What a blessed day!' said Zahed.

3

After my martyrdom, I feared enormously the uncharted liberties my wife might take—as soon as the news of her recently entrusted widowhood reached her. I dreaded, no, I knew for a fact that as soon as the news of my death reached her, she would end up turning the peaceful Cemetery House into a darkened whorehouse.

She would advertise herself on billboards and in newspapers, warranting an A-class sexual experience for anybody who might be ready to dispense a few thousand rupees for the fuck of a lifetime. And then, travellers and rogues from across the nation would begin showing up at my estate on the pretext of being lost in the city of Nalanda. Homeless men begging for alms and various mistaken milkmen would crowd my gate as soon as dusk settled on the town, and with the dying, dark night, she would commit even darker deeds.

In fact, at the front gate itself, she would get a small dormitory constructed, which could be used to receive visitors of enormous wealth. And also a hired gunman to protect her from malicious, non-paying invaders. I also felt that she would remove my family's surname from the main epistle and instead install something European just to outrightly highlight her enterprise—Madame Noel M'oron of Nepal.

So, I thought it would be a good idea to keep vigilance over her for a few days before I could go away and figure out my own afterlife. To enjoy her outrageously sad sobs of widowhood or to bust her fucking a stranger and then mauling both of those bastards to their instant death. But Zahed advised me against it as I could get caught. In the passion of catching her naked, there was more of a chance that it would be me who might be caught spying on her, and then my dreams of destroying her would be turned against me—so violently that I would be forced to escape this town once and for all. Zahed said that 'now I must take a train to an unknown land and then a ferry from there to another tropical island and begin a new life'. He said that if I could become a fisherman, I could scavenge enough mackerels to keep myself going for months at a stretch. He said more than anything else, I might find unexpected solace in agrarian life. In pastoral life. He said that it was time to embrace solitude. It was time to let myself be enthralled by the greatness of nature and mother earth and not beg for validation and pussy.

To which I retorted, 'It might also probably be easier to find a village girl in a famine-stricken village and fuck her for a solid year if I were to find a remedy for my broken heart.'

To which Zahed replied defeatedly, 'Yeah, that too, Moron. That too.'

But just the idea of leaving Nalanda to embark on a pastoral orgy scared the wits out of me. Leaving this land—which had accepted me after my arrival from Boston—leaving the university, my dissertation, my father's grave, Zahed. Leaving my whole life for the unknown.

'I am not going anywhere,' I announced. 'I am not going to leave Nalanda.'

'So where would you take your refuge, Moron?'

I surveyed the endless expanse of the old gangster-ridden land of Nalanda through the window of my dorm. How does one become invisible in his own city?

And then poor Santos walked up to me, and putting his hands on my shoulder, he said, 'Sir, you remember how I had told you to fuck a nice prostitute in the red-light district of Chaturbhuj? Right after Ms Noel was stabbed, and you came like a madman wanting to dismiss me from my job?'

'Yeah, Santos, I do. You even offered to pay for my intercourse with your humble salary. What about it?'

'And you didn't take my advice? You remember that?'

'I do, you mad fool. Why bring that up right now? Are you trying to take some second-degree revenge on me after all these years?'

'No, sir. I just wonder how nice and happy your life would have turned out to be if you had listened to me that day.'

'I guess, Santos,' I said, looking at my dear Zahed and then at Santos.

'Listen, you sisterfucker,' Zahed snapped at Santos. 'You go and wait for me in the car. Your pay grade and your lifestyle don't permit this much brain usage. Just fuck off. What are you trying to do to my friend?'

'Santos means no harm,' poor Santos justified, referring to himself in the third person. 'It's just that I have a similar sort of advice for Moron ji today.'

'What is it?' I asked, feeling a ray of hope. 'I will listen this time. Santos ji. My senior. My guru. My teacher. I shall listen.'

'Well,' Santos said, coming up to stand right in front of me and blocking my view of the magnificent outside. He began surveying the expanse of Nalanda with thoughtful eyes. After about five minutes, he said, 'More than the need to disappear, you need to fuck a nice tight pussy right now.' Then, grinding his teeth, he made an artificial pussy with his hairy hand and inserted his other hand into it with enormous passion. 'Right now! Moron Ji, as a dead man, you need to be invisible, for unos. Somewhere the hands of the law can't reach you. And dos, if you wish to keep your sanity intact, you must fuck for a few years like a sex-deprived addict on death row, while remaining invisible and inaccessible.'

'You mean to say that fucking a nice prostitute will repair my broken heart? How is the penis related to the heart, Santos? You think a nice prostitute could fix the great damage that only a wife could have caused?'

'Hmm.' When the difference between the need for love and the need for sex was explained to the loyal manservant, Santos paused for a minute. And then, with a fierce grip of optimism, he said, 'Or better yet, Moron ji! Let us find you a second-hand wife. Somebody who would yield to you and your mad desire for mating as and when you please. And I am not talking about just any wife. I'm not suggesting that you go out in this afternoon heat and seduce an average girl and make her fall in love with you all over again only to have your tiny, little heart broken again. What I'm suggesting is that you find yourself a nice Ukrainian or Russian wife. A tall, golden-haired girl who would not speak English to pester you but would fuck you like a madwoman. I suggest you sell your house and buy yourself a second-hand wife.'

I rubbed my lips, swallowed my saliva, and looked at Santos as if he were a total rascal. I felt like slapping that mad bastard right there. But then, what would I have gained from it? He meant no harm, after all.

'I have read in magazines,' Santos continued, 'about the prized market of virgins in Bulgaria. Nice virgins are sold at weekend markets for the purpose of marriage. I'm sure they would be docile and much better than your horrible missus. Imagine this new wife of yours; she won't know anybody in India. How would she fuck anybody else if she doesn't know anybody else?' Santos said.

'I guess that should be a good start, Santos, no doubt. But such places only exist in those cheap roadside magazines you read while waiting for us in your car, Santos. I could go to a sex paradise—Phuket (I always dreamed of visiting Phuket), Moscow, Ukraine (I couldn't really go there due to the great war happening in that great nation), or even Bulgaria. But after my death certificate is published, how am I supposed to take an international trip? How would my visa get clearance? How would they stamp my passport?'

'Well, you tend to underestimate my smartness, Moron ji. You forget that I'm a humble servant to you. The most loyal and the most dedicated. I used to drive your dead papa around the city while he was still alive. You think that Santos is some cheap, talcum-rubbing, shit-eating driver who doesn't know that a dead man can't go on international vacations. But if you must know, I'm also the best friend of a doorman who works at a place like the one I described to you just a few seconds ago. Someplace where girls are flooding in and waiting to be fucked.'

'What doorman, Santos? Which door? You live on Champasari Street in a 2,000-rupee rental room. Do you smoke crystal meth or inhale whitener at night? Are you losing your sanity?' Zahed asked.

'No, Zahed ji,' Santos said. 'I work another shift. When I'm not driving you or your great papa, I have a different job altogether. I work at Bahubali's mansion. Yes. I suggest that you go and take refuge at Bahubali's house. I could get you in. Sure as fuck, I could get you in. He met your papa once, Moron ji. I still remember that day. Our great master Bahubali had come down to the university for some rally, and your father greeted him. They just met and immediately became friends, talking for hours that day.'

Suddenly, I was reminded of the day when I was almost killed by a cavalcade of some forty unruly SUV cars that sped past the tea stall on Warden Road and the uncanny commotion Bahubali had caused merely by doing something as simple as driving past us.

'What? He knew my father? That Bahubali?' I asked incredulously.

'Sure as hell, he did.' Santos nodded his head with absolute assurance.

'Where does he live now, Santos?'

'He has a mansion right across the Rabti River, just as huge as yours,' Santos said. 'Only you have accommodated just one prostitute in your household. But Bahubali's house is replete with whores. Sir, what can I say? If you threw a grenade inside Bahubali's guarded compound, nine out of ten people who would die would be underpaid whores. You throw a slipper like this,' he said, taking off his slipper and throwing it at the ceiling fan, 'it will surely land on a whore's head. But your slipper can't reach his compound. Neither can a grenade. Hell, not even a bird can enter Bahubali's mansion if he doesn't want that little birdie to.'

'Why is that, Santos?'

'Because it is public knowledge. Bahubali's mansion is highly guarded. Oh, my bad!' Santos said. 'It used to be heavily guarded until last month before his horrible court trials began. He had over fifty-five commandos in black turbans guarding his estate with light machine guns. Hell! It used to be quite a sight.'

'Gunmen? For what? So that he could fuck his whores nicely? I have heard he is old. How do you know that he fucks so many whores? Is he a routine whore fucker?'

'No, Moron ji. Ahh, what dog shit! Ahh, thoo, thoo,' Santos said, pinching his ears. 'No, no. He hasn't fucked one single whore in his lifetime. I mean, he has one. But that one was a mistake. He fucked her after he married her. And he didn't know she was a whore until she acted like one. Just like yours. Bahubali sahib is a godman with ill fortune. He is an emperor just like yourself, but it seems that his empire is falling just like yours.'

'But why does that emperor have so many whores in his compound?'

'For the same reason he is facing all the legal trials. Oh my God, Moron ji,' Santos said, rubbing his eyes in disbelief, 'I can't believe that a man as scholarly and informed as yourself keeps away from the newspapers. It's everywhere. Every news channel is running the feature on repeat. He used to make films, Moron ji. You know those dirty, third-grade, once-in-a-lifetime erections featured in porn films. He still does. He is working on his last, very promising masterpiece right now. But I suggest you don't use that word in front of him. "Porn". I'm sure he will make you disappear if he hears it. Just say "art", Moron ji, when you meet him.'

'Hell,' I said. 'Does he still have those guards?'

'Not anymore.' Santos' face fell in dejection. 'If you recall the *Deccan News* article that came out the day before yesterday, the mansion is unguarded now. The state has withdrawn the security. He has been kicked out of the ruling party.'

'Why?'

'Well, sir,' Santos said, 'that is something that goes right over my head. I suggest you ask him directly when you meet him.'

'So what if somebody just walks into his mansion and kills that poor guy, Santos? Now that he is not guarded?'

'I mean, that's not entirely true. He still has his own personal army. Of course, these affairs can't be published in the newspaper. But there are rumours that he still has over 34,000 bullets encased in the trunk of his bed, along with a few brand-new AK-47s. Also, there is the old, loyal Durban ji, a very reliable manservant just like myself, still guarding the compound. But apart from that, his empire is on the verge of its downfall. Just like yours.'

After hearing Santos' fantastic story, I thought, *What harm could there be in giving his plan a try?* After all, all that a passionate madman has for himself is another madman.

So, when the loneliness and despair of a broken marriage hit the owner of the former empire (yours truly), he corresponded with the owner of another brazenly mysterious empire (Mr Bahubali) through a fervent letter that he had written with passionate enthusiasm:

Dear Bahubali sahib,

Don't freak out when a letter from a dead parishioner ends up in your hand, ha!

Then, believing that lunatic number two might not fail and might be enthused to receive a letter from lunatic number one, I wrote that I was his biggest admirer. I praised his unique line of work. I said that his films had helped me to not commit suicide after discovering that my wife had slept with her estranged lover. I wrote that his films had been my most promising and reliable companion during my difficult childhood in Boston, facing loneliness and racial discrimination. I told him that I had just returned from a great university in the West and that it was my dream and life's goal to work for his great filmmaking enterprise from now on. At the end, as personal connections go a long way in securing jobs or bails from prisons, I gallantly reminded him of the time he had marched down Secretariat Road and had shaken hands with my father and said that my father was like his own brother. (In reference, he had also presented you with a small bottle of very expensive ittar.)

And that it might be reported in mighty sorrow and aghast horror that his brother is now dead. That he died a year ago and that the nephew (don't scowl and laugh now—if he had called my father his brother, wouldn't I become the natural nephew?) is enduring a difficult marriage. And that the only remedy now is to fake his death.

Santos stared at my letter with great attention and asked me to make a few alterations here and there. 'Add that you were inspired by his great films after Santos had asked you to watch them while you were still in the US.'

I did.

After the letter was finalized, Santos called his doorman friend at Bahubali's house and talked for about twenty minutes. After hanging up, he smiled and said, 'You are all set, Moron ji. You must go and see Bahubali tomorrow itself. As it happens, Bahubali has been in a deep state of meditation for over a week now. Some sort of exercise for tomorrow's shoot. But the first thing he will do tomorrow is consider your case.'

'What if they shoo me away, Santos? What if the guards don't let me in? Can you come with me?' I said, fearing that maybe Santos was indeed a madman after all. Maybe he wanted me to visit Bahubali's house because he himself wanted to see the great mansion once in his lifetime.

'No. It's your journey, sir. I can't drive you there,' Santos said. 'I'm your driver and manservant. No doubt about that. But now that you are dead, you must not be able to talk to me. You are not a ghost after all, right?'

'That's not how it works, Santos. How will I survive if I cannot talk to people?'

'That's the whole point, sir,' Santos said. 'You are not surviving anymore. You are dead. I strongly suggest that you follow the lifestyle—oh, my bad—"deathstyle" of the dead. Otherwise, I'm afraid that if you don't pretend to be dead, two days later, you will end up calling your stupid wife again. Because that's what heartbroken living people do. Rules are rules, Moron ji,' Santos said, nodding his head sagely.

'Just be present, Santos.'

'I'm afraid that even if I am present there, I would not be able to entertain you. As you see, I have a totally different job there. A totally different identity. I'm not even called Santos there. I'm called Chota Khashoggi. A pun on the celebrated polygamist and arms dealer, Adnan Khashoggi. It is because I have two wives, sir.'

'What the fuck!' I said, startled.

Zahed widened his eyes and gaped and repeated right after me, 'What the fuck? Why didn't you tell this to us before, you rascal?'

'Because poor Santos was never asked.'

'Anyway,' I said, 'that's not important right now, Zahed. What's the criteria for getting a job at his mansion? I'm sure they won't just let anybody take up a job. What should I do?'

'What would you do to get any job? Prepare a CV and do some mock interviews.'

So that night, as Zahed announced my most tragic death to the world, I began researching my afterlife. While an obituary about me was being printed in the *Hindustan News*, I was writing the course of my future.

Before my death could be announced, Zahed snuck me into the trunk of the Sumo and had me driven to a shabby motel near the state highway. An ideal hiding place for rapists, murderers, or imposters. There, I sat in a dimly lit room, and, ignoring the flaring pain in the valves of my heart, I focused on more practical and hopeful matters for tomorrow. Noel inevitably crossed my mind a few times. I wondered what she would be up to right now. Would she be heartbroken? Would she go mad hearing about the tragedy of my death? Would she turn into a notorious whore? Would she run back to Herman or bring unknown men to our marital bed to cope with the grief of my death? Would she be lonely and suicidal?

I sighed as my thoughts raced. How did all this matter anymore?

I sat in deathlike silence and prepared answers to any questions Bahubali might have upon our first meeting.

Say, if he were to ask, 'What qualifies you to take domicile in my private residence?'

I would reply, 'Well, I'm a renowned scholar of psychology, having just earned my bachelor's degree from a great university in the West. I can dedicate all my hard-earned knowledge and scientific temperament to conducting A-class research on your great artwork. I can publish reports and provide evidence on various behavioural trends in society in general. For example, I could run a T-test or regression analysis to determine the type of actresses you should hire for your great films. You know, big-breasted? Small-breasted? Pointy-breasted? Things of that sort ...'

'Out of all the jobs you can possibly get around the world, why do you want to work for my great enterprise?'

The truth was, I was going to Bahubali to buy a second-hand wife for myself. But I couldn't say that out loud. Not at the beginning. So, I figured I would need to work on this part for some time.

To maintain some dignity, I thought it would be a good idea to avoid discussing the greater details of my failed marriage should he ask. If he got to know everything about Noel and my tragedy, he might think of me as an outright fool.

The next day, I arrived at Bahubali's mansion following Santos' directions. I had to take a rickshaw from the state highway and was peddled here by a sickly man who was surely suffering from tuberculosis as he kept coughing and groaning for half the journey. When I reached my destination, I found a crowd of curious old men and boys milling around the boundary of Bahubali's compound, trying to catch a glimpse of the activities inside the mansion. From what I could gather, there was a giant crane with strobe lights swinging through the air. And there were large cameras being installed on dolly tripods.

The crowd was so thick that it was absolutely impossible to enter through the main gate. I looked around helplessly, wondering if it was nothing but Santos's lifelong desire to enter Bahubali's palatial estate that had gotten me stuck in this mad brouhaha. Helpless and defeated, I put my backpack on and was about to retreat back to death when suddenly my eyes fell upon a small shiny gate—another passage to the dreamland mansion. This gate was on the opposite side of his house. A backdoor! Only this door didn't have people milling about. There was, however, a guard with a lathi stationed at the entrance. Somehow, the crowd was only buzzing at the front door, leaving the backdoor almost unattended.

'What the hell! I'm already dead. How low can I go now?' I wondered and walked to the backdoor.

Throughout my childhood, I had been a good imposter whenever the situation demanded it. Once, I remember accidentally witnessing a semi-famous Hollywood actress make love to her scandalous lover in the grand presidential suite of the Beverly Hills Hotel. I was seventeen then, and I had just completed my first drug run in the United States. I was staying at the Beverly Hills Hotel for the night, loitering through the empty corridors, when I ended up right in front of the door to the presidential suite, which was being guarded by a sleepy security guard. With a strange sense of authority, I was able to breach the security. And thereupon I entered the suite, where I saw for the first time a semi-famous pop singer and actress make love to a jacked-up model from LA. This passionate and scandalous sight, which people would have spent a fortune to see photographs of—only if I had managed to capture it with my Polaroid. But such glimpses are reserved for those who can disappear even when there is nothing to hide behind.

Anyway, I walked past the old guard at Bahubali's door with the same sense of authority. I took out my silver Macintosh laptop, my face reflecting the sternness of such authority that seemed to say, 'I'm here to mind my own business, and it would be good if you mind your own business, you fool!'

I kept walking, my back straight, because I knew I was being observed. I opened the latch on the back door when suddenly the guard said, 'Where are you off to, dear sir? Are you going to the Ministry of Revenue?'

Ministry of Revenue? Is he a contorted idiot? I thought to myself.

'No. I've been called by Bahubali himself. I'm a foreign correspondent and an art dealer,' I said, trying to make things sound too complicated for his comprehension.

'Oh! You are here to shoot the film?' he asked.

'Oh yes. I don't come until I'm called. And Bahubali is waiting for me. In fact, he is quite impatient.'

'Ah,' he said, pointing at my silver Macintosh laptop, 'so you are going to shoot the film with that?'

'Yes, of course,' I replied.

'Ah! Off you go, sir. Must hurry then. The shoot is about to start. I suggest you go and report to the Ministry of Entertainment.'

As I would learn later, the various ministries of Bahubali's estate managed the affairs of his life and household in a manner similar to how the government manages a nation. There was the Ministry of Revenue, which focused on terrorizing and collecting security money from local shopkeepers as well as from the sand and alcohol mafia. There was a special unit under the Ministry of Revenue that specialized in collecting money from corrupt state officials. Then, there was the Ministry of Justice, which specialized in killing any son of a bitch who dared raise a crooked little finger at Bahubali. The Ministry of Justice had two units: the QRT (Quick Response Team), a gang of designated killers commissioned to eliminate any rascal within twenty-four hours of Bahubali's announcement, and the SS (Strategic Services), which specialized in assassinating renowned politicians and powerful public figures whose ideologies didn't align with Bahubali's. Rascals who dared to question Bahubali in the state assembly were killed four months to a year after they had done so. They were made to die in an accidental building fire or, say, by having the petrol tank of their vehicles explode while being refuelled at the local gas station. The SS worked closely with the QTR on special instances, for example, when it came to violating the women and widows of Bahubali's enemies after the main target had been killed, to set an example for others. Then there was the Ministry of Entertainment—the one closest to his heart and soul. This enterprise was dedicated entirely to providing hospitality and alcohol to prostitutes and handling the latest film production technologies that Bahubali might require to shoot his porn.

Anyway, I entered the compound. I was unaware of what awaited me on the other end. Once inside, I felt the realms of the real and surreal merging at one point of existence, where the dimension of time bent and mixed itself into the expanding space. I thought that instead of entering a mansion, I had entered a state of pure dream. The mansion was no longer a mansion but a market. Yes! An empty market with unattended stalls selling fresh vegetables and dead fish and croaking roosters to nobody in particular.

'Have I been shot by some rascal? Am I actually dead? Am I in hell or heaven?'

And suddenly, out of nowhere, a bare-breasted woman who was practically naked toppled down. A fairy of a woman who walked past me to the stall, not even bothering to look at me. I thought if I had lost my sanity. Why the fuck was I seeing naked women all of a sudden? Was this heaven? Papa? You there?

And then suddenly, another missus appeared. A taller, fairer, bare-breasted woman whose crotch had an enormous amount of pubic hair.

'Hello, miss,' I said out loud. But then, the woman didn't seem to care at all.

I looked around in amusement and kept walking when suddenly there was a terrific scream: 'Cut! Cut it! Some rascal has barged into my set. Cut!' I looked around nervously, and my eyes met the angry gaze of the man I had only been dreaming of all along. Bahubali. He was a tall man, almost six feet in height. He was wearing a white shirt, white flannel pants, white shoes, and a white hat—a vision in all white. I noticed a scar on his head, so deep it could qualify as a bullet scar.

'Are you a fucking moron?' he screamed from afar.

'Yes, sir. Absolutely. How do you know me?'

'Cut it!'

It turned out that I had walked right into Bahubali's set while he was mid-shoot.

'Oh hell! I must apologize vehemently. I'm sorry, Bahubali ji. A father figure to me. My God. I'm sorry!' I screamed. 'I didn't mean to disrupt your shoot.'

I feared that I was going to meet my instant demise right then. No really, I thought it was time for me to die when Santos emerged from behind Bahubali's shoulder, whispered something in his ear, and then a sudden expression of warmth appeared on Bahubali's face. I felt as if I had been accepted into the afterlife.

'Come here, Moron ji,' Santos called out to me.

I went.

'This is my master, my god, my guru, Bahubali.'

I bent down and touched both of Bahubali's feet.

'Very well, boy! I have just been told by Santos that you and your wife had been married for six months and that she slept with some serviceman from Delhi without even letting you fuck her during the entire marriage. Is that true?' Bahubali asked me. His very first question about my state of existence was posed in front of some twenty-five of his sidekicks.

'Yes, sir. It is,' I said defeatedly.

'Hell! That's outrageous, boy. Just outrageous. And that you have faked your death and come here? Why is that, boy?'

'It's because you knew my dead father. Your brother. Here, please read this,' I told Bahubali, taking out the letter I had written for him last night.

Bahubali unfolded the letter and read it aloud. He stared at the letter blankly for a second, and then he began to get all teary. 'What a great misfortune, son. What a great misfortune. First, the death of your loving papa. And then the misfortune of seeing your wife sleep with somebody else.'

'Yes, sir,' I said, tears smarting in my own eyes.

'And what terrific English you write, boy. Like a damn Englishman. I wish you could work for me,' Bahubali said.

'I wish that too, sir. I really do,' I said.

'I remember your father. What a learned man,' Bahubali said, all emotional now. 'I remember meeting him outside the university. And we spoke. He just spoke about you. He just went on and on. He also gifted me, very humbly, a very nice-smelling ittar. In fact,' he said, 'it's such a coincidence that I happen to have put it on this morning itself. Here, smell your father's present.' He raised his right hand and invited me to smell his armpit.

I walked forward and shoved my nostrils into his armpit, and my senses were brimming with the same musky, fruity scent of my dead father. The cologne he used to apply when he was alive. The olfactory senses, as they have been discovered, are said to be the strongest and most receptive when it comes to human perception. I don't know if that is empirically true or not, but as soon as that scent entered my nose, I was all teary. I just couldn't hold myself back. Seeing me in that state, Bahubali hugged me, slapped me on the back, and asked me to stop crying like a schoolgirl.

Once I calmed down, he paused the day's shoot for a while and had a brief interview session with me.

'So, nephew, do you desire to stay with me from now on?'

'Only if I could be of service.'

'Santos tells me you have come from a foreign land. What do you think I do here, nephew?'

'You make films, sir.'

'Well,' Bahubali said, 'not just any films. The thing is, people think that Bahubali is a third-grade degenerate pervert. They think he likes seeing people fuck. He likes sodomizing helpless, poor people. But what I'm trying to do here, nephew, is create a cure. Porn is not just recreation. It is what keeps the ailing at ease. Porn is not for people who are already happy with their way of life. Porn is not for people who are already fulfilled. Porn is for the broken. The thirsty. The starving. Porn is for the desperate, who might go mad if they are not given hope. Porn is for the generation that is crippled under the weight of unnameable and unthinkable maladies.'

Hearing his speech, his sidekicks started clapping and cheering. Bahubali continued, 'There are desperate men on the streets. Hidden in the darkly lit alleys. There are hungry, starving men who would turn this world into a revolving rape house if they were not served with porn. I say, free the porn. I say, let there be liberation.'

This was followed by more 'wah wah's.

'Oh, what a genius, Bahubali ji.' The sidekicks joined in the chorus, acclaiming their boss' brilliance.

'So,' Bahubali said, 'do you actually want to serve my greater cause, or do you just want to fuck my prostitutes and be gone and complete your journey towards enlightenment by yourself? I'm fine with either,' he said, raising both his hands and shaking his head vehemently.

Unable to think of an answer, I looked at Santos in confusion. He pointed his eyes towards the letter, suggesting that I follow the usual.

When silence still reigned, Bahubali asked again, 'Are you visiting us to drink rose sherbet and fuck a prostitute, or is there anything else you would want to do?'

'I'm not here to fuck your prostitutes,' I said, jolted into my senses. 'I'm here to find enlightenment. Something that only you can lead me to. I'm here to become your loyal manservant, Bahubali ji. But I won't stay if I can't make myself useful to you. I'm not a freebie.'

'What's a freebie?'

'Those who eat and fuck for free. I'll eat if I earn, and I'll fuck if I earn. No freebie stuff.'

'Ah, I see.' Bahubali seemed quite happy with my explanation.

'You have written here,' Bahubali said, looking at my letter, 'that you have been educated at the most prestigious institution in the West.'

'Yes, sir,' I said. And when the name of the great institution was muttered, a wave of frenzy passed over everybody gathered there. Bahubali closed his eyes, raised his head, took a sharp breath, and looked at me again with a fresh resolve.

'So you have come from England? All the way from England? Just to work and intern under me? Under this small enterprise?' Bahubali said, mistaking the United States for merry old England.

'Yes, sir' I said, 'it has been a dream.'

'Tell me more, son!' Bahubali said.

I told him about Tania and about Boston. About Harvard. About Mukesh. And then, sensing that I might end up outperforming his wits, Bahubali began speaking and raving about England himself. He recounted a bright summer in 1999 when he had gone to England with his wife. He was on a trip to receive an honorary doctorate from a renowned university, which was later rejected because, as he said, they cut his name off due to his Indian skin.

Among his gawking sidekicks, Bahubali raved, rambled, and recalled the time when he went on a voyage to England.

'The place was a dream,' he said. 'The bitches were merrier, the food dreamier. Everybody was lining up in front of my hotel room to have sex with me. All these bitches were sneezing from their crotch because they were hella mad that I had come to England and was planning to leave without fucking anybody into pregnancy.'

'Oh damn. Why is that, Bahubali ji?' one of his sidekicks enquired.

And Bahubali explained, 'They wanted Indian kids. They wanted me to have sex with them and inseminate them so they could have Indian blood running through their white-skinned children. So that their children could be as strong as an Indian. And they could make love with the might of an Indian. And they could die for their country and kill for their mother's honour,' Bahubali said.

'Oh hell yeah!' screamed one of Bahubali's sidekicks.

'Praise to Bahubali ji. Our master and our father.'

'Did you fuck anybody in England, Bahubali ji?' Santos asked sneakily.

'I would eat pig skin, but I couldn't touch white skin. I didn't. I threatened to kill those bitches or at least beat them with my rubber slipper if they tried anything fancy like sneaking into my room and trying to steal my dear semen.'

'Oh lord!' cried one of the sidekicks. 'Weren't you scared?'

'Usually, I ain't scared of anybody. But when there are some twenty or twenty-five mad bitches outside your door, ready to tear you open, you will be scared. My wife and I barely slept that day. Guarding ourselves with a slipper in one hand and sheer fear in the other. We made it out alive and safe,' Bahubali said in response to our question.

'How much does it cost to go to merry England, Bahubali ji?' asked a cameraman.

'You sell your house and your wife, and you will probably reach halfway with that fare,' Bahubali said, guffawing. Then he looked at me and said, 'And this boy has come from a place that is prettier, mightier, and more sex-deprived than England.'

'Oh my God.'

'Yes. And thus I ask him—I mean, I request that he turn my home into England with his English brains.'

'Oh hell, Moron bhai! A classy English fellow! Oh hell yeah!'

The men were so happy after hearing Bahubali's praises about me that, if I had demanded to fuck their wives right then, they would have run home, fetched their wives, and happily let me do the deed.

'But what am I supposed to do, Bahubali ji? What service can I offer to your great estate?'

'Well, you're a smart man,' Bahubali said, 'Why don't you tell me yourself?'

'Well, I'm a renowned scholar of psychology, having just earned a bachelor's degree from a great university in the West. I can dedicate all my fathomed knowledge and scientific temperament to performing A-class research for your…' I had only begun my pitch when Bahubali began descending into a state of deep thought. Then, all of a sudden, he interrupted me and said, 'You are hired! Not because you seem to be an A-class pervert. But because you are one of the most cuckolded men I have come across. The story of your life surpasses the darkest of tortures I can think of committing on anybody. You are hereby commissioned to work exclusively and entirely for the Ministry of Entertainment. Your job will be to scout for me the sexiest and most desirable girl a man could come across. A girl upon whom, when your eyes fall, you wouldn't be able to help yourself from masturbating right then and there. Who somebody might desire to drill or watch getting drilled. And we will buy her off from her family, and with her, we will shoot our film. For if my art can cure your broken heart, I am certain it would cure anybody.'

With that speech of his coming to an end, I was hired by Bahubali to serve in his enterprise as a full-time pimp.

'But what am I to do, Bahubali ji?'

'For starters, you can help me finish this porn you interrupted. I am still worried about these actresses. I need more good-looking porn stars. The most desirable ones. You can go and find them for me.'

I raised my head and surveyed his crew and team in confusion. His case really was hopeless. Inside Bahubali's mansion, the reality of the situation was so destitute, his staffers so hopeless and idiotic, that I figured all the exclusivity, the phenomenon, and the rumours surrounding Bahubali's mansion were fabricated by the outside world. The inside of his mansion was a welcoming place for madmen and the heartbroken. Initially, I had thought I would never be able to meet Bahubali. And here I was, asked to take care of his most private business. Just a simple swear of lifelong loyalty over my forehead was enough to win mc his counsel.

So even though I had been envisioning myself running after Bahubali with a pen and notepad, presenting him with data on various trends and regression analyses about the perfect features of titties on a prostitute or the most attractive hair colour on a prostitute's head, I learned that more than theoretical inquiries, I was to handle the field research for Bahubali. Instead of conducting a natural or quasi-experiment, I was to travel to nearby villages with his hired gunmen to audition and scout a few prostitutes for the shoot, which was scheduled for the upcoming weekend. Instead of playing the scholar, it was time to play the pimp. And so, a pimp I became.

Over the next month, I travelled through half of north Bihar under Bahubali's powerful penumbra, scouting villages and ghettos for the dream girl for our next porno. I showed up at mid-wedding ceremonies to take a look at the orchestra dancers (magnificent women, really, who were called from Kolkata and Nepal to dazzle the crowds). I was, in fact, reverently put under the nomenclature of Kotha Naresh. The whorehouse's gatekeeper. I dressed comfortably in a white denim T-shirt and black denim jeans, and I travelled with an entourage of eight SUVs, which had tinted windows and silver-rimmed tyres. For security, I had six gunmen with semi-automatic rifles. Santos was my secretary, and such was my unquestionable power that if I had merely lifted a finger in a household, its residents would have been set on fire and their generations of dreams would have gone extinct. With my newly acquired job, I also developed a plan to teach Noel a lesson very soon.

My job had me marching gallantly through the extremely depraved, unsanitary ghettos of Nalanda and adjoining cities. I traversed the dangerous township of Munger, where women in veils would melt iron and manufacture working-grade AK-47s in their courtyards. Elsewhere, there were dancers in supremely perverted shiny dance troupes. Just like Noel's house at Namchi, their houses were thatched, and children lingered and gawked at me in confusion and awe as I hopped off the Gypsy in my black Ray-Ban shades, accompanied by a few gunmen to protect me from the calamities of these impoverished areas. Initially, I would be mistaken for a gangster myself, and many of these ghetto people would come running and scampering, bowing at my feet, and giving me salutations as their lord and father. But when I made my intentions clear, they would giggle and laugh, leading me to one house or another. Most of the prostitutes I met wore spandex tights up to their knees. They wore anklets and smelled of sweat and human discharge. They had blade marks on their wrists. They were mostly short, heavy, and busty with many children (some didn't even know who the fathers were). When I offered them the once-in-a-lifetime opportunity to star in an upcoming cinematic masterpiece, they would laugh nervously and retreat. Overall, it was really tough to come across a willing prostitute ready to tear herself apart for the greater good of Bahubali's film.

Within months of arriving in Nalanda, I had seen Bahubali crossing Warden Road with his massive entourage, which had filled me with awe. Now, it was me sitting in that tinted SUV, travelling with my own entourage. In my hunt for the actress, I came across pimple-afflicted teenagers and wannabe gangsters (just like I had been) gawking at my passage in amusement and awe. I had to ensure my identity remained concealed as my staged death would have otherwise been in vain. In fact, whenever we approached a busy intersection, I would hide in the back trunk (like a magician creating the illusion of being invisible) and only emerge when our SUVs reached the open, silent highways.

During the course of the month, we patrolled the borders of Nepal, from the village of Ghodasaan (famous for its semi-virgin Nepali orchestra dancers and gold smugglers) to the drought-ridden and famine-stricken land of Mothihari—the birthplace of a great English writer who later left India and wrote a few stellar masterpieces. In search of finding the perfect girl for Bahubali, I travelled to the nastiest red-light districts. Even Santos' much-desired Chaturbhuj (finally), where a few plump women surrounded me, teased me, and played with my nipples; some even offered to fuck me for free. Because, as they said, they were in love with me. But there wasn't a single girl—not a single one—whom I felt a mad desire to possess.

Hell, the clean-shaven, cross-dressed men who were famous for their 'launda naach'—dancing and shaking their asses with the might and sensuality of a woman—were more appealing to me than the sad-looking girls selling themselves in these late-night orchestras. After repeatedly failing with the prostitutes and bar dancers, I shifted my energy to a more promising prospect. Housewives. I think it was more of a sublime revenge I was taking on Noel. Handpicking housewives to act and fuck in front of me. I was trying to create a misery of the commons with the housewives, hoping to know that there were other housewives who had sex with men other than their husbands. This would have probably reduced the pain I had endured from my own cuckolding.

One might wonder: didn't my conscience ever stop me from doing all this? Not even once? A little sawdust fairy did materialize on my shoulder, asking me to introspect about turning into a broken wild pimp when I could have shifted to some agrarian drought-stricken land or enlisted in the military after a traumatic heartbreak, as the film industry professes. It did, though not much at the beginning. But shortly after I began to recover from the shock of leaving Noel alone in this world at my ancestral home, it did.

And one day, after a lot of aimless squandering and wandering, this sisterfucker of an old villager approached me from a darkened corner of the ghetto, and instead of taking me to an unchartered province with mystical, big-breasted girls who spoke foreign languages and fucked in Polish, he began telling me to do something principled with my life. He told me that Bahubali was crazy. That he was a crooked, shrewd man, and that I, too, was an unwise fool really to be doing this nocturnal trip of depravity for him. He told me to become a school teacher and asked me to count from fifty to one in reverse. And really, he sort of tormented me with this preaching attitude. Thus, no wonder, I slapped him as soon as he was done. I slapped him so hard that his intellectual eyes popped in disbelief, and he would have been utterly depressed about it, but then I slapped him again. Then I pulled him by his hair and asked him to show me his home. He did. And I said I would incinerate his home right there if he ever told anybody in this village about what they should do with their lives. With this vengeance, I terrorized the ghetto into complete surrender.

You see, I was not merely a pervert strolling through a Babylonian market, whipping and fucking girls here and there. The fact is that I was a virgin and manically depressed, but people also stayed aloof because Bahubali's sidekicks were known for committing outrageously heinous crimes. And though we patrolled and surveyed the villages, people would sometimes look at me in askance and wonder, 'Really! All this spinster has to do in broad daylight is gawk at our wives and sisters, and then next moment they would be fucking for his watching pleasure?' It was futile to explain to them that this was all being done for mere art.

At the conclusion of my first month as a dead man and a pimp, I returned to Bahubali's mansion with a total of eleven girls. Eleven plump prostitutes. Were they the best and dreamiest of girls one could think of? No. To be quite honest, they were not even my pick. They were more of a consolation carried on by my many sidekicks and guards. They were women my sidekicks would have enjoyed seeing drilled but not me. And then came the day of Bahubali's shoot.

Porn 1, Scene 1: Bahubali's Second-Last Attempt at Making the Magnum Opus

Location: The Backyard of Bahubali's Mansion—A Lawn Turned into a Marketplace

There is a cardboard house set up on the front lawn. Outside, our well-built jock and porn star, Johny Boy, is performing spectacular bench presses on the front lawns of his cardboard house. He lives with his single mother in that cardboard house and sells drugs on weekends to make extra money. In our film, Johny Boy suffers from the deadly and embarrassing ailment of erectile dysfunction. At the beginning of our scene, our director and cameo actor, Bahubali, can be seen handing Johny Boy a magic tablet. This is the Grenade tablet—Bahubali's secret to owning the world and also our sponsor for the day's shoot. Shortly after ingesting the Grenade, Johny Boy gets up from the bench and takes a stroll towards the evening market.

'Fry the chicken, ma. I'll be right there,' he screams as he exits his house and heads into the evening market.

'Be home soon, Johny!' The voice of an elderly woman—his mother in the movie—is heard from inside the cardboard house.

In the marketplace, Johny Boy can be seen strolling with pride past the raw fish stall and the fresh fruit stall. A group of women has gathered to chat and share intimate problems about their husbands. All their husbands do is come back home and go to sleep. As Johny Boy listens to the women complain, he sneakily takes out his magnificent cock. There is a shy sort of excitement in the director's eyes. Johny Boy is supposed to act smart. He can't just pull out his dick and make it explode. It is supposed to be a slow process. A sly unravelling of his giant weapon. So he simply pulls out his dick and starts caressing it. Slowly. Softly. Profoundly. Fresh blood is being jettisoned into his existence. It's bulging and ready to shoot! But wait, because all this is an act. The character of Johny Boy is supposed to simply urinate. As men often do in the corners of the market.

'Why the fuck is he caressing his dick?' Bahubali screams. No one listens. Johny Boy proceeds to flash his dick prominently, but none of the porn stars have noticed. This is the scene where one of the vegetable sellers is supposed to scream in disgust, but as she slowly gets a proper look at his dick, her screams die in her throat. In fact, her nipples are supposed to pop. And Johny Boy is supposed to fuck her behind her stall until more women take notice and start pouncing on his dick.

But what the fuck is this?

'Son of a fucking whore has started masturbating!' Bahubali screams. 'Oh fuck no. Cut, cut. Stop!' Bahubali comes down to the set as Johny Boy stands with an unbearable, hard-on erection.

'Start fucking these women,' Bahubali orders. Johny Boy starts fucking the women as his mother comes out from the opposite side, announcing that the fried chicken is ready. But Johny Boy can be spotted fucking a dwarf, a five-foot-two-inch plump vegetable seller behind her stall, and the 35 mm camera zooms in to capture the monstrosity. There is a pissed-off customer at the counter; he has been waiting to get his change back for the vegetables he just brought. But there is no stopping now.

Pump. Pump. In an open marketplace. Could this be a magnum opus? A public fucking scenario? The loud announcement of a woman screaming and reaching her climax. Johny Boy finishes with his first woman and pounces on the next. This one is a Bengali fisherwoman. Another plump breed with an unopened, disastrous feminine passion that no one has been able to unlock. But today is the day of her redemption. Johny Boy is nowhere near stopping. Bahubali is clapping slowly with pride.

'You see my line-up, ha?' he asks me.

'Damn fantastic, sir,' I announce.

'This shit is supposed to last until eleven women. Eleven women handpicked by you. My pimp,' he says thoughtfully.

I wait for the third.

'Is he having a heart attack, sir?' I ask suddenly because I notice Johnny Boy acting weird. He is nodding in disapproval. He is twitching. His forehead is sweaty. His vest is drenched in sweat, but he won't stop.

'Oh fuck!' Bahubali screams. 'No. No fucking way, you stupid fuck. You can't cum right now.'

'I think the Grenade is going to explode, sir!' Johny Boy screams nervously.

'Not now. The model class is yet to come. The housewives.'

'Sir, I can't control it anymore.'

'Control! You fucking mad dog, you fucking piece of shit. I will chop off your dick without giving it a second thought,' Bahubali warns.

I feel like laughing. But that, too, would be a disaster.

'Sir, I'm going to cum.'

Bahubali suddenly turns and vanishes inside his house with his hands pressed against his ears.

'You fucking wait, you son of a whore,' he mutters furiously.

Johny Boy is trying to slow down. But the heat has taken over.

Everyone is utterly confused since the director has left the set. Some five minutes pass by in this fashion. I anticipate this to be another of those wasteful days until Bahubali comes running out of his house with a fucking shotgun in hand. He goes near the in-action Johny Boy and points the barrel of the shotgun five inches from his forehead.

'The moment you cum is the moment this trigger gets pulled.'

Frightened for his life, Johny Boy keeps pumping. Keeps pumping. Non-stop.

'This is true art,' Bahubali yells in jubilation. The Bengali fisherwoman is bent all the way to the dusty floor. Fearing Bahubali might shoot Johny Boy in the head, the cameraman distances himself by a few steps, just in case there is a splatter of blood.

Pump. Pump.

There is no denying it. Like death, orgasm is also inevitable for Johny Boy. At this precise moment, I realize that if anyone is to stop Bahubali, it has to be me. I walk up to him peacefully, like a dead spirit, and slowly mutter into his ear, 'Sir, if you shoot this poor man, the whole movie will shut down. Probably no one ...' I rephrase, 'Probably people will be scared to act for us in the future. Let him go, sir. I beg you. Let him go.'

Bahubali looks at me with disappointed eyes, then pulls the barrel away from Johny Boy's forehead.

'Alright, fuck it.'

And Johny Boy collapses on the floor, having fucked two of Bahubali's paid prostitutes, rendering no pornographic masterpiece at all.

A Look Into Bahubali's Past and the Inception of the Idea of Making a Pornographic Masterpiece (As Told to Me by Santos)

That evening, after the porn has ended, a driver for a dwarf is jumping and screaming in front of the car garage because he wants to fuck a prostitute I had brought from the land of Chaturbhuj. This is after Bahubali has gone inside, and the crew is busy packing up. There are a few staffers who have haggled a deal with the prostitutes and are having a mad siesta fucking them inside the garage. For fun, they have locked the door from the inside, leaving the dwarf driver outside. And this driver is all agitated and furious. He is jumping comically. Like an impatient dog. He is begging them to open the door, saying he is in love with a particular prostitute and must be allowed to fuck her first (given she agrees). But they just won't open the door.

Santos and I are resting beneath a peepal tree. The red warm sunset's light falling on our features.

'Santos ji,' I say, 'what's the deal with Bahubali? Why does he do all this? Why doesn't he fuck these prostitutes himself? Just putting so much money into nothing?'

Santos pinches his ear in horror, eyes wide. 'Uf, chee chee. Bahubali sahib is not a pervert, Moron ji. What dog shit.'

'Then, Santos?'

'I think he is impotent,' Santos says. 'I have never heard any news of him sleeping with any prostitutes or actresses.'

'Then? What's the deal with him, Santos?'

And Santos enlightens me with the history:

There was a time, not long ago, when Bahubali was a man of political greatness. A so-called leader, if I must say. He would wear a white kurta and a fine line of cold sandalwood chandan on his forehead, and when he walked into a room, his sidekicks and secretaries would stand up at once, urgently, in deep horror and respect. They would bow to him, pinching their nipples or slapping their chests, as if no earthling on earth deserved their respect as much as he did. When he drove out of the compound of his mansion, there would be a minimum of seven to eight cars in his convoy. Media flocked to capture his arrival at the secretariat. The Opposition dreaded the questions or rants he might unleash against the failing government systems. Sometimes his own party members were jealous because there was not a post in the bilateral government system he could not hijack if he set his mind to it. His days were filled with public events and philanthropic events. Cleanliness drives and hunger strikes. Sometimes he was so passionately busy in working with his people that the media journalists could only watch from a safe distance.

One time, a journalist asked him, 'What do you think about this government?' and his irritated, quick reply was, 'What government? This is a dick-sucking government.' People pinched their ears in horror because the adjective 'dick-sucking' was too fucked up to be said on national television. Despite the grim state of governance in Bihar at that time, politicians were still known to maintain a certain decorum while addressing their opponents. 'Dick-sucking' was not a respectable adjective. In fact, it was perverse. And then at another instance, right before the Lok Sabha elections, someone asked, 'Sir, what would you do if you win these upcoming elections?' To which he replied, 'Oh! I would sit in big planes and fly around.'

And then there was the time when he was being sent to jail right before his election rally because there were suspicions about him hoarding some 3,400 rounds of AK-47 ammunition in his house. 'What do you think will happen to your elections now that you are being sent to jail?' someone asked. To which his savage, futuristic reply was, 'It will only be better for me, my dear sir. Otherwise, I would have needed to traverse my constituency, and there would have been an obligatory need on my part to visit every nook and cranny of my constituency to beg for votes. Now I can simply sit behind bars and win the elections without even taking a single round.' People were such huge fans of him that he actually did end up winning the elections by a sweeping margin of 25,000 votes. This put the media in a state of constant awe of him. Here was a man who said he would fly big planes if he won the election instead of acting like a mediocre, well-tempered gentleman who would only show you dreams of clean, potable water and promise you fifty-rupee jobs as part of his bigger religious responsibility. 'I will just fly around in big planes', 'This is a dick-sucking government' and so forth.

Until one day, it all came crashing down on him. While all this chivalry inspired millions of rough-tongued goons and stood as a masterpiece comedy gig on our smartphones, the bigger whore hole was in his own house. I'm recalling the day Bahubali's wife was suddenly kidnapped. After learning about his missing wife, Bahubali was not a savage, none-fearing fuck-you-all public figure. In fact, he was like a twelve-year-old schoolgirl who had never had friends apart from a one-eyed, red-dressed doll, and who had now lost her as well.

Like a heartbroken maniac, he looked for his wife everywhere. National highways were sealed. Railway trains were commanded to halt for extra hours. Police patrols were everywhere. But the real drama was happening inside the mansion of Prakash D, the leader of the Opposition. Around midnight, Prakash D and Bahubali's wife mingled into each other like theirs was a newfound love. The first night of copulation. Heavy breathing and grunting filled the air as cool breeze and sirens drifted in from the outside world. While the police rushed from street to street, promising the public they would go to any extent to recover Bahubali's lost wife, his lost wife was indeed totally lost to Mr Prakash in the oblivion of an orgasm so intense that she herself had chosen to make it known publicly that her love for Bahubali had extinguished and that she was now in love with the great Mr Prakash D.

The media discovered her two days later in a scandalous half-dressed state right in the mansion of Prakash D. Despite what had been happening outside, she seemed to be playful and at ease. Prakash D too was simply sitting in his lawn, sipping tea while his lover confided to the awe-struck reporters as she plucked jasmine from the lawn: 'That man always likes melodrama. All that hit him was that I had been kidnapped. Didn't it ever occur to him that maybe I had simply run away?' To which Bahubali's sole response was an attempt at suicide by firing a bullet across the anterior of his forehead.

This saddened the nation. There were male protestors and even women screeching on television, calling out the cheap stunt Bahubali's wife had pulled. So now, as Bahubali struggled for life and death on the ventilator at PMCH, his supporters mourned in silence. Rose bouquets and jasmine garlands surrounded his bed. 'The infidelity of his wife was a matter of national shame.' 'What crooked whore would do such a thing?' Rickshaw pullers were heard gossiping, 'National whore number one, absolutely, sir. That man had given nothing but love to his wife.'

On the fourth day of his stay, when the doctors came out of the ICU amidst a clamour of journalists, they announced, 'Miracle! Pure absolute miracle! He shall survive with no detrimental consequences. Our Bahubali is in ecstatic peace.' The response was a magnificent celebration outside the hospital.

'But poor Bahubali sahib was still in love with his wife,' Santos said.

'What? How do you know that, you fool?' I asked Santos.

'Because after recovering from the wounds of the bullet, that was the first thing he told the media.'

'That's so depressing, Santos.'

'It gets sadder, sir,' Santos said. 'After hearing this, his wife was even more enraged. Instead of feeling guilty, she was consumed by anger because, somehow, Bahubali had won in this drama. She called up the *Deccan Herald*'s office that day to simply announce, "Fuck that eunuch Bahubali!" And finally, Bahubali's response was that it was time for him (because God had whispered to him in his comatose state) to supersede the capabilities of a common man and, in fact, unify himself with the eternal singular power of God.'

'And how do you think he would do that?'

'By creating an erotic masterpiece. A film that would liberate a generation. His dream—The National Porn of India, Moron ji,' Santos said.

That evening, after the horrors of Johny Boy and our eleven failed prostitutes had ended, I stood on the roof of the Ministry of Homeland Security while Bahubali was on the roof of the Presidential Palace. This was after the crowd had dispersed and even the cleaners had cleaned his house and left. So there was me staring at the landscape of Nalanda from the roof of his compound and him walking on the adjoining roof. A few minutes later, when I couldn't stop staring at the landscape and he couldn't stop staring at me, he invited me to come and join him on the roof of his house.

'Well, that was that,' Bahubali sighed, referring to the disaster of the afternoon.

'I tried, boss. I really did.'

'It's not your fault,' he said dejectedly, and without pausing continued, 'It's nobody's fault. What your wife did to you. What my wife did to me. What Johny did to these women. It's not our fault.'

'But we were not able to shoot the scene, Bahubali ji. I spent months in the heat and sun, and we couldn't make the great porn film!'

'Do you think we will ever make the national porn of India? Any great artist,' Bahubali said, referring to himself as an artist, 'can only chase perfection.'

'To be quite frank, Babhubali ji,' I said, 'I myself wasn't very impressed with the line-up I had gotten. I just got them for the sake of getting somebody. They didn't drive me mad with desire. Like Noel used to. I don't think we will be able to make the National Porn of India until the star cast makes us fall in love with them. In fact, Bahubali ji,' I continued, 'I have learnt and realized this one night while I was in solitude, stargazing on the borders of Ghodasaan, that we can't have great porn until we have real love. A real person. A person somebody could fall in love with. A person who would be a pleasure. And then, of course, getting to see them have sex would be a pleasure by virtue.'

What I was trying to tell Bahubali was that there can't be great sex until there is great love. Otherwise, without love, the entire act of sex would be so mechanical. So detached. For great sex, there needs to be great passion, fear, and uncertainty. The fear of death and the uncertainty of losing each other at least.

'We need somebody,' I said, 'who can personify sex and love in the same frame.' I, as a learned virgin pimp, informed my master dutifully.

But all we got in return was a wave of great frenzy and uncertainty. All I was saying was just deep poetic stuff. Hell! Finding someone like her would have been like finding a new life for myself.

We kept staring at the endless expanse of Nalanda. And as the evening dawned upon us, Bahubali said, 'I'm just happy that there was a day and a lady who thought of us as worthwhile to get naked in front of us and suck our dicks.'

After the exhaustion of a month of expedition, I slept soundly through the evening in my small studio room. Unbothered. The sight of Johny Boy fucking the eleven whores to waste flashed through my dreams. When I woke up, I was startled to find Santos at my door. He had come to bid me farewell.

'Goodbye? Where you off to, Santos?'

'Poor Santos here is to take Bahubali on a very deadly journey, sir. Right now. Bahubali may never return after this,' Santos said.

'What the fuck,' I said, jumping from my iron cot. 'Bahubali sahib? Uncle? Uncle?' I screamed and ran outside, hunting for my hopeless boss and messiah.

When I reached the portico, I saw Bahubali sitting in his black SUV. They were departing for some place. His eyes fixed on the front gate, his bullet scar facing me. 'Where are you going, dear sir? Santos tells me that you may never return,' I blurted as I ran towards him.

Bahubali rolled down the window of his SUV and, without even looking at my tear-filled eyes, announced, 'Bhanja, you are the sole owner and caretaker of this house. For the next two days. You take good care of my estate. I will be back soon.'

Before I could ask anything else, he rolled his window up, and when I turned back to look for Santos, Bahubali's car was off to the city. Apparently, Santos had pulled himself up using the door of the last car of the procession and was also gone with Bahubali, leaving me and the grand mansion to our vices.

After they were gone, I had to spend my time all by myself in that huge house. I believe that was the first night I spent in solitude after faking my death. The horrors of

Noel and even my dead father revisited me. I roamed around the mansion like a dead phantom. And when the sun rose from the horizon, I slept again, clutching to a spare pillow as my only companion. The afternoon was again ghostly and silent. In the evening, they were playing some loud Nepali music from a distance. Probably another boy like myself was being sacrificed to the mysterious land of Nepal. I sat, sulked, and ate some leftover bread from Bahubali's fridge.

I didn't know when he was going to return. If he was ever going to return, Maybe I ended up killing him too. Maybe my presence just killed anybody who treated me as their child. I lay motionless on my cot and thought of Zahed. Of Noel. I don't know why, but I even thought about the great Ms Staci. And before I could know it, Mother Sleep had taken over.

The next morning at 4:30, there was a loud banging of the gate, and the doorman ran towards the main entrance to receive our master, who had come back in the same clothes that he had been wearing two days ago. Only now he seemed more at ease with himself. When he was leaving, it was a different story; I recalled how he was utterly confused, his mind in complete turmoil, which I could not appease. But now, here, this was a mighty, renewed man with a new energy. On seeing me, Bahubali grabbed me by my shoulders and drew me inside. It was as if all this time he had been keeping something in his stomach, and now was his grand occasion to spill it out.

'You said that we needed regular, everyday women who can personify natural sex. You wanted me to bring regular, good-looking women? Daily regular women on whom daily regular men could sprinkle their lives?' Bahubali said, his eyes sparkling with excitement.

I nodded in approval.

'Well, guess what?' Bahubali asked, and then looking at the car door that was still open, he whispered, 'Shut the damn door.'

I shut the door.

'I have finally found that breed. And now young nephew, tomorrow morning we shall have them at our doorstep, and then you shall see that the greatest porn in history is made in no time. Porn so great that every living breathing man of this century shall be in possession of an erection of a lifetime.'

'How is that, sir?' I asked mystified, starting to worry about the purpose of his trip.

'You shall see. You shall see in no time, nephew.'

I was very confused about how Bahubali had managed to break this great matrix. There are only limited right answers to a puzzle. And in my case, I have been through them all, but nothing seemed to work. I knew Bahubali was not stupid enough to recreate a similar answer (which had previously fetched me failure).

As the grizzly sounds of crying birds subsided around sunrise, a fresh, cool breeze filled the air, dewy mist clung to the leaves, and a renewed sense of hope emerged. My riddle was solved when a red Omni van pulled up at the door of the compound.

Bahubali emerged from his room and breathing in the cold mist of the morning air, he directed the doorman to let the car come in. Once the door of the van was opened, the answer to our riddle was presented in the form of three innocent-looking, extremely fair and delicate, but very evident from their faces: extremely poor-looking girls from the borders of Nepal, whom Bahubali had brought at 2,50,000 Indian rupees each. I almost felt like banging my head on the street. This was mighty genius. Because here we had materialized in front of ourselves, not prostitutes who had no shame about sex and weren't respectful of the intimacy of sex; neither were these rebellious schoolgirls who would only shriek and feign in horror mid-sex scenes only to realize that their ass is not meant to get fucked raw by a totally strange poor man. But these were real innocent and decent girls who were poor, but that did not really matter because these girls were extremely beautiful. One of them had a certain movement of a dancer in her for she was quick and energetic with her movements. Once she had gotten out of the van, she had crossed her arms because she was cold and stood straight. Her hair was dark brown. The second girl appeared curious and was trying to figure out this new place. This one, to my utter delight, was voluptuous with big breasts and round buttocks. The third one, who seemed to be the eldest of them all, was not even of Indian or Nepali descent. Her skin was gleaming in the sun. And as a provocative man, I was taken aback by delight when I saw her sweat droplets evaporate and trickle through the creases of her delightfully white and blushing breasts. This was a Russian or Ukrainian. It had not come as much of a surprise because, after the latest invasion of Russia in Ukraine, Ukrainians were too much of an exotic rarity in the market.

'Holy shit,' I said to myself 'here is the second-hand wife I was on the lookout for'.

'March in, ladies' Bahubali said, directing the girls to go inside the mansion.

They followed his command with docility.

In the evening, I was battling two emotions. As an impatient virgin, I was excited and almost neurotic at the prospect of fucking any of those three newly trafficked women as soon as they would be instructed by Bahubali to start yielding themselves. But then, as a professional pimp, I worried that these girls weren't great actresses, and expecting a full-fledged show of carnal indecency from them as their first job after being bought was a far-fetched idea.I voiced my concern to Bahubali as we sat down for supper in the verendah.

'In the black market,' Bahubali narrated, looking at the sunset, 'they are mainly sold for domestication or marriage. They are sent off to a rich sheikh in Dubai who would only put them as one of the many jewels in their jewellery or to some lonely obese American fucktard who is nearing death with high cholesterol as his arteries are jammed with cheese and lard. But today,' Bahubali continued, 'they have been brought here to work in a profession. Here, they are our budding artists. Not some saphic doomed creature who will only be subjected to our ruthlessness and savagery.'

'But I just am wondering if these girls would be any good on screen?'

'They are raw seeds,' Bahubali admitted. 'They might, or they might not. But if it's a might-not-case scenario, then we can definitely train them. We can train them for the specific purpose of this art.'

Later, Bahubali explained to me in even greater detail how he had actually travelled through the borders of Nepal and India—he had taken a private six-seater, single-propeller airplane (on which your chances of survival are sometimes near half because of the Himalayan terrain and currents)—and had gone to an obscure forest on the foothills of Muktinath. This was the mystical village, The Enchanted Forest of Virgins, a village full of young sweetheart girls, fresh Nepali lassies who would welcome guests with a homely smile. And if you were to pay a good amount to their family, they wouldn't straight away permit you to fuck their daughter in daylight. But you would be locked away in a separate cottage with the girl in the secrecy of the night, whereupon you might festoon your tentacles into the lassie and cure yourself from the most harrowing of diseases. Also, they would only open the gate once you and the lassie both have announced that you both were 'satisfied'.

'So have you borrowed the girls or bought them?'

'Oh, these girls were not into the sex thing,' Bahubali explained. 'They were not even close to starting. They are not prostitutes. Their mothers probably. But not them. They are very young, fifteenish or something. I had to buy them.'

Had Bahubali made his intentions clear that he desired to transport three of his young actresses from across a different nation and harbour them in our domicile, I would have joined him on the voyage and helped him scout the best talent myself. But I believe in some way

Bahubali did not believe in his own idea at that point in time. He was harbouring it—sure as hell—but then very few people have really succeeded in finding the enchanted market of virgins in the first place. But we sure had a fabulous time indulging in the vivid descriptions these girls provided of their lives at the dinner table. They spoke of their hygiene—guaranteed in fact that they used to bathe in the first of the water that fell from a distant miraculous hill back in the village. They said that their clothes were washed in the hot spring water while their skin was energized with rich zinc and charcoal which could be found only in the waters of Nepal. They said that they were the finest of all merchandise mankind would ever topple across—and then, when Bahubali had told them that they may not fear now—that the families had been paid handsomely, and there is no need to oversell themselves now—they giggled and narrated briefly how they are coached to worship their husbands as their kings and emperors. They proclaimed that they could commit any outrageous crime—from stabbing a man to setting themselves on fire if the need arose—to protect their husband's honour. And when their account was over, all of a sudden, I remembered my sorrowful days in Nepal, and somehow from being the most sinister place on earth, it gained my ultimate reverence.

'Alright', Baahubali clapped 'Alright, this is the most superstitious and fantabulous fable I have heard. I think I have just stumbled upon what would come to be known as my Masterpiece. You three are going to star in the national porn of India' Bahubali said, looking at the girls.

Before dinner was concluded, Bahubali accosted one of the girls and asked, 'Did you, young lassie, just mention our mothers?'

To which she replied, 'Oh yes, sir.'

'So you mean,' he said, pointing at the Ukrainian girl, 'that she happens to be your sister?'

'Yes, sir. My mother took her in after she lost her home back in her country.' Before Bahubali could say anything, she added, 'It's great of her, sir. We don't have much food to eat back home. Fuck, we don't even have a toilet back home. Not a latrine to shit in. Can you buy that for us, sir?'

'Wow, that is something, isn't it, Moron?' Bahubali said, turning to look towards me.

'Yes, most definitely, sir.'

'Even Moron's wife didn't have a toilet back at her home. He told me this once. Didn't you, Moron?'

'Yes, sir.'

'Did she have a shitter to shit in, Moron?'

'No, sir. She didn't. She used to shit in the backyard forest.'

'Did you girls also have a backyard forest?'

'No, sir.' And then, explaining the great deed of her mother, the Nepali continued again, 'but as I was saying, sir, my mother took her in because she was a girl child. A lot of people came to the bazaar. Asking her to be sold alone as she is from another country. Her skin is of a fairer complexion. So it automatically increases her demand. But my mother was dead clear that we would be packed off together.'

'That is so great of your mother,' he said.

'Yes, sir,' she said.

'Anyway, coming to our work scene. Do you happen to know what I do for a living?'

'You must be a charade of many cards, sir. I'm sure there is not a profession you are not an expert in.'

Bahubali looked mightily pleased with this reply.

'I make films,' he said. 'Do you like films?'

'Yes, sir. Very much, sir.'

'Have you ever seen a film?' he asked.

'Oh yes, sir. There was this girl from our village who was packed off to a bar in Kathmandu. She was a hell of a dancer, sir. She did come back home one day and show me a film she had worked on. She seemed to be enjoying a lot of the film, sir.'

'What was the film about?'

'Sir, it was about her having sex with the owner of the bar back where she worked. Terrific, terrific acting indeed. She wanted a raise. And her boss wanted more than what she was willing to give. In the end, sir, she gave it all, and it turns out she liked it.'

'You mean,' Bahubali said, a sly grin appearing on his face 'You mean...okay, how long was this film?'

'I don't quite remember, sir. All I remember is that she showed that film to me in the utter secrecy of the night. And she made me put my hand over my head and swear that I don't tell this to anyone.'

'Oh, that is quite fantastic. Would you yourself want to make a film like that, dear?' Bahubali asked.

'It will be a dream come true, sir. She was so happy in the film that it almost made me combust in jealousy, that Bitch.'

Cue in: Porn 2, Scene 1: The National Porn of India

The Set- A battlefield, which has been set in the backyard of Bahubali's mansion. The floor is covered in cotton for snow. There are a few huts and a few piles of wood for hillocks.

Starring: Johny Boy as Captain Messiah (A soldier and a captain in the Indian Army. Nepali number 1 as 'Miss India' who happens to be Captain Messiah's wife. Fortunately or unfortunately, the Ukrainian and the Nepali number 2 have been asked to simply chill on the sets.

The camera is rolling. And…Action!

So soldier Captain Messiah has just been deployed with an artillery of three Bofors guns and seventy marching troops to the isolated highlands of Kashmir to battle Pakistani militants who have infiltrated the border across to India. This is something the soldiers won't tolerate. Captain Messiah has been appointed as the senior commander of the troop and is the personification of all bravery and chivalry. His wife back home (the eldest Nepali) is worried. Too worried this time because she has a bad feeling about this. Anyway, Captain Messiah, being the zealous messiah of the nation, is squatting now behind a giant rock on the Indo-Nepal border. The Pakistanis have kidnapped a few villagers in their own homes. The troopers are supposed to storm into the village and kill the terrorists and save the hostages.

The ghatak commando force goes first, giving a clean fire with their INSAS assault rifle. But only wait and watch this catastrophe as the twenty-year-old Pakistani terrorists have blown away the heads of these six-foot-tall ghatak commandos with the firing of a light machine gun.

'Fucking sons of bitches,' Captain Messiah screams.

Only last night he had gotten a hinge in his chest. In his dream, he had visualized his daisy white of a beautiful silky-haired wife cheating on him with a moustached banker from his neighbourhood. This was just a nightmare. And right now, Captain Messiah is gorged with another nightmare. The ravishing infinite fire of the light machine gun, which is spurring bullets like twists of chanas being sprinkled on starving ducks.

Captain Messiah rushes into stark cover. Gun clenched tightly against his breasts. He speeds and speeds hastily, slyly entering the enemy region. He finds himself there all alone. Our captain has resolved that if he returns home from this battle—after which he will be submerged in garlands and medals of honor—he will retire and cherish the enchanting wiles of his wife until his last breath. It is the elixir of love that has taken our Captain Messiah in its grit. By the time the firing from the light machine gun subsides slightly, he finds his troop making its way to him in the same sly manner. So Captain Messiah takes another step. He pulls out a grenade from near his buttock, unpins it with the aid of his tooth, and throws it right inside the house, knowing for a fact that the hostages are not in the same room from where the terrorists are giving off the LMG firing.

He has acquired this secret knowledge because when he looked around the house, he saw and registered that on a wire mesh there were pink and blue undergarments of young five-year-old children being dried. What this meant was that if the terrorists were firing LMGs in the stark presence of these five-year-old kids, the kids would have screeched and wailed so loudly that the young Pakistani terrorist boys would have shoved the grenade pin right through the eardrums.

When the grenade explodes, two Pakistani terrorists and no Indian hostages are flung out from the window. With practiced ease, Captain Messiah rushes to the next house. But only wait. He has cut his left leg by scratching it against a barbed wire. This is fucking painful. He feels like he is urinating in his uniform. But this is only blood. Yet to double check, Captain Messiah excuses himself to the washroom mid-warfare to take a peep inside his pants. What he notices gives him a tiny heart attack. It's not only the leg but also a fair size of the penis, which has been severed by the iron filament. He looks at his dick, which is slightly hurt and fast asleep. Thanking God that the injury was not bad enough to castrate him to a female housewife, he closes his shutter and comes out of the washroom, resolved to kill the three remaining terrorists. Captain Messiah reloads his INSAS and fires at the rooftop of a nearby house from where a sniper had been aiming at his approaching troop. The troop, which is way ahead of him, pauses mid-fire and salutes him in honor. Captain Messiah limps to the other house. He gives a fantastic cover fire as his boys save another household with the aid of three hand grenades. This house had caught fire. It's burning, and you can hear the shrieks and wails of the hostages who have been tied in their own house against their sheer will. The flames are leaping with hunger. Ready to eat anybody who may dare enter the house. But Captain Messiah, a former fire trooper, made famous in the entire infantry because of his bravery, hereby having won for himself the name Messiah, hops inside, and there is savant silence for another five minutes.

The troop boys look at each other with wide, puzzled eyes. Has the Messiah roasted himself in the hills of Kashmir? Is this the end of life? The end of an era? Is this the poignant reward of bravery?

Five minutes or so pass as the troops watch in absolute puzzlement as the hostages make their way out of the house in deep relief. Captain Messiah is right behind them. When they have returned back to the base, Captain Messiah, instead of reporting to the high command, straight away goes to the Infirmary and reports the feeling of a bad burning sensation in his pants.

Back in New Delhi, he is honoured with the sovereign Veer Chakra by the Vice President of our homeland. His wife is all tears. He himself is all tears. What a brave man! What a brave husband! A national hero indeed. But what pains might a soldier endure to keep up this honour? This gallant. He spends the next one month in the Cantonment Hospital, where the staff and doctors attend to him and nurse his gangrene. His rotting leg. The cuts and bruises were exposed to the frigid cold for too long. And now around his groin, you might spectate how the harrowing disease of black fluidy gangrene can eat up a man's body within days. His leg and some shreds of his privates have swollen to immeasurable intensity. The swelling takes a week to subside. The doctors are running antibiotics way over the recommended dose to stop the disease. They have performed three minor surgeries within a span of six hours. The whole nation is worried about whether the Messiah will survive or not. There are visits from local news and the governor himself. In the end, the doctors have managed to stop the gangrene from reaching his upper body. But they will have to castrate our Captain Messiah. They will have to remove a considerable portion of his penis. He might or might not have children because his tissues are still safe and hanging. But it is a matter of fact that he will never be able to copulate with his wife; he will never be able to ravish on her feminine gifts from the point his dick is removed. So in the flower-bred room infested with 'get well soon' cards and wishes from young girls and elder brothers, fathers, and forefathers, the private curtains are pulled up. In the secrecy of the chamber, he is given exactly three days to fuck his wife to the levels of eternal satisfaction before he might come and get his penis surgically severed. That's the cost of life.

Cut to Scene 2: Porno!

To Bahubali's wild delight, the scene was closing perfection. Finally, we have on screen-the sex between the sick Captain Messiah and his loving wife. The thunderous thumping and slapping of the flesh. Captain Messiah's thighs slapping against his wife's open legs. Captain Messiah's butt rising and attacking. Rising and attacking. Sataaak! Sataaak! Sataak!

And one must keep this in mind-this, on screen, is no old, worn-out flesh of a random prostitute. This is sensual purity. Because herein there is no display of a rough gaping asshole. In fact, this shy girl over here, who is delightfully and deeply in love with this macho man, is still wearing thigh-length, tight grey shorts as her lover is entering her by not totally removing the shorts but just slipping it enough to let the gangrene ridden penis slide. Miss India's (Captain Messiah's wife) hair is falling perfectly to her waist. The viewer may in fact feel the softness and smell the freshness of the hair by simply staring at the screen of his device. And now I may hereby pull your attention to her breasts. Wildly gorgeous. Soft. With three remarkable moles. One humbly huge and then two small ones. Moles in porn are as rare as a twenty-four-year-old virgin prostitute on the side streets of Phuket. Watch as her beauty emanates from her face, her eyebrows, and her breasts as she rides her lover. One can almost smell the fluid of lovemaking that is dropping from her pelvis. That is what love would smell like if it were a flower.

Bahubali was not a bad man. He was a sincere artist. A devout follower of his art. But on this glorious occasion, when I stole a few moments to look at him, even he had acquired a thunderous erection. This was the first time he had had an erection on a porn set. Not to mention, I only imagined that this was his first thunderous erection since his wife had left him for good.

Also the day after the shoot, things eased up around the mansion. And shortly thereafter started my stint of endearing for myself-a second hand wife. My eyes inevitably fell on the Ukrainian. Her name was Clarissa. The bare-breasted Clarissa. Bare-breasted because after settling into the routine of the mansion, Clarissa began living in a way that she had been accustomed to back in her village. Bare-breasted. She had a royal blue bra hanging from her bosoms most of the time, and her nipples would be erect because of the cold. She was a playful girl with beautiful hair and glossy skin. Later conversations with her revealed that her past had been as tragic as mine. Her house in Kyiv (the Capital of Ukraine) had collapsed under the attack of a random missile which was dropped a few miles away from her home. The impact had instantly killed her family while she survived for she was in school (a few miles farther from the site of impact). Once the missile had gone off, she hid in the rubble of her school building for three days. Most of the children had succumbed to death by getting smashed beneath the collapsed ceiling. On the fourth day she was rescued by some volunteering group who sent her off to a Refuge Camp in some distant land. From that camp, she was traded to the island of Phuket in Thailand (bought at a hefty fee by some pimp) and had then been sold to a dance bar in Bangla Road in Phuket.

There she grew up a healthy girl among other grown up strippers for dancers (who, as you would have guessed, were famous for their topless pole dances). These dancers barely wore a top themselves. For them, the breasts were as normal as any other part of the body. Which now might explain why she preferred being topless. In Phuket, she stayed in a squalid flat (right behind the club) and the dancing mothers trained Clarissa to become a dancer herself. But more than a dancer, they taught her how to become a woman. They taught her the things which men desire. Things for which men would sell their houses. And things of that sort.

I remember one evening Clarissa had told me that 'the strippers are the most powerful types of women a man can come across. Because a stripper knows "what she wants", and she also knows "how to get it".'

Clarissa was a sweet girl really. At another instance, I remember, when I got a little too excited myself and I shared with her my love for the Jagermeister and the Pina Coladas (while telling her that I can't drink a lot of those cocktails anymore, for the mixers have a lot of sugar and I'm trying to lose weight), she told me that there is another way I can drink my favourite alcohol without worrying too much about my weight! I can mix the spirit of my choice with coconut water.

'Hell damnit' I said.

After a few more conversations, Clarissa was all playful with me. At random instances, she would jumpscare me by popping out of a vacant room, and then I would have to act all scared and thereafter she would let me fondle her breasts.

At night she slept in an unlocked room with her breasts still popped out. I desired to fuck her with aplomb. But then when I would try to sneak inside her room, scheming to fuck her by surprise, I would just be taken aback by her sweet innocent sleeping face and my desire of fucking her unwarranted would change into the desire of letting her sleep her sound sleep. What else can heal a war-famished girl after all? Sound sleep and the Young Moron!

Anyway, that is all about the bare breasted Clarissa. I'll come to her very soon again. But right now, we have a more urgent matter to attend to. Bahubali.

The real problem with Bahubali started, not after he began making the porn, but after he had finished it and now had to release it.

The problem being: 'Who the fuck was going to watch the National Porn of India?'

Could a porn which was shot in the backyard of a house become the National Porn of India? Would it be played on the television or be talked about by intellectuals and the founding fathers of our Country? Would it become a masterpiece until people would call it a masterpiece?

I assume it happened on the day after the shoot of our porn. That Bahubali, in the solitude of his room had decided to premiere his masterpiece in Hollywood directly. For this, he had fetched some Hollywood agent's number from the internet. And after doing a few rehearsals, he had called the agency. Once the receptionist had answered, he had in fact introduced himself with roaring pride, as if, if there was something these Hollywood cats were waiting for, it was for his phone call. And when there was no response from the Hollywood agency, just a stern white secretary hanging up the call after saying a few irritated 'hellos', it belittled our porn to some one week local havoc instead of a global masterpiece.

After this, Bahubali became a true madman. Drawn into the fierce dream of breaking free from the constraints of being a local phenomenon, it must be put in the readers and my fellow sufferer's deepest concern that Bahubali began chasing the fame and success of global measures.

And hereby I was summoned to his bedroom again, whereupon I was asked to use all the knowledge I had acquired in Harvard, to release his porn and publicize it among the masses.

'But what are we aiming for, Bahubali ji?'

He looked at me as if the answer was obvious.

'Fifteen years I have put into making this film. Fifteen years of sincere work. I'm only an artist. I know how to make the porn. But I don't know how to make a masterpiece out of it.'

'We can upload it on a few websites and see, Bahubali ji,' I said.

'Yuck thoo' he spat on the floor and looked at me with sad eyes. I won't lie, I got a little scared for my life.

'That' he said 'I have already done yesterday. There are 1,649 views on the website on which the masterpiece has been uploaded. Five likes. Two shares. And two people have commented something which I'm not pleased about.'

'What have they commented, Bahubali ji?'

'They didn't say anything. They have just posted a link of their own porn. That's all.'

'Well fuck. What do we want, Bahubali uncle? What are we aiming for, sir?'

'What would any man want after putting his fifteen precious years into something? Global dominance. I want to become a global leader.'

'Holy shit' I said 'I will see what I can do, Bahubali ji. I will do my best.'

The next day, when I opened the internet, there was no stir around his porn. Just another few hundred views and a comment saying 'Nice'.

'Nice?'

I think more than a matter of fame, it was in fact shameful for Bahubali that by the second day of him putting his porn on the internet, his porn had not mastered the hearts of people that he thought were going to travel from different states and even continents to shake hands with him, once his masterpiece would be discovered. This is what Bahubali had meant by global dominance.

He wanted national newsmen and even global world-trotting celebrities mobbing his doorstep. He pictured private full-fuel jets landing at Nalanda airport for the first time to meet the man who had brought a sexual liberation to our civilization. The American President calling him and congratulating him because, even if his principles were wrong, the United States supported his First Amendment rights. 'Please, you must accept our elite team of marines at your security, sir,' he had imagined Donald Trump begging him over a concerned phone call, 'We can't afford to lose a man of your creative acumen.' He wanted his house to be embraced by personalities of eminence. Grand famous movie producers and music composers. The BBC wing from the United Kingdom and Al Faqr News from Iran. He wanted his house to be brimming with Iranian chai and dates. Turkish delights and Swiss chocolates. But here to his sheer discontentment, it was just a bunch of live video views and a few jobless media boys who were milling around his house (more so to catch a glimpse of the Ukrainian than to cover his porno) with their faces jam packed with rose-scented ghutka.

On the next day, I was explaining to him 'Sir, it will take time to spread around the world. Rome wasn't built in a day. This fortune and fame you have found today is among these local chappies and the internet community. They will put the news to the outside world.' and more incessantly, 'First there is local fame, and only then there is national fame. And then international fame. These are steps to the fame game.' But he madly rebutted the idea, claiming that he had already put in his best and mustn't stop doing whatever is there in his capacity to get people to watch 'the National Porn of India'.

That morning, a list has been drawn from the internet archives of 'Hollywood's biggest talent agencies'. Driven by the enigma of his newfound fame, heraldic phone calls are made after he has memorized his introduction and his pitch by line. He didn't want to get into the major details of his work per se. He just wished on luck that his voice would be recognized on the other part of the continent, and thereafter he would simply ask them to connect him to the boss slash owner slash master of that agency. But most of the calls were sent to the answering machine. So now his phone, in accordance with his expectations, was answered very warmly and humorously by the recorded voice of the boss slash owner slash the big dog, and he was asked to send recorded messages. One of the poor agency ladies who did end up answering the call told him to drop and email, and when she was told hereby that 'I am Bahubali, don't you know me?' and 'This is a matter of greatness of which your boss must be made aware', she promised him that he would be made aware of it as soon as the mail reaches him.

'But how much time would it take?' Bahubali asked, all neurotic now.

'Yes, sir, please do send your work at once. Our general reply time is five to six months.'

'Five to six months for a bloody review on a fifteen-minute porn?' Were his dreams to die in the shambles of these digital waitlists?

When no favourable response has been received over a phone call, Bahubali asks me to get a few thousand pamphlets printed. Informative pamphlets about the National Porn of India. And a few preview CDs, which he plans on mailing to every big institution across the globe.

I do as I'm asked.

A nice glossy vinyl pamphlet and a CD that has all the three favorite porn pieces of Bahubali's mansion.

After that, my job has been changed from being the pimp to becoming the postman. So as per Bahubali's instructions, I stand in front of the local colleges, distributing Bahubali's pamphlet and handing over the CD cassette to more mature-looking professors and voyeurs who might enjoy watching the porn for free. When this doesn't have an impact, I'm sent to Nalanda Primary School and Hail Bishop Kindergarten, where I'm asked to put the pamphlets and CD drives in different comic books in the library.

'Why target the children, Bahubali ji?'

'So that they grow up in reverence to me and my art. So that the National Porn of India can become a part of their culture. They after all have the most imprintable mind, if you must know, Moron boy'.

And then one evening, I'm asked to mail the pamphlet and the CD to every goddamn school and college I can come across.

'Should I also send it to the Ministry of Education in our parliament... and see if they would be interested in making this erotica a part of their school's curriculum?'

'Send it to all the ministries. Every damn senator in the upper and lower houses. Hell damnit, send it to the Chief Justice of our Country.'

I do as I'm asked.

The next morning, an incident happened that was going to change the course of our future. Only, we didn't know it then. At ten in the morning, a bespectacled man came rapping on the doors of Bahubali's home, escorted by two newly recruited young policemen. Our gatekeeper had let them inside the compound because that fool had mistaken that Muslim porn-hating bastard for some media personage of International Acclaim.

The man had heard some rumours and enquired about the origins of our star cast. Only my messiah Bahubali welcomed them to join him for a tea. They joined. Then, Bahubali made them sit and watch his three pornographic masterpieces, while also explaining in greater detail the small travesties and providing fantastic bloopers to those innocent-looking men. Bahubali had even paused in between Miss India's scene to show how complicated and artful it really was 'to eliminate the actress's pubic hair' to make her look young enough to be seventeen and still leave a fair patch of bush behind to make her look more human than some mythical sex doll.'

'It's all just art, officer,' Bahubali said after the scene ended. 'I'm just a madman artist. I'm wondering, what does my business have to do with you? It's not like I'm harbouring a dangerous terrorist in my basement, is it?' He glanced at me with sly, contented eyes. Then, he added, 'Would the detective also like to interrogate our pornstars?'

'By all means,' the officer said, nodding.

Our pornstars, mildly irritated by the bright sun contrasting their darker world, were lined up—unbrushed and unwashed.

'Sit, sit,' the detective requested more than commanded.

They giggled and sat down.

The detective pulled out a small notebook and produced a pen from behind his ear. 'How old are you?' he asked the Ukranian girl.

'Twenty-three.'

'And where are you from?'

'I'm from Ukraine,' answered our talented, bare-breasted Ukrainian.

'Do you have a passport?'

There was a sudden twitch of Bahubali's ears. 'Wait, Officer. I thought you were more of a fan, an admirer of their hard work and labour. But your questioning threatens and scares my little girls.'

The innocent, wide-eyed detective looked helplessly at his police escorts. There wasn't much he could do at that moment.

'It's alright, please ask your questions,' Bahubali said as a goat wailed in the distance.

'Where are you from?'

'They are from the ghetto of the pure and unbred in Nepal.'

'Would madam mind showing some form of an ID? Some proof of citizenship to our motherland?'

'Is it absolutely necessary?'

'I'm afraid so,' said the innocent detective.

'In due time, they will,' Bahubali replied. 'In the meantime, would you like to touch their breasts? Play a little hickory-hankey-pankey? We have enough to serve all our guests, don't we, Miss India?'

'Mhmm,' Miss India groaned playfully. But much contrary to his fantastical porn, this was real world. The detective suddenly began complaining of an aching pain in his groin and left politely (promising that he shall come again and definitely feast on Miss India. That bastard even patted Miss India's cheek to prove his absolute determination.), and then the three men of the government walked away in the hot scorching sun.

Once they were gone, Bahubali said, all excited, 'Woah, Moron boy. Nice work. People have started showing up. Haven't they?'

'They have, sir' I said, as I retreated to my room.

We thought that more people will follow. Buses packed with people. Fans. Admirers. Voyeurs.

And finally, two days after having the National Porn of India floated across any conceivable office address and email address, finally the fame, the fortune, and the dream of Z security did materialize in front of Bahubali's mansion when a police gypsy pulled up on the outside door, and three policemen came rushing inside the mansion. I rose to share this exciting development with Bahubali. But then I saw another gypsy (this one darted right inside the compound, and a few more angry-looking men rushed to the inside of the house, baton in hand); they smashed and kicked open the door of the living room. I muffled my voice and sat back on the sofa from whence I had risen, and ten minutes later, after innumerable curses and screams, my master Bahubali was dragged into the front porch. What surprised me delightfully at that point in time was that my master had really been a PR-trained person all this while. What no one could have possibly conceived at that unpredictable hour—Bahubali had asked the police to wait for five minutes so that he could put on his costume. And when he was put in handcuffs, he dressed in a newly ironed suit, and on top of that, for the first time in my life, I saw a yellow tie hanging from his neck. And he smirked all the while as the policemen dragged him insultingly to the gypsy, and a few media folks took his clandestine photographs with their flashing cameras. When our eyes met, I thought faintly that the divine hour had come for me to boast my own loyalty to my boss, so I rushed to and haggled with the policemen, trying to dissuade them from really arresting Bahubali.

'Aihh, he is innocent. You let him go, police ji!' I pleaded with the policemen.

However, just at that moment I saw another of those fancy anti-riot police vans pull up in the front porch, and out popped a bunch of masked policemen with MP5 automatic machine guns, and I realized that this was not just a minor arrest. This was a fully planned raid of Bahubali's mansion. A public prosecutor jumped out of a gypsy and began reading a memo out loud 'four bloody counts of human trafficking, one count of kidnapping, two counts of child prostitution, and two acts of making and distributing child pornography over national and international media'. Just the number of counts made me speechless for a solid half hour while some random hand groped my collar and dragged me to the police van. A great many important men have been arrested in the past, and none of those arrests have been this glamorous if you ask me.

The last thing I remember before leaving Bahubali's mansion forever was the sight of the sedated Miss India standing with crossed arms covering her bosoms on the front porch of the mansion, pretending as if we were just burglars who had attempted to burgle her house, and here she was embraced in the penumbra of Bahubali's mansion, watching us thiefs being carried by the responsible police and protectors of the moral society.

We spent a sleepless night in the lockup. Me and Bahubali. The policemen were cooperative towards my boss. They offered us tea and biscuit. An 'A class VIP treatment' that day, for Bahubali was still a dreaded gangster (rumours of some 34,000 bullets hidden somewhere in his house. Enough bullets his gang can use to fight an entire army battalion let alone a police station). They even asked if we would like to have food. We refused. Asking instead for freedom. But that was something we could not have. As the policeman explained to us 'I can do whatever I can personally. But the matter is quite serious, sir. There are calls coming in from Delhi. The opposition is involved. We can't let you out. There are a few people from the special forces keeping an eye on you.'

'To hell with it,' Bahubali said.

After spending a night in the lockup, we were presented to the local judge in the morning. Bahubali was made to sit in the front row while thankfully, they ignored me enough to fairly place me in the last row of the courtroom along with the remainder of the crowd. An arrangement I was thankful for because otherwise my identity was at a risk of getting disclosed.

When the hearing started, the public prosecutor rose up, adjusted his black coat, coughed twice, and declared, 'Sir, we are hereby pressing charges on Mr Bahubali for two counts of aggravated assault and three counts of child pornography, that is the making and distribution of it. One count of distributing illicit 18+ material among civil schools (primary and secondary), one count of creating propaganda, one count of...'

The courtroom is breaking into laughter.

'Three counts of human trafficking, three counts of trafficking minors for the purpose of child prostitution, and one charge of housing a terrorist under his basement.

'Spreading propaganda, is it?' The judge asks, gawking at us in bemusement.

'Yes, sir. His pornographic collections have made rounds through the honourable higher and lower houses of our nation. There are speculations of his work being watched by our great ministers (two to be precise) whose names can't be taken in this honourable court.'

'Will the defendant be please presented on the podium?' Babhubali is held and placed for the purview of the courtroom.

'What do you have to say about this, Bahubali?'

'Sir, if I may say something, I must point out that the conditions in these state-run lockups are detestable. There are mosquitoes and cockroaches—believe it or not, sir, I found a cockroach crawling on my thighs this very morning. Such treatment for an innocent person like me, who has been respected as a leader and a scholar? It's degrading, my lord. I would have come willingly if you had sent an invitation, but instead, you subjected me to this third-rate treatment.'

The crowd in the courtroom erupted in laughter, but Bahubali's face remained serious, filled with furious anger.

'Do you think this is the face of a guilty man, my lord? This, right here?' Bahubali asked.

'Very well, Bahubali, before we proceed,' the judge said, 'I just want to confirm that you have chosen to represent yourself in this case, without any legal aid?'

'Absolutely, sir,' Bahubali nodded his head in determination. 'My lord, I don't consider myself a criminal. I haven't assaulted an innocent girl or distributed pornography in schools. I mean,' he paused, 'I have, but my intentions were very different.'

'What do you see yourself as, Bahubali?' The judge looked Bahubali in the eyes as he asked the question.

'Well, a chemist. A healer. Porn isn't for people who are already content with their lives. It isn't for those who are sexually fulfilled. My lord, porn is for the broken ones, for the generation crippled by unnameable, unthinkable maladies. There are desperate men out on the streets, in dark alleys. These are hungry, starving men who might turn this world into a revolving rape house if they aren't given access to porn. I say, free the porn, my lord. Let them watch. Let them be liberated. All I ever did was shoot a porn scene, and to be quite honest, I can swear on my heart,' he said, slapping his chest, 'that, my lord, I have never touched any of these girls. Never. I'm a man of principle. A family man. I have to set an example for our children. I am just an artist making my art. I'm just doing my job, my lord, just as you are doing yours.'

'What the hell is wrong with you?' the judge said with indignation. Suddenly, an electrical buzz filled the courtroom. The journalists, who had been half-yawning, sat up attentively and watched with anxious interest. Notes were being scribbled furiously in diaries and legal pads. 'How can you suggest that we have the same job? That you and I are doing the same respectable thing?'

'I'm sure you've accidentally let a convict go free sometimes. Maybe you've even sentenced an innocent boy on charges of sodomy or rape. These are the unfortunate sides of our professions. I guess it's the same thing.'

'It's not the same thing. You can't just walk into my court and accuse me of making bad judgments in my life. You can't point your crooked fingers at our legal system, son.'

'I'm sentencing this man to ten days in police custody until all the evidence is collected and reviewed by the court. The next hearing will be in ten days,' the judge declared as he passed the order of the day.

Nine days in lockup—nine long days away from the world's glamour—we lived in almost complete silence, marking time by the cycles of the sun and moon. Every knock on the door seemed like it might be from some distant journalist, but on the fourth day, we woke up to find our cell overflowing with fan mails, letters, and gifts. The blue bra of the braless Ukrainian had become a cultural symbol. A random clothing brand even printed her topless image on white T-shirts, with the blue bra draped over the collar. Our Nepali actress was being sold as a blow-up doll, and even Johny Boy found his niche audience, with tank tops and T-shirts bearing his name. Letters poured in, thanking Bahubali for saving a generation—letters from bored housewives detailing how the National Porn of India had intensified lovemaking in Indian homes, since no one knew when it might be their last chance. Though we received a wave of support, there were also outraged letters from activists in Delhi. I remember one particularly that condemned Bahubali's film as an affront to public morality. By the fifth day, security at the police station had to be tightened as journalists from across the nation swarmed the place.

'Just wait, Bahubali sahib. What has become a state-wide phenomenon now will soon be national.' A senior editor from a major media house even called the station with a special request to interview Bahubali by phone.

Bahubali replied, 'It's just art. But I've come to realize that this civilization doesn't want men to be happy. It would be a vigilante horror show if any man found true happiness.'

The night before our scheduled hearing, we sat in the oppressive silence, mosquitoes buzzing around our ears, a big, fat moon hanging just outside the small window of our cell. I asked Bahubali, uncertainly, 'What do you think will happen to you, sir? Do you think they'll put you in jail?'

Bahubali said, 'Even if they do,' and he paused as if realizing something profound, 'look at Gandhi, Mandela, Nehru, Bhagat Singh—every great revolutionary has been imprisoned within these same rotting, urine-soaked walls.' He was right; the place was a cesspit.

'How do you think you'll make a legend out of yourself? Right now, you're just seen as a perverted paedophile. No offense, sir. But how will we rise? How will they worship you?' I asked anxiously.

'It's not about me. I've done my part. I was just a means to an end. It's them—the media. They're going to turn me into a legend. If the media says I can fly, then trust me, even if I don't know a thing about flying,' he said, 'I can fly.'

'I think it's going to go downhill, sir. I don't doubt your abilities, but I've seen it with my own eyes. This is our downfall.'

'Boy,' he said, 'the day you realize that what you see on the screen—the beauty of those sizzling heroines, the scandal, the love, the passion—it's not just two-dimensional, but three.'

For a moment, I thought he'd gone insane, but then he continued, 'What you see on the screen, even the girl you fantasize about, she's real. She's out there in the world, and if you play your cards right, there's a chance she might one day fantasize about you too.'

For some strange reason, I was reminded of a black-and-white Onyx eau de toilette poster of Ms Staci.

'But to meet my dream girl, I must be a free man,' I said, my anxiety mounting. 'I don't think they'll ever let me out of jail, sir. The judge seemed very angry.'

'You'll walk free, boy. I won't let you go down with me,' Bahubali said.

'It's not the arrest I'm scared of. It's ... what if my wife finds out that I'm alive?'

'Well, you tend to overthink, boy. Just wait and watch,' Bahubali said, then suddenly snapped his fingers at a nearby watchman, who then disappeared for a moment.

'What's going on?' I asked. And if that was not enough to satisfy his excitement and my anxiety over my prospective discovery, the watchman returned bearing in his hands a broken wheelchair, which apparently Bahubali had been able to arrange for me from inside the lockup.

'What's this?' I asked.

'From now on, it's your throne,' Bahubali replied sagely.

'A what?'

'It's a throne. For yourself. This is your bail card. This is your free pass.'

'Sir, am I supposed to drive away in this? A bike would have been better. Or at least an electric wheelchair,' I said in dejection.

'No,' Bahubali said, 'From now onwards, you are a slobbering contorted idiot.'

'I'm sorry?'

'From now on, you are a mentally deranged man. You don't know shit about yourself, myself, or anyone. You don't know anything. You are a retard. You are a retard whom I discovered loitering around in my front lawn one day. And I took you in. And see these bastard policemen; they just carried you inside this lockup along with me. Poor you.'

'But how will that save me from jail time?' I asked in confusion.

'Well, you're an absolute fool,' Bahubali replied. 'The court can't do anything to a mentally handicapped person like you. You should know that. The law protects people with mental disabilities, Moron boy.'

'But what if they interrogate me? They'll find out, right? My name, where I come from—things like that?'

'You don't know anything,' Bahubali said, shaking his head. 'In court, you'll sit there and count imaginary birds flying across the room. You'll claim to be in a state of partial amnesia, so out of it that real migratory birds come and whisper Arabic in your ears. You can't speak, you can't understand, you can't do anything. Just a poor, helpless idiot.'

'And what will we gain from that? What if they publish my photo in the newspaper, asking people to identify me?'

'They won't disclose your identity. In fact, they'll keep it private for once. They won't send you to jail, just to a madhouse for a few weeks, maybe. But not jail. It's surprising, really,' Bahubali said, 'that you used to teach psychology at Nalanda, yet you don't know about the Mental Health Act. You can't be imprisoned, and your identity can't be disclosed. All you'll face is a little "fun time" in the private ward of a madhouse. So relax, Moron boy.'

The next morning, we had our trial at the colossal High Court compound of Patna. A bulletproof anti-riot vehicle escorted Bahubali and me to the court. The morning's paper announced that today was a pivotal day for our civilization to determine what was acceptable and what was not.

In the first part of the hearing, the public prosecutor—a sad, yet energetic old man—marched around the courtroom, speaking as if he were the ultimate guardian of morality. He didn't condemn porn because it corrupted young minds; instead, he argued that it degraded the pure connotation of love. He blamed Bahubali for contributing to the rising crimes against women, despite the letters of praise he had received from women who admired his work. It was truly a lost cause. My master had trafficked girls from Nepal, filmed them in broad daylight, and created scenes intense enough to make even a widow experience an orgasm. What more could be said?

The Indian Penal Code states that any material that appeals to the prurient interest of men shall be deemed obscene. In the United States, courts have developed scales—much like those for depression and psychopathology—to measure whether porn is truly arousing or just mildly stimulating. During my Harvard days, I had learnt about one particular scale devised right after the Miller v. California case, which is widely used to quantify the 'sexiness' of the porn in question. The National Porn of India was obscene. It depicted women in a degrading, lascivious manner. So, the prosecutor passionately argued his case, insisting that even a life sentence wouldn't suffice for the heinous crimes we had committed. He wanted to make an example out of us, advocating for 'zero tolerance towards porn and sex'. Before concluding his speech, the prosecutor dramatically produced a piece of chalk and drew a line across the courtroom floor, declaring, 'This is where we draw the line against obscenity. We must protect our children by putting that man behind bars. We must set an example.'

Then, a member of the jury stood up and said, 'We hereby appeal to the honourable court to impose a nationwide ban on the National Porn of India with immediate effect. We propose this in the pure interest of public morality and decency.'

The court's verdict was swift: 'Yes, by all means. Urgent. Pronto! Ka-boom—the National Porn of India is hereby banned.' But no one really knew what the implications would be because people were still going to watch it—ministers, schoolchildren, you name it.

During lunch, Bahubali turned to me and said, 'What is great art if it can't survive the test of time, boy? A ban? Incinerations? The day people masturbate to my porn even if their house is on fire—that's when I'll know I've created something truly great.'

By this time, whether the National Porn of India would continue to be watched was a matter of national interest. The prosecution had even requested further embargoes, including prison time for anyone found selling, buying, or even watching it.

After lunch, we were entering the second and final hearing of Bahubali's case.

'So you're going to send every masturbating citizen of our country to jail for jerking off to my porn, huh?' Bahubali asked the judge, while still seated on his chair. This was in reaction to the matter of further embargos they had asked about.

'Not just yours,' said the judge informally, while still entering the dais 'Bahubali. Anybody's. We are trying to fix the society here. Don't think you are anybody special.'

All the while, I sat in the last row of the courtroom on my squeaky wheelchair, thoroughly improvising my act as a retard. I had even managed to produce a thick foam of white saliva that drooled from the corner of my half-open mouth.

'Will the defendant please come to the dais?' the judge called out, hereby motioning that the court was back in session.

Bahubali was presented at the dais. He was now carrying a giant polythene bag in his hand.

'What's that, Bahubali?' the judge asked.

'My defense,' Bahubali replied.

'I am not sure I understand you,' the judge said, looking confused.

'I have here a collection of 793 erotic films and magazines,' Bahubali said, pulling out a pile of trashy erotica from the polythene bag and stacking it on the floor. 'All of this has inspired my work to a great extent. All of it was made and produced on this very soil in the last few years. I'm just left wondering—where the hell were you when they were producing these? And why am I here today and not the creators of this? Just because my porn features pure virgins while theirs is limited to worked-up prostitutes? Because mine looks real and theirs looks substandard? Because mine has virgins and theirs do not?'

The judge pounded his gavel, shouting, 'Order!' as the courtroom erupted in laughter.

'Members of the jury,' Bahubali began his speech, 'this system will create havoc, but it will never allow a man to be truly content. When was the last time you had the divine pleasure of enjoying a daisy-fresh virgin girl? Are there even any real virgins left in this world anymore? In fact, just a month ago, I conducted a random survey in our village to find the average age at which a girl transitions from being a virgin to becoming, well, not a virgin. It's approximately at fifteen years that a girl loses her virginity. You know, they give in to their dying, torturous mating call—maybe jumping into the bamboo forest with their lovers and admirers every once in a while. The village landscape is, in fact, dotted with places of fine concealment. The infinite fields where the brazen sun strikes the half-ripe fruits of youth. A moan from the cool rice paddies here, a slap of the pelvis by the lakeside there. By the time a decent-looking girl is married, she's lost her virginity to over twenty men, each of whom would have ravished her at least a hundred times. Then she gets married. That's the state we live in.'

'What does any of that have to do with this case?' the judge snapped.

'That virgin women are as imaginary and fascinating as unicorns and fairies,' Bahubali replied.

'So?' the judge pressed.

'So, just because I was able to find one doesn't make me a damn terrorist, does it? Then why the hell am I being used as a scapegoat?'

The courtroom again broke into laughter.

Bahubali continued, 'I'm being convicted of tarnishing the family values of our Indian households by so-called saintly, church-visiting, gospel-reading housewives, when the truth is that the foundations of these very houses have been built on farce and infidelity. If these women were as pure and principled as they claim to be, then, my lord, they would be at home raising children or raising hell on their husbands for forgetting their anniversaries. But these women here, they want to fix everything wrong in this world except their own households.'

After that statement, a very angry lady suddenly leapt out of the audience and attempted to assault my master by throwing a handful of red chilli powder on his face—despite all the security and barricades. A fresh whiff of chilli powder struck his face. Modern police forces are equipped to handle all sorts of threats—bombs, bullets, stones, and petrol bombs—but not spices and chillies. My master coughed and croaked as if he had suddenly been struck by pneumonia, while the judge, ignoring everything that had just happened, simply retorted, 'The courtroom is a place to express your general opinions, Bahubali ji, not to complain about your wife and how she treats you.'

Thereafter, Bahubali was made to rest in the side chamber, and then, quite unexpectedly, I was called to be presented on the dais. My wheelchair was wheeled in among the gawking, curious spectators. The whispers grew louder, with people narrating and asking questions in hushed confusion, but I remained as calm as a sedated fox. My life had been so pathetic that if there was a fitting description of me that day, it was that of a helpless, drooling retard. When the judge asked me for my name, I groaned and hummed, making desperate attempts to put my emotions into words.

'He is only a helpless invalid, my lord. I saved this poor soul one fine afternoon after seeing a beautiful, magnificent creature like him begging in front of strangers,' Bahubali said from the corner, the chilli powder still stinging his teary eyes.

'Is that true, boy?' the judge asked me, clearly confused.

That day, I learned that voices can be made not only from a man's mouth but from various other paraphernalia as well. I croaked like a bullfrog and then looked around the courtroom, avoiding eye contact with the judge and the prosecutor. All of a sudden, the poor judge became warm and fatherly towards me. He might have been planning a good civil education for me in some orphanage or perhaps thinking of all the ways society could tamper with my helpless youth. I kept on whimpering and mumbling incoherently, just to emphasize how vulnerable I really was. The truth is (which I learnt at a much later date) that the poor judge himself had a disabled son, who was truly disabled and not an imposter like me. After much stammering and fidgeting, when I finally managed to utter a word in court, I said with a lot of emotion in my voice, 'Bahubali', and then the entire courtroom became depressingly silent.

'Have you made him watch the National Porn of India?' the judge asked Bahubali.

'I felt,' Bahubali said, 'that if my porn could salvage him, then it could salvage humanity.'

'But why would you want to save anybody, Bahubali? The only reason you make porn is because you were unable to make love to your wife as a man should. And, therefore, she abandoned you. Isn't that right?'

The judge's personal comment seemed to unsettle Bahubali completely. Still trying to remove the red chilli powder from his eyes, he wailed in exasperation, 'Oh, what horse shit, my lord! My dearest lord, my majesty, if you want to know the absolute truth, then I'm just an artist. Just a curious artist. And I very much like to examine everything. I would, in fact, very much like to see you grunt as you make love to your cherry of a wife in the darkness of this night. It is because until you have not seen a man grunt while he fucks you can't estimate what material he is made of.'

I broadened my eyes in surprise. People from the audience, while stunned too, could be heard muffling their laughter.

Bahubali continued determinedly, 'I would very much like to see the flames of our constitutional rights, the rigour of our jurisprudence per se in your grunts, my beloved lord. Show me a video of you fucking your own wife. Or better yet, call me home tonight, and I shall give you good evidence on whether I'm a good fucker or not. Your wife shall roar and tell you personally after a night of the great Bahubali fucking her.'

The judge retorted in spasmodic horror, looking confused. He exchanged glances with the guardsmen, his own scout neatly dressed in his morning court attire. Then, in bewilderment, he rolled his eyes, fumbling as he said, 'This here is a depraved madman. This man would bring shame upon our prisons, upon our petty criminals. He is too dangerous—sorry, I rephrase—too disgusting to be put in our civil jail. I command and sentence him to a state-run mental asylum for an indefinite period of time, along with that mystery Moron sitting right there,' the judge commanded, first pointing his finger at Bahubali and then, towards me. I just sat and gasped in delight because, after all, my identity was still concealed. And I was to be sent to a real madhouse. I couldn't wait.

4

Back in 1857, when the British oppression of Indian sepoys reached unbearable and inhumane lengths, India finally fought back with its immense, optimistic forces. What began as a sepoy mutiny in Bengal quickly spread across the entire nation. There was significant military activity in the Kanpur Cantonment, followed by another uprising in Jhansi led by the Rani of Jhansi. Essentially, every plain along the holy river of Ganga was under attack. So, when the British Crown decided to finally anchor itself firmly on Indian soil, they needed a new Anglicized way of taming the so-called 'Indian revolutionaries'. That's when they thought, 'Oh! Hold on a sec! Who in their right mind would want to fight us? We, who ride on these long Persian horses with .35 Colt rifles, and these barefoot bastards think they can beat us? They must be insane! They must be madmen!' And so it was resolved that, aside from the already prevalent 'Optimism Pandemic' in Mother India, another growing pandemic was the 'Pandemic of Insanity'.

The British Crown began constructing modern, futuristic jails for revolutionaries, idealists, and freedom fighters. However, they didn't use the term 'prison'; instead, they called it the Insane Asylum. These were epicentres where sane revolutionary minds were captured, dehumanized, and subjected to electric shocks, frontal lobotomies, soul-cleansing rituals, and other brutal methods until the revolutionary in question was finally 'liberated'.

Clemency's was India's first and oldest asylum, spread over 220 acres of lush greenery near the Agra Fort. Much of Clemency's grounds offered a decent view of the Taj Mahal (a monument marking the undying love of the Mughal Emperor Shah Jahan for his twenty-second wife, Mumtaz—a fact that made my inability to secure even one solid wife for myself all the more painful). A larger part of Clemency's merged with the Agra Cantonment and the Agra Fort.

During the British Raj, it was common for a revolutionary man to leave his house in the morning with a bristling idea of mass revolution brewing in his head. He would ride his rickety old bicycle to the ruins of the Agra Fort to attend a clandestine meeting of one of the many revolutionary committees that had sprung up during the freedom struggle. Suddenly, midway, he would be stopped and questioned by British police officers about his destination. Unable to come up with a quick lie, he would be beaten into insignificance, dragged by his neck, and shoved into their van to be locked up at Clemency's. Some false charges of molesting a five-year-old child or a seventy-year-old decrepit woman in the streets of Agra would be slapped on him. There, they would teach him the true meaning of freedom by incarcerating him in a one-by-one isolation ward, stark naked, in the harsh winter of North India. He would be dipped in freezing water over a hundred times a day by the interrogating officers until sanity deserted him forever. Once he had forgotten his name and his mission in life, he would be sent back to his house—a harmless man, capable of doing nothing.

Ironically, the less dramatic parts of the Agra Mental Asylum are now designated as the Agra Central Jail.

Right after the judge's verdict, we were taken to the Asylum on the same day by a state operated Government bus. There was a police escort which followed us halfway. The first imprint of the asylum in my mind is as follows- The bus wheeled forward, dragging itself along, and before we could enter the asylum, much before that, we came across the giant, endless walls of the asylum that ran along our right side. From the look of it, the wall concealed a forest of madness within. I tried to gauge the space inside by making rough calculations. The wall must have been over thirty to forty feet high, with barbed fences running in multiple layers. There were watch posts (vacant but altogether eerie), and though there was a forest of bushes and city garbage on the outside of the wall, the inside seemed mysterious.

We made a few turns around the corner, and then our bus came to a halt. A few guardsmen shouted something, the driver pulled out our paperwork, and the doors of the asylum were swung open by an unseen force. The two guardsmen looked at us with detached curiosity.

The environment inside was cooler, with sunlight barely escaping through the overgrowth of giant peepal and juniper trees. A few madmen walked lifelessly in blue and brown robes, mouthing unintelligently and staring at us with mild amusement, while a few chased the bus.

The inside of Clemency's looked like pure magic—like a distant mirage, nearing us from obscurity. As we got off the bus (me and Bahubali), a madman accosted us and shakily asked if we could show him the way to the train ticket booking counter.

'Right there, boy!' Bahubali said, pointing his finger to a dismal land, even before I could fully absorb our first encounter with insanity.

We were then led inside the Mousley Ward, as the plaque on the wall mentioned. A flash of panic swept over me as I wheeled my chair passionately, playing my best imitation of the same contorted invalid as I was supposed to be. Somewhere deep down, I feared that this might eventually become my primary identity—this pretended retardation.

A few nurses led us, and I recall the hurried commotion of nurses appearing and disappearing under the bright white panel lights. We eventually stopped inside a vacant room where a ward boy and a nurse stood, evidently waiting for our arrival. A small wooden plank was placed at the centre of the room.

I sat in my wheelchair, examining that curious place with the gape of the retard I was supposed to portray. Meanwhile, my master Bahubali let himself loose and went ahead to confidently shake hands with the doctor, who was sitting behind a screened porch. But before Bahubali could say anything, the guardsmen and the ward boy stopped him near the centre table, lifted him some seven feet into the air, and placed him on the tabletop. His eyes widened in shock as he found himself practically on all fours. Before he could utter a word, he was stripped to stark nudity, his penis limp like a dead seahorse. With his eyes still wide and his legs spread-eagled, the ward boys performed a full-fledged cavity check on his body. When no threats were found—a sharp iron object in the anus? No. An iron nail hidden in the hair? No—he was made to stand up and face our doctor.

Let me quickly register my first impressions of Dr Dean (it was only later that I got to know the name of the doctor). Dr Dean was the head doctor at Clemency's. A singular man running the madhouse. And from the sight of him, a truly depressing man indeed. He had dark, tanned skin and a permanent glaze of glistening sweat over his bald forehead. He wore smudgy, white-rimmed glasses—smudgy, of course, because they were soaked in his disgusting sweat most of the time. The first time I met him, he was wearing the same light navy-blue shirt that I would see him wear on various future occasions.

He had acknowledged our entry subtly, still engrossed in some official paperwork. He told us to sit down—well, he asked Bahubali to sit down, for I was already permanently seated on my throne. He then extended one arm and rang a call bell to summon a pretty looking secretary from the depths of his chamber. Insanity was nothing new to him, so we didn't excite any curiosity or wild fascination in him.

'Well, let's see what we have here, shall we, Shelly? Oh, Ms Shelly, my darling?' he said, addressing the slim skeleton of a nurse. I believe Ms Shelly was there to assist him with his job.

Ms Shelly smiled at us with mildly curious eyes. 'So, how are you gentlemen today?' the doctor asked.

'Absolutely fantastic, sir,' Bahubali replied.

'And you?' the doctor asked, smiling and looking towards me with sympathy.

'Yeew yeee yeee hawwww,' I responded.

'Well, yea, yeee eye haw it is, boy. What's your name?'

I remained silent, scared, as panic built inside my chest. What if he could tell that I was just pretending?

'He's Moron, sir. Mason Moron,' Bahubali said.

'How do you know that?' the doctor asked, turning his attention away from my face.

'We named him Moron as he is stupid. That's why,' Bahubali said, now staring at the ceiling and trying to hide his nudity with his thighs.

'Well,' the doctor said good-naturedly, 'I've been informed by the authorities that in a bout of insanity, you kidnapped and sodomized three virgin girls in your backyard. You made them mate, filmed the entire act, and distributed it among our civil schools and even the Honourable Parliament of our nation under the pretence of bringing about a sexual revolution, Mr Bahubali?'

'Sexual liberation sir. Not revolution,' Bahubali corrected.

'Yeah, whatever. Well, here's the deal, boys,' the doctor said. 'I run this asylum with all my heart and care, along with this fantastic team. How you're treated inside will solely depend on how easy you make it for us to complete your treatment. What happens to you here depends entirely on you. If you behave civilly, you'll be treated civilly. If you act like an animal, you'll end up in the animal farm. As you must know, you've been sent here for an indefinite amount of time. This could mean the course of your lifetime or, at minimum, a few years. This is your new home. Treat it like your new home—your own home.'

'Yeeewww haaaw,' I said, perspiring and exhaling in defeat. I hadn't expected the judge to send us here for the entirety of our lives. I couldn't even ask the doctor whether we'd be discharged anytime soon. Damn! I couldn't even look at Bahubali in surprise. He had assured me it would be just a week-long treatment, all that nonsense about the Mental Health Act and such. Now, here I was, entering Clemency's without knowing if I would ever be free again. All I could do was mutter, 'Yeee haaaw.'

'Well,' Bahubali said, suddenly adopting a very official, formal tone, 'I'm Bahubali. I was the Member of the Legislative Assembly from Nalanda. Now retired. And Dr Dean, I surrender myself to your capable hands.'

I couldn't believe Bahubali was saying this. I hadn't imagined it even in my wildest dreams—our Bahubali, surrendering himself to a government doctor. But there he was.

Bahubali then extended his hand for a handshake, though by that time, the doctor was already scribbling something into our admission form.

In the days that followed, much to our dismay, the sanatorium proved every word Dr Dean had told us on the first day to be painfully true. Large barbed fences stretched endlessly across Clemency's, with signs warning of high-voltage currents running through them. Depressed riflemen wandered aimlessly but cautiously from the post-meridiem hours through the night. People had grave faces and dull days. They seemed bored and agitated but responsible.

For the first few weeks, it was just Bahubali and me in a single, plain, white-washed room, with a door that could only be opened from the outside. From the inside, it was a hopeless plain yellow metal door, shut indefinitely until some poor, helpless nurse would come to administer our prescribed medicines. Though the clouds rumbled and the sun made its usual course, we were deprived of outside noise. Bahubali lay in silence under the weight of his great misfortune. He lay plainly against the hardness of his metal bed, staring at the ceiling. Every now and then, owing to the miraculous effects of the drugs, he would close his eyes peacefully, reflect on the great deeds of his life until his eyes moistened again, and then he would fall asleep. This was permanent—the shut door and the blank, unchanging walls.

Sometimes, when he was awake, I would ask him if he was alright because, honestly, it was a little scary. But as the days passed, his speech started to become more distorted.

The most prized possession of a madman is his collection of leaves—rusty, crispy, fallen leaves that he gathers all day from the front lawns after recovering from his mental breakdown. Perhaps after committing a few murders here and there. Inside the madhouse, he roams around in his brown hospital robe, collecting the crispest and freshest leaves, which he hides up his sleeves.

This is shortly followed by his penis. Cut off a madman's penis, and the crazy will go crazier. When a madman isn't collecting leaves, you'll find him playing with his penis. That was the routine rhythm of the madhouse.

After spending an indefinite amount of time in the observation room, we were sent to the General Ward. Clemency's had three wards—there was Ward A, the Acute Ward, an extremely dangerous territory filled with loud and aggressive madmen whose only desire in life was to tear you apart and eat you raw. For a very, very long time, I didn't get the chance to visit Ward A. Then there was Ward B, reserved for general IPD patients and even the geriatrics. In Ward B, the nurses used to sit in their chamber behind an iron grill, playing cards all day long, while the doctors made their routine rounds. The ward overflowed with the smell of fresh phenyl and cleaning detergent. My strongest impression from Ward B is of Mr Ashmit, our very old, very civil sweeper, sweeping and mopping the floor throughout the day. Then there was Ward C, an upscale VIP ward attached to the administrative block, reserved for madmen of eminence—a subject I'll come to very shortly. All I can say right now is that it took me half my life to find that ward in the first place.

So there we were. It took us a while, probably an entire season, to settle into the routine rhythm of the madhouse. Of course, we were sent to Ward B. The ward remained silent throughout the day. The afternoons were dull, with patients mumbling to themselves and sleeping on their iron cots. We had a common ward, with rows of iron beds lined up next to each other. There was no door to the bathroom; they had been removed because there had been instances of patients trying to hang themselves from the flush vault after locking themselves in. The ward boys would play the TV on mute while the inmates slept or collected leaves all day.

During mealtimes, we would line up in the posterior section of our ward near the back lawn. There was an indefinite expanse of land behind us and in the far distance, the restricting sight of tall barbed walls. During dinners, we would stand against the backdrop of a red sunset, with noisy birds retreating home above us.

First, there would be the medicines, followed by plain, tasteless food. Afterward, the ward boys would lock the common entrance to our ward, and we weren't allowed to leave our beds. All you could do, if you felt good about life, was stand at your own bed and holler, but no one would care.

In my early days, I made friends with an unusual man—a middle-aged banker who had worked at the Reserve Bank of India before being admitted to Clemency's. He told me he had been working at the Ranchi branch of the RBI. During our later encounters, when I asked him with great curiosity about what went into printing money, including the pink 2,000 rupee note, he explained that sometimes the printer wasn't set to the right alignment, leading to the accidental printing of a series of useless but still authentic 2,000 rupee notes. This incident reminded me of my own experiments with printing private currency. He told me that printing notes wasn't as fascinating as it seemed. Inside the heavily guarded walls of the RBI, they were printing a commodity they could never practically touch. The sight of infinite currency inevitably led him to be brainwashed by a group of communists who convinced him to set fire to the RBI itself—on India's Independence Day, no less. He did exactly that. And then, to avoid jail time when the Central Police Forces showed up with their pumped-up MP5 sub-automatic guns, he tried to hang himself from the ceiling of the RBI Printing Unit with the shirt he was wearing. Later, upon his arrest, he was diagnosed as severely bipolar and, for some funny reason, schizophrenic.

Apart from him, there was Ahmed, the depressed poet—a mechanic from the village of Samastipur in Bihar. He used to write and recite poetry to me in the evenings. Whenever I was returning to my bed from the bathroom, Ahmed would leap out of his bed, and in pure excitement, narrate to me the most heartbreaking poetry he had written for his amazing girlfriend—a girl half his age, whom he missed terribly. He would always ask me for some cash because he wanted to mail those romantic letters to his girlfriend back home. One time, when I went to Dr Dean and asked him to help Ahmed mail his letters, I was informed that our deranged Ahmed was serving time for murdering his own girlfriend and her entire family with an axe. Only his mind wasn't willing to accept this harsh truth.

I'm not telling you all this to highlight how amazing or amusing our Clemency's was or how unusual and adventurous my encounters with the many patients were. I'm telling you all this because it had me wondering just one thing: what was I to do with my penis in this helpless madhouse?

No wonder, with the passing days, the mystique of my wild youth would have died right inside this asylum. I had learnt from an informed psychiatrist—a senior and more tantalizing colleague of mine with a brilliant mind, if I must say so—that true and passionate manhood can only be experienced in the ages of youth. During a visit to Clemency's, he had told me that a man seriously experiences the fierceness of his manhood while he is young. It's no wonder, then, that the young often end up getting mixed up in a lot of sexual misdemeanours—all of which are the result of various miscalculations made in the throes of youth. And it was particularly this that I feared. Not that I would spend the rest of my life in this mental asylum. Maybe, someday, fifteen years from now, the iron gates of my ward would creak open, and then an industrial truck would unload me one windy, dusty afternoon on the edges of an industrial township. And then, when I would be sixty-five, my eyes would no longer be popping, and I would be sitting against the afternoon sun, fixing screws and making machines with a dick that doesn't work anymore. And hell, that would have been bad.

I developed a void inside me, as vast and hollow as a human-sized chasm. Every day, I sat and stared across the deserted landscape of Clemency's, while the infinite rows of orange blossom trees burgeoned in the springtime heat. I gazed deeply and meticulously at the ancient walls of this asylum, and I felt an overwhelming certainty that my life was falling apart. I was awfully and indefinitely stuck in a void of maddening rage. At night, I shuffled and sweated profusely in my bed because the fire in my groin refused to extinguish. I had days consumed by harrowing anger and days of regret, laced with vivid memories of the topless Ukrainian. And the tormenting reality that, even though she was there, right in front of me, I never fucked her. I never fucked my wife. I never fucked Tania, the Ukrainian, Miss India, Neonika, or the Russian hooker who waited for me in LA when I was a kid. Hell!

The most idiotic consolation I offered myself when maddening rage rose inside me was this: Yes, maybe I haven't inserted my passionate soul into a living woman, but I have stood at the conception of a sexual history in the making. Yes, I was present when the National Porn of India was being made. Yes, I was there when Miss India was being fucked to eternity. Even though half this nation is now masturbating to the amazing rump of Miss India, I had seen, felt, and touched it in the real world. So maybe I haven't fucked anybody. But I've been present at every historical event in the realm of sex. Can't it be the case, then, that I was never meant to fuck in the first place and have been compensated in other ways?

Do madmen masturbate in sanatoriums? Do madmen shamelessly exhibit themselves among screaming and wailing nurses? Do madmen fuck the cavity of their mattresses, screaming and exploding in orgasm? And what happens to these creatures of unrestrained libido?

Yes. Yes, they do. Absolutely. But what happens if an unsuspecting nurse walks in on them in the throes of pleasure? Eternally terrified, she would wail, run away, and report the incident to the senior doctor. Afterward, the madman would be carted off to Ward A, where he would be left among other masturbating, flashing madmen. Once inside Ward A, his brain would be electrified, his semen dried up, and within a week, he would sit in a haze, unable to walk or even wither.

Had I touched my own ablaze dick in the privacy of the washroom or the changing room, and had an alerted nurse walked in and caught me, she would have been horrified and screamed, and I would have needed to run for my delicate life while the ward boys stormed the shower room.

'This sex-crazed madman has just dropped a load of his disgusting semen and hidden in that corner,' she would have screamed, her fingers pointing at my naked legs. I would have been chased by furious ward boys with flaring batons and whips, and the rest of my life would have been spent in the ghostly isolation of Ward A, where I would rot in my own semen and discharge, with nobody even to spit on my living corpse.

So that is what became of the masturbating madman in a state-sponsored mental asylum.

You only tell me, what could I have done with my penis? Or my unextinguished passions of boyhood?

Apart from being under constant vigilance, there were other things that made it tough for me to masturbate in peace. Inside that madhouse, I was ridiculously scared and aloof, always wary of the other patients. The fear of someone pouncing on me in the dark of night, or attempting to bite the flesh off my neck, haunted me. By the end of my first year, I began to plan my exit from the asylum. I realized I was one of those early-age chalet idiots, a fine specimen of a fool who had locked himself inside a sacred castle without knowing how to operate the door. What had likely started as a latent, laid-back approach to life—me giving up pimping and surrendering to the asylum—had morphed into a desperate craving for girls and freedom. These two things became my utmost desires.

In an asylum, the lines between sanity and insanity are totally blurred. I figured out that the less I spoke, the more I risked spending the rest of my life in this madhouse. So, what was my solution? I spoke. Finally, after a solid year of enduring the haze, a year after making my first miraculous recovery inside the asylum, I fell under the influence of psychiatry and produced 'speech'.

Now, the act of producing speech might not amaze people otherwise. In fact, inside the asylum itself, I've seen nurses cursing and sometimes wishing that a particular patient couldn't speak at all because of the vile filth he would hurl at them. He'd shout, 'Fuck this', 'Cunt that', 'Fuck off with your warm smelly cunt', 'Fuck off with your hillbilly horror show cunt', and so on. Some patients in my ward could get really nasty, urinating in the lobby or writing their names with their excrement in the walking area, so the hospital would reek of hell for a good two or three days. All the sweet, tender nurses of Ward B could do was duck behind the nurse's station and wish for dreadful silence. But when I spoke, there were celebrations and cheers.

I muttered a simple syllable: 'Papa'. I couldn't think of anything else. That single word had brought eternal solace to my years of suffering. Two syllables, one word: 'Papa'. As soon as the word escaped my lips, the corridors of Ward B erupted with claps and joy. Nurse Ms Shelly, our janitor Janice, and even Dr Sherpa ran and leapt from their rooms, assembling around me in great jubilation. They hugged me and hugged each other for I had validated that their treatment was working.

'There has been speech, Doctor. Damn good job. Mission accomplished. We've made the moron speak.' Ms Shelly had reported to Dr Dean when he had come for his rounds that evening.

That evening, an important meeting was held to discuss this occurrence of a lifetime. By then, I had blurted out a few more words. My transition from 'Yeeew haaw' to 'Papa' had been so spectacular that sweets were distributed in the ward that evening. With perplexed, inquisitive force, Nurse Gabriel asked me, 'How do you feel, Moron? Speak, Moron' as if I were a tiny crawling child. I replied, 'Fine', and she almost broke into tears of happiness and sadness.

And then the strict ward boy (who never spoke to anybody) asked me, 'Do you know where you are?' I replied, after some thought, 'Hospital. I'm at the hospital.'

'Oh, damn right you are, boy. You are in the hospital.'

I had given up my wheelchair only a few months ago. After making progress in speech, I was able to resume the usual routine of the madhouse. The next day, feeling miraculously healed, I walked to the dining hall of our asylum in high spirits, a swelling bubble of faith and excitement in my chest. I was looking forward to meeting Bahubali and having a real conversation with him—my first real conversation with a real person after a year of silence!

The dining hall had a celebratory atmosphere during the afternoons, with clumsy madmen eating with their bare hands (forks and spoons were forbidden, as even these objects could be used to commit suicide or murder—or both). The madmen sat and ate, scattering food all over the floor. Literally everywhere. A madhouse dining hall doesn't look much different from a playschool—food spilled everywhere, people with overmedicated, bulging eyes tending to their meals with the innocence and ignorance of toddlers. The loud clatter of iron utensils echoed in the background. Access to the dining hall was limited to patients who were showing good progress and could be left unsupervised for a short while.

The day I went to the dining hall to meet Bahubali, I encountered Harrison Brown for the first time.

Our encounter wasn't as simple as one might expect. To tell you the truth, I had heard Harrison Brown's voice for the first time three days earlier. He had recently been shifted from Ward A to the isolation of Ward B. He had a habit of emitting loud, deafening screeches that echoed through the halls of Ward B—at random intervals without any warning. Suddenly, there would be a loud, shrill scream from this boy echoing across the second floor of our ward, whether it was day or night. His screams just wouldn't stop.

So, feeling miraculously healed, I entered the dining room and saw my master Bahubali sitting there, eating his plain, tasteless meal. He didn't even bother to raise his head or look around. I sat at the other end of the table at which he was sitting and tried to make a sound to get his attention. From his appearance, I couldn't tell whether he was still the same old Bahubali or if the treatment had changed him. So I sat there, trying to make a noise, but my voice was drowned out by the loud whirring of an industrial exhaust fan overhead. The clatter of the broken fan was deafening. It was a massive fan, installed in our British-era dining hall, and it made things even more challenging for me. No human sound could compete with the clattering of that industrial exhaust.

Just as I was about to get up and shake Bahubali back to consciousness, there was a loud scream from the corridor, but this time from a man who seemed to be in immense pain. A wave of anxiety surged through my chest. I was terrified. As the metal fan clattered louder and louder, the screams grew more intense. It wasn't a deep, booming scream from some loony's stomach. No, these were screeches, shrill and painful to the ears. With every increase in the fan's clattering, the screams grew louder.

And then I saw Harrison Brown for the first time.

He was being carried into the dining hall by three ward boys, his hands and feet bound with rope. Harrison Brown. In the days to come, he would become my most devoted sidekick, also known as Harris Boy.

Later conversations with Harrison revealed that the major issue with his brain was related to a murder. Now, I'm not afraid of serial killers or murderers; I've learnt that they, while seemingly twisted, have their rationale for their actions. But in Harrison's case, there was no clear reason for his descent into paranoia. On his seventeenth birthday, in a moment of breakdown, Harrison stabbed his mother to death—with a cake knife.

I tried to psychoanalyze his case. Perhaps it had something to do with his mother creeping him out while his father was at work. Maybe she scolded him or treated him with cold hostility, and this poor boy developed an acute fear of her. Imagine Harrison's young mother, creeping him out by randomly peering at him from darkened rooms while he was playing with his toys. Maybe she was depressed herself. Who knew? But something happened on the day of his birthday that drove him to stab her (with a damned cake knife). And when he saw the grotesque finality of death on his mother's face, he must have been driven into an absolute frenzy. So he pulled the knife from her belly and stabbed her again, and again, and again—eleven times in total.

The horror of his crime was so shocking that neither his Youth Welfare attorney nor the juvenile court asked him any questions. They sent him directly to a mental hospital to be cured and nursed back to sanity.

'Oh Lord, what a poor, helpless child,' I thought to myself. I wondered what kind of mental illness could result from such an act. The murder must have made him feel utterly wretched, consumed by the belief that he had done irreversible damage. There is no cure for bringing the dead back to life, after all.

It took me a long time to understand his condition. Apparently, all he could say was that he wanted to send more people to his dead mother so she wouldn't be bored in heaven.

If only I had known that day that he was secretly planning to kill everyone in the asylum so his mother wouldn't be alone in heaven. He believed that was his only path to redemption. He couldn't undo his crime, but he could send her some company.

'But we can always send a few more people to them so they don't get bored, Sir Mr Moron,' he would say.

Anyway, after that first speech on my part and a massive celebration on theirs, after my first encounter with Harrison Brown, the next day, I was told to attend the 'Groups'. Informed rather by caring Ms Shelly who had come to my bed and after her failed attempt to probe into my memory (she asked if I was ever married or if I remembered what my parents looked like—I didn't, of course. Instead, my eyes became moist, and I showed her that the patient was beginning to panic), she patted me on my shoulders and told me to come to the Meeting down in the Prayer room by 6 p.m.

'6 p.m., okay' she said as if she were talking to some deaf rogue rather than to some savant idiot '6 p.m., Moron. Okay?'

When it was 6 p.m., she came again and told me that 'It's 6 p.m. This is 6 p.m. Look! Look outside the window.'

There was the normal evening red sky with beautifully scattered clouds. '6 p.m.,' I said. 'Yes.'

I figured if I had said something more, she would have gotten so excited that she would have fed me her own breastmilk, I tell you.

The prayer room on the ground floor was really just a circle of iron chairs around a Styrofoam armchair, with a giant picture of the Jewish Jesus overlooking his children. We were his children.

There stood Dr Dean, Nurse Shelly, and Nurse Gabriel under a dim golden light. Among my fellow patients were the RBI banker, Bahubali, and a few dumb geriatrics. It was a little dark, so I couldn't see much anyway.

As soon as I sat down, Dr Dean began, 'Okay, today I'm going to tell you all a fantastic story about a guardhouse and the guard.' The session had just started.

'The guardhouse?' I repeated, mimicking him deliberately.

'Yes,' he said. 'Oh, Moron boy. What a pleasure to hear you speak, son! Everybody, this is Moron,' the doctor said.

A chorus of 'Oh hello, Moron' came from the crowd.

'Yes, sir,' I said, smiling, hoping that after hearing my firm speech, they might consider letting me out. He didn't seem to notice.

'So,' Dr Dean continued, 'I'm going to tell you the story about a guard from the nearby Agra Prison.'

Everyone shifted to the edge of their seats. Even the lady in the black dress—wait, there's a lady in a black dress. How had I not noticed her all this time? Maybe she was a new admission. Hell! A stunning lady in a black dress in this madhouse. After a year of peacekeeping, a year of silence, here comes a woman with an ample bosom and a lovely face.

Dr Dean continued, 'So, during the British era, in the old prison of Agra Cantonment, there was a tiny guardhouse where an old guard lived, with all thirty-two of his teeth fallen and mixed into mother earth. Once the British left, much of the prison was deserted, serving as a part-time prison and a full-time museum with British Raj artefacts and black-and-white photos stored for the exhibition.'

Hell! I just couldn't help but stare at that big-breasted motherly lady from across the assembly. I had already counted three moles on her neck, and from the look of it, it was promised that she had a few more hidden around her chest. Goddammit!

'As you all must be aware, museums are usually closed to visitors at night. So, this old guard from the British times stayed back to do his guarding. Only, a few days into it, he became a sort of recluse. He stopped speaking to anyone from the outside world. He stopped going home to his dead wife. He even refused to see his ignorant, third-world grown-up children. It was as if he were stuck in time. The poor guard still cooked and lived in the same old guardhouse, and every night, he disappeared for a few hours to some pale, secret place. He never slept at night, only during the day when the sun was bright and the world was safe.

'One day, a few idiots from the local media thought of interviewing him. They turned up with their broken mics and their handicams to have a candid conversation with this guard. They thought it would be a hilarious ten-minute showpiece with that twisted recluse of a guard muttering bullshit. But, mid-interview, that guard started speaking such fine brilliant English, such superb non-stop English, that you would've slapped your forehead, believing you were witnessing the reincarnation of Lord Clive. Imagine a stupid illiterate guard speaking non-stop English! He revealed scandalous secrets and wept, laughed, and finally, in the end, he said that the ghosts of the dead and tortured visit him every night. He claimed he was already half-dead and had witnessed true torment. He said that, on multiple occasions, he had been dragged by his feet in the middle of the night to the closed arsenal of the museum. He had seen the tortured ghosts of depressed English soldiers, whose pipes never went out.'

I kept wondering what she would look like without her clothes. Goddammit, listening to this story, even this woman seemed afraid for her life. She scratched her neck with *her* delicate fingers, and our eyes met. She gave me a sweet, tender smile.

'Anyway,' Dr Dean said, 'no one from the local village visited the deserted premises after dark. If they did, their families were famished and tortured, and every damn body committed suicide within a year of visiting the haunted museum of Agra. So life went on. The guard did his rounds, and thieves stayed aloof because who in their right mind would trespass into the waiting arms of a semi-depressed, bewitched spirit? But sooner or later, civilization reached the outskirts of the city. In the blink of an eye, there was new construction happening all around the British Museum. Walls were torn down, the museum was demolished, and the iron from the cellars was sold for scrap. But the guardhouse remained intact, standing among the construction workers in their yellow helmets.

'They hammered iron pieces together, and a flyover was halfway completed last year. Giant halogen lights lit up the area, and darkness was thrown out from that place like a murdered prostitute hurled from a speeding car. But the guard and the guardhouse stood throughout the construction. In fact, the guard was given the duty to watch over the new development, despite his old age. With this new responsibility, miraculously, all the ghosts disappeared. After all, who would want hypertension and migraine in a new civilization? So the ghosts vanished, and the workers built and fucked and ate and shat and lived their lives. But the guard remained the same—scared, desolate, haunted, spooked, and aloof. Why?'

Hell if I knew why. I was going to talk to that beacon of hope the moment the assembly ended. I knew, just by looking at her, that she was a butterfly waiting to be *fucked* in this asylum. *Gosh!* Why is she even here? A beauty like her.

'Because,' the doctor said, 'the ghosts began dwelling inside his head. Ghosts can linger in people's minds for ages. So even after the museum was demolished, the ghosts remained alive in his head. The traumas of your life are over. What you did—how many people you murdered, how many times you ever shat in front of an amused crowd. It's over. What we want in this group is to eliminate that ghost. Now, I know we can't do this right now. But one day, not far from today, I, your humble doctor, will have kicked that ghost out. And you will be free, loving people in the normal world.'

The beautiful woman had been staring at me for over five minutes now. Every now and then, she listened intently to the tales of the British era, the bewitched ghosts, and the supernatural forces. But every few minutes, she glanced at me as if she was as curious as I was about her.

After the group session, I walked to the dining room and waited for the lady to show up—impatient, aroused, and nervous. When she didn't appear, I felt disheartened, as usual. But once again, life was as pale as a virgin's summer night. I grabbed my plate, scooped two giant spoonful of the bland, gooey food, and sat beside Bahubali—again. The food here wasn't meant to excite anyone; it was comforting, just enough to help us absorb our medications.

There was a strange, comforting silence in the dining room that night, the giant exhaust fan still clattering noisily overhead. I wondered why no one had protested or tried getting the fan down until now. It really did give us the creeps. If there was somebody who really protested and screamed against its booming threat, it was our Harrison Brown. However, after a few days of mixing with the rest of Ward B, his habit of screaming and scaring everyone was replaced by another evil trick. Now, he barely screamed casually. Realizing that his effort was going in vain, Harrison began preserving his energy for something more sinister. Now, he would creep up to an unsuspecting dumb madman (there were a lot of them wandering in and around our ward, all knocked out of their senses), and then before his presence could be sensed, Harrison would tap the madman on his shoulder. Unsuspectingly, when the madman would turn to look, Harrison would screech with such maddening intensity that the dumb guy would be knocked back to his senses only.

That evening during dinner, he tried this stunt with my boss, Bahubali. But instead of leaping and shrieking in horror, Bahubali simply stopped eating his sandwich and looked at the poor bastard as though he'd interrupted some very important train of thought. With nothing else to do, Harrison Brown then quietly sat in front of Bahubali, his feet dangling and shaking in the air.

After that incident, I forgot about the mysterious lady. Instead, I joined Bahubali and Harrison Brown for the talks. I'm glad I spoke to Bahubali that evening for it was the last time we were talking to each other. Soon after, the infamous cot incident occurred, and Bahubali was sent permanently to the Ward of the Acute.

I remember that sunny afternoon vividly—it was a Sunday. We knew because Sundays were reserved for rearranging our iron cots and cleaning the stinking, unreachable corners of our ward. My master, Bahubali, was standing on the front lawn, soaking in the morning sun and gazing at the mystical landscape of Clemency's. He was too tired of not being himself lately when, suddenly, the mad RBI banker hurled an iron cot from the first floor of our ward. It crashed onto the ground below, missing Bahubali by a mere seven centimetres.

Did it startle him? Not really. Bahubali was not one of those maniacs who would be startled by a gunshot or a plummeting bed aimed at his head. But at some point, Bahubali raised his head, looked up at the sky, closed his eyes, and, I presume, had some kind of ultimate calling because after a few minutes had elapsed, he walked up to Dr Dean's chamber. The sincere doctor was sitting in his chamber and was engrossed in reading medical literature. Suddenly Bahubali slid down his drawers and began masturbating violently. When the cursed doctor came out of his chamber, everyone thought Bahubali would stop—but he continued, violently and helplessly because he was on the verge of ejaculation. It was, after all, his first in probably a decade.

'What the hell are you doing, Bahubali? You told me you were a very important politician. Do good politicians flash themselves like this?' the doctor said.

Mid-process, Bahubali looked up—his hands still stroked his penis and he professed loudly that he wished to examine the doctor's mother's birth canal, to see how great healers like Dr Dean were made. The doctor, who had only recently lost his mother to a harrowing disease, was shocked at first. However, he went ahead and hugged Bahubali with passion. Hugged him with both hands. But that marked the end. The man who was once meant to transform the nation into a socialist paradise had ended up getting himself transported to the distant land of Ward A.

With him gone, Clemency's lost its meaning for me only. After staging my death, Bahubali had been my only constant. I didn't know him that well, but I knew him enough to anchor my life around his existence. Wasn't I his son and favourite pimp? Hadn't he taken me in when no one else would have given me a spare room? Hadn't he kept me safe from Noel and other great misfortunes that this world hides under its sleeve? And hadn't he kept my secret—that I was still alive—only a secret through all these years?

Once he was gone, there was nothing left for me to attach myself to. I thought I'd fall into a stupor after his transfer. That I would give up food. Hell! Probably I would have refused to leave my bed only. But his departure had the opposite effect on me. Instead, I became a wanderer. An explorer. A curious spy embarking on an unknown mission. For after he was gone, I began using the aid of my feet and a mind, which was still in good working order, to explore the vast premises of Clemency's.

The more fearless feats I took on myself, the more I discovered about that mysterious place. I learnt, for instance, that all the humming and buzzing that spooked my brothers in the ward wasn't the result of some whimsical transportation of souls to a place where helpless men were beaten and turned into pigs. It was just the huge, broken-down geyser in the ECT Chamber on the floor above us. The secrets about the ECT Chamber also for instance. Though earlier, waves of frenzy would sweep across a poor madman's face when the name of Electro-Shock Therapy was blurted out by an irritated nurse or cruel doctor But a nightly glimpse into the ECT chamber led me to discover that there was nothing fancy about the ECT. It was just a normal room with a simple iron stretcher, a small HP desktop, and a bunch of electrodes hanging from a small machine. That was all there was to it. A bed and a computer. Yet, you should have seen how the madmen surrendered themselves at the mere mention of ECT. Most of the things we fear aren't the things themselves but the ideas we weave around them.

Of all my little expeditions, my night routine became an all-time favourite. The night gave me the luxury of the most silent and uninterrupted of hours. I could crawl out of bed, quietly exit through the front door (pretending to head to the bathroom or on the lookout for some cold water), and wander endlessly through the ivy-covered corridors. On one of those nights, I came across the Records Room in the Administrative Block—a chamber where every madman's personal file was kept. On another sad night, I discovered the very sad mortuary, a vacant room with a single iron stretcher and some embalming agent, kept there to preserve the corpse if someone committed suicide in the asylum.

Not all my findings were depressing, though. Some nights, I'd encounter a semi-nude ward boy sneaking into the janitor's room with a senior nurse. Once, in her impatience, a poor (probably, unfaithful) senior nurse had dropped her undergarments in the corridor itself before disappearing into the janitor's closet thereby lending me a sight of her smooth broad back. When it came to fucking the nurses, our nurse Gabriel, in fact, was a routine fucker. In fact, I had seen him sneak into three different janitor closets with three different nurses on three separate occasions. I swear, the nurses loved getting themselves drilled in the madhouse. Maybe it was a fantasy for them—like getting it on in a nursery or a day care. They were young, bored, and had nothing else to do at night, so they fucked as if they had absolutely nothing to lose.

Apart from the routine fuckings, of course, there were other moments, too. Times when I'd eavesdrop on a ward boy playing out his wildest dreams for a bunch of orderlies or when the nurses would joke and curse among themselves. It was surreal, the way they behaved in front of us madmen and how they acted when they thought we were asleep.

Apart from that, there were these very adorable, very sweet moments too. For instance, if a ward boy had his birthday, in the night, he would distribute chocolates and sweets to the entire staff. Or when a newly recruited nurse was too afraid to cross the small bridge from Ward B to the Administrative Block in fear of being pounced on by a madman, she would be happily escorted by a muscular ward boy with animated musculature across the small bridge.

Things were altogether falling into a fine order. My days were dull, but I always had something to look forward to at night. During the evenings, I used to play badminton with Harrison Boy in the Dutch Church. We had an 1857-built church inside the premises which doubled as a badminton court and a library. There the madmen used to play badminton or pretend to read various newspapers. Really, things were going altogether fine.

And then one night, while I was on my usual expedition, I overheard Nurse Gabriel telling Nurse Shelly about a very important person who was being brought down to Clemency's for her treatment.

You see I had kind of readily begun accepting Clemency's as my new home. And then Nurse Gabriel told Nurse Shelly that Ms Staci, the great actress, was being brought down to Clemency's under mysterious circumstances and I, fortunately or unfortunately, ended up overhearing that news.

5

I was dead until now, Staci. But now I am alive. There's fresh air in my chest and new life in my heart. If nothing else counts now, then at least I have hope.

With her name muttered that night, I began my wild hunt for Staci in the real world. With the knowledge that probably Staci was lurking somewhere only a stone throw away from my existence, such a restless frenzy had taken over me that I couldn't even sleep for one second. I had turned into a full-time vigilante. During the night, when the ward boys patrolled the corridors, I lurked in the shadows. If they passed by our dormitory, I would rush to the washroom, ensuring that even if my absence was discovered, I'd only be found innocently at the urinal). No wonder, I spent endless nights just to hear her name again. Her onyx de eau toilette advertisement plaguing my insomnia and filling and refilling me with a brand-new life. What would this world become if I would have had Staci all for myself? But her name never came up again—not for weeks.

The real mass of shock came one unsuspecting afternoon during lunch as the industrial exhaust rattled in the dining. They had put the television set on (not for the interest of the hungry mutes, but for the extremely bored nurses). I remember vividly how I was in my own peace, was heartily eating my flavourless meal, the idea of Staci evaporating from my memory like a ship disappearing in the fog. I remember I was at such peace that I had even tucked a napkin around my neck. And then suddenly something occurred on the TV screen, and I felt a sharp pain through my abdomen. And the pain shortly flared into wild excitement. My heart raced and lungs filled with more air than lungs are supposed to carry. When, God forbid, what your dutiful spy couldn't muster in ages was now a news of national acclaim. The broadcast of a pretty news-lady announcing that the star of our nation, Ms Staci is off to take some private time for herself (the time of her return, unknown. Future film commitments have been cancelled.) and her PR folks had just left a statement saying that the 'star's privacy must be respected as she is going through some hard times'.

And hell damnit! There it was. At that time. Not on the television set. For the news almost always lies but in the knowing smiles of the ward boys, who despite being silent were smiling an evil smile. They knew. They knew where Ms Staci was. And I remember the food I had been ingesting had now began choking my throat, and after almost escaping death, I knew for a fact that if Ms Staci was to be discovered anywhere in the world, it was here in Clemency's, no more than 500 feet away from me.

In Nalanda, I couldn't imagine life without Noel and her hill house in Sikkim. Her wickedness had turned me into a helpless fool who couldn't even touch his own wife freely. But then Staci liberated me. And I hadn't even seen her yet. But just the idea of her being around in the same sanatorium as me liberated me so completely that I felt my heart was going to explode.

What torments I've endured for you, Staci, now that you're no longer an illusion. How long those endless hallways felt, how dense those buildings, hiding you from my eyes. No medicine that I know can numb me now. The tranquillisers are meant for neurotics and not for people who are mad about finding their Solace.

I wandered helplessly in my passionate search for Staci and wasn't I lent the most mystical of surprises which nature only unfolds to a lost wanderer; for instance one cold night a white owl flew by me as I wandered through the endless arrangements of tall junipers right outside Ward B. And then one night when I was entering Ward C, there was a sudden power outage, and because things remained on the whole calm, I sprinted further to the restricted premises of Ward C and almost reached the forbidden door of Staci's bedroom, and a sharp fruity perfume filled my nostrils, and I was practically able to get a glimpse of her in real life even though I hadn't seen her yet. That olfaction remained to haunt me even in my sleep. As far as sleep is concerned, that too was becoming a rare occurrence now.

Maybe I was becoming insane. Maybe I could have not even been able to tell you the difference between what was real and what was unreal anymore. The case with that bedroom of Ward C for instance. That night after the power outage, for the entirety of that night, I had rejoiced and tumbled around in my bed for I had figured that I had finally found the door which would lead me to Staci. But then on the next day when we were returning from lunch, I came across the same bedroom again; this time it was less like an illusion but more like a storeroom from where the staffers were coming out with boxes of files and office supplies. It was as if on the previous night, in my spell of craziness, I had ended up building a dream of that bedroom only. And probably it wasn't even a bedroom at all.

I think I might have continued her search for an entire week. And I suffered cruelly for I could feel a permanent void building inside my chest. A permanent vacancy in my embrace. For every particle of my existence longed for Staci. And then when the suffering became unbearable, in a moment of wise judgement I altogether abandoned my pursuit. With that dying hope, the winters toughened, and our night outings became even more limited. Clemency's was grim in winter, a season of suicides and despair.

I have many stories to tell. In that season of cold, we lost two geriatrics, and a nurse fled with an interning doctor after they were caught mating in Dr Dean's cabin. But none of them matter anymore. Here's what really does:

One evening, after giving up on the idea of finding Ms Staci, I remember I was simply walking near the Dutch Church. It was during the early sunset (I was probably on a lookout for some warm sunlight) that I don't know what impulse hit me, but I spotted Mr Len, a very senior nurse, standing aimlessly by the library. Without thinking much, I walked straight up to our unsuspecting Mr Len, and gathering all hope, I said the unspeakable: 'Mr Len, have you by any chance seen Ms Staci?' And then I saw his face turn all clueless. As if he intended to say 'What the fuck? What? Oh! You too, Moron boy! Getting all schizophrenic. Hallucinating about the presence of great actresses now. Must go to Ward A now, boy.'

His face had a blank expression. I thought I'd ruined everything, but then I added, 'Dr Dean is looking for her.'

'Oh, alright, boy!' Mr Len said, now easy and friendly as if he were not being molested by a madman but being enquired by a devout and sincere volunteer of Clemency's. 'Oh, yes, she must be in the recreational room right by the church,' he said. My heart leaped. I ran to the men's room, fixed my hair in the useless iron mirror, and headed towards oblivion, where madness was to meet the supernatural.

There she was. Her long hair concealing her radiating face. Her presence, brighter than my entire future. She was sitting by the window, painting on a canvas a picture of a small hummingbird. She was wearing a light denim shirt and a pair of dark denim jeans. And years of suffering and ailing came to an instant conclusion. For I knew that maybe I have been dead all along. But at that moment when I saw her for the first time, I felt like how I would have felt when I was born.

'Ms Staci,' I muttered, hoping not to scare her away. She didn't seem to care.

'Ms Sta...' I tried again, and this time, her eyes met mine, stopping my heart. In that moment, I found a new respect for myself.

'What an amazing painting, Ms. Truly brilliant.'

'Do I know you?' she asked, clearly threatened.

I realized I had made a mistake by approaching her while she was alone. Poor Staci, she must have felt scared. Must have thought that she was about to get murdered by a useless madman.

'Not really, Miss. I've been sent here by Dr Dean to give you company,' I said, trying to win her trust. She must have thought I was some kind of doctor. After all, I had studied the great subject of psychology myself. Hadn't I?

'How have you been, Staci?' I asked, dropping the 'Miss' subtly.

'Fine, I guess,' she replied, looking out of the window.

I don't remember how the rest of our conversation went. The mental faculty is incapable of registering such humongous and overwhelming amount of sensory input in one go. But by the time it had begun growing dark outside, she was all friendly.

Reeling from the shock of that encounter, If I'm to replay the conversation we had on our first meeting (accurate or inaccurate), it went something like this:

'And where do you live, Miss?' I had asked. I just could not let go of the 'Miss'. It must have felt unusual. But then what was not?

She said that before she could come here (after her admittance to some madhouse was assured) she had run away from her home in Los Angeles and had made a tent in the backyard of an unnamed locality. She said that she dwelled in litter and ate burgers from a burger joint which served stale fries. She said that there was a community church near her tent where she served every night. She said that she enjoyed her freedom for nobody knew her in that unnamed land.

By this time, I had taken a stool and was sitting right next to her. The girl I saw up close, through my ardent eyes, was not at all the Staci the world had grown to love. Up close, she was no longer the Staci of my dreams.

Not anymore, at least. Her face was uneven and freckled. Her hair, once wide, silky and hypnotizing, was now a tangled mess—like that of a homeless woman. Her eyes were filled with anger and sorrow. She looked utterly defeated by a war no one knew she was fighting.

'So what if she has gotten this miserable?' I recited to myself cheerfully.

I was surprised by the ease in my voice, especially since I had grown so accustomed to talking to her in my dreams that doing so in reality felt like second nature.

'Oh, that's a very sweet mockingbird you've drawn, miss,' I said.

'You really think so?' she replied, and the way she said that 'you' was the kind of solace I could only dream of finding on this planet. It wasn't some hollow, meaningless word—it was directed at me, by Ms Staci herself. The first time when my existence had been acknowledged by a star.

I think I was silent for a few moments, caught off guard. Then I said, 'Oh yes, miss. It looks terrific. I especially like the murky shades of green you've used to show the distant trees. Are you going to put it in a cage?'

'You think I should?' she asked.

'Oh yes, absolutely. A broken cage. Only, the poor bird has forgotten how to fly,' I responded.

For a moment, I feared she would get up and slap me for daring to offer advice on how to paint her own portrait. After all, she was a successful actress—the best in the industry. Who was I to say anything? But instead, she continued drawing in silence.

Zahed would always tell me to keep my mouth shut because I was vulnerable and capable of saying the most despicable, disastrous things to a person by merely being frank with them. You see how preposterous the situation was. If I would have said anything else and if she would have not replied, I knew for a fact that tomorrow I was not going to wake up in my familiar bed in Ward B. That the able psychiatrists would surely conclude that I had tried to molest Ms Staci upon catching her off guard, and boy! My life—and my hope—would have been crushed faster than an annoying housefly in a Indian household.

Sulking, I retreated to a distant corner of the room, sitting and pretending to read a book. 'Call me Ishmael…' Call me the biggest, most foolish bastard to ever walk this earth, born from pig excrement and the mind of an ideological fool.

The silence seemed endless. At that point of time, I would have gladly picked a fight with half the sleeping men in my ward, just to have them mob and kill me, had she not spoken to me right then.

But she didn't.

I was just about to get up and walk out when I felt a soft, tender tap on my shoulder—the light touch of a pretty woman. I turned around and saw Staci standing there, holding her painting with sincerity.

'Do you think this cage looks nice?' she asked.

'Make it golden, miss. Just like this enchanted evening.' Before she could return to her painting and draw the golden bars of a cage in which she had captured my heart and soul with just a tap on the shoulder, I added, 'I'm Mason Moron, miss.'

'Moron? Haha!' she laughed softly, and her face illuminated—so blessed, so gorgeous. Then she said, 'It's a really funny name. Is it your real name? Moron! Oh God!'

I chuckled. 'Yes, miss.'

'I'm Staci,' she said. 'Staci Silverstone.'

'Just like the great actress?'

'Absolutely,' she replied, breaking into laughter.

'What are you in here for?' she asked, more out of curiosity than judgement. I could tell she was trying to assess if I was dangerous, maybe preparing to leave if she thought I might do something unsettling.

'I lost my father, miss. I think the shock of it drove me into lunacy.'

Imagine the palpable rush of excitement coursing through my wasted life. After all the years of misery and after being stuck in a miserable marriage with someone as hopeless as Noel, here I was—standing before the woman of mankind's dreams, Ms Staci, having a conversation. Such moments of pure joy cannot be captured by even the greatest of writers under the greatest of passions and inspirations. Words can't capture the essence of such fantasies. A century of massacre, an unexpected freedom of a tortured nation, Jews escaping from a concentration camp with several thousand dollars and a ticket to a massive ship could only explain some part of my bewildering joy.

Staci left that evening without giving any hint about how she might take our 'romance' forward. I stood there, wondering if I would ever see her again. As I was exiting the reading room, Harrison Brown suddenly appeared in front of me.

'Oh, geez, Sir Mr Moron, where are we? This is the first time I'm seeing you here. What is this place?'

'This here is Clemency's,' I said. 'And that over there is Bombay,' I added, pointing to the cornfield. 'And that there,' I continued, pointing to Staci, who was rummaging for her slippers near a poisonous bush, 'is the new reason I have to live.'

'The heroin addict girl, sir? She makes you this happy?'

'She's not just any girl, Harris. She's the great Ms Staci.'

'Right now, sir,' Brown said, 'she's worse than the average girl. Look at her, scavenging through the garbage.'

'It doesn't matter, boy. It doesn't matter.'

But Brown couldn't understand why I was so enamoured with a woman picking through trash in front of us.

'Forget about it, boy. She's had a rough time. She had to stay in some roadside camp for a while. Old habits die hard. She probably doesn't even remember who she is.'

'Whatever, Moron sir. It's just the first time I've seen you this happy. So damn happy about some retired actress.'

'She's not retired, boy. She's just on a break.'

'Whatever you say, sir,' Harrison replied. After a pause, Harris said that he wanted to attach himself in my exploration for whatever I was seeking because I seemed 'truly alive after making my first contact with the supernatural'.

And since I was feeling mighty passionate, I told Harris 'I am in love, boy. It's a mighty conquest.'

'With what, sir?'

'With...the invisible.'

His childlike curiosity made me want to reveal my heart's deepest desires to him.

'You can tell me, sir,' Harrison urged.

'Absolute silence!' I said, widening my eyes and placing a finger over my lips.

'Yes, sir. Mum's the word.'

'Well...' As I shared my feelings with him, I felt exhilarated. Just speaking of it made me feel as though I had already won Staci's heart. 'Me and Staci—we're falling in love.'

'You mean that garbage-picking lady?'

'Yes, boy. Just now we met in the painting room. I think we're falling in love.'

The words, though completely fictional, felt magical. It was as though a celestial light of acceptance had descended upon me.

'You're delusional, sir. This morning, she came to our ward and spoke to several people, even the wheelchair-bound Mosheed. In fact, after her gone, Mosheed told me he's her chosen suitor. He said that she had in fact come to the ward in the first place just to sneak a glance at him. He said that the matter must not be disclosed.'

'What else did he say, boy?'

'Sir, he's narrating the story right now in the common room. You can hear it for yourself.'

In the common hall, Mosheed has flung his wheelchair into the air, pretending it was a mighty airplane about to take off. Somehow he has also pulled his pants down, and his weapon of destruction is erect. And he is shouting and narrating about his beautiful marriage to Ms Staci. He recalls how they were wedded in a white-marble church whereafter he was suffered to leave the real world and go to the asylum after a bout of madness had made his life worse. He said that he was mighty happy to have her visit him after a year of painful separation.

Seeing him, I felt so hopeless and defeated that I felt like pushing that bastard off his wheelchair only. But that would have alerted the ward boys. 'Patient shows extreme signs of hostility towards fellow patients' they would have written in my file. And thereafter I would have begun getting electrocuted over the weekends in the ECT chamber.

It also took me by surprise, if you want to know the truth. That while I had been searching for Staci on the grounds, she had visited our ward itself. What a horrible situation really. It was absurd. In hindsight, I realized it was probably Dr Dean who would have advised her to socialize with other patients while she was here, as a way to fight her depression. Perhaps that's why I hadn't spotted her in the beginning. She'd been in the Observation Room in Ward C, just as I had been in the Observation room of Ward B when I first arrived. Now, she had been moved to the Private Suite in Ward C, and Dr Dean likely encouraged her to make friends with the other patients to combat her feelings of hopelessness.

The situation was utterly preposterous. Not only had the nation's greatest actress made contact with me, but she was now going door-to-door in the asylum, befriending half of this lunatic asylum (I'm having to stop here because a roaring madman is approaching from behind, singing 'Happy Birthday' while carrying an uprooted plant. Happy birthday to you too, dear sir!).

That night, I stood at the window of our ward, gazing out over the vast expanse of Clemency's. Though I was trying to come to terms with my past—with Noel and my dead father—my thoughts were consumed by Staci. Imagine my amazement, realizing that this dream, once a cry into the abyss, had materialized into a living, breathing reality. Staci was no longer just a fantasy; she was a real person, sound asleep, though trapped in her own suffering.

From the next day, I began stalking Ms Staci in the asylum. Talking to her was out of the question, especially after realizing it would have meant nothing. She talked to every damned madman there, so it would have made no difference. Instead, I sought control over her life by watching her silently. I convinced myself that by tracing her every step, I could bring myself closer to winning her over. I tracked her movements, following her through the asylum.

During lunch, I would sit in the dining hall, waiting patiently for her. She would arrive in the late afternoon, and my heart would swell with emotion as she would enter, laughing and gossiping with the RBI banker and the heartbroken Abdul. Then, Dr Dean would arrive, shooing away the others to sit with her. Then, they would eat and talk, and afterward, he would lead her to his private chamber.

I knew when she bathed. I knew when she dined, when she visited the library. By obsessively tracking her every breath, I deluded myself into thinking I had some control over her life.

In the evenings, I would watch her play badminton with Abdul and the RBI banker. It was a quick, seven-point game. Abdul, oblivious to who he was playing with, would jump around, his robe flapping like a ninja as he took shots.

During dinner, she would sit with Dr Dean again. To my dismay, it wasn't him talking this time—it was Staci, endlessly babbling about her world to Dr Dean.

Most would have abandoned their chase after witnessing such disappointments. But I just couldn't help it. I would grow envious, I would get hurt, and lament because of her sluttish attitude towards our inmates. The way she would so easily talk to any and every madman in the asylum. Still, I clung to her life like a nasty parasite.

'You only tell me, Staci?' I asked in my mind. 'Why offer me a glimpse of heaven only to snatch away the ultimate solace?' My feelings toward her turned bitter. Was it possible to abduct this 76kg non motile statue of beauty, run across this expanse, escape and hide her away in my basement forever?

Evenings were spent wandering the lawns. I paced back and forth, passing the bougainvillaeas and menthol tea plants, aware that I was being watched by other inmates from the windows of Wards B and C. There is a lunatic who has done the miracles of planting these trees across the asylum. In fact, in some of the portions you would find beds of roses, daffodils, sunflowers, and even lilies overgrowing each other in a giant mess. Because apparently the problem with this lunatic was that he believed a goddess had commanded him to beautify the asylum to his best extent. He'd been here for two years. He is a nice decent chap, who is not extremely harmful to anyone. He just sits and plants trees all day. Sometimes he plants trees even at night. It's tragic that he never took a moment to enjoy the garden he created.

As I walked, I felt insignificant. Was I just another lunatic to Staci, as insignificant to her as we were to the invisible state that sponsored this asylum? What were my odds with her? Even if I played my best game, the most I could hope for was to be noticed, maybe even to become her friend. But would there be anything more humiliating than being just a friend to the nation's most prized beauty?

I had already killed myself. I can't go any lower. This is practically rock bottom. I couldn't fall any further.

Sometimes, when I worried about Staci, I would close my eyes and let the cool winter breeze of Clemency's touch my face. In those moments, I imagined a younger version of myself, my toddler self, back at my Cemetery House. I could see the long juniper and peepal trees, the raspberry bushes. I remembered how my father and I would take early morning walks through the plantation. I'd be so proud of myself for keeping pace with him on his daily ten thousand-step routine. The roads would be covered in crushed berries and vegetables, their scent mixing with the fresh air after the rain.

I'd close my eyes and picture myself standing in front of the gate of my Cemetery House, and suddenly, my panic would turn to sadness. The winds of home would sweep over my forehead, reminding me that I wasn't just chasing an unattainable beauty—I was an orphan. I had fallen into a loveless marriage, had had my heart broken, and now, the least the universe could do for me was bring Staci to me.

And then, one night, I decided to do something about it. It must have been midnight because everyone was fast asleep. I quietly slipped out of my bed and made my way to the Records Section of our Asylum. I figured, if they kept everyone's files, there must be one on Ms Staci too.

The Records Room was generally inaccessible to the inmates. But then again, it was only inaccessible to madmen. I was not a madman. I was only mad about Staci. I didn't know where they kept the keys to the room, but I had seen a window through which I could sneak inside. So, I walked down the corridor (empty, well-lit), took a sharp right from the descending staircase, and reached the Records Section. The front door was locked, but thankfully the window was half open. I climbed in, my eyes scanning the piles of dusty files—centuries of records on brilliant and unusual madmen.

A closer inspection led me to the dedicated section for Ward C. I searched for a while, but finding the file was as difficult as winning over Staci herself. I spent a good hour looking. It was unbearably hot inside, and my fear was mounting—I was on the verge of a coronary occlusion. I was terrified. Imagine being caught before I'd even had the chance to kiss Staci! After what felt like forever, I gave up and started walking towards the window. But just as I was about to leave, I saw her file lying on a work desk. Of course! She was a recent patient—why would they have filed it away yet? Dr Dean must have kept it on his table to get familiar with the case.

There it was. Ms Staci's file in plain sight. Her entire life, all her secrets, her maladies, her diagnoses, all stored in a thick file of about a hundred pages. I figured if I mastered that file, I could master her life.

But I couldn't just steal the file. Had I done that, the doctors would have been alerted, and Staci's entry to Ward B would likely have been restricted due to a suspected threat to her security. So, I used my wits. With the Xerox machine in the Records Room, I made a copy of her file. Slowly. Stealthily. Hoping the sound wouldn't escape the room. It didn't.

By the time morning arrived, I had Staci's life in my hands. I believe, at that moment, holding her past, I had entered a new world. Knowing her secrets, she could finally be mine in a way no one else could claim her.

A look into Staci's world

I didn't know it then, but nothing was going to be the same after this. Watch as the stealthy hands of a thief flip through the pages of her life—a silent entry into the sanctum of her mind.

Why hold back now? Let me let my imagination run wild and tell you everything there is to know about Staci. She had the body of an Olympic gymnast—extremely flexible and playful. My Staci was just as attractive as she looked—like the perfect girl from around the corner. In one of her movies I had watched a few years back, she wore a heavy Indian dress, making her appear older and more beautiful than her age. In another, she wore short skirts and ballerina slippers—delicate, delicate Staci. In this film, she played the role of a confused, lost, but know-it-all girl who had fallen hopelessly in love with a spy.

In another movie, she was a street-smart neighbourhood girl, set to marry the brother of an eligible working-class bachelor, only to realize that she was in love with the brother of the groom. Then, there was one movie where most of the nation thought they had lost her—her romantic ordeal with the star on screen was so powerful and beautifully tragic that we all believed she would marry him in real life.

But now, seeing her before me in this mental hospital of lost souls, I realized that during all those roles, she had never truly been herself.

To understand her puzzling stay at our humble sanatorium, you must follow me, not from the psychiatrist's chamber but from the very beginning of Staci's life.

Staci was born to Ms Staci Senior, an actress herself, and Ismail Jaffaria, a renowned screenwriter and producer in the city of Bombay. They lived in a grand white marble mansion on Bandstand. Staci Senior was of British descent, while Jaffaria was a Kashmiri who had struggled immensely before finally making a name big enough to win over Staci Senior. This was back in 1983—a time when my father hadn't graduated yet, and I was far from being born.

The mansion where Staci grew up was called 'Jaan', meaning 'Life'. It was a giant, multi-storeyed mansion overlooking the Arabian Sea. She had a healthy, loving childhood, surrounded by film stars as aunts and music composers as uncles. The house was always lively with card nights and jazz dance parties on the sea-facing terrace. A steady stream of elite, gold-studded friends and families arrived in expensive limousines for evening gatherings. The elders danced and laughed, sipping lively mimosas while listening to melancholy Sufi music on vinyl.

But it wasn't what happened in the light that bothered her—it was what happened after the guests left and the mansion doors were locked.

This is something nobody knows. At four years old, my Staci walked in one day on her beaut of a mother, the delectable Miss—Staci Senior—being beaten by her husband. This incident followed after Staci the Senior made the tabloids for irresponsibly getting into a car and cosying up with her new lover boy, Sultan, who was fifteen years younger than her and had a reputation for being a hell of a playboy. He was a saintly good-looking man, this Sultan, who had at least slept with seven of his co-stars and daisy-fresh of actresses.

At first, the idea of starring in a film with the infamous playboy seemed like a ridiculous farce to everyone in the mansion. But Staci Senior was seeking a rebirth in the studios, wanting to reinvent herself as a young actress. So, eventually, she took the role.

On the first day of the shoot, Sultan arrived on set in his new red Cadillac, dressed in a black shirt and pants, looking more like a feared gangster than a suave, immature lover. Staci Senior was captivated. However, this 'lover boy' was a lover only on screen. Behind the scenes, he was an A class gangster and opium trader—Sultan Bhai—who roamed the city with fifteen to twenty gunmen. The duality of his persona—the smooth lover and the dangerous criminal—was enough to sweep the ageing actress off her feet.

Eventually, when Sultan made advances towards Mrs Staci, she rejected him with a sharp 'I'm a mother, you son of a bitch.' But soon, she introduced him to her husband, Jaffaria, and the two men formed an unlikely friendship. Sultan and Jaffaria's bond grew to the point where one was essentially lending his wife to the other for the supposed 'greater good of cinema'.

They began hosting regular cocktail parties at the villa's piazza, with evening tea and card games by the fountains. The couple thrived in the limelight once again. Staci Senior was content, believing her career was on the verge of a new chapter. Her husband was equally satisfied, still the leader of their peculiar new circle. On the surface, everything was 'tip-top class', as the Mumbaikars would say.

But it was the lure of morphine—administered in hidden alleys and dimly lit rooms—that finally led Staci Senior into Sultan's bed. Naked, vulnerable, and trapped in addiction, she gave in.

Cue in the sight of Sultan Bhai suggesting to Mrs Staci that she take a hit of heroin whenever she would be worried about her wrinkling skin or her nearing downfall. But because she had already kind of accepted Sultan Bhai to her household, she let him play his desires on her eventually. So now the dealer himself injected Mrs Staci the Senior with a shot of the cursed morphine. She gasping and moaning with pleasure, he bodyguarding her decency and not to mention, the opium injection necessitated her to remove parts of her delightful blouse (so that the injection spots could remain hidden from the frenzy of the media and reporters), and one day he couldn't stop himself from kissing her on the bare back of her body. She giggled in confusion and later in the opium ridden pleasure, kissed him back.

Three days later, they were practically lovers. Sultan Bhai would now administer her opium right down in between her belly button and her pelvis. And she would ask him to eat her out. There was a point when she confessed to him that she had never let her husband eat her vagina. That was the day when they rushed into the car, and Mrs Staci the Senior was found fixing her blouse in the car while Sultan Bhai drove her off to her villa.

Cut to the final shot: It is the night when their clandestine pictures have finally found their way to the tabloids. Ms Staci walks in on her mother getting thrashed like a street dog by the hands of her father as the chandelier of the living room glistens and reflects light of sorrow; Ms Staci, the teen daughter who was at the age of catfishing boys into her love den, was consumed by fear and dreaded loneliness. She thought she was going to be an orphan. That nobody would love her. And then one day, when husband and wife were nearing divorce, when finally Mrs Staci had announced that she was going to marry Mr Sultan Bhai aka the lover boy, Sultan bhai had found his soon-to-be-young-daughter Ms Staci in her bedroom, sitting idly in the bed lamenting and playing with her Marilyn doll. Sultan bhai smiled at her as if he had already accepted her as his daughter. He treaded towards her cautiously in the dullness of the light, lifting her in his arms, smiling at her with his friendly smile. She smiled back, and then he kissed her on her lips. Only funnily the kiss lasted a little too long. He started inspecting the entrails of her mouth with his tongue. He even paused in between, cooed out 'Allah you look like your mother's purer younger version' and then began kissing her again. Biting her lips with his masculine power. He manoeuvred into her dress. Placed an arm inside her frock and felt her heartbeat. Mrs Staci, who was supposed to be passed out in her vile sleep with the aid of two opium shots, was sadly wide awake. She appeared at the door of her daughter's room as the soon-to-be-father molested his soon-to-be-daughter in the rancidity of the night. But the opium haze was too strong. Unable to comprehend most of it, she passed out at the door itself while Sultan Bhai smiled at his soon-to-be-daughter, now totally alone with her and with nobody to interrupt him.

I like washing my face sometimes early in the morning. If someone was to ask me to mention the best thing about this state-sponsored mental asylum, I would tell them it's the cold, frigid water they supply early in the morning. At one point of time, not very long ago they used to treat insanity with cold freezing water. They used to strip a person naked and blast them with jets of ice-cold water. Sometimes, they'd tie the madman to a rotating chair and shove his head into cold or hot water until he ran out of breath and swore never to act insane again—until a wild, crippled lunatic would swear to be docile and loyal to his master therapist. Today it only runs in the pipelines of Clemency's.

I had in fact spotted the old water treatment facility at two distinct times. Now the concrete drainage is overgrown with mosses and plants. Before they used to cage the lunatics in grilled, see-through rooms. The heavy metal doors of which could only be unlocked from the outside, requiring someone to reach through a hole in the wall, locate the latch, and unlock it. There were also these things you would call the group cages. These was meant for men who were caged together in just one big cage instead of a single room. These set ups were built outside in the lawn or the common areas, and there were barbed wires fixed around them to prevent inmates from climbing over the top like chimpanzees and jumping to their deaths. Now, it was all just a grim piece of history.

The cold water, however, had a calming effect on my wretched soul. The only days I truly suffered were the ones when I couldn't see Staci, either because she was tied up in her therapy session or sometimes when she simply chose not to come out of her room. On those occasions, I missed her as much as the other patients did. Time passed in a dull haze, with no sun, only clouds welcoming peacocks and distant migratory birds to our madhouse. When Ms Staci didn't show up on such days, it was unbearable. Otherwise, just catching a glimpse of her beauty lifted half my ailments, and I ended up feeling ambitious—despite her current condition, she was, after all, Ms Staci.

One afternoon, after lunch, I spotted her walking alone toward Dr Dean's office. Normally, I would have just observed her from a distance, but this time, I rushed over. She greeted me first.

'Hey, you,' she said.

I froze, then suddenly some surge of energy shot through me. 'Hey.'

She was wearing a plain black skirt, a white shirt, and a pink sweater over it, looking more like a fresh college student on her way to submit an assignment instead of a madwoman going to see her doctor inside a lunatic asylum. She had her therapy reports and files clutched close to her chest.

'Why didn't you come for lunch today?' I asked, immediately regretting it. I feared I had just crossed that thin line between normalcy and insanity. Why did I say that? Now she'd know I'd been waiting for her. I hadn't spoken to her all week, but I had been waiting for her. *Way to go. What the actual fuck*!

'I had my therapy,' she responded, laughing apologetically. 'But I'll see you at dinner,' she added politely before walking away.

I was left wondering if she really would join me for dinner or if she now thought I was a dangerous madman—so dangerous, in fact, that she'd confide in Dr Dean about my threatening behaviour, who would then order three ward boys to beat the life out of me, cage me, and torture me until I stopped making advances toward her.

When she did show up for dinner, I waved at her from afar, and she came and sat directly across from me. This time, I felt terribly sad, hoping my sadness might make me appear more serious, more mysterious—not some empty fool. Through the flickering lights overhead, I saw her wide, beautiful eyes as she nestled into her arms, resting her head against the cold, industrial metal of our dining table. She stared at me endlessly, nudging her head like a bored puppy. I swear, she was an incredibly beautiful woman with ample curves.

'Were you waiting for me, Mr Moron?' she asked, comfortably seated across from me.

'Very much, madam,' I replied. 'It's been a long day.'

'Oh, what did you do all day?' she asked.

I wanted to say, 'I spent all day cursing myself for falling in love with you. I'm just an idle man hopelessly in love with you, miss.' Instead, I told her I had been missing my late father.

'I detest my father,' she said, catching me off guard. I knew exactly why she hated him.

'Why is that?' I asked, feigning ignorance. Dear Staci, I know he molested you. I know he did terrible things that made you sick to your core. But who am I to know these things?

'Do you like the food here?' I asked, quickly changing the subject, hoping I hadn't already crossed the line.

'It's okay. There was a time in my life when all I ate was raw fish and vegetables—salmon, sushi, broccoli, beans. That was pretty much it. So, compared to that, this is a treat,' she said, breaking into a light-hearted laugh. I laughed along with her.

From about five metres away, I could see the soft opening and closing of her cleavage as she laughed like a carefree child. I saw her glistening white teeth, the cuts on her wrists, the sleeplessness in her eyes.

'This is the love of my life,' I thought to myself. I wanted to hold her hand. I even placed my hand on the table. How wrong could it go? After all, she was just a girl. She noticed and told me I had nice, long nails, almost touching them with her own fingers.

'You could stab a nun with those, Mr Moron,' she laughed even harder. I saw the roughness of her cuticles—bitten down from anxiety or uncertainty. When she noticed me observing the imperfections of her hands, she stopped laughing, withdrew her hands, and began eating in silence.

'What did you do all day?' I asked her.

'Oh, so much work. Therapy, then group therapy, art therapy. Why did I ever take that stupid shot of opium?' she laughed again.

'Are you enjoying the therapy? Are they any good?' I asked, slipping into my educator role, having been a professor of psychology myself.

'Oh, yeah. It's like school homework—simpler, and you can be sure of the outcome. Anyway, I'm leaving tomorrow. I think I'll really miss this place.'

'Where are you going?' I asked, stunned.

'We start shooting again tomorrow, for a month or so. I don't know if I'll be able to continue treatment here.'

That night, it rained so heavily that the flood alarms blared around 1 a.m. I wondered if Staci would be busy packing her luggage and if by the time I woke up, she'd probably be gone.

As the alarms buzzed, alerting the guards to monitor the electrical fences (now disabled), a commotion erupted in the hallway.

'Code Purple' echoed over the central announcement system. 'Code Purple at Ward C.'

That was Staci's ward. Code Purple occurred when a patient tried to harm a doctor, one of the nurses, or themselves. The nurses' station had these neon stickers listing the different codes and their meanings. Code Red meant fire, Code Blue meant someone was dying, Code Pink meant a child had been abducted, and Code Purple meat a patient had harmed themselves or those around them.

It turned out that Staci, deprived of opium, had felt so helpless that she had gone too far. She was accustomed to making small cuts on her hands—a habit, as the body releases natural morphine when in pain—but this time, she made a much deeper cut on her wrist, nearly fatal. I could only imagine her lying there, a broken wreck, surrounded by her own blood. Enough blood to make a new nurse shriek, pinch her ears in horror, and possibly faint right on the spot. When the blood flowed outside the door, it must have alarmed the other nurses, who rushed in to find Staci barely clinging to life.

She did survive.

The next morning, Clemency's was in turmoil. Nurses rushed hurriedly from one room to another. Before breakfast, the entire staff had disappeared for a tense meeting in Dr Dean's office. A few outsiders had arrived, and their cars were parked opposite the front porch, visible from my window. Just after breakfast, a police van pulled up, and a sharp-looking officer came to collect documents from Dr Dean. By lunchtime, the meeting had been dissolved, and the nurses returned to their stations, eyes dried from tears but still carrying the weight of uncertainty about what lay ahead.

The reason I'm telling you all this, dear reader, is to let you know—sadly—that I was certain that even if I resolutely decided to see Staci, it would have been simply impossible. It was impossible because I knew she would not be leaving her ward for at least the next few weeks. Even if her stay at Clemency's was extended indefinitely, she was as deeply hidden and protected as one could be in those huge premises. Though she was right near me, she was unattainable—highly guarded, a valued secret beyond the reach of patients like us, even in our wildest fantasies.

That evening, despite the constant rain and the winds shaking and bending the trees outside, I sat and stared at the silent corridors. Nurses patrolled Ward B, administering medicine and making rounds while Dr Dean remained in his meeting.

Cautiously, I slipped out my long-dreaded secret—Ms Staci's file—from the bottom of my shoebox. I sometimes worried whether I should alter the forms, rearrange her file, her life's records, so that if someone happened to find that folder in my shoebox, they wouldn't be able to figure out it was hers.

On the tenth page, I saw that she had scored brilliantly on her TAT (Thematic Apperception Test) and RAT (Random Association Test), revealing her to be a creative genius, something I'm sure half the planet is already aware of. On the eleventh page of the TAT, she described two converging black leaf-like shadows as 'a demon about to zoom from the sky and snatch someone's life away'.

Then there was an entry: 'Patient shows high levels of creativity in Random Association, though the State Anxiety Inventory reveals inconsistencies in her belief patterns regarding her creativity and creative pursuits.'

Ha! A classic case—a fearful, anxious beauty slaughtered by the hands of a hundred men before the movie of her life ends.

The truth is that Staci's anxiety began the day she returned to India after pausing her studies in London. This was fourteen years after the night she was violated by her stepfather, Sultan Bhai. After that horrific incident, her mother sent her to London to stay with her aunt while she stayed and married Sultan Bhai (The poor woman had nowhere else to go.).

Staci grew up in London, separated from her mother, who still lived with that evil stepfather, too addicted to him—like morphine—to leave. Fourteen years later, dreamy-eyed, she landed at Chatrapati Shivaji Terminal on the British Airways 445 flight and found herself being driven to the very mansion she called the 'House of Darkness'.

A heavy sea of sadness swelled under her heart as she viewed Mumbai with travelled eyes. The slums were being replaced by multi-storied apartments, yet these new towers were still inhabited by the same slum dwellers. The once-hidden homes now toppled over one another.

The car garages of Sultan Bhai and Joe D'Costa (an A class gangster in Bombay), filled with fifteen hundred stolen cars, parts mismatched and sold, still thrived. D'Costa's garage had a record speed of turning a stolen car into a different model in just fifteen minutes. Staci could sense the vile energy of Mumbai—the crores of rupees flowing through its gutters, as reported on the front pages, and the dirty underworld money being funnelled into film production houses. Her mother, once a beautiful actress, was now being thrown around from house to house, because she was a decrepit heroin addict, no longer a heroine, but a has-been who was now consumed by the drug that she used to consume long ago.

Staci left the house as soon as she entered. Sultan Bhai, her stepfather, was still lounging in the front veranda, smoking and playing charades with the other vile bhais of the city. Her father had remarried an actress as young as Staci herself and was now the country's most dreaded pervert. As for her mother, whom she still cared for—she was nowhere to be seen. Staci rented her own apartment near Bandstand, where the ocean waves constantly washed the city's dirt ashore. She moved in and started reconnecting with people she thought she had left behind.

Before Staci became the woman we know today—half human, half universe—traversing the globe in leather tights and oversized Italian hoodies, swooning photographers with her walk and smile, before she made headlines leaving random airports in Barcelona and was mobbed by the media and fans, before she learnt to smile at the camera and listen to the trendy Punjabi music dominating Bollywood, before she danced like an angel and ate cake with a spoon, glinting at the camera—my Staci was a semi-shy, semi-extroverted girl. A beauty, dwelling in the loneliness and wreckage of her seaside apartment at Bandstand. Though film money had placed her in a dream home, she found her new house being haunted by a different disease: loneliness.

She reconnected with filmmakers from her childhood days. Her fondest memories were from that time—when Jaffaria was her real father, and their house was filled with Mercedes limousines and Cadillacs. Film magnates crowding the villa in the evenings. The game of teen patti and blackjack over evening teas. The talks of work intermixing with those of scandals. On some evenings, her house had become the spot for some massive Bollywood scandal, with actors and actresses meeting and falling in love. There would be evening soirees in which, black-suited servants served orange mimosas and local bhel in silver cutlery, while a pianist would sit and play a grand sea-facing piano. In those days, her uncles and aunties danced in romance.

But after the morphine curse crippled her family, friends drifted away. Staci's family became a faint, delightful memory to everyone. Bollywood is a fast mess. People learn about new budding people fast and then unlearn about them even faster. So when after ages, a phone call was made by the young puerile Staci, whose voice has now gotten coarse and 'only meant business' they recalled her as this sweet young girl, showed love towards her, invited her for tea and disconnected the call cordially offering their condolences for whatever hell the opium had brought on her family.

'You are born to be a star. And so we are only poor talentless filmmakers whose job is to turn you into your real form.'

'Of course, you are like our own daughter. Come to our studio tomorrow first thing in the morning,' her first film director, Subhas Shah, told her in the living room as his own toddler was loitering on the floor, bumping her head on random corners and nibbling on her daddy's screenwriting pen.

The next morning, sweet Staci arrived at the Ramouji Film Studio in the midsummer heat. It turned out that half the people who had signed her were themselves becoming redundant in the cinema line. She received scripts of Bombay's cheap melodramatic gang wars. She was offered item songs and ad campaigns for local toothpaste brands, but she did them all.

'If I have to thrive, I must put my everything in every role. No matter small or big,' Staci told Mrs Shah with firm passion, who was now concerned because if this movie failed, she herself would have to leave her plush penthouse and move to a cheaper accommodation.

A few days later, while she was sitting in a silver fake diamond-studded bikini, still getting her make up fixed, a co-star had told her, 'All it takes to sit in people's heart is that one role. That one shot. That one glimpse of the genius, and then you will rule forever.'

And in the anticipation of that one role, she started taking numerous projects and chased unknown upcoming directors and filmmakers from studio to studio.

And now, I moved to a part of her file that made me feel foolish for ever thinking I could have endeared myself to Staci in the first place. We came to the case of her current boyfriend and lover: Zafar.

If fear had a name, it was this peculiar lover of her's from her past—Zafar. Though they had separated early on, Staci had remained incredibly close to him, even after their year-long break-up. Recently, just two weeks before her arrival at our humble madhouse, she had been corresponding with him again, her emotions mixed. This was mentioned in her reports as well, so it must have held significance for it to end up in this file. Even the media had caught wind of their recent encounter at an award show in Cannes. There's a photo of them crossing paths randomly at the event.

On that breezy evening at the Cannes Award Show, they collided, exchanged pleasantries, and before they knew it, some nosy media person snapped a picture of them whispering to each other. That very photo was in the file. It must have unsettled Staci deeply for it to be included in her medical records. In the picture, Zafar was dressed in a matte black three-piece tuxedo while my Staci wore a black, backless gown.

Then there was another photo, taken the next day by the paparazzi, showing them hand in hand on some random beach at the French Riviera. Staci was in a white two-piece bikini, while Zafar wore black surfing shorts. They were walking, hand in hand, with Zafar glancing at Staci's backside as she headed toward the warm sands after a dip in the ocean. The headlines read: 'Staci and her long-term beau back together?'

Staci and Zafar had met when they were just young, aspiring actors—when Staci had recently moved from

London to Bombay, and her newfound success was beginning to make waves. Back then, she would drive around in her limo with her chauffeur and her manager to the Rama Arts and Film Studio, where she was co-starring in a political drama, *Hindustaan*, set in the northern part of India. Her co-star was the son of a prominent film mogul, Salim Senior, the producer of *Hindustaan*—Zafar. Zafar starred opposite Staci, and with his cocky charm and honey-hued complexion, he was the upcoming heartthrob of Bollywood. Staci, the emerging angel of the industry, was his perfect match, and the two were dramatically and madly in love, both on- and off-screen.

By the time filming wrapped and the movie became a success, they had moved to the United States. Staci and her Zafar were living together in a sprawling, floor-to-ceiling glass apartment in Manhattan, apparently taking a course together at the New York Film Academy. Cue in the picture of the two starlets of our giant industry copulating in a foreign land. Where they didn't have to worry in the night for what the next day was going to bring. They had infinite time and an insatiable hunger for each other—a passion so intense that you'd never want it to end, feeding it with every breath. Picture the New York skyline as these two beautiful lovers fuck the living life out of each other with wild abandon, while, in some distant and irrelevant land, I was busy trying to get Noel to behave.

At this precise moment, I was feeling utterly clueless and dumbfounded for I had failed to realize that probably she still belonged to Zafar. Just like Noel belonged to her Herman. What the fuck was I doing here? Reading the past of somebody else's girlfriend?

I was still not aware if this Zafar did ever show up to meet her at Clemency's or if he had simply left her here alone like some cold, decaying meat. If he had ever come here, she would have mentioned something about it in her records.

Anyway, her file was now thicker by merely three pages which was followed by a note on the fourth page in Dr Dean's spaced-out handwriting: *The patient is being more silent than usual. Her replies are getting concise. Patient seems disinterested in communicating. Meal intake has reduced. Patient is probably contemplating suicide.* There was also an attached prescription—apparently her dosage now included an additional dosage of methadone (a substitute for morphine, administered during the early phases of rehab) and another seven days of complete bed rest.

Looking at her life up until now, I could only imagine Staci dying slowly inside, filled with regret. Here, in the madhouse, she was loved because people were paid to love her. Out in the world, she was loved more fiercely, with craziness and passion, and she knew that she earned that love.

Now that she had lost that legitimate real-world love and she had chosen this lame love which our madhouse has to offer, she must be detesting herself. *How do I tell you, Staci, that if there is some real love in this world, it is right here in my swelling, aching heart?*

By the fifth day of her absence, when the maddening spell she had cast over me finally wore off, I realized with frustration that I couldn't clearly remember Staci's face anymore. This had been a recurring problem since childhood. Whether it was Tania, Noel, or any other girl I had been obsessed with, I just couldn't recall their faces when they weren't with me. Maybe my anxiety blurred my memory when it came to women—or attachment in general. Who knows? In any case, it was a painful discovery. In her absence, when I desperately wanted to paint her face behind my closed eyes, I simply couldn't summon the image of the woman I claimed to love.

This left me no choice but to make another trip to Ward C. An expedition I was undertaking with the purpose of simply seeing her and memorizing her face to burn its features into the canvas of my mind. Also, after everything I had been through, I was growing less cautious, less terrified of making advances towards Staci. Hell, I had nothing to lose anymore. What was the harm in breaking through the silly boundaries they had erected between Ward B and Ward C? Also, it's not really apt to presume that I would have landed in trouble if I were caught entering Ward C. It could have been an accident as well. I figured clumsy men like Harrison Brown must lose their way all the time and end up near Ward C's entrance. How was I any different?

So, I did what I never thought I'd have the courage to do—I crossed the boundary from Ward B to Ward C in broad daylight. As I walked, excitement mixed with dread, I passed through a hidden alley, steeped in silence, and soon found myself standing before her room. But sadly, my Staci wasn't there. Her bed was neatly made, the brown blanket that covered her soft form folded carefully at the bottom. Fresh cellophane-wrapped flowers sat on the table, but her bed was empty. A wave of fear washed over me—had she left for good? Just disappeared like the wind?

Then, after hearing a small commotion, I glanced toward the front lawn. There she was, sitting at a table, drinking coffee with a smart, slender man. They seemed to be admiring a distant pond—and each other. She leaned in to say something, and he kissed her on the cheek. She then moved to sit on his lap, and in that moment, I realized that Zafar had never really left the picture.

This wild discovery—this cruel humiliation—was a revelation. A direct insult to my small, loving heart. I resolved at once to turn back, retreat to my chamber, and declare myself mad and dead. Maybe then they would make me disappear. But before I could begin this march of self-destruction, Dr Dean appeared right behind me.

'Young Moron, have you been looking for me?' he asked.

'No. Not exactly, sir,' I replied. At that point, I wanted to get caught. To hell with it. 'I wasn't looking for you. I was looking for Ms Staci.'

'Ah, I see,' he said, his eyes not even widening in surprise. Instead, they became a little numb, a little quiet. 'Go on then. You're her only friend in this place. Go and greet her,' he added, nodding toward the pitiful scene of Staci and her lover wrapped up in each other.

I walked away in shame and despair, realizing that I had an awful habit of stepping into love stories that were never mine to begin with. It was a track record. Time and again, I had walked in between two lovers, interrupting their relationship. And not just that—I'd even managed to win over the woman in question. I'd been with her, enjoyed the affections that had once belonged to someone else. I'd even ended up marrying one of them. But once their old love was rekindled, I was discarded—trampled and forgotten—so brutally that it took a fake death or feigned madness just to heal myself. That's what happened with Noel and Herman. Hell, that's what happened with Tania and her Sarge. And now here I was again, a stupid fool about to interrupt another connection—this time between my lovely Staci and her Zafar.

For two solid minutes, I stood dumbfounded, watching them nestle into each other's arms. I was glad that I could now clearly remember Staci's face. It was much younger and slender than I had imagined. I felt relieved, thinking I could carry this image of her in my mind for longer. But then, I felt the sting of foolishness, knowing it would be pointless to ache and reminisce over that face anymore. And just as I was drowning in those thoughts, they both looked at me—at once.

'Moron,' Staci squealed, still holding Zafar in her arms. 'How have you been?' My dear reader, my presence didn't bring any difference to their romantic act. She seemed at ease.

Her soft Bollywood crazying legs climbing all the way to Zafar's shoulder. Those legs belonged to him. And her robe, which was quite loose at the top, permitted me to see a fair amount of her cleavage—far more than the whole wide world had seen. But those breasts, which I so madly wanted to see, belonged to him. But I felt fortunate that I had seen Staci's cleavage. I felt like I had smartly broken a definitive law of the universe. No one was allowed to see that much cleavage of Ms Staci. It was only upon our civilization to imagine them and masturbate to them, but I had seen them.

'This is Zafar,' she said.

The automatic response that comes when one encounters a celebrity—whether they are your nemesis or the object of your envy—slipped out: 'Oh my God! I'm a huge fan, sir.'

What the hell? I wasn't a fan of Zafar.

'Moron here is making a solid recovery in this institution,' Staci remarked, not addressing anyone in particular.

'Oh!' Zafar glanced at me with pity. 'That's quite wonderful. How are you holding up, boy? You seem alright—what's the issue?'

Even Staci looked at me with curiosity, realizing that she didn't actually know why I was in this madhouse—an unusual place for someone who seemed as sane as I did.

'You see, sir,' I began, 'the doctors tell me I've had it rough since my father died. They say I'm manically depressed, and I don't remember much of my life before his death.'

'It's something they call amnesia,' Staci chimed in, sinking more tenderly into Zafar's arms.

'Hell, even I don't remember much from my younger days,' Zafar added with a laugh. 'Does that qualify me to stay here too? Wouldn't that be terrific, baby girl? We could stay together all the time.'

'Do you think it'd be cool if Zafar stayed here with us, Moron?' Staci asked, but before I could answer, she kissed him on the neck.

I wanted to stab that man right then and there. Harrison Brown would've had the time of his life ripping his guts out or maybe stabbing him with a cake knife the way he did his own mother. Insane men can't be imprisoned, after all.

Later, when it was dark and nearing dinnertime, Staci's secretary, a slender woman with a high ponytail and a sizeable rack—Jeremiah—came to pick Zafar up. Apparently, he had an early flight to New York, and Jeremiah was flying with him. Staci grunted in irritation when she realized he had been going around with her secretary without even bothering to consult her. I saw a flicker of regret cross her face. She must have thought, *why did I kiss him and cling to him so shamelessly today?* This, of course, would have led to an even bigger, more philosophical question: *Why did I ever cling to heroin even after it had killed my saintly mother?*

Why do we people cling to things which we know are bad for us? This is something I find inspiring about men like Zafar They always know how to confuse a sweet, charming woman like Staci. Even if she had just cut open her own arm three days ago. If Staci could do that, she could certainly endure the sight of Zafar and Jeremiah exchanging glances and their half-hearted goodbyes in some fancy lobby of some hotel in Manhattan.

But right before they left, something funny happened. Zafar rolled down the window of his S-Class, called me over while Staci stood there, half angry and half confused. 'Take good care of her, young Moron. And yourself too,' he said. He expressed sympathy for my loss and said I must complete my journey toward redemption with 'his Staci'.

I agreed completely. The journey of healing would undoubtedly be better if Staci and I undertook it together. In fact, we should begin our process of healing immediately, starting from this poignant moment.

Years in ailing had conditioned me to a point where I could wait and wait and wait for days in a row before making a move on someone I loved. But now, with Zafar having casually delegated the responsibility of taking care of Staci to me—even if he said it only to sound polite or as a throwaway line in his goodbye—the very act of delegation gave me an unexpected surge of strength. I was learning to be more willing, unashamed, and bold in my advances.

Still, I had no intention of making my feelings clear to her, not because it might scare her into retreating further into isolation but because if I confessed my love for her in broad daylight, she would simply put me in my place. I'd be no different from the countless other men who had lost themselves within Clemency's walls or, worse, from the scores who had gone to insane lengths trying to woo Ms Staci.

There had been thousands of attempts to win Staci's favour. Some men sent her threatening letters while others lavished her with outrageously expensive gifts. Gifts so extravagant that they would cost a regular man his home and his wife just to afford such delectable presents. Paintings by renowned French artists, leather-bound first editions of Dickens (this happened right before the release of her movie which was based on a Dickens novel), gold-plated cars, Persian cats—she had seen it all. Many of these gifts arrived without even an explanation or an attached note detailing what the sender hoped to achieve by offering such an opulent present. Some came from a mysterious man living in

Monaco who promised to reveal himself when he felt that she was in the 'right frame of mind' to marry him. Others were simply wishing her the best for her next film.

And then there were the stalkers. Mild to severe, these fans followed her every move, obsessively tracking her through her fan pages. This particular lot knew everything about Staci—her brother's carpentry business in the UK, her sisters, even the school her sister's children attended. Yet most of these stalkers were so destitute they could hardly afford an internet connection, so acting on their research was a distant dream.

I was both fearful and excited at the thought that one day, one of these stalkers or paparazzi might show up at Clemency's and catch me sitting close to her. I imagined the scene: Staci hugging me or resting her head on my shoulder, when, at that very moment, a faint-hearted stalker—a boy or girl deprived of any real connection, obsessed with the world's most sensational actress—would show up. Most of these stalkers weren't dangerous, testosterone-fuelled criminals, but average-looking individuals, heartbroken and disillusioned. What would they think if they saw how comfortable Staci was with me?

In that moment, I envisioned myself being worshipped by them, a sort of strange reverence. I couldn't help but wonder what my widow Noel would think if she saw me like that here at Clemency's with Staci. Would she react like a wife catching her husband in the arms of another woman? But that thought seemed ridiculous—Noel was insignificant, a bitch, and the idea of even putting her in the same picture with me and Staci felt like a disgusting, spit-worthy notion.

The evening brought about a miracle that is still hard for me to express in mere words. All I can say is that on that particular evening, I realized I was born for greatness. I was suffering because I was a lonely star in this infinite nebulous sky. Otherwise, why else, as I lay on my cot, stomach pressed against it (eagerly anticipating my next meeting with Staci), would she have appeared on my doorstep herself? She had come in person, crossing the boundaries of Ward C, entering Ward B, and—so I like to imagine—under the wild, confused stares of all the nurses, stood near my cot. She wore a cute little black dress, looking as damned beautiful as ever.

My heart fluttered in surprise. I remembered countless moments with Noel when she had the ability to induce a similar mild heart attack in me—whether she was taking off her bra in front of me or holding my hand in the evening market. But here I was—truly confused. Was I so captivated by Staci because she was the eternal Ms Staci, or was it because I was in love with her? Or both?

'Hello, miss,' I said. 'Please sit. Why trouble yourself standing at a distance?'

'Hey,' she said faintly, stepping two feet closer. 'What a huge ward. How do you manage to stay in here all day? You don't even have a damned smartphone with you, do you?' She was full of questions.

'I believe my own mind is enough to keep me entertained for a while.'

'Ah. So you sit and think deep, dreadful thoughts, Moron?'

'Not really, miss.'

'What do you think about all day, then?'

Hell! All I think about is you, Staci. What else?

'Should I bring you something, miss? Some snacks? A strong coffee?' I asked, not wanting to fail as a delightful host.

'Nothing,' she said. 'I still have to stick to my diet, even in here.' When I looked at her, she reminded me of her dead mother—beautiful, but tired and weak. I couldn't understand why she'd be on any diet. That wasn't the face you could sell in cinemas anymore—not the face she had today.

'I wish I could be on the same diet as you, miss. I'd look all perfect and glowing,' I said, making her laugh. She loosened up and said, 'Let's go to the group therapy session. I don't feel like talking to a lot of people, but the last thing I want on this planet is to walk there by myself.'

'Certainly, miss,' I replied.

When we entered the group therapy room, I was rather delighted to see my old friend, my master, Bahubali, after a solid month of absence. It was an emotional moment for me. Normally, Bahubali would've stood up, shouting and screeching in surprise upon seeing his 'dead' sidekick walk into the blessed hall with the most dazzling woman a man could ever lay eyes on.

But he didn't even flinch.

This saddened me.

I whispered intimately into Ms Staci's ear that Bahubali was being treated for trafficking three girls from Nepal and for being criminally obscene and insane. She listened with half-hearted attention before walking off, leaving me behind.

Though it didn't matter at the moment. I was more astounded by how things had gone with Bahubali. I wanted to know if he even recognized me anymore or if he simply didn't have the energy to acknowledge me, even if he did. I looked at his three-quarter bullet-cut head and imagined it being electrocuted and fried so severely that now, after numerous electro-convulsive shock therapies, he sat there—dumbfounded.

I then stood next to Staci, who, I'll proudly admit, even shifted a little to make room for me. In that particular hall, at that particular time, I knew I was the centre of the world. I was born for greatness. And despite being a dead man—despite the disrespect I had endured from my wife not long ago—I was making things happen.

In the night, I was again plagued by my rampant sweaty dreadful dream where I was visualizing my Staci as a handicapped dwarf who is dying every five minutes with my dying breath. In my wakefulness, I realized that the reality was harsher than the dreams because in my dreams she was still surviving, and I knew that this funny looking angry dwarf was not exactly my Staci. When I was awake, I knew for a fact that Staci was nearing death. You see, all my encounters with her until now had happened when she had wanted then to happen. Or at least when she had been outside her room. If her roaming and loitering around the corridor of Ward B was true, then even the fact that she had tried cutting her hand only a week ago was also true. If her being able to eat her tasteless meal with the other madmen was true, then her deadly green vomits (her stomach emptying itself every five hours) was also true. If her being capable of standing and smiling next to me was true, then even the fact that when she was not with me, she was getting mad cold chills and vomiting green vomits and sweating excessively, was also true. Afterall that is what morphine does to your body. It's a treat when you are on it. But not so much when you get off. Morphine is said to be the strongest of drugs in the world. At least a sub-category of morphine including fentanyl. The withdrawals are considered to be deathlike. Scary. And almost every time requiring a trip to the madhouse. So I knew that she must be shivering and dying of cold or otherwise sweating profusely. This was the truth. My Staci is thinking that she is dying, and it won't come as a surprise if she did end up taking her own life (like she had formerly tried to with impressive precision), and in the morning, all that would remain in Clemency's would be a thick black plastic body bag with a pointed face and angry toes curled up in death being carried to an ambulance and then being flown from the Delhi airport to the Chatrapati Shivaji International Terminus, and before one would know it, my Staci would be mournful news on the National Media among thousands of brave young horny men vehemently beating their chest and masturbating at the disturbing thought of digging up her body from her grave and making hot, hot love to her.

Around 4:30 in the morning, when I finally managed to get an hour of wondrous slumber, a distant, more sensible dream came to me—one that would change the course of my life in the coming days. In the dream, I saw myself as a fit and able Mason Moron, taking an ambitious walk in the gardens of Cemetery House. (Mind you, in the dream, Cemetery House was completed, looking bigger and more beautiful than it ever had in reality.) It was a joyful, dusky evening, with clouds rumbling in the distance. As I strolled through the gardens, I saw not one but two wives—or perhaps it was my current wife Noel and another, soon-to-be wife, Staci. They were either sitting in armchairs or standing in the veranda, looking at me with admiration.

They spoke peculiar words. One of them said, 'I fell in love with him after he so masterfully saved my life back at Clemency's.' To this, Noel responded with a hint of jealousy, 'I'm glad he saved you. I'm glad you both are together.' These two women—two incredibly fine women—were talking about me with a sense of dignity, something I had never experienced before in my life.

When I awoke in the morning, I resolved that I would volunteer at Clemency's, and perhaps, in doing so, end up saving Ms Staci's life. That was the only path to my redemption.

During breakfast, Mr Len broke the most dreadful news to me—that one of my friends had died. I assumed he was referring to Bahubali, and I broke down into uncontrollable sobbing. Suddenly, Harrison Brown entered the room. Upon seeing me cry, he too began to weep. I held Brown by the shoulders, crying and screaming, 'Fuck, Harris boy! Why am I alive? I should have died with him. I feel like contemplating suicide!'

Hearing this, Harrison Brown cried even harder. Then, without asking me any questions, he abruptly left the dining room.

I continued crying.

After some time, Mr Len managed to calm me down and explained that he never realized I was so close to Mosheed, the man in the wheelchair.

'What the fuck, Mr Len?! What are you talking about?'

'Hell yeah,' he tried to explain. 'Mosheed is in a better place now. He had cancer. Poor guy. He had a tough life, Moron.'

I calmed myself down and wiped my tears and left without telling Mr Len that if there was the least amount of fucks to be given on any day, I would give them to the dead Mosheed.

That evening, I arrived at the group session just as it was ending. I had spent a solid hour in my room, waiting—or, more precisely, dreadfully hoping—for Ms Staci to show up at my bedside like she had the last time. That would have eased my mind completely. I imagined her walking toward my humble room at least twenty-seven times. Each time, I positioned myself comfortably, carefreely, often with my leg propped up against the wall as I lay with my eyes closed. On three occasions, I caught myself staring out the window with my arms crossed. But when no one came, and the lobby fell into eerie silence, I simply walked and walked, my heart pounding, a daring plan forming in my head.

I decided to announce my plan to volunteer at the asylum—not in the privacy of Dr Dean's office but publicly. If Bahubali could propose an art studio, I could certainly offer to volunteer and be of use in Ward C. But making such proposals publicly was risky. Take Bahubali, for example. He had asked Dr Dean for an art studio, and, unsurprisingly, they had given him one. But where was this studio? Not in the open comfort of Ward B. No, it was in Ward A, the isolation ward. They even gave him a camcorder and crayons to draw with, but all in isolation. What if they sent me to the isolation ward, suspecting I was suffering from a manic-depressive breakdown? That would be the end of my game—kaboom! A damned holocaust.

When I finally reached the assembly, I wasn't surprised to notice that everyone seemed to have been waiting for me. I was an hour late, but no one questioned my delay. Instead, Dr Dean stood, walked up to me, and hugged me just like Staci had done the evening before. As he embraced me, I glanced over his shoulder to see Staci sitting in a chair next to his vacant one. Her nose was red from the cold, and she looked sublimely beautiful. Harrison and Ms Prerna (the mysterious lady with those three moles) sat at a fair distance. When Dr Dean released me, I was asked to sit in the centre.

'Young Moron,' Dr Dean exclaimed.

'Sir,' I nodded, confused.

'I've been told that you were seen crying in the dining hall today. Harrison Brown here tells me you contemplated suicide and even discussed the idea of assisted suicide with him. Why are such thoughts coming into your head?'

I looked at Harrison in disbelief. 'I didn't ask him for assisted suicide, sir. It was just a figure of speech. I thought Bahubali had died, but it was Mosheed who passed away, sir.'

'Have you been feeling depressed more than usual, Moron?' Dr Dean asked.

'Not depressed, sir. I wouldn't go as far as to call it depression, but I do feel sad.'

'Why do you feel sad, Moron?'

Realizing the group therapy session was underway and it was my turn to open up, I said, 'Sir, my saintly father—God bless his soul—passed away five years ago. My mother died when I was a kid. You tell me, what am I doing here on this planet? Sometimes, I feel like a burden to all of you. And this burden is growing day by day, crushing this humble institution under my rotting, useless weight.'

'But that's the most absurd thing I've ever heard, boy!' he said. 'In fact, just now, Ms Staci, Ms Prerna, and Harrison were telling the group how beautiful you've made Clemency's with your delightful presence.'

I inspected everyone's faces in confusion. Harrison had tears in his eyes once again. 'It's all my fault,' he said. 'Why do I always end up doing the opposite of what I intend?' I stared at him in surprise. Before things could escalate, I continued.

'It's just, sir, if I could make myself more useful to this institution—help my fellow patients and healers find the path to redemption—I think I'd feel a little better.'

'But just your solemn presence here is a grace to all of us. You don't need to go out of your way to be of use. You see, you are of use.'

'I meant more practically, sir. Like if I could do a job—clean the lobby, maintain the garden, or take care of my fellow patients.'

'Ah! I see,' Dr Dean exclaimed. 'That's a most welcoming thought. In fact,' he added, 'there used to be a time when hundreds of state-sponsored patients volunteered here, looking after this unattended 220-acre ghost town.' He closed his eyes, exhaled, and seemed to imagine Clemency's in its former glory.

'Put him in Ward C,' and, my beloved reader, I can't—just can't—describe the elation, the sensation of triumph that washed over me when my most beautiful Staci uttered those words with her perfect lips. 'Put him in Ward C. He can look after all of us. He's amazing company.'

At that precise moment, my dear reader, even if Dr Dean had placed me on a frying pan and fried my brain to uselessness—no matter how painful that might have been—I would have died in peace. Because, with Staci's single line, I had won back the last five years of my wasted life.

On my first day as a volunteer, I was fully determined to become a promising and responsible worker—irreplaceable, if that were even possible in the realm of volunteering. Throughout history, there have been great volunteers—older men and women dedicating the remainder of their lives to distant deserts in the Sub-Saharan region. I remember coming across an advertisement in a magazine at the Nalanda University library: 'Volunteering opportunity on the coral-fed islands of the Maldives', where volunteers were tasked with conserving the biome of manta rays and stingrays. Even on the bustling streets of Bodh Gaya, saintly Buddhist volunteers could be found, working for various royal monasteries, chauffeured in gleaming foreign cars from one monastery to another.

In this brief sojourn on the planet, I had stumbled upon the most exotic and fabulous volunteering role of all: serving in the Private Ward of Ms Staci. Although Ward C wasn't technically her ward and there were over twenty other people there, it felt like her private domain. It housed Dr Dean's office, the real nurses' station—where during office hours, the nurses, dressed in pink frocks and white slacks, rushed about the lobby, speaking in quick shorthand. There was the mysterious, always-locked Log Room (which I learnt was simply locked to prevent pests and rats from chewing through two hundred years of Clemency's history). There were also two empty Press and Conference Rooms, and at the far end of Ward C, the fabled, dimly lit suite of Staci.

The downside of volunteering in Ward C, however, was that it was mind-numbingly boring. I spent hours sitting on one of the benches in the lobby, watching the evening commotion. Occasionally, a nurse would pass by, pause briefly to greet me from a distance, then continue on her way even faster. My primary task was to serve tea, coffee, water, and sometimes snacks to anyone who requested them. Apart from that, I had the freedom to wander aimlessly, sometimes into Ward B, where I'd stand beside Ms Shelly as she diligently organized her files, the medicine cabinet, and the rest of the nurse's station before clocking out. During the night shift, I would still sit idly watching the quiet chaos of Ward C unfold around me.

After referring me to Ward C, Staci herself hadn't stepped out of her room. Today, during lunch, one of the designated nurses had taken a tray of lunch to her room and had returned with the tray still full and her food still foiled and untouched. I knew what was happening inside. She was nearing death. Not practically. But she thought she was nearing death. She would be welching over her commode, vomiting the dreadful green venom which she was afraid to vomit. Or she would be sweating profusely inundating bedsheets after bedsheets with her dingy sweat. In the late evening, they had run inside with an electric fan. And then in the evening they had to replace that with a double coiled heater. There was a funny sounding bell that she would ring anytime she needed anything. On the first day of my job, it had rung twice. I learnt by the evening of next day that the most interesting part of her day in itself was the group therapy. That was the one spot where the spotlight fell on her for a while, and even though she never muttered a story about herself, never opened up about herself, she enjoyed the rest of us meekly sharing our anguish.

The next day, I realized that it wasn't boredom I was feeling during my aimless presence in Ward C—it was the absence of Staci. I had imagined that my proximity to her would be a sound possibility once I started working there, but that proved to be far from the truth. I quickly learnt that I was at the very bottom of the organizational hierarchy governing Ward C, with volunteers having the least amount of 'organizational liberty' in the hospital. In fact, it was the senior nurses—those neatly dressed individuals with trim moustaches and thin eyebrows—who had regular access to Ms Staci. Twice a day, they brought her breakfast and lunch. When Dr Dean visited her suite, he was accompanied by two other nurses in grey hairnets and white slacks, carrying writing pads and files. Outside of that, there was no regular contact with her.

Dr Dean, of course, had the authority to interact with Staci in a medical capacity, though I imagined he was either too horrified by the responsibility or too innocent to think of anything beyond that.

By the third day of my shift in Ward C, however, a series of events unfolded that shattered my illusions. I came to the painful realization that any hope of wooing Staci was a distant fantasy and that my so-called proximity to her was merely an illusion.

It was in the afternoon—about six days after I had last seen Staci in her usual space in Ward C—when a sleek black Mercedes Maybach rolled up to the front porch. The tires clung firmly to the gravel road as Zafar, dressed in grey joggers and a black t-shirt, stepped out. This time, he had come for his delightful afternoon siesta.

And my dearest reader, I can't put in plainer words how that silent afternoon was turned into this siesta of carnal indecency, as soon as that man had come to the ward, had entered Staci's room, and had locked it's door from inside. I heard for the first time, the sound of Ms Staci's pleased painful moans. There were not many moans per se. Only a few. Some occasions when her usual voice was converted into a squeal and accidentally escaped from her room.

On the third day of my shift in Ward C, I heard the eternal Ms Staci being fucked to eternity by Zafar. I heard her massive orbs being slapped by Zafar's thighs. I imagined her bare nipples dangling against her hospital bed as she lay offering the gifts of her stardom to this young foolish star boy who had the keys to her reminiscing heart. And this was a pure dreadful scandal. What I hadn't even dreamed of thinking in my entire life and this guy simply drove in a Maybach, copulated with the most beautiful, damned creature on the planet, and then in another fifteen minutes, when they stepped out, I saw Ms Staci again after an interval of six entire days.

After they had ravished each other, they sat in the front lawn. Her hair was all messy and frizzly. Zafar seemed more at ease, more relaxed than how he had been when he entered the room. When their eyes fell on me, I was sitting on a stool in the front yard, with both my hands resting on my lap, and then there was a quick snap of the fingers.

'Can you bring her some coffee, Moron?' Zafar asked. At least he remembered my name.

'And some diclofenac gel for him,' Staci giggled, holding the lower end of his spine. I rose up to get her coffee, suspecting that he must have sprained his back while devouring on our treasure.

When I returned from the kitchenette, I was greeted by the same cinematic scene I had come to despise: Staci nestled in Zafar's arms. As I handed her the coffee, I noticed Zafar's hairy arms wrapped tightly around her waist. She had her eyes closed, resting her head on his shoulder. He took the coffee on her behalf, and as I glanced at her one last time, I discovered something unsettling.

What initially appeared to be a playful love bite—a toothmark implied only to alleviate the process of procreation—was not in the usual place one would expect. No, this was something far more sinister. Even though I might still be a married virgin and despite the fact that my own marriage had denied me certain delights, I knew what I was seeing. The mark on her shoulder wasn't a hickey—it was a poorly injected shot of the cursed heroin.

And in the throes of passion, she had forgotten to conceal this dreadful truth from my depressed, manic eyes.

And as I walked back to my bench, I realized in dawning horror that Zafar was no mere lover boy. He was not somebody she could have grown to love. He was not here simply to fuck Ms Staci. This was history repeating itself in deadly circles. That Mrs Staci the Senior was simply replaced by Ms Staci. And the vile Sultan Bhai was replaced with Zafar. Here, Zafar was simply her drug mule. And despite what she had been going through, she has never been off from morphine herself.

Upon further calculations, I came to the conclusion that whenever Dr Dean's prescribed treatments began to take a toll on her—when her chills became too severe or her fevers too unbearable—Staci would call upon her boyfriend, who would discreetly provide her with a fresh supply of heroin. In return, even though the world knew Staci had left him long ago, he would ask for nothing more than a few moments of her company to satisfy his own desires. It was a purely transactional arrangement, much like many relationships in the world.

After I had started my volunteering in Ward C, a few more rewards had come tumbling in, all because of my great recovery. Apparently, I was shifted from the Common Ward of Ward B and was given my own dedicated Room (still inside Ward B). It was a decent seven by seven room with grilled windows and a shiny metallic sheet for a mirror. I had my own iron cot and also a cupboard. Though sadly, the door to my room couldn't be locked from inside.

So, at night, I roamed around in my room, from my bed to the window as the thin sky above Clemency's shone in blue with drizzling stars and a mild scented wind blew outside. Life is either a series of plain dull monologues or a tragic downfall of events which may sometimes dramatize itself as a good heavenly matter of substance. I thought that under the presiding circumstance, I anyways don't have her. I can never have her. Because either Zafar or Opium would have her for some time. And then it would be either the end of her or her way back into stardom which would further make it even more tough for me to even step onto her shadow.

So during that crazed bewitched hour as we neared midnight, I drafted my first letter to Staci. Now the reader must keep in mind that Staci would have received over a thousand letters everyday with expensive gifts and sometimes even suicide threats. So she must have developed some resistance towards the implying effects of these letters. It would not be the magical effect the writer thinks his words might have on the apt reader as he sits and scribbles foolishly, poetically. But somehow, I wrote the following:

Dear Ms Staci,
I'm no man of greatness. On the contrary if I define myself as something, it is that I think of myself as an orphaned useless moron who has no business writing a letter to you like this one. But even in the worst scenario, after reading this letter, if you and Dr Dean decide to put me in Ward A whereupon my brain will be fried with electrocution, I will commit suicide and my life would be over for good. So I thought that it won't really be a terrible idea to try to make your life better as I am on the verge on ending mine. Ms Staci, I don't know why we love things which we know deep down are bad for us. Why are we drawn to things which are simply mediocre when we can be striving for greatness? I don't think of you as a glamour sized poster girl actress, Ms Staci. I think of you as your mother's daughter and your brother's little sister. Even if I'm dying and I hear your name, I would very much like to imagine you or a version of you playing around the fountain of your Bandra mansion instead of you having to drive your way through this crazy world. Ms Staci, I know that Mr Zafar brings you heroin every time he visits you. And all I would like to remind you is that you are not meant for this. A man sneaking in heroin for you while you are rotting inside a third-grade government-sponsored rehab like a little mouse can't be a

man of good intentions or a man of substance. You are anyway suffering. I just hope you will make the best of it and would actually heal yourself. You don't need any heroin to survive and function. You see, you are the heroin (Ha!).

In response, I imagined a series of responses which could have ranged from total silence and then my sudden disappearance into Ward A to all the way to 'I don't think you are anyone to judge this situation or to interfere between me and my beloved.' That was, if she would be kind enough to reply to me before getting me off to my own ward for good.

I also imagined a scenario wherein she would simply hand over a chit to me after the group therapy with a polite 'Thank You!' and a probable heart sign drawn around it. That would be, if she were sensitive enough to prevent me from committing suicide.

But having written my letter in such a wondrous heartfelt capacity, I didn't wait until morning and instead decided to slip it beneath her door in the middle of the night. I did assume that she must be having her deep, deadlike sleep at that hour because it was probably after a week-long interval that she had finally gotten her fantastic treat of heroin again, and today there would be no night sweats or a pang of disgusting chills to haunt her in the night. But while I was in the process of sneaking in her letter, I heard an immediate thud from across the door, and it was Ms Staci's feet running towards the door, probably to fetch what had been sneaked inside her room. Hell! Inside, she was like a contained desperate ghost. Extremely unpredictable. One moment she could be sleeping like a baby, but it would only turn out that she was brimming with the energetic passion of a cruel animal. I got so scared of this suddenness of her nature that I ran back immediately to my ward, turned off my lights and feigned sleeping, knowing that even if this was the last day of my sane life, even if I was to be wrecked to helplessness just like my master Bahubali, after this sneaking incident, I would heartily accept my fate.

Hours had passed, and a faint morning had begun to creep in. When I went to the nurse's station to check the time, it was 4:30. Having briefly fallen into a restful sleep, I wondered if Staci had woken in the night, perhaps to use the bathroom, and whether my letter remained unread. Maybe it had fallen into a pile of her green vomit, never to be read. I considered heading back to Ward C to begin my usual early morning 'chai' round, as the nurses liked to call it. My job was to serve hot, fragrant tea to everyone in the early hours. Upon seeing me enter the nurse's station with tea in hand, they would always exclaim, 'Ahaa! Chai!'

After serving the nurses, I stole a quick look at Staci's health record. They had taken her temperature at 2 a.m.: normal. Other symptoms? The patient had requested an extra blanket. There was no mention of my letter. It hadn't stirred any response from her. My words had likely faded into obscurity, unnoticed. I had to accept the reality: I was a delusional, manic-depressive soul, oblivious to the mysterious workings of this world.

As I stepped out of the nurse's room, a cold chill slapped across my chest. The night seemed to fuel a manic energy in me. I returned to my designated bench, which felt warmer than usual as if someone had been sitting there while I was gone. I glanced at the darkened room where Staci rested, wrapped in her extra blanket, and imagined her auburn hair gently cascading over her soft neck as she slept peacefully. I didn't realize when my own head drooped, and I slipped into a deep, exhausted sleep.

By the time the sun rose, I was sprawled out on the bench, dead to the world. I assume that when Staci finally emerged from her room, she must have felt some strange amusement seeing me, a helpless figure asleep on a cold bench, drooling in my sleep. When I opened my eyes, there she was—her magical face near me. She squatted on her feet, making funny shadow puppets with her hands over my face, her eyes gazing deeply into mine. Then she whispered, 'You're already dead. Welcome to heaven, Moron.' I knew she was joking, but I also understood that she had found comfort in her chaotic life, one that my silly letter could never have offered.

By the time I fully regained my senses, she was already walking back to her ward. Her swift, youthful steps carried her away, and I noticed her slippers—an adorable pair with large, expressive eyes and wide ears, resembling a grey chipmunk. I recalled reading a fancy article in Vogue that mentioned she had purchased them from Harrod's in London for a staggering £1,750.

When I lifted my head, I noticed that she had quietly slipped a yellow, tightly-sealed envelope into my lap. Expecting to find a few thousand rupees, perhaps a bribe or even my transfer papers into Ward A—delivered personally by Staci—it turned out to be something far more amusing. Inside was not money, but a thick, three-page love letter, written by none other than Dr Dean himself, addressed to Staci just a few days earlier.

In the letter, Dr Dean had expressed his affection, declaring that if she allowed him to share in her world of insanity, a fabled realm where magic intertwined with reality, he would be forever grateful—a devoted maniac living within the boundaries of her heart, worshipping her with the limited knowledge he had of the human mind and its capabilities. He ended the letter meekly suggesting that if she disapproved of his love and didn't imagine a scenario in which the great actress and a humble psychiatrist can live together, he was just otherwise happy to accept a job under her as her personal psychiatrist.

As I turned the pages of the letter with astonishment, stunned to see even Dr Dean joining the legions of competitors I had for Staci's affections, I saw another scribbled note. This time in Staci's handwriting.

Dear Moron,
You are hereby summoned to take a brief walk with me today before our group therapy so that I may kill you somewhere near the far end of Clemency's. Also, I already called Zafar and told him to never even dare come around me anytime in this life span.

And if that was not enough, she had also taken the courtesy of dropping in a tablet of finely packed Zoloft anti-depressant in the envelope.

A narrow, almost mysterious yet beautiful, shrubbed alley stretched from the front of Ward C, and the trail ran endlessly to the very edge of Clemency's. It was a charming path, shrouded in cold mist during winters and buzzing with insects in the summers. Around five in the evening, about an hour before therapy, I found myself lingering in this very alley, waiting for Staci with a pang of uncertainty. Would she actually come for her promised walk, or was I better off lying in my room like a careless freak? I imagined myself on my humble bed, staring at the ceiling and whistling, only for Staci to show up at my door and say, 'You forgot about our walk,' upon which I would have jumped up with wide eyes and an 'Aha!'

But instead, I waited and waited. When I finally couldn't wait any longer, and even the nurses began to worry that I might be planning an escape from the asylum (my job at the Ward C was for limited hours), I mustered the courage to walk to her room. I knocked on the door—a respectful, yet demanding knock. Then, in a moment of irrational paranoia, I grew tense. What if she had poisoned herself or hanged herself? The panic turned into a vivid image of Ms Staci's two lifeless feet dangling, accusingly pointing at her murderer—me.

Just then, Staci appeared at the beginning of the alley in her new joggers and running shoes. 'Are you trying to break in?' she asked.

'Yes, miss.'

'What for?'

I wanted to say, 'To steal you, miss,' but instead I stood there, confused.

As we walked along the aimless path, I asked her, somewhat puzzled, 'So, what is the purpose of this walk, miss? I mean you were definitely joking about the killing part.'

'I have been known to kill men before, you see,' she laughed.

'I bet, miss,' I said.

'Well, I have come here to tell you that that the letter you wrote to me accusing me of taking heroin was the most fantastic letter I have ever read.'

And my eyes broadened in confusion.

'But then why would you write such and such things about Zafar, Miss?' As we walked further and further, I could feel her soft auburn hair brushing against my arm. Suddenly, her smiling carefree expression vanished, and there was abrupt silence.

'Anyways, mister, what did you use to do in the real world before coming to this asylum?' Staci asked.

'I used to teach.'

'Really?! Teach what?'

'Psychology. At Nalanda University.'

'Oh, I'm just hoping that you are not some underground researcher, researching on the effects of mind-altering substances on us cattle then?'

'You mean like Project MK Ultra?'

'Yeah.'

'How do you know about MK Ultra?'

'I had a series offer once. This script. Pretty disturbing things you psychologists do out there.'

'So,' I said with a smile on my face, 'What did you use to do in the real world, miss?'

'Heroin,' she said and broke into hysterical laughter. I laughed with her.

'Well,' she said 'I'm glad that you confronted me about this heroin thing. It was very sweet, you being this brave for me.'

'Are you sure you would be able to live without it?'

'I'm not sure. I stopped imagining my life without it like after my seventh movie. But we all can just try at the end of the day.'

'It doesn't sound like you, Ms Staci,' I told her. 'It doesn't sound like what a girl of your will would say. You must be absolutely sure that you can be better off without that. You know it can kill you. Like you will be dead.'

'I know you won't let that happen. I'm just glad you confronted me. I just hope you will be there when I'm falling.'

'I will be, miss,' I said, 'I will be.'

As we walked in silence, she started singing out loud this heroic love-making song from some old Bollywood movie as if to tease me on having ended up on this romantic walk with her. After a while, she asked, 'Why didn't you wear your shoes, Moron?'

'Why should I have?'

'Because as you see the matter at hand is that we will be jogging for the next two kilometres in this scary, wild jungle and run for our lives.' And, assuming the role of a jogger, she took off, almost leaving me behind on the confusing trail. I ran after her.

Halfway through, panting, I yelled, 'Is it okay if I just cross you at the intersection, miss?'

'Whatever.' And she kept jogging and jiggling her fine bottoms; my dedicated Ms Staci while I struggled to keep up with her. After a while, Ward C and any recognizable building of Clemency's had completely disappeared from my view. All I could see was Staci running like a seasoned athlete. Every now and then, I'd jog a few steps, then walk and pant. My chest burnt from the effort, and I wanted her to stop, but she kept going relentlessly.

Suddenly, she emerged on a road which was parallel to mine but separated by a patch of rough land. I leaped across, and once again, we were side by side.

'Fuck! I forgot to bring water,' Staci exclaimed.

Slowing back to a walk, she slung her arm around my shoulder carelessly, and her smooth, sweaty underarm brushed against me. A man might have sold his house and his wife to jog with Ms Staci as I did. No, that's a shameless exaggeration. I didn't jog. I chickened out. But a saint might have given up his lifelong wisdom for Ms Staci to drape her arm around his neck. This was the woman I had heard making love to some strange, evil man just the previous afternoon, and yet, despite that, I felt helplessly alive, hopelessly falling for her. Even her armpit seemed charismatic.

All of a sudden, after last night, she seemed to have gained this unbreakable unfathomable belief in me.

But let me interject with a sensible thought: Once, when I—Moron—was happily married to a wife of mediocre beauty and ample bosoms, I was so deep in love that it was practically that part in a song where the singer yells, 'Oh! I'm so horribly in love with you! My heart and life belong to you!' And then what? She slept with some estranged married lover from her past. And now, looking at my stupid idiosyncrasies, I could see myself headed down the same road again.

Because, after all, hadn't Staci just spent the previous evening with her lover, Zafar? There was a huge possibility that she had refused to see him only because of some minor tiff that often breaks out between crazy, inseparable lovers.

And then what?

One day, she would go back to him, and I would be reduced to a substance of insignificance. I'm already at the lowest point of significance in my life. But then, a saner thought prevailed, and I chose to believe in the eternal plan of God. I imagined that she might never see Zafar again. But then, there were a thousand men with huge mansions, Rolls-Royces, and even truly unconditional loving hearts, waiting for her in the real world. A newspaper headline like 'Ms Staci marries her heroic life-saver from the asylum, Mr Moron' seemed logical and possible, and I even found amusement in imagining the horrified confusion on my widow Noel's face as she read this fantastic headline.

But there are a thousand men out there who would give up everything, even their pride, because their beloved Staci had fallen for an insignificant rascal like me. If I did fall in love with her, I knew for a fact that some princeling would come along and sweep her away. Like a hawk snatching a beautiful little rat from the jaws of a poor, skeletal cat.

And then, as if from some random corner of the universe, just as the sky darkened and the screeches of eagles and crows turned into a haunting, scrawny horror, Staci looked at me and asked, 'You know what heroin has taught me?'

'What, miss?' I asked.

'That the most beautiful kind of love in the world is the one you fall into knowing it will turn your life into a nightmare. And when it does, you won't have anything left to lose,' she said, her voice filled with a strange serenity.

Bear with my poor soul as she continued, 'I had that kind of love for Zafar. And even for heroin. And you took both away. What should I live for now?'

'Um,' I hesitated, trying to think.

'Don't give me that "live for yourself" nonsense, young man.'

'Umm,' I replied, 'Live for the day you'll walk out of this shithole, miss. Out in the real world, as the real Ms Staci you once were. I'm sure you'll find a better Zafar and a better drug next time.'

She sighed and said, 'Then you must live with me. Don't give me that suicide scare again.'

How much self-control it took not to mutter, 'I'm already dead, miss. I faked it five years ago.'

At night, I sat by the edge of my window, struggling to understand if there was any possibility of having Staci in my life. I knew this wasn't going to be easy. There were so many challenges—most of all, the very law of the universe, which would never allow a man as mediocre as me to even dream of being with someone like Staci. But then something strange happened. Out of the mess I had created in my head about her, about my life, my father's image came to me. His grave, vivid in my mind, as if summoned from nowhere. And I thought—hell, Staci is going to end up in the same place my father is. She's going to die one day. And then, I'll die one day too.

The image of my father wasn't of his composed self. I could see his body had degenerated. His skin had dark, rusty flakes. In some places, there wasn't any flesh left at all. His meditative, loving eyes, by now, were probably eaten away by maggots. The grave is not a very beautiful place after all. And I realized—Staci would end up like that too. We all would. So what was so special about her? She was going to die and decay, just like me. Why shouldn't she have someone who loved her for who she was?

I wondered why I wanted to be with anyone in the first place. Wasn't it, in some way, so I could let them go? I wanted to have sex because I wanted to feel like someone was mine. But the daunting weight of this challenge didn't last long—surprisingly so. There was no struggle, no fight to fight. No law to stop me. Staci was mine. Staci could have been mine. It wasn't that difficult after all.

As I sat there, staring into the starry, full-moon night, I was overcome by the depressing beauty of love—such despair, such a majestic force of surrender. It energized me. And when I looked at the distant cluster of stars from that humble madhouse, I saw my father's face. I realized I didn't need to be with any woman to let him go. Even though I would never be able to converse with him again, his love for me was eternal. It would remain, beyond time and body. And then I wondered—was there any harm in loving Staci in that same way? In surrendering to fate, knowing I had already fallen before?

The file I had taken from the doctor's office had made me realize no one had ever loved Staci outside the cameras. If she were a normal human being, she didn't even qualify as such—she was a glamorous dream held captive. People had tried to own her, but the only way to have her was through love. And I figured that if I could give her that, she might never escape me. In fact she might get so obsessed with me that I might end up becoming the one who would need the escaping while she would be trollopping pregnant in the rose gardens of our villa.

With that realization, I knew—if I truly loved her, I had to free her. I had to let her go. I had to let her escape Clemency's and trust that eternal love would remain eternal. I knew it was time to let her go.

And with that realization came another memory from the past. I began looking after Staci, just as I had once looked after Noel after she was stabbed.

A week or so passed, and what had felt like a once-in-a-lifetime occurrence soon became a routine, filled with passion. I would wheel around the lobby of Ward C through the night, bringing hot coffee and chai for the nurses during their tea breaks. When Dr Dean arrived for his night shifts, I always made a point of looking busy, as though I was truly living for this lame graveyard shift at Ward C. Sometimes, I would hear his car approaching and quickly grab a cloth to start wiping the windows of his office. Other times, I would dash through the corridor, mop in hand, singing the hymn he'd taught us: 'Praise to those brushing lights of healing falling on my graceful head from the heavens.'

Once he was gone, I'd head over to Ward B, where Ms Shelly often left the nurse's station on my watch to catch a few hours of sleep in the resting room. After everyone was settled, I would sneak back to Ward C.

On my shift there, the nurses had started learning my name and greeted me more empathetically than cautiously. The group therapy sessions became something

Staci and I looked forward to, even though we shared most of our stories with each other during our brief, animated walks. In the group, we mostly listened to the other patients. It was an opportunity to step out of the chaos—one only we knew we had stepped into.

A few days into it, Staci gave up jogging altogether. Instead, she was content to stroll a few paces with me. During these walks, she would recount stories from Bollywood like a faithful storyteller. It was impossible to interrupt her; her narrations were always sequential, often accompanied by spot-on character impersonations. I learnt so much about the booming artists of our time.

One of the funniest stories was about a man, newly famous after starring in three successful films, who proposed to her in the middle of an award show. Initially, it seemed like a joke, and everyone laughed, assuming it was part of a skit. But five minutes into it, after Staci had played along, the man turned all serious. His face sulked like a lover who had spent too much time fantasizing about her. Even Staci was taken aback. She admitted that she had seen potential in him and might have given him a shot sometime in the near future. But after a date, when he saw her 'real heroin', he freaked out, broke all contact, and moved to Hollywood in search of fame elsewhere. She said it wasn't funny at the time but was hilarious in the grand scheme of life.

'The bigger picture of life, hmm,' I thought to myself. That was a perspective I had never had.

Then, she asked me about my father. 'Do you miss your father?'

Another thoughtful, careful question. My eyes teared up—not from sentiment, but in a childish way, and my eyelids fluttered uncontrollably. Suddenly, I felt unbearably lonely. Helpless. I had no one in this damned world. Not a single person I could call if something went wrong. No bed where I could sleep without worrying whether the blanket covered me all the way to my chest or not. They don't do that in orphanages—or in mental asylums, for that matter.

I told her I never let my father cross my mind.

She shared that her father had died just two days before her mother, in different cities, on opposite sides of the world. Neither knew of the other's death when they passed. 'I'm a creation of that distance. That nothingness,' she said.

I thought if she had shed a tear at that moment, with a beautiful red sunset in the background, it would have made for a hell of a scene in some melodramatic film. But she just smiled at me. And—though this memory is fuzzy—I think she put her arm around my neck and asked me to wipe my tears. I did and only then realized she was shivering, terribly cold.

And then, one day, when her chills became unbearable, she invited me to her room.

For a few days, I did go to her room. But it wasn't something which was entailed in the job description of a volunteer. Probably I was not supposed to visit her in her private suit. Had it been somebody else, then maybe they would have had no problem with it. But it was after all Staci's room. Even this rascal Dr Dean was in love with her. I figured he might go crazy upon finding that young Moron was spending time with Ms Staci in her damn bedroom! And then somebody might have spotted me walking into her room some evening because shortly after that, in the groups, I was denied entry into Ward C during the night shift.

As mighty historians might one day recount my significant feelings, it had been only me—Moron—who had the privilege of enjoying Staci's profound company. But on the seventh day of her withdrawal, when it became unbearable, Staci made it public that she was feeling 'terrible ... absolutely terrible from the inside'. She described a sensation of something trembling in the lower right part of her head as if that area was corroding. This was accompanied by a profound phase where she felt she was sinking into a vast sea of sorrow. She likened it to the way an experienced diver feels the weight of the mighty ocean blocking their ears with every ascending dive. With each passing second, she felt herself becoming more erratically sad as though she were continuously submerging deeper into this sea of sadness.

I refer here to Staci's bouts of neurosis, which are quite typical during withdrawal. When deprived of morphine, the neurons and neuroreceptors in the brain long for something to bind to them, leading to these intense feelings of sadness.

There was some logic to her making this public announcement. Perhaps she feared Dr Dean wasn't providing the best treatment, and she wanted to spark concern among the nurses. Or maybe, on some level, she already knew what Dr Dean's response would be.

'You need a distraction, madam—Staci,' Dr Dean said, his audacity now allowing him to call her 'Staci'. 'These are typical withdrawal symptoms. They will worsen. We need an excellent distraction,' he continued, clapping his hands during group therapy. What had been a private exchange between him and her now turned into an announcement. 'I'm thinking of introducing some new recreations into our programme. Perhaps some occupational therapy. We could start a film club. The patients can watch a movie at night and discuss it verbatim afterward. Your critique, with her genius.'

'But,' Staci interrupted, 'I'm already taking evening walks, and these symptoms are most excruciating at night.'

'Maybe we could arrange for someone to engage you after dinner?' Dr Dean suggested. My heart fluttered at the possibility that Staci had made this complaint in the first place because she longed for my company even at night. But then, with a devious kind of calculation, Dr Dean surveyed the room, purposely avoiding eye contact with me, and instead proposed, 'Would you like Harrison Brown to play board games and discuss life with you at night?'

Staci seemed agreeable to the idea, and her lack of consideration for my potential companionship made me realize something. Despite getting to walk with her and spend my evenings in her presence, it would be Harrison Brown spending nights with her. From that point on, I would be reduced to a mere peasant, a spot boy—the chai waiter, the floor cleaner.

Anyways, so there it was. Harrison Brown was now given the task of looking after Ms Staci, every night from

9:30 p.m. onwards. While very smartly, my visitations to her ward had been limited to the evenings.

That night, after our group session, a growing fear took hold of me. I began to worry that Staci might have finally collapsed. Perhaps her complaints weren't merely for attention or comfort. Maybe she truly was suffering. It could have been her final day—the moment when a bright, brimming light from Jesus stood before her, ready to lead her into eternal calm. I imagined her head sinking into an ocean of tranquillity, slowly drowning, the last seven minutes of her life passing, and in that time, I—just an irritating speck—would be non-existent in her dramatic death flashbacks.

Then, at around 9:30 p.m., Harrison appeared in the corridor. I watched him with absolute distaste in my eyes. Harrison taught me something about doors that I had never considered. I used to be cautious, even scared, of approaching Staci's door. But Harrison, with his newfound audacity, let out a soft screech (a mild one because he didn't want to alert anyone in Ward C), knocked on the door of Staci's room once, and then opened it shamelessly. It's like with Dr Dean, having instructed him to spend a few hours with Staci, had essentially given him permission to enter her room without hesitation. I wondered if I too could have walked through that door all this time.

For two solid hours, my dear reader, two pristine hours, Harrison was in the company of Bollywood's biggest star. I imagined the intimacy, the gloom, and his small triumph. Perhaps she cried, and he wiped her tears. Maybe she changed her robes, and he assisted her. After all, in her mind, he was just a child—a mere guilt-ridden boy.

I wondered if they spoke about me, our walks or if it was Zafar who filled their conversation.

The next evening, I cancelled our usual appointment under the guise of needing to focus on my own healing. In truth, I wanted to withdraw from Staci before she could have thought of withdrawing herself away from me. Instead, I spent the evening playing an intense game of volleyball with the RBI banker. But later that night, something fervent took hold of me. I thought, if there's pain in love, some passionate dissatisfaction, then it was here now. I was just a jealous lover, willing to go to extraordinary lengths to win my beloved. After all, what is love without war?

I twirled and walked past the dimly lit chambers of Ward B, entering Ward C, where a kind young nurse greeted me. My only goal was to reach Staci's door before Harrison Brown. But there he was, the timid boy, already sitting outside her door, waiting for the clock to strike 9:30.

At 9:35, Harrison stood up, dusted himself off, fixed his hair, and entered Staci's room. Another two solid hours passed. I felt the growing pains of a man watching another man take what was once his. With Harrison inside her room, I was flooded with the same despair I had felt when my wife cuckolded me. I could only imagine what they were doing inside. I felt so powerless, so helpless that I wanted to flee.

But then, as I gazed at the enchanted garden outside Ward C, a sudden sense of dignity washed over me. I began to feel like a mighty warrior. I thought to myself, 'Hell! Even Staci will slip from my grasp someday. So what? It's time I let her go.' She was just a girl—British, maybe, beautiful, certainly—but the world was full of beautiful women. 'There are so many girls in the world hell dammit!' I told myself.

When Dr Dean arrived for his rounds, I grabbed a broom and began sweeping the front corridor. We exchanged a helpless look. 'Why does he look so helpless?' I wondered. You can always see the dying love in a mad lover's eye. Dr Dean had proposed to Staci just a few days ago. I couldn't help but think about his wife—did she know? Did she even care?

After Dr Dean left, I waited patiently for Harrison Brown to emerge. The uncertainty gnawed at me. After two sleepless nights and two days of near starvation, I began to worry that the staff was keeping tabs on me, possibly planning to transfer me to Ward A by the end of the month. Whenever people around me started being too nice, ignoring my major mistakes, it usually meant they were plotting something.

When Harrison finally emerged at around 11:30, I saw the lights in Staci's room had been switched off. I ran towards him like no madman had ever run towards another.

'How is she? Harris? Is she okay?'

'Oh geez, Sir Mr Moron, you need to relax,' Harris said.

'No, really. You must tell me!'

'She ain't good, sir. She is not doing good.'

'What did she say?'

'Nothing, sir. She doesn't say anything, and to be honest, I'm scared of her.'

'Stop kidding around. What do you mean that you are scared of her?' I demanded as we both sat on the bench.

'She just lies there and looks out of the window. She doesn't even tilt her head, Sir Mr Moron. I saw today that her feet were cracking open.'

'Cracking open as in?'

'As in she is going to dry off like a clay doll and wither away, and she knows it. I think she already thinks she is dead, sir. Not a word. She just sits like a damned angry locked-up ghost.'

I could see in Harrison's eyes that this boy was a good poor soul who had suffered more than his share of horror.

'But I will try, sir. Will try to keep Ms Staci in a good humour. All we can do is try at the end of the day.'

'Did she speak about me?'

'Yes, sir. She told me to tell you … ah I don't remember exactly,' he said, rubbing his eyes in confusion and yawning. 'Something about your walk … she said that you should practice jogging. And something about a secret.'

'I want to meet her, Harris boy. I want to be next to her.'

'Geez, Moron sir,' Harrison stammered.

'What?'

'I think you … ah, never mind, but I think you want to…' he said.

'I think I love her, boy.'

'Well,' he said, 'you and a million others.'

'It's different. Just make me meet her.'

'No, no, no,' he asserted vehemently in a sing-song voice.

'Please.'

'Why do you want her?'

I can never quite grasp what overcame me at that moment, but with each word I spoke, I felt an immense relief, as if my heart, frozen for a year, was finally thawing. A heavy emotion filled my chest as I said to Harrison, 'I'm twenty-six years old. I've yet to truly live, and I've done nothing of significance in these twenty-six years.

I might as well admit to myself that my late, simple father never saw me achieve anything of note in his lifetime. And now, I realize, I must have her—Staci. That is my only redemption. Ending up with her is my only salvation. I can't see any other way out of this.'

'You want to do it for your dead father?'

'In a weird way, yes.'

'I want to do something for my dead mother too, Sir Mr Moron.'

I still regret to the day that I never asked poor Harris about what exactly he wanted to do for his dead mother. Sometimes we are so occupied with our own quest that we fail to notice things which might just ruin everything forever.

'I want to do something for my own mother on my upcoming birthday. It's next week. Ah! Practically next to next week because it's on Monday.' Harrison Brown said.

'Didn't you kill your mother on your birthday?' I asked tentatively.

'Yes, sir,' Harrison said, 'and I'm going to give her the biggest gift of her life on my birthday. Until then,' he said finally answering my question, 'you can have her, Sir Mr Moron. By all means. From tomorrow I will take you to her room along with me. I will play a good child for a few hours, and then I will be gone, and you and Ms Staci will have each other.'

'That sounds splendid, Harris boy. That's in fact quite a genius plan you have just made.'

Then Harris looked at the distant end of the pathway on which Staci and I used to walk. He raised a finger towards that gravel trodden path and told me, 'I have the same exact view from my room. I like how you and

Ms Staci used to walk there like two filial fools in a universe. I just want to ask for one favour in return.'

'Anything, Harris, anything.'

'I just hope that when you both elope and run away from this place, you and your heroine lover, I hope you will not mind taking me along. We can live happily ever after.'

I realized that this was also just an orphan just like myself. I was sad because my wife had broken my heart. He was sad because, funnily, if there was someone who was to be held responsible for his orphanship, it was he himself.

And right on the very next day, as per his promised verdict, I had the pleasant chance to enter Ms Staci's room. No, it hadn't come that easily. First, I had to wait because Harrison Brown wasn't served dessert after dinner—they had run out of it. I don't know why everything seems to fall into disarray on the most important days of my life. But after their blunder—when they finally gave him his dessert, which he ate with his plastic spoon—he walked into Ward C. I eagerly got up to run to Staci's room, but in his calmness, he suggested we wait for Dr Dean's rounds to finish.

'Let that fat fool go,' he said, giving an impromptu command. We both nodded in understanding. Dr Dean, luckily, had come earlier, completed his routine round, entered Staci's room, and came out composed. I felt some relief seeing him walk back with his usual calm demeanour rather than like a panicked schoolgirl, which would have implied that Staci might be dead.

His round in Ward B was even quicker, and on his way out, he seemed to be in a tense rush. Sweat covered his forehead, and before I could begin my little dance of relief, he quickly got into his car and drove away.

At around 10 o'clock that night, Harrison Brown slipped into her room with the stealth of a cunning criminal. After checking the nurses' station and noticing they were all gathered around a desk, I hurried inside. I was immediately greeted by the pure, fresh scent of an extremely expensive perfume, a smell I knew would define Staci for me even on the day of my death.

'Look who's come to see you, Ms Staci,' Harris announced.

And my fellow reader, three days of her private transformation in that private ward of Clemency's had put me in a state of ambiguity so deep that not even the most fervent force of passion could have brought me back to my senses even after a good fifteen minutes had passed.

Just the mere sight of Staci was so damn unsettling that I almost thought for a moment that instead of being the most desired woman on planet, she was a cross-dressing psychopathic sixteen-year-old boy who masturbated with his cock not shyly but nastily on peoples' faces.

For one, she was losing weight, and for the rest she was so deeply and helplessly sunk in her bed that I thought for a moment that a man of my weight might just sleep on her and not be able to tell the difference if there was another human body beneath his own self or not.

'Young Moron!' Staci exclaimed. I'm still somewhat proud to remember how she sat back in her bed, taking a little support from the edges of her bed, and her voice was still the same rudimentary sound of an archangel who had haunted me for years now.

Somehow when I looked into her eye, I could still figure out that it was the same Staci, and that reminded me that if that was the case, then she could very much be the same Staci again despite the fact that right now she was looking like a helpless nerve-wrecked Thai stripper whom you won't fuck even if you were being paid a million dollars to do so.

In my experience of living with a woman, I had learned that they are not always as beautiful as they seem. I had learned from Noel that she had an outdoor, clean face, and then a homely, boyish one that took pleasure in arguing, shouting, and secretly farting in relief. Yet, when it came to lovemaking, you couldn't tell the difference. When life is fresh and there's still a hint of false optimism in your heart, you tend to look deeply into your lover's eyes during those moments. Men stay shaven and tidy, while women don't remove their makeup. These passionate, secretive encounters happen before the lovers find true comfort in each other.

But once they have been tied in marriage and the marital bed has begun to go stale, the husband then barely looks at his wife's face. He just sinks his face deep in the bed, placing his ears next to hers, with his face down, and he copulates with her like missionaries, all the while grunting and telling her how nice her pussy is. But he never really looks at how horrible and deathlike their marriage has become until one day their eyes open and they see that, and they have begun making what can be termed as short mistakes and distractions in otherwise a long and stagnant life. My wife—though never gave me the pleasure of consummating my marriage or consuming anything worthy for that matter—did teach me that women tend to look (not ugly) but normal and humanlike when they are ill or pissed or simply at home. I still remember how, when Noel was sick and her face was plain and full of shame, I felt an inexplicable passion for her. But with Ms Staci, it was just very different. I mean, I still somehow did manage to get that emotion, but I was devastated to see that she was tumbling down, and if she were to go out in the world with this face, no one would even recognize her, let alone demand a damned photo or an autograph from her.

I don't exactly remember how my conversation went with her for the rest of the evening, but when I was able to walk out of my brief chain of thought, Harrison Brown was leaving, having crowned upon me the opportunity of looking after Ms Staci.

After him gone, I asked her how she was feeling.

She looked at me in confusion. I thought I might have asked this question only a few moments ago in my daze.

'I'm fine,' she mumbled.

'No. Really. Ms Staci, a fine won't do. How are you actually doing?'

'I feel like dying. Sometimes I am sweating like a geyser from the sub-Sahara desert, and then at other times I'm frigid as if I am in Alaska, all alone with no food and blanket.'

'You know I have read that it subsides within a few days. Like a week or so.'

'Where did you read it?'

'In the library, miss.'

'You went to the library for me?'

There was no library in Clemency's. Only the recreational room with a few illustrated books and cookery books and the giant painting affair. 'Yes,' I said to comfort her.

'That's such a sweet thing,' she said, 'Also, I think I'm forgetting most of what we ever spoke of. Or anything for that matter. It's just,' she said, putting her head in her arms (sweat glistening and dripping from her neck), 'it's just I wish, I really wish I could get something which doesn't make me miss that heroin.'

'How will you go back to the real world if you don't stop missing it?'

'I can just walk,' she said. 'Walk out of here. I'm involuntary. See,' she said hopping off her bed and then walking around. She struggled and limped, but she kept walking. Then, after a while, she tip-toed and let out a mild 'Akh!'

'What is it?' I shrieked in horror.

'Ahh ... that hurts so bad.'

'Hell, Ms Staci, you twisted your ankles.'

'So fucking bad,' she groaned.

She crept onto her bed like some grievous schoolchild. After that, there was silence in the room. She was looking out her window. I was looking at her.

'Why are you staring at me?' she asked.

'Because you are a dream,' I said.

'I don't think anyone would even dare to compliment me when I look like this dreadful ghost, and we both know it,' she said.

'You are still Staci.'

Every night, I sat by the edge of her bed, and I saw her fighting death. I couldn't remember anymore the last time I had slept soundly. Sleep came to me in these soothing dream-like episodes. When the body is giving up on morphine, it ends up thinking that it's nearing death.

In the night, sometimes she would sweat herself into madness. And then I would be woken up to the sight of Staci standing on her bed weakly, fanning herself with both her hands. Her robe would be drenched in sweat. Her body had lost a deadly amount of salt. In these instances, I would have to go and fetch her a new robe. And she would change and redress like an impatient child while I would be asked to look to the other side of the room.

'Don't you dare, Moron. Don't you dare turn back,' she would say, still changing her robes, her eyes broadened in amusement and funniness. And then sometimes, after the sweating would be gone and dear sleep would have embraced me again, she would begin to shiver. The shivering used to be the most daunting of sights. For then her body would turn pale white, as if the blood had stopped running through her existence only. And then I would have to pull another two or three blankets from the almirah and cover her body with that.

'The heater…' She would say, 'Can you please bring the heater closer?'

Apart from that, there were instances when I would wake up to the sight of Staci welching and vomiting green vomit.

'Oh my God!' I would squeal and stand up.

But she, who would be vomiting and crying simultaneously, would draw one of her hands out and would direct me to 'Look that way. Stay away.'

How could I have, Staci? If only you would have let me, I would have carried you away from this madhouse, this world, into a brand-new world where morphine would have not existed only.

Sometimes in the night, say after a terrible episode of sweating or vomiting, she would just sit straight and look out of her window, and there would be deadly silence all over again. But even in that silence, I could listen to the echo of her downfall. Deep down, she was getting restless. She was uncertain, sorry, and ashamed, as if there were many versions of her surrounding her and mocking her, 'Look! Look what you've done to yourself, you miserable dying fool.' And then probably there would have been a sight of her inside her head: that she was withering and collapsing and vanishing. How would the world be without any Staci in it? Would it be any different than it is now?

While the going is good, I'm hereby noting a few more things I learned about her. My Staci was a disciplined, sincere child when it came to handling her life. Even though her beauty had come to her naturally, I was sure that it needed some discipline from her part, a proper routine, a workout routine, a fancy diet routine, and that her life had been chained to a series of nerve-wracking and expensive routines. I remember when we played a board game, Monopoly, for instance, she always stacked those fancy small paper notes very tidily. The fives went in one section. The twenties in another. And she would scoff and scold me, saying, 'Oh noo! you don't put the twenties there with the fives.' So passionate was she about maintaining the rules of snakes and ladders that when I one day showed her my talent of bellowing the ludo ball with my feet, she wiped it with her robe and looked at me with disgust and in disbelief.

She told me that she hated the food inside, not because it was bad. She said that we should be grateful that we got to eat something while there are tribes in Africa who would attempt battery just to get a drip of water. It was just that she was concerned about her diet. But she wouldn't let these concerns stay with her for a long time. Unlike most women, she wouldn't cry and dread and be melodramatic about it. She would simply acknowledge it and then move on with her natural predisposition of maintaining happiness and, more than that, a fierce need to follow the rules of every big and small game.

We don't fall in love and then get lucky by the enchanted beauty of the lover in question. We are greedy animals who fake the dramatization of love, often drawing inspiration from movies, literature, and myths, so that we can devour the beauty of the lover. Her sweet moan and her call for longingness. The stark realization that 'this person right here, this beautiful eternal lady, lets me have sex with her shamelessly. And the reason I love her is because I am the only one, the chosen one, who gets to appreciate her beauty for the remainder of my life.' So the ideology of love that way is shadowed by possessiveness. The real unbinding universal love comes much later. When the two lovers have gotten used to each other and have become a habit for each other. It's easy to kill memories but very tough to kill a habit.

If I were to use this general philosophy of rule on Staci, I realized that Staci was used to being surrounded by a lot of usual faces on each and every day of her previous life. So, I thought I must do something extravagant. Something that would make her eyes pop out. But the thing is that her eyes were already popping out, and contradictory to my notions, she was this pleasant, welcoming girl who shared much of what was hers with me. She was a good girl. Simply put, if all her beauty was removed, she was still a good girl. So I really thought that it was a matter of only time before I would be able to stir the notion of love in her heart.

I had drawn a very carefully planned trajectory, having tried my best to avoid any miscalculation that could arise because the fire in my chest was very intense to keep my sanity intact. If we progressed like this, if she let me stay near her feet every night in this same composed fashion, then I was calculating that somewhere around the end of this month, I would be able to tantalize the air inside her ward to such an intense sensuality that finally my intercourse with her would become a possibility. For now, I just thought that it was a good idea to make her more and more habituated to me.

Things didn't always go as planned. There were times when she would simply ask me to leave early, also while simultaneously turning her back towards me as I walked away, and she would just grunt softly, 'Please, turn off the lights as you go.' Sometimes she would throw a tantrum, which was too harsh for my mild heart to digest. One time I remember I had gotten her a glass of water, and looking at the finger marks on the glass, she said that I should really wash my dirty hands before picking up the glass.

I thought it would be a good idea to maintain my calm and our cordial harmony in these difficult times because if I simply would have stormed off, then really, I would have vomited shame on my trajectory and my chances of sleeping with her would be reduced to a fair zero.

Only if I would have learnt at that time how seriously wrong I was. That things were not going to run as per my plan. That in the outside world, I was not allowed to love Ms Staci.

Sometimes while laying her down (this was when she needed somebody's assistance to even lie down on her bed), her face would be a few inches closer to me, and I would accidentally be mesmerized by this sight (illusory or real) that I had entered into one of those primetime scenes where I was laying this beautiful, delicate, nationwide recognized, adored face of Ms Staci on the bed.

An imaginary voice of a journalist lady would be asking me, 'And how was the pleasant experience of handling her, Mr Moron? Did you see any worth in your life, in your fortnight of an otherwise extremely long life, in caring for Ms Staci?'

I dreaded it. To be honest.

Not because it was bad but because it was good, and it might get over soon.

And then another imaginary (this time, really horrible) dream sequence of a ticket counter lady: 'Your fun fourteen-day amusement pack is over, sir.'

'Can I enter again, Ma'am?'

'No, sir, our policy is one guest, one round.' I practically heard an imaginary ticket lady barring me from entering Staci's room one sudden evening.

But for now, to put it in poetic terms, it was just me and my Staci, her beauty and my stupidity and the darkness of the night, the calmness of our souls, and a few billion galaxies over our heads that had made this meeting a possibility.

One day Staci told me about everything she wanted to do if she got out of this place alive. She wanted a peaceful, married life. Wanted to have children. She wanted to pack their tiffins. She wanted a house in the Swiss Alps.

And I listened to her with teary eyes.

In the middle of our conversation, she closed her eyes and exhaled in relief as if we were two tired soldiers fighting this tiring war against the agonies of time. I reached out for her and began caressing her forehead. It felt good. I felt like here she was. My distant phantasm. I thought she might have opened her eyes in surprise and would have laughed, but she just kept it closed and asked me to caress it like her mother used to. All the way from the front to her back. She took my hand and directed it towards her hair and then the back of her head. Now my arms were caressing her head, all the way to her back. I was running my fingers through her fine hair.

'In a non-romantic way,' she said, 'there is this hairdresser of mine. This Rakesh dada, he gives such good head massages.'

I kept quiet.

'I mean, he is very old, you know. Like seventy-five.'

I laughed.

In the course of the last five years, I reconciled that I had myself had a fair share of enlightenment and in fact as a young booming man of this 21st century, I had found myself at the disposition of some of the most fascinating and atypical women of our times. My heart is ballooned with pride; my dearest bare-breasted Clarissa: I thank you mightily for being this remarkable (if not very famous), lady, and I hope you will enjoy learning the fact as you dance over some random shiny pole in your country that yes, I remembered you while in the process myself of endearing the heartthrob of our nation. You have the most fantastic pair of breasts mankind has gorged its eyes upon, and I would very much like to fondle them if you somehow show up in my ward. I wonder if Bahubali remembers you though. And to the little schoolgirl Alia: I hope to tell you that you had an amazing ass, and I hope that you will take good care of it. I'm glad you left porn (mid scene) and returned to school. Who else? Hmm, while I remember … Noel: You were a disgusting whore akk thooo … and yeah now finally I bow down and enter into my long tedious road to redemption as I'm about to make my glamorous proposal to my future wife and also gracefully my mother because you are going to give me a new birth: Ms Staci. We met at uncertain times and learnt to love each other when we ourselves are withering away. One of my good friends and another actress in Bahubali's film who once chased me with a mutton chop knife in order to stab me, Andy: said that it is real love when two broken people heal each other. Now I really have flushed her image out of my mind, but this line of hers remains.

A few days before her discharge, I asked Ms Staci to come on a walk with me one afternoon. I suspected that she had agreed only because she felt that she owed me something for having taken such fantastic care of her.

I expected her to simply show up with a semi-healed face. Smile. Express her gratitude. Shake hands and be gone forever. But contrary to this dullness (love is after all just a heavy bag of surprises), when she showed up, Staci seemed at much ease. In fact, she had already been waiting for me in the front foyer in her robe, which looked clean. Her hair was dangling playfully over her forehead, and her feet were dry. I was happy that she had been sensible enough to hide her genius forearm. We were, as vividly as I can recall, going for a walk this time, not on our walk on the usual nostalgic path. Instead, we were going a little far into the Garden of Wonders.

Now as far as the story of this funny 'Garden of Wonders' is concerned, there was this insane man in our Ward B, this old, foolish, almost lost in modern world chap named Firoze, who had come down to us from the distant borders of Rajasthan. The issue with him funnily was that this Firoze one day had fallen in love with a goddess. No, it was the contrary. This goddess had fallen in love with Firoze. And thereafter, she had told him to do something of greatness with his life. In this regard, this Firoze, much like Bahubali, became a madman artist and started painting across his village in Jaisalmer, Rajasthan. Only one day out of some randomness, inspired by some low-budget Indian sci-fi TV show, he thought it would be a good idea to drink the entire bottle of oil paint in his possession and become a sort of god in himself—all brimming with colours and paintings. The amount of lead and cadmium as well as volatile organic compounds (VOCs) in oil paints is almost half toxic. When they finally saved him, he was somehow packed and sent to Clemency's for being a stupid schizophrenic. In here, along with Bahubali, even this madman artist was enjoying his gallant redemption by having a shot at his recreational activity, which was planting and gardening. Literally over one winter and summer, he had planted over one hundred thousand flowers in the damned lawns of Clemency's itself, so now Clemency's was brimming with all sorts of blue and red and daisy and maroon flowers. His schizophrenia though never healed in totality. It kept getting worse. Firoze would be heard sometimes making a static sound from his mouth and then whispering daily in the men's room. Since he wasn't really doing any great harm with his personal conversations with the goddess, everyone let him be. Until one day, while on the usual evening round, our poor Dr Dean had to use the restroom immediately and chose to enter the washroom of Ward B. Only to find that instead of a mere static noise that Firoze beatboxed from his throat, he was actually in possession of a fully functional, bigger than usual transmitter and a satellite phone. There were long curled-up wires, a sound box, and a walkie-talkie curled up inside the least used (and therefore Dr Dean's preferred) bathroom. It turned out that this man had been an imposter. He was a Pakistani spy who had taken up his adobe in our humble Clemency's. Dr Dean was so horrified and ashamed of this guy that instead of sending him over to the police, he just simply shipped him off to Ward A, and his brain was fried in electrocution.

But that really didn't simplify the matter. In fact, the electrocutions made it even tougher for Dr Dean because right after he thought that he was going to die, that is, when the nurses were preparing him for his seventh round of ECT in the ECT chamber, this man announced that he had to see Dr Dean on the most immediate basis. Dr Dean was called, and now before him, Firoze Maqtool Ansari confessed, 'Because Doctor Sahib, you have been stupid and reckless enough to not even ask me what I was doing with those wire transistors and satellite phones, I have come to think that you are more of an anti-national Mother India hating bastard than those bosses of mine,' and he continued in his strange soliloquy, 'Doctor Sahib, I am one of India's most wanted men. Last time we checked, I was at 27. I am the right hand of India's most deadly sleeper cell. But you see, today I'm feeling a little romantic, so I'm going to let it out. Two years from now, on July 16th, there is going to be a series of 16 blasts across India. Delhi. Mumbai. Bangalore. Pune. Even Ranchi. Tell RAW to hunt down for Seedhi maachis,' he said.

Dr Dean slapped that rascal and told him to stop muttering nonsense.

I don't really think Dr Dean had even given that information out in the world until now.

'And what has been the problem with you, boy?'

'I'm manic depressed, sir.'

And I wondered how easily he had bought it. Just like that. Puff, one less inmate in Tihar.

I have never proposed to a woman before in my life. Even Noel, for that matter (goodness, please forgive me for having brought up that horrible name now when I'm at the end of the tunnel, and the promised light gleams in front of me). But even with that unnameable merciless lady, I never proposed to her. We fell in love (pardon my writing), and then one day we just kissed, and I thought that a passionate kiss at my father's grave did qualify as love. So we were just married one day. Just like that.

So I don't really know what the ordeal was. With the entire proposal thing.

My tender Staci and I were walking side by side in the enchanted garden of Wonders. I thought it was a matter of some pride and gravity that I have learnt to love this woman not at her best but probably at her worst. And really, I have a sincere concern for her. My forehead was aching because I was deeply worried about her sweats. And then, even yesterday, when I was just a fool, running my hands over her forehead, I felt that she was no great actress of our generation. She was just Staci. Staci had a playful, light way of walking, as if her legs knew she was very slim and athletic. At one point, when we encountered a puddle of water with small swimming tadpoles in it, Ms Staci shrieked with laughter and clutched my hand. I then took her hand completely into mine. They were no longer as soft as they used to be, but they were Staci's hands.

In my quest for love, I had learnt to be unafraid and bold, assuming that was the least I could do for the person I loved. So, I didn't let go of her hand even after we crossed the puddle. I noticed that after trying twice in a weak, indecisive way, she stopped trying to withdraw her hand. Then I told her to go and smell the jasmine, this wide, white bella. She didn't. Instead, she plucked a few of them and put them against my nostrils.

And then, my heart began thumping with distress, a feeling as if my soul was clambering up to my chest, when she muttered, 'You know the funny thing about life is that we don't give enough time to love for it to grow. We just become so obsessed with consuming the other person, and then it all becomes a waste.'

The mere, stupid but somehow realistic proposition I put forward was, 'It's like the market. The other person has a demand, a need, a want. They see who can fulfil it, and they go for it.'

Then, trying to fit ourselves into this notion, I said, 'We met at such an unusual time in our lives.'

She asked me how much I had paid some weird organization to make such an arrangement.

'It's a law of the universe. We would end up breaking it if we somehow ended up together. Funny, right?' I said.

'What law? Do you really think there are laws in this universe?'

'Yeah,' I said. 'Like this one law that won't let a man like me end up with a woman like you.'

'How is that a law?'

'You are Ms Staci. I'm just a fool. Do you see us crossing paths anywhere?'

'We did, didn't we?'

'And honestly, Staci,' I said (I always used to call her Ms Staci, but right now she was just Staci), 'I did end up falling in love with you. Here I am, successfully putting myself on that long list of people you've rejected in the last five hundred years.'

'What if I don't want to put you on that list?'

I said, 'I do love you. I know I'm confined here in this asylum. And you will be gone soon. And it hurts, but I want you to go. And so there will be no prospect of us together.'

'Well, if you say so.'

'I mean, do you see any other way out of it?'

'Are you actually proposing to me?'

'Yes, and I want to take care of you like this for the rest of my life.'

'Do you think I will be able to take care of you like you take care of me?'

'Yep.'

'Well, I guess we are going to break a law of this universe.'

'Can I ask you something?' I asked tentatively.

Silence.

'Why did you give yourself this much time to fall in love with me? When you knew that I would be gone. And the reason why I would be gone this soon is because you stayed around. But you still did. And now you will be stuck here, and I will be gone. So how do you propose that we will end up together?'

'I mean, I can always escape. Right from there.'

'And then will you be fine outside? Just the way you are? When I will be at shoots and award shows with strange people … sorry, men. Strange men. How do you think you will take it?'

'I will trust you. And well, if you see, technically I am seducing an actress. This extraordinary person as yourself, so what makes you think that you will be the one surrounded?'

'Can you take honesty?'

I nodded.

'You know I have already fallen to rock bottom. I met you at the lowest point in my life, and you helped me. You helped me get up. But I don't really owe you my love only because you have helped me.'

'Why would you say that?'

'The truth is... can you imagine if I walk out of here one day along with you by my side, you will stay. This place will stay. People will ask, oh! How did you meet? Where did he come from? And then you will be there like this reminder of my fall. You don't know how this world works outside. Even here, really? No, please, let me. I like you because you were there for me. Otherwise, really, you are literally,' she said, distancing her eyes from mine, 'you are nobody. I don't know anything about you. All this is too weird. Can I please just go back?'

'Sure' I said, unable to think of anything else to say.

And we began walking all the way back to Ward C in humiliation and shame. She didn't even mutter a word. And over that she was walking ahead of me. I thought of catching up, but really then until when would I have tried to catch up with her?

I have been stupid enough for this one bitch to already have humiliated me a long time ago. Be it Staci, this was not going to be another of those bitches really.

And then suddenly, out of nowhere, right when I was about to enter death, I heard myself saying the most unbelievable thing.

'And your mom,' I screamed from afar, 'she ended up with extraordinary men. Famous men. Powerful men. Where is she now, huh?' Words of outrage spilled from my mouth. 'I know she haunts you every day. I know your stepfather haunts you every day, Staci. I knew you were broken inside. But really, I don't think I'm stupid for falling in love with you. Because I knew everything, and still, I tried. So smart of you to walk away. Wow! Everybody, look at her heroin-free walk. Wow, where's the press? Oh fuck, no one's looking at Staci.'

There was still no reply.

'Well,' I screamed 'I hope your PR folks will send you a reply to this. They are always there, aren't they?'

And her walk stopped. I could see her fine brushed hair dangling and bouncing as she was walking. But now it was all still. And Staci turned back to look at me in disgust.

'Wow I did stir something up' I thought. What was the loss now anyway?

She then began walking towards me. Her walk getting faster. Hell! She was almost running towards me with her absolutely beautiful athletic composure. I just reminded myself not to end up pushing her or punching her at any moment while she would be beating me as if I were a street dog. Even if she would have slapped me seventy times. I just had to keep my hands in my pocket so that they may not flounce out of some sort of reflex. And once she had come closer to me, she gave me a sharp punch in my stomach. It was not really intense. And then another one. And then one more. Two three in repetition. Nothing wrong with a girl fighting for her honour, I thought. And then before I could really laugh it off or cry it off, she grabbed me by my face and my dear reader, *I urge you to close this literature right now because I really don't want any jealousy out there*. We broke the law of the universe and before I could get a chance to breathe, Staci's face was all mine, and her lips were all mine and she kissed me. My beloved heroin addict champion pressed her lips against mine, and the sun gleamed, and she had tears in her eyes. But she kept kissing me. I had to remove my hands from my pocket to hold her face. It was warm. She was shaking and crying, and I could feel that I myself (I didn't even cry when my father had died) was crying, our tears were mingling, and my own face was flushed, and I knew at that precise moment that falling in love with the right person felt like there is nothing to lose in this world.

When we were returning to her room, Dr Dean was standing in front of the nurse's station along with a few other important-looking men. And having kissed Staci for the first time only some twenty metres from there, I wouldn't practically be surprised if he did see us in the act and knew that Staci was taken.

Though whatever the practical matter might be, when he saw Staci, he glanced at us, bowed in respect, and the three men walked around and encircled her.

'I hope you are doing good, madam.' There was this mildly dark, grey-haired, yellow-toothed gentleman who looked more like a nuclear scientist and less like a scholar. The three men stood around Staci and looked at me with curiosity. She said she was doing good. Then they chatted for some time about her discharge.

Her discharge was due in a few days. Which really had me wondering, what the hell was I supposed to do after she was gone?

Anyways, they chatted for a while. Smiling nervously and struggling to act all suave. And thereafter their attention fell on me.

'And that there,' Dr Dean said pointing his fingers at me, 'is one of our fine patients, Mr Moron, who looks after her fantastically.'

'Quite fantastically,' Staci said and broke into a sweet smile. Only if I would not think of flying every time I looked at her rosy, sparkling lips.

Just to give you a small lesson on the taste of my lover's lips: they were sweet. They were wet. Fuck! I recall that our teeth somehow funnily collided at one moment of passion. Her teeth felt small. Her tears were salty. Her face, when touched, felt hot but not exactly feverishly hot. It was more like passionate hot, but still, there were a lot of tears.

Anyway, after the conversation ended, Dr Dean called out to me while walking away, 'Come to the 6:00 p.m. group therapy, son.'

'Son?' I thought, '*You practically would be working under my shoe, you fool, had my Staci accepted your proposal that day.*'

'Sure, sir,' I said.

I left for the group therapy session after having taken a beautiful ecstatic shower in my ward. I started contemplating that I must escape this place before Staci's discharge. Because Ms Staci was a voluntary admission here. As a result, on the day of her discharge, she would be let out as a free roaming spirit with no one to stop her until she chose to. But if they were to find out about my romance in the meantime, I would be kept under very tight scrutiny. People would fear that the Moron might escape to get to his lover. And then I realized that until now Staci hadn't really made any commitment to me. Maybe she didn't even love me. Maybe she just took offense because I brought up her dead mother (about whom she had opened up in a moment of anguish), and she had kissed me only to fool me into thinking that she loved me. Maybe she was plotting her revenge, thinking that she would walk out of here, leaving me behind to rot and die in loneliness.

Maybe she wanted me to do something crazy. Make a bad decision and reveal my heroic love for her in the coming days in front of everybody. Then there would be close inspections. Dr Dean would take a personal offense if he were to find out that I was in love with her. He might try to put me in Ward A for a while, from where my escape would be impossible. Just the very thought that soon she would be free and I would be here rotting was making me anxious.

Then, there was a saner, more realistic explanation, which hit me when I was about to enter the group therapy. What if it's not Staci's fault at all? What if it is Dr Dean?

Just indulge me for a second. There was the Garden of Wonders in Clemency's, and behind it, there was this story of the magnificent sleeper cell, Firoze. Firoze was no fabrication. His wire transistors and his satellite phone were real. As real as I myself was. As real as Ms Staci. As real as our kiss. And if there actually was a satellite phone, then why was Firoze in Ward A? Even after spilling his secret, still, why was he really in Ward A? Why was he not in some third-grade torture chamber of some military camp in Rajasthan? Because Dr Dean didn't want him to leave. Because, had Firoze ended up in prison, people would have also discovered that Firoze, the dreaded sleeper cell, was simply chilling in Clemency's all this while, using it as a part-time vacation resort. And then they would have reprimanded our Dr Dean for this. For his negligence. So Dr Dean hid him inside. Fine!

Now it wouldn't have really hurt Dr Dean or anybody, if I were to add into this equation that maybe he didn't want Staci to leave either. I thought, why was he being all calm and tender? Why was he acting fine with me taking his secret love on those long, distant walks? Why hadn't he done something when he saw me kiss Staci this afternoon?

And then one genius 1 million rupee winning answer: What if Staci is never off the heroin? Why does she still sweat on every third night? Why does she still have fevers, and why does she look so miserable and dreadful? The sweating episodes, no matter how they had made my love possible, should have stopped within the first few weeks of her being admitted inside. It had been three months, and her sweats had not stopped. Perhaps Zafar was still running the course for Staci? But it's been a month since she met Zafar. Why were her withdrawal symptoms not going away? I had to run a check on her schedule. Her file, after all, the only harpoon that had led me to her, was still incomplete.

It had been my virtuous trademark to show up late to these group therapies. I figured if I would get late today as well, then I wouldn't be deviating from my normal behaviour. So I stood for a while in the empty corridor and kept thinking. The thing about heroin withdrawal is that apart from treating the symptoms, they really don't run any real medicines on the patient apart from methadone, which somehow mimics the exact mechanism of heroine. And then you really just taper down the dosages of methadone for a while, and then you stop it all of a sudden. That's how a successful morphine deaddiction program is performed. By substituting the deadly drug with a medical grade cocktail which somehow mimics the drug. Otherwise, if you simply put someone off heroin all of a sudden, they might actually die because that is what opium withdrawal does. It really will kill you if you suddenly stop taking it after prolonged use. At least this is what I had been able to put together based on my own doctoral research—thank God for the crazy paper I had chosen to write back in Nalanda.

But even methadone is stopped usually after a month or so. So why the fuck was Dr Dean still prescribing her the same old methadone? Why was she still on drugs? What if Dr Dean wanted to own her as badly as Zafar wanted to own her?

What if he is not even running methadone on her? What if it's just morphine? Really? A derivative. OxyContin? Fentanyl? How many people does that bastard have to report to anyway? Nobody. There is practically nobody Dr Dean is afraid of. Nobody he is supposed to answer to. He could just do whatever he feels like doing to anybody in Clemency's. Look at what he did to Firoze. Or Bahubali!

Call it a pure fantasy, this pure stupidity of a deranged mind, but I did something that day, which I should have done long ago. I walked up to Ms Shelly's chamber. From there I filched a bottle of my own antidepressants (it was kept in an orange medicine vial). And then I went to the nurse's chamber of Ward C, which I reckoned was completely empty (the nurses were down in group therapy), and because the front door was locked, I had to sneak in from one of those funny old, 19th-century wooden windows that never used to be locked. I went to the file cabinet (Staci's file had been moved from there) and then towards the medicine rack. I looked around a little. And then my eyes finally spotted it. There it was, right in front of my eyes. Ms Staci's drawer with just one orange vial of some drug they were running on her. I was just glad that her drug bottle was after all exactly like all of ours. No special treatment policy over there. I took her vial, felt sorry for holding it in my hand and sneaking it in my pocket, I put my own set of harmless, useless antidepressants in the drawer. Upon close inspection, really, one could not tell the difference between my Nexito and her Methadone or OxyContin tablets or whatever the fuck it was that Dr Dean was keeping her on. Afterall, from the look of it, most of the drugs look alike. At least the generic ones do. They have different salts and different compositions and everything, but they look alike. Just a plain white tablet. That's how it is done in the asylums. I think that's how Dr Dean was able to run morphine on her despite the fact that it was not his personal job but the job of the various nurses to give Staci her medicine. Because all the generic tablets looked alike. No poor nurse could have suspected anything.

Anyways, then taking the same exit out, I went back to the nurse's station in Ward B. Ms Shelly, my humble pirate, was all pitiful and had engaged herself in the group therapy. There, I slipped Staci's pills on my rack, and hereby, with this mere trifle, there it was. Apart from one kiss, now these two of your humble lovers, dear reader, also shared one another's drugs.

As soon as I entered therapy, I saw Staci. There was an empty chair between her and Dr Dean as if that special place was reserved for me. Her eyes met mine, and I was reassured again that she was totally in love with me; a sea of calmness took over my feverish head. I knew that she was all mine, and I knew that somewhere this trade-off between our drugs was a sensible knock into the universe.

Should I go and sit on that chair? I wondered, looking at that vacant spot, and when I looked up, Staci's eyes directed me to this spot next to hers. I walked across the roundabout gathering, putting my leg across the RBI Banker, and stomped mid-assembly to sit on my throne. Ms Staci leaned back and whispered that she loved me. Somewhere, stealing it from across the abyss of my charm, I told her that I loved her more. And then, because this peasant, Dr Dean, had been sitting right next to me and I really didn't want to raise any suspicion on his part, I crossed my arms and sat waiting for the assembly to start when Harrison Brown stood up at once.

'Good evening, sirs and mams,' he said.

We all muttered, 'Good evening.'

'Dr Dean sir,' he said, 'as you all must be made aware of, my birthday falls in the next twelve days.'

'Yes, Harris boy, that's A-class news,' I muttered.

'Sir Mr Moron,' he said in anger, 'Welcome, but you are not to interrupt.'

Before I could apologize, he said, 'Dr Dean, on my last birthday, if you remember, I had fallen extremely ill. I had a fever, and I had to make repeated runs to the latrine, sir.'

'Yes, boy. We all know. But this time I propose to make it different for you,' Dr Dean said, 'Would you like a ball in the lawns, Harrison? In fact, we have all been planning a ball anyway. Ms Staci's discharge is on the same day.' I skipped a heartbeat here. *Holy shit! I realized that Staci would be gone for good in the next twelve days.*

'No, sir. Just like Mr Moron, I am feeling that with growing years and repentance, I must also make myself of use in this humble hospital, sir.'

'You mean to say that you are growing responsible with the years? Well, that's wonderful news, son,' Dr Dean said. 'What would you like to do?'

'Anything, sir. Wipe the toilet. The corridors. Anything at all.'

'But Harris, we already have an excellent staff to wipe the toilet and the floors. In fact, these floors have been shining so colossally lately that a man like myself must close his eyes and cross the corridors because otherwise it shines so much that I fear I might go all blind.

'That is indeed true, sir,' I muttered and then felt sorry because Harrison would probably scold me again. But contrary to that, he said, 'Sir Mr Moron, I don't know gardening. Where else do you think I can make myself useful? What about cleaning the cars, sir? I was looking outside my window the other day, and I noticed that all your cars stand dirty in the gleaming sun. And with your busy schedule, I know that you won't probably have time to drive your car to a carwash, so if you don't really mind, would it be okay if I wiped all the cars in the parking lot, sir?'

Dr Dean was pleased with the diligence of the demand.

'Well, if that is what you wish, Harrison boy. By all means. Please take up this important duty from tomorrow itself.'

In the evening, Staci walked towards her room with her hands stuffed in my pocket. I put my fist inside the same pocket so that now I could feel the soft, supple back of her palms in my palms. We conversed for a while. Something about the weather and the kind of clothes I liked to wear in the real world. 'White T-shirt and black jeans,' I said.

'I just really hope that I will be able to face these cameras when I'm out in the real world,' she said.

'Well, you are good at it,' I said.

'Was,' she corrected.

'No, you did still know how to act,' I said, and then, recalling a great dead pop star's advice, I told her, 'You know it's not really you who produces the art. To be a great artist, you should just know how not to get in the way of the art.' And then, immediately, I felt like I was being a foolish, advice-spilling farce. But then I felt her wrist turn, and she held my hands inside my pocket. 'I'm glad I fell down,' she said, 'I'm glad I met you.'

Her lips were gleaming wet. She looked up to be kissed. I took her to the corner, right around the entrance of Ward C, and looking at that same empty spot from where I had crept inside the nurse's chamber, I kissed her quivering lips while also simultaneously wondering if it would be a good idea to tell her about this pharmaceutical trade-off.

At a distance, a crow from the Garden of Wonders was screeching, and it sounded faintly resentful. When we paused our kiss to inspect, I saw her failed lover, Dr Dean, walk into the nurse's station. And I knew that probably he had seen me and Staci kissing. And just the sheer thought of stopping us midway, of interrupting us in betwixt our passionate throe, and the horror he would have invited upon himself if Staci was to belittle him to his non-existence would have mandated him to walk straight and unbothered. When I did let go of her slowly, my palm still throbbing with the sensation of Staci, Harrison (who I assumed must have seen us) came and announced that we were to be on the 'special list of guests' for his birthday.

When Staci, a little embarrassed, asked him if there were any other special guests, he looked at her sadly and told her that she and I were the only two special guests. I told him to make an exception for Bahubali as well, upon which Staci looked at me in confusion.

'Bahubali? That slipper-eating looney?' Staci asked.

'He is a good man,' I told her, 'A madman artist who couldn't help himself,' upon which Harrison Brown muttered some gibberish and vanished into Ward B.

After dropping her back to her room, as I walked back to my ward, I was plagued by this peculiar thought. You see, I had been fine with almost everything that had happened in my life ever since I faked my death. It was just this one thought which was really unsettling. That in twelve days Staci would be gone from here. Hell! I had to figure out my own escape from this place. Who knew if I would ever be able to escape? I knew I had switched her drugs. Probably I had saved her from Dr Dean. In that case, she would actually be able to get a discharge. But then there was no apparent logic to it. With Staci's discharge being made public, maybe it was just stupid on my part to change her drugs. Fuck it. The drug was a different problem. What counted right now was that Staci would be gone while I would remain inside Clemency's, rotting for eternity.

How could she have just kissed me, knowing that she would be gone? Fuck. She didn't even have a plan for helping me escape. It's not like, once she was out, she could have used her industry connections and called some powerful attorney in the government who would have gotten me out of the asylum. I wouldn't have wanted her help in my escape. If she had tried to free me, our love would have collapsed. The reason it would have collapsed was that once she tried setting me free, she would have gotten her hands on my criminal record. I couldn't have simply gotten a discharge at Dr Dean's discretion. My discharge would have required a district judge to review my case. And then Staci would have figured out that I was a liar. In fact, that I was a married man. That I had married a Nepali woman whom I later abandoned under mysterious circumstances. And apart from that, I had trafficked three girls from Nepal to India. That I had taken indecent liberties with three underaged girls. Hell. I mean, I hadn't. But that's how my life was accounted for when seen through the eyes of the law.

And then Staci would have asked, *'If you never did any of those things, if you really were innocent, then why did you hide this from me?'*

'Hell, Staci, I hid it because I was waiting for the correct time. You were in deep shit yourself,' I imagined explaining this to her loudly.

I was probably in the deepest of troubles I could have possibly gotten into.

As I was walking past the bridge of Ward C into Ward B, I had another catastrophe fall on my head. Bam! Right out of nowhere. I saw the same old Mercedes Maybach roll in again. Zafar had come to Clemency's!

Hell! It was her discharge. Of course, she was going to call her Zafar.

If you want to know the truth, I have seen so much after faking my death, so much insane stuff that I barely get breathless anymore. Most of the horrors of our civilization are just a laughing joke to me. But probably that day, after six years or so, I remember, I finally found it hard to breathe. Just the sight of his Maybach made me go numb. My legs were shaky. I felt nauseous as if I were nearing death. I don't know how I managed to walk back to Staci's chamber that evening. But when I did, I saw the door to her bedroom was wide open. Zafar's car was parked right outside her ward.

So there it was. The misery of my life finding its final culmination. How else could this have been really? Staci was Zafar's. Zafar was Staci's. Who the fuck was I?

I didn't really pass out that evening. Instead, I thought I would kill that mad bitch with my mere words.

I went to Ms Shelly's workstation (she hadn't returned from the group therapy yet). There, I took out a pen from her drawer and tore a piece of paper from the visitor's logbook, and in that paper, I wrote what, God forbid, no sane man would have ever thought of writing to an unfaithful wife.

I cursed Staci for being mean and selfish. I told her that no matter how beautiful she might look, she was just like any of those miserable people this world is already full of. I told her that she should be thankful to me for the remainder of her life that I kissed her even after seeing her getting kissed by that sewer-eating Zafar. I accused her of attempting rape on me. I told her that she had tried to kill me by playing with my heart. That probably I would end up killing myself. Or not. But whatever the case may be, I wrote that she should really just leave this place and commit suicide once she was out. I told her that whatever shit she had faced in her life, she was deserving of it.

And after writing my letter in mad anger, I slipped it under the door of her room. The door was locked now—probably she was fucking Zafar. Just like Noel did when she met Herman after our marriage. And because I wanted her to read that letter right away, I gave an astounding bang on her door and left in madness and anger.

However, I hadn't even properly crossed the nurses' station when I saw that Zafar wasn't inside Staci's room at that point of time. He had never been inside Staci's room. Instead, he was in the Records Room with Dr Dean.

The two were talking in a low voice. I didn't know what I had missed and what I hadn't. But from the sight of it, Zafar was handing Dr Dean a very thick wad of cash. It might have been a fortune. Hundreds and hundreds of two-thousand-rupee notes. What is happening? Is he bribing Dr Dean? I wondered. There it was right in front of me. The hands of the starboy Zafar giving a fortune of money to the sly Dr Dean. The sly doctor receiving the fortune with his sly shameless hands. Then, before he could leave, Zafar said this to Dr Dean verbatim: 'Ensure that she is never off her heroin.

Not until her discharge. I want that bitch under my proper control when she's out.'

And Dr Dean decorously and dutifully nodded and said, 'Yes, sir. Absolutely.'

So apparently that has been the entire case with my Staci and her heroin. It was Zafar, paying Dr Dean to keep Staci on morphine so that he could own her for the rest of his life. So that he could tame her, for there was no other way for him to tame this dream of a generation. And here I was. The biggest rascal, the most famous Moron to have taken birth on this planet. For I had ended up writing that horrible letter to Ms Staci without knowing what the situation really was.

What the actual fuck?

I thought of retrieving the letter from Staci's room or probably barging in and snatching the letter from her hands and then running away with that letter to the farthest end of the madhouse and never coming back again. I could have gone and at least tried explaining everything to Staci. But how would it have mattered? When I tried walking to her door, I was stopped by our favourite, Zafar himself. Apparently, he had seen me run away while he was exiting the room. Which means he had caught me spying on him.

I'm reminded of a fancy article that appeared in the Bollywood Times a few years ago, which ranked Zafar to be among the hottest men in our country. It's quite shameful to be rated as the hottest man in a country, to put it bluntly. In that article, there were these funny round boxes at the bottom of his picture wherein these crazy sixteen-year-old girls had commented that 'they were mad for his nose', 'What a baby nose? How cute. shreiks', and then 'Oh God! His face! His nose! Awwww!'

It was said that after this article, he had insured his nose at some 1.5 million rupees, and I feel somewhat ashamed to confess that in that glistening afternoon, as he stood, one foot away from me, his breath was partially blowing my hair back, 'Moron boy! You dare enter Staci's room again, and I will send you to a shithole so deep that you will choke on your own life. Let's just pretend that you didn't see or hear shit. Okay?'

'Funny poetry, Zafar boy' I said, getting all breathless, 'You are too good at allusions,' and then, I'm quite ashamed to confess, I took such an amazing swing at Zafar's nose (I have never used my fist on any man or woman before), but today, I reckoned that this one gallant swing across this lover boy was such a damned punch that I made him sit down on the street in front of our Ward C. And I looked at Staci's door and wished that she might come and see that epic scene right then, but she was too engrossed, probably in reading my stupid letter and breaking her heart. When he stood up, he looked like a daylight zombie. There was blood around his face, and funnily, he hadn't noticed it yet. He tried to move forward to hit me, but his movement and his close brush up against me let out a big snot of blood from his nose, and it splashed on my white t-shirt. 'There,' I thought, 'even the act of breaking his nose was a dent I had somehow made in the universe.' Tomorrow the tabloids and the news will change, and people will believe in the lies he would tell them about how he broke his nose.

'I'm feeling dizzy,' he announced. When I looked at my hand, I realized that I had cracked open my own knuckle. There was blood on my hand. I simply left, leaving him behind, funnily recalling the day when he had asked me, rolling the windows of his Maybach to take care of myself and Staci right after fucking her for an entire afternoon.

It's true, the more time you waste fucking around, the more somebody else fucks your future wife.

For two days now, the mists outside had clogged the view from my small window. The windows in Clemency's couldn't be opened from the inside, except in Ward C. After the punching incident, they had permanently closed access from Ward B to Ward C, which meant that Staci was absolutely inaccessible to me now. Every morning, I sat cross-legged and wondered how it felt to lose the love of your life even before you had made her entirely yours. I remembered her warm, flushed kiss. Her hot, sweaty, teary, helpless face resting on my virgin arms. And I thought about her eyes. Her hair. Of love. Of owning her. Of owning our lives together. And then I felt at ease for a few seconds. And then she disappeared. In exactly ten days, she would be out of this place, and I had come to the conclusion that my life wouldn't be possible after that. In my own strange sentiment, I also had glimpses of Harrison Brown excitedly running around the lobby of Ward B ten days before his grand, stupid birthday was due. Every morning, right after we had all lined up in front of the nurse's station to pop our pills, I would need to immediately lie down and shut my eyes because, after all, morphine could be felt in full effect only after you took it, lay down, closed your eyes, and imagined yourself floating. Yes! With that mere switching, it was me who had been taking the morphine while she had been kept on some sad antidepressant. In my morphine-induced dream, I would have acquired the ability to fly, cross the many walls of Clemency's, and talk with the brilliance of convincing anyone of anything without actually having a real conversation with them. And then Staci's face would appear in front of me, and just the mere sight of her would send a chilling ecstasy through my spine. Just the thought of Staci was more debilitating than her real self.

When on morphine, I felt as if I had stolen Einstein's brain and had fitted it into mine. I figured that my eyes would be rolling uncontrollably, and I would feel and live in its truest essence the meaning of true ecstasy. And then my dream would be broken by the heavy thudding of Harrison's running feet, which would quickly stomp across my room, and then his thud would die and become faint as he would make his exit from Ward B with the solemn purpose of wiping Dr Dean's second-hand Wagon-R car and, apart from that, any other cars that would have been parked around.

At night, I would wake up from my half sleep three to four times just in fear of not getting strangled to death. I knew Zafar was not going to let me live.

What presumably could have been his revenge? Maybe it would be something as plain as an arrangement he would make with Dr Dean, wherein I would be packed off to Ward A on the same day as Staci would be discharged. Or maybe Zafar was a hasty, impatient bastard who might ask Dr Dean about my case. After all, after receiving that gallant punch, he would have figured that I was an imposter. And after the shrewd doctor would have somehow given him my link with Bahubali's, he might get a lead to unravel my every secret. Hell! Bahubali had gained some notoriety in the media three or four years ago. This Zafar (after reading a few articles on Bahubali) might even end up going to Nalanda or at least sending somebody (like I once sent Santos to Delhi) for investigation. And then after knowing my secret—my Cemetery House, my days of pimping (those were not hidden from anybody in Nalanda or the adjoining villages for the dreaded pimp I was)—he would show up in a week or so after having a clean file about my secrets and then I would be sent off to jail and Staci would be made aware of my past. Thereafter, she would be systematically made to fall out of love with me. And really, Staci would readily unlove me too. Because, after all, I would be a damn fugitive in front of her. An impersonator. An adamant pitiful criminal who assisted Bahubali in kidnapping three innocent children from a foreign land, trafficked them, and used them for the illicit purpose of making our cheap third-grade sex film. So there was that. Either way, I was fucked.

Bahubali told me one day that we don't end up marrying the people we truly love. We can never end up with the people we truly love. And then we can't always fall in love with the people we end up with. And this obvious truth, which he muttered so solemnly, so plainly, gave me the mightiest of a heartache. This is a sad truth about our lives. And it's sad because every time we hear it, it stirs up something unusual in our hearts. Listen to it again.

I remember asking my dear old friend Zahed once, 'Why does it happen, Zahed? Why can we not end up with women we truly love?' And I remember his response, 'Because with time, they just see the clear logic in changing beds and sleeping around once they see the appropriate happiness they would get when they are not with you.'

Ten Days Later

Ten days I have spent now, Staci, without making any real contact with you. I have spoken with you multiple times. We have had a lot of conversations, honey. But then I believe they have happened in my dreams. I didn't know that morphine taught you how to dream. That morphine taught you how to fly. Hell dammit! I spent ten days—ten entire days—unable to meet you or explain anything to you, Staci. I didn't know if you were alive or not. All I knew was that my end was near.

I still remember how on Harrison Brown's birthday Zafar came specifically to my ward. He was wearing thick leather boots and a fine alligator-skin leather jacket. As he stood there, a smirk lacing his tired face. It was the face of a man who had travelled into the life of another man, and now here he was, looking at me as if I were the hero of his latest story.

Our eyes met—mine afraid and silent and his tired and happy. He muttered a name that had long ago vanished from my head. Our memory is reconstructive in nature. It is a matter of great shame and wild amusement that we don't really recall the exact occurrence of an event but only the peripherals. We don't live in memory. We only exist on the outline of a memory. And people just like names are prone to getting forgotten if not tended to every now and then. A sly closing of eyes, a deep exhalation of breath, and then the name was muttered: 'Z-A-H-E-D'. Dr Zahed. As happy and torched up as I was to hear that old familiar name, it took me by surprise, quite obviously.

Zafar told me that he had personally requested my file from Dr Dean, which did reveal my association with Bahubali. The fact that I was brought to Clemency's with Bahubali. Now that obviously was public knowledge. The fact that there was a contorted mute who had been wheeled into Clemency's along with Bahubali. But what stood out for Zafar was how this helpless mute had been able to endear a lady like Staci? That was something which he couldn't understand. Thereafter, he did some research on Bahubali—the famous pervert that Bahubali had been in Nalanda. And then, he travelled to Nalanda where the old guard at Bahubali's house gave out a few details about me. Including the fact that I was close friends with Santos. Once Zafar heard that I had close friends in Nalanda, he himself began acting like one. He went to Santos's house and met him and his wife and in fact had a lunch of mutton and rice with them. Then Santos took him to Zahed (now a psychiatrist at RML Hospital), where Zafar cried and lamented that his dear friend Moron was suffering in a mental asylum. My friend Zahed had been foolish enough to reveal most of my secrets as soon as he heard my name because he had been afraid all this time that I had actually embraced death and that my metaphorical death had merely foreshadowed my real one. Zafar told me that, in fact, Zahed had been so happy upon hearing my name that he told Zafar he planned to visit me very soon. He also said it was a matter of surprise, and I should brace myself for the best.

'You are just a sly, scared cockroach head,' Zafar snarled at me. 'Does she know you are a married man? It amazes me. Here I was thinking that I was the bad guy for some time. That cheap villain in my movie, but it turns out it was you. You fucking son of a bitch.'

For a moment I pretended as if I didn't know what he was talking about. But of course, a fair description of the Cemetery House, my father's grave, and how I had lost it all just to chase something without which I could have lived anyway—Noel—got me all teary. Instead of fighting back and probably knocking him unconscious, all I could manage was to get a few tears out. And then some more. And then there was a stream of hot, sad tears rolling from my eyes, and I looked at this man in disbelief as he told me about Bahubali. About how I was a registered mute, a retarded manically depressed man of no substance in the real world.

'How do you know all this?' I asked, crying.

'As I said, I'm your best friend, you bastard. So Zahed told me everything He even told me that he is a fan of my movies. Asked for my autograph as well. He just couldn't help. That emotional fool.' It was true. Zahed was an emotional fool. I could picture him crying and getting all depressed and sharing my past with Zafar out of the virtue of care. It was so easy to fool that bastard, I tell you.

Once he left, slamming the door behind him, the echo of which persisted in my teary face for a while, I sat and thought to myself, 'It is time to finally give up.'

I remember the day when Zahed asked me, after my father's death, what difference it really made if I had to spend the rest of my life with people who didn't share the same blood as me if they were willing to love me the way someone who did share their blood would. I looked at him with teary eyes and found in him a friend for a lifetime. Only a month later, Noel swooped into my life, and I forgot about Zahed and that question forever. After Noel, and after my wedding, all my conversations with Zahed became simply 'The Noel Conversation'. It was as if we were two profound scholars discussing the giant matters of the cosmos and its most extreme and rare phenomenon, 'Noel'. After Noel, the next great phenomenon of the cosmos was his greatness, Mason Moron. I found myself moving from Bahubali's mansion to Clemency's, and it made no difference at all. And now, no matter how sad and anguished I felt, I knew I had to flee again. Even though I was going to miss Clemency's and Staci, neither would truly accept or love me—not after knowing my secret.

The 220 acres of the unmanned stretch of Clemency's could have given me a hiding spot for years at a stretch. There have been no cases of an escape before as far as my knowledge was concerned. There was no search block of sorts as one would have imagined in that British-aged mental asylum. I thought I would retreat into one of those huge bushes that lay beyond the crying eagle's park. And then I would slowly retreat towards the giant walls. I would find a definite passage to the outside world, and then I would be a free man. But as soon as I imagined myself in the free world, roaming around the edges of Yamuna, behind the crematorium of the Taj Mahal, I wondered what I would do about the finances. Beg? Beg, really, after kissing the most sensational girl on this planet and making her fall in love with me? And then I thought that maybe I would lay low for a few days and then see Staci in the real world. Sneak into her fifteenth-floor flat in Mumbai. Climb over her terrace and vehemently apologize to her. That still seemed to be a sensible decision. So I simply walked. I got out of Ward B and saw Zafar's Maybach parked in front of Ward C. 'There!' I thought, 'That is a solid man right there.' Zafar was picking out some files from his car while it was Harrison's routine car wash time. I saw Harrison go near Zafar in wild amusement. On seeing him, Zafar tossed his keys into the air, and Harris boy seemed delighted to have gotten this opportunity of wiping Zafar's Maybach that day. I waited for a good five minutes, walking aimlessly, fearing that Dr Dean was already aware of my preposterous and fairly unbelievable plan. I didn't think my great story after all was small and believable enough to have been told over an animated phone call. And apart from that, Dr Dean's car was not parked in the parking lot, and then I remembered that he had gone to Agra for a conference. There was supposed to be another enigmatic young doctor joining the brilliant psychiatrists of Clemency's today itself. A new doctor joining to assist Dr Dean. And I assumed that I wouldn't be fortunate enough to meet him. I also felt funny that I would be the most important man in Clemency's tomorrow. How Dr Dean would slap his bald, sweaty forehead upon learning that his biggest rival Mason Moron had simply walked out of the asylum one afternoon. And how this new young fellow, this new doctor, would be all embroiled in my search along with Dr Dean and a bunch of ward boys.

I saw Zafar walk up to Staci's room. Only he did not enter immediately. He crossed her closed room and sat on a bench outside Dr Dean's office with a yellow parcel held tightly against his belly. Once I suspected that no one was watching, I leapt across the small partition between

Ward B and Ward C and sneaked towards the road that connected Ward B to Ward A. Then, lost in Staci's haze, in the middle of another heartbreak, with tears in my eyes, I walked straight. Non-stop. Behind me, I felt the giant, colossal affair of Clemency's drawing me towards itself. The buildings behind me were getting smaller and smaller. I kept walking. Past the eagle ground, which was now empty, and then straight into the giant bushes. The farther I walked, the more I missed Staci. Her soft, elegant smile. And then I imagined her packed suitcases, all ivory white with sharp silver edges, set for tomorrow's departure. Tomorrow would be a new morning, and my life would turn again into a meaningless, Staci-less misery until I was dead. I would never kiss or touch another greatness of that magnitude.

So I let the tall brown dried grass wave behind me. When I was a kid, I realized all of a sudden that I was a pyromaniac. I got an edge by setting things on fire and watching them disappear into the sky. Into the greater nature. And then I reckoned that day in Boston, I had been daring enough to set ablaze the tent under which my dear uncle was getting married. And I remember how people leapt out of that tent and saw red fire on that red afternoon as I walked away slowly, unaware that I had the capacity to set such a huge fire to things in general. I didn't ever think I would end up in some giant unknown jungle of some random mental asylum, but here I was. Walking away from the greatest feat a man can ever get his hands on.

The human body, after all, is about degeneration. Today's greatness will be tomorrow's waste. It shall stink and ooze and be history. And then the bush behind me shrieked and waved, and Harrison Brown emerged, pitiful little boy running out of his poor breath.

'Sir Mr Moron,' he said, 'Not today. Not today, sir. Not until my birthday is over.'

'I must go, Harrison boy,' I said, quickening my pace, almost trying to run away from this psychopath, but he ran behind me.

'No, no, Sir Mr Moron, you and Ms Staci were on my special list, sir, no way, sir.'

'No, Harrison boy. They know my secrets now. She won't love me anymore.'

'What secrets, sir?'

'I faked my death, Harrison. I ran away from my wife.'

'Wow, why is that, Sir Mr Moron?'

'Because my wife didn't let me have sex with her, and then after we got married, she cheated on me, boy, and then I forgave her, and she still didn't let me have sex with her.'

'Oh geez, I know that story, sir. I just didn't know that you quite literally ghosted your wife after that. Geez! What genius!'

'Thank you, Harrison boy. Please take care of Ms Staci as I'm going to abscond again.'

'But you love Ms Staci.'

'I know, but what can I do? I should have told her then. Too late now, boy, I must run.'

'You can still try, Sir Mr Moron. It's not your fault.'

'But Dr Dean had been giving her heroin all this while amping up her dosage. Dr Dean doesn't want her to leave. That Zahed doesn't want her to leave.'

'And you will run away?'

'What else, Harris boy? They will fry me by electrocution. They will turn me into a dumbass useless person like what happened to Bahubali.' And now unable to escape from him, I stopped and crashed on the floor and held my head while Harrison came and squatted in front of me.

'Do you believe in me, Sir Mr Moron?'

'I don't know Harris boy. Yeah, sure, I do.'

'Then don't go,' he said. 'I will myself tell Ms Staci.'

'But she thinks you are a looney; why would she believe you?'

'Because I will tell her the looney way. Even she is a looney.'

'Okay, Harris boy,' I said, 'Whatever you say.'

And I followed Harrison Brown back to Clemency's, thinking that this was the boy right here, who had knifed his own mother and cut her open like a moving living birthday cake only five years ago.

'Be there, Sir Mr Moron, for my cake cutting after dinner,' he announced without looking back.

'Will be there, boy, at all costs.'

The alleys of Wards B and C felt unnaturally cold. There was some commotion I could hear in the dining hall. I noticed that they had taken off the gigantic fan from the wall so now there was just a giant circular hole. And I remembered how Harrison Brown used to get so frightened that he would shriek and wail like a schoolgirl when he would enter the hall and see the fan where it was placed. I figured it was Harrison Brown who would have asked Dr Dean to get that fan off (as a birthday present). After all, the fan was his old nemesis.

In the dining hall, they were arranging more than the usual number of plates on the dining table and also an extra row of empty food containers, which made me wonder if they had actually set up a ball of some sort.

'Last day, innit?' I thought to myself. I noticed that because of some special arrangement, today they had unlocked the gates of Ward A. Contrary to how I had expected the corridors of Ward A to be, sticking with linoleum and meruchrome and white powder chemicals, the floor and the doors were pretty much similar to that of our own Ward B. Again, taking the liberty of being a twisted, helpless, hazed-out madman, I simply wandered into Ward A on the lookout for my lost friend, my Bahubali. The further I walked, the more scared I got because it wouldn't be a shocking surprise if at any moment a madman with superlative human strength pounced upon me and tore at my chest. But upon coming across one of the madmen of Ward A, all I saw was a deep sense of fear and sorrow in his eyes. Apparently, there was this old, disfigured man sitting on a bench silently meditating and getting more and more sad. He twisted his neck to look at me with gravely devastated eyes, and then, after looking like 'Oh, here is another useless bastard', he simply gravely turned back and resumed his meditation.

From a room at the far corner of the ward emanated a dispersed yellow light, the same light that had attracted me a few days ago into the semi-art studio in which Staci sat and painted her bird. And then, as I walked towards that light, I became breathless as a strong, undeniable scent of paint and paint thinners emanated from the room. I saw an easel and a drawboard with a palette thrown to another side of the room. This must have been Bahubali's room. I was hella sure about it. It's just that Bahubali was not to be seen anywhere.

'Has he escaped?' I thought.

Dreams can be so pacifying sometimes. If right now had been a dream, then I would have seen Staci right here in this art room, and we would have started all over again. Instead of telling her my name, I would have straight up told her that I was a desperate cuckolded virgin and I had to run away from my disgusting wife. Staci would have broadened her eyes and said mutely, 'What?' in a faint exclamation, and nothing would have changed.

But this was not the art room. Staci was herself a helpless victim of Clemency's, and when I looked back, Bahubali was standing right behind me. The same old Bahubali with his familiar face and the bullet scar, standing and looking at me in plain confusion. His face almost said, 'Can I help you, sir?' but then, because he had forgotten to speak, he simply walked inside his room with his same 35mm static handicam dangling in his hands, and I reckoned that overall he was a happy man inside Clemency's.

'I fell in love with the great Ms Staci,' I told him, still standing at the door. If he were fine and this was not Clemency's, Bahubali would have gotten up, laughed maniacally, and then would have pulled me to his chest and hugged me. But he just sat, not even bothering to look at me. Instead, he was taking a chip out of his camera. Right next to him, there was his chewed slipper.

'She loves me back as well. We kissed,' I said.

There was still no response from Bahubali. 'Are you coming for Harrison Brown's birthday celebration?' I asked, and then still when there was no stir in his humongous body, I simply left with the sole thought of fixing things with my Staci.

By now, the dining hall was lit and decorated with silver ribbons and colourful paper bands. I saw

Dr Dean standing in the middle of the arrangement as if it were his wedding day, but he was busy on his cell phone. I avoided being spotted by him (if he had stopped me at that point in time, I would have died with my faint heart) and ran to Ward C. Staci's door was now open, and a dim white light was emerging from it. Zafar's Maybach was still parked right outside the ward, and it appeared that Zafar was probably inside. I thought that again I had been reduced to just a minor mistake in their otherwise solid and mature love. In a moment of dull confusion, I even went as far as to think whether that wad of money Zafar was giving to Dr Dean was to get his own hands on some medical-grade heroin, OxyContin, amphetamine, benzos, or whatever worked for him!

Late that evening, I could hear the loud croaking and cursing of the eagles, a maddening sound that came from the deserted land. The sun was now maroon at the edges of Clemency's, and the dining hall was a gloomy, crowded affair with the rattling of plates and cutlery. The outside bonfire was now ablaze, and there was the static over the PAS, asking all patients to assemble duly in the dining hall for there was a special occasion to kick in in the next fifteen minutes.

No, really, however tense and grave the situation was, Harrison Brown's birthday was to be a giant, colossal affair for which the preparations had begun two weeks ago. It would be exactly five years now since Harrison boy had knifed his own mother. A solid five years since guilt had eaten his heart, and today, for some peculiar reason, he seemed happy. When he emerged into the lobby, I saw an alternate illusion in which we were trotting like horses, brimming with excitement and happiness. Staci appeared a few minutes later, and I stood unbathed, all soaked up in my own misery. She however appeared her usual self—the casual flickering of her eyes and a sweet, tender smile on her face. Perhaps she had still not been made aware of my well-kept secret. She just seemed a little uneasy, that's all. And then I scanned for Zafar, but he was nowhere to be found.

I would always recall Harrison Brown's birthday as a sort of tumultuous emotionally harrowing day for me, for I found myself so near to shedding tears of guilt and horror. I cried again, this time because Staci looked so charming and beautiful in a long black skirt, revealing an ample of her cleavage (all three of those blessed moles), the cleavage of a goddess. I think it was probably for the first time that I was seeing a Staci who was not being treated at Clemency's but a Staci who belonged to the real world. And then Dr Dean clapped and announced to everybody that we are hereby summoned today because three grand occasions were happening under the blessed roof of our humble Clemency's.

'For one', the doctor said, 'it is, of course, Harrison Brown's birthday, and he has made quite an excellent recovery in these five years after killing his own mother and popping her eyeballs out.' Everybody looked at Harrison Brown in excitement. 'Second', the doctor said, 'our own great inspiration and heartthrob, Ms Staci, is hereby healed, and tomorrow she will be leaving us.'

I looked at Staci with sadness. She was all composed. *Why the fuck did I write her that letter?*

'So now,' the doctor said, 'apart from a mere birthday celebration, it is also the farewell of Ms Staci Silverstone. And third, later in the night, a great mind just like myself, another psychologist of some local renown and in fact quite a young impressive chap, is to join us at Clemency's as I have been thinking of retiring sometime around the upcoming fall.' The nurses look at each other with moist eyes.

So three destinies were announced in that brightly lit hall among us madmen. Three grand happenings, and still a question was left unanswered: what was to become of us? Of the remaining? Of people forgotten and left behind? Why are there no celebrations for people who remain static? Why is change such a cause celebre?

And as we gathered around the centre table beneath the glittering strings of paper, I looked at Staci, who was now having a conversation with Dr Dean, and then our eyes met again. Oh! How she looked at me through those long eyelashes. There was this sense of sudden pride in her existence—that she had learnt to stand up on her own two feet now and that tomorrow she would be a free woman. I wondered if she actually ever loved me and if a stupid letter was sufficient enough to break her heart. Or she might have had it bad with a series of crazy fanboy lovers, one or two of whom previously did manage to topple down in her life, and then she had to brilliantly erase them and spit them out of her existence to keep her mind in sane working order.

'I have an announcement to make,' said Harrison, seizing his birthday hour.

'Oh yes, do go ahead, Harrison,' said Dr Dean.

'I had appointed two special guests for my birthday. Two and only two people who would be let go tonight.'

'Let go tonight?' asked Dr Dean.

'Yes, sir, of a game that we are all to play.'

'Oh! Go ahead, boy!' said Dr Dean, his body relaxing.

The two guests were requested to climb on the bench on which Harrison was now standing. Staci, laughing and quite embarrassed, stood on the bench while I was on Harrison's other side. Harrison then grandly announced, 'Oh! We are in the presence of greatness,' and pointed his hand to the entry of the hallway.

Zafar stood there, looking all tired but still fierce enough to attack me bare-fisted. Only I knew he wouldn't do it now. He simply came and joined in with the crowd.

Before the cake cutting could begin, I was reminded funnily of that one solemn day when I had rushed out of that poor fortune teller's dwelling in Nalanda, and about how my dear friend Zahed had paid her to scheme me into believing that I would ever be able to have sex with the most beautiful, most gorgeous, and the most famous girl in the world. Here we were. Side by side. It made me wonder how married couples feel when they are invited to stand on a stage whenever it's a wedding or a birthday celebration of not themselves but somebody else. And they are expected to participate in that occasion together in oneness.

So after the crowd had settled, coupling and pairings established, Harrison Brown took us outside the dining hall. Staci, our orphaned Harrison and I, walking hand in hand, troddled down a path that had been trampled and walked upon by insane men for generations. Zafar followed us with the rest of the mad crowd—walking steadily and trying to remain in Staci's purview.

Once we had gathered at a corner of the asylum (near the front lawns), Brown announced that he had made a special arrangement for his birthday. A late insane party game, if we may please, and that he would be cutting not one, not two, but three birthday cakes—one at each corner of the asylum—because today he was ready to embrace the entire circumference of the asylum as his 'home'.

'Won't that be a really, really long walk?' the RBI banker enquired, all worried.

'Not that long. Well, we are not covering the farmland, banker ji. Just the buildings. Also, they are all three different flavours, sir. You might not want to miss the red velvet one, which is the third one.'

So we followed. The entire procession. The banker and Ms Prerna (they seemed to be in love), Ms Shelly and Dr Dean, and the South Indian brothers. They had light music on the outdoor lawn, and the bonfire was all ablaze. And as Harrison cut his first birthday cake with a red plastic knife (of course they would not give that poor boy a royal kitchen knife) and we clapped and celebrated, I caught Staci looking at me and smiling, and I knew that this was probably the last time we were seeing each other. I would have to spend the rest of my life on today's memories. That this right now would be a memory of eternal greatness, and I wondered if this should be sufficient to reminisce upon as I would be either begging on the streets of Agra tomorrow or otherwise be getting my brain all combusted in Ward A. Speaking of Ward A, as we sang and praised Harrison boy, I could see from this distance that they had opened a door of Ward A as well so that the patients from Ward A could come and become a part of his celebration.

As Harrison cut his second birthday cake beneath the sharp yellow moonlight, I saw Staci and Zafar strike up a small conversation. Zafar was whispering something to Staci, and Staci seemed teary and confused, and I began contemplating my end. As a faint image of my near probable future popped into my head, I saw Harrison mutter a small verse to himself, as everybody was busy singing Happy Birthday. He kept on reciting inaudibly and then muttered a verse in which for the first time I heard his mother's name, 'Rita. Ms Rita Brown.' Hell! even my mother's name was Rita, it suddenly struck me.

My ears strained cautiously, and I twitched and flicked my forehead unknowingly. I assumed that because of my special position on the special guest list, it was only me who had heard him mention his mother's name. Staci might have heard it as well, but she had left and gone to the end of the procession.

I knew then that Harrison Brown was planning something. In one of his faint reveries, I recalled a story he had told me about the enchanted heaven of the dead pet dogs and how everybody's faithful pet dog (who has died or has been euthanized) awaits for its owner's arrival in that heaven of theirs. 'Right on the entrance, Sir Mr Moron,' he had said, moving his tongue like a dog.

Now my reunion with my dead pet dog would have brought a soothing comfort in my existence, but when I thought about it from this young boy's evidently insane frame of mind, I reckoned faintly that it wouldn't really be a surprise that in his psychopathic head, he himself had pictured his dead grieving mother waiting for his arrival at the gate of some random heaven, whose address was totally undisclosed to humanity until then. And then I thought, what if he were planning to kill me? That being his special guest really meant being his sacrifice on this red full moon night. But then Harrison Brown had also told me that he would ensure that I do end up with Staci, in which case I assumed that I was safe and invincible under his watch. All I had was this psychopath's word for it.

So we proceeded to Ward A now, which was the third and last corner of his birthday celebration. One might wonder about this curious cake cutting. Things like, which mental asylum would allow such nonsense? Aren't there protocols and regulations that govern the running of a mental institution? A doctor indulging in a patient's birthday? Things of that sort. Well. Sometimes insanity is not an isolated phenomenon. There have been reported cases of mass hysteria and mass psychosis. A family of eleven in Delhi had hung itself from the ceiling of their house a few years ago with the futile agenda of retrieving their dead father from the heavens. One insane man over a period of time can let his insanity creep on many. Sometimes entire nations have been known to have gone insane. Historians would argue that such was the sad case of Germany in Hitler's era, for instance. And today, as I walked with Harrison Brown in this weird seven-person procession, I realized that at some point, after all these years, we have so utterly lost grip of reality that this was not even a mental asylum anymore. That the laws of sanity and existence in itself have totally disappeared. I raised my head in order to survey the nearby grounds and the buildings and the sleepwalking patients. And furthermore to take a look at this great actress, Ms Staci—but hell, Staci wasn't there anymore. Neither was Dr Dean. Nor Zafar. They had left the procession under the watch of a few nurses and ward boys. I looked at Harris boy in disapproval, but he assured me, 'It's alright, Sir Mr Moron, we are finally at the end of the tunnel.' And considering this as a goodbye, I left them and walked towards Staci's ward.

I still fail to reckon if I happen to be one of those very few, rare people in the world who can sniff an ocean or a lake somewhere around the harbour as soon as there is actually an ocean or a lake nearby. There is something gentle and uncertain about these water bodies. The calmness of it. And I don't quite remember if today what I felt was probably the same calmness when I ran towards that unknown ward in the most unknown of times in the most unknown of places. I did somewhere find myself at ease. Not because Harrison Brown had after all given me his word for it. But somehow it just felt right, and I learned that when too much built-up anxiety relieves itself at once, all you can feel is euphoria. Inside Staci's room, Zafar was standing, arms on his waist, while Dr Dean stood on the other corner, slightly embarrassed as I made my roaring entry. My grand entry was not really met with shock or surprise. It was as if they had been expecting me. And everybody raised their heads in disappointment as if to convey, 'Why are you so late?'

Then Zafar said, 'So you will just be with him then? You really choose him over me?'

And my heart began beating faster as if the last, most powerful rays of the bright, hopeful afterlife had finally embraced me.

'I just want to be left alone. I just want to start all over again. Or probably, never again,' Staci said, crying. 'I don't want anybody. I can't give you anything. I don't even want anything. It's all the same. You used me for your own happiness.' And then pointing at me, she said, 'He used me simply as a means. Just like any other man would have.'

'As a means?' I said, dumbstruck.

'Yeah, just like any other man would have. They all lie and scamper and feed on the bits of the eternal waste.'

'What the fuck did I do?' I asked.

'Well, for starters, Kotha Naresh ji,' Zafar said, 'You kidnapped and harboured three underaged girls with that looney small-town gangster Bahubali a few years ago, and then to escape jail time, you came here.'

I stood there in silence. I hadn't heard that title in ages.

'Look at this article, my dear Staci,' he said, presenting a newspaper article about me that had appeared a few years ago: 'This moron is not even Moron. His real name is Kotha Naresh. Having pleaded guilty to three counts of slave trading, three counts of human trafficking, two counts of child pornography, and two counts of distribution of child pornography among public institutions, three counts of sodomy, and one count of harbouring a fugitive terrorist in the basement.'

Dr Dean raised his sweaty forehead and gave me a look of pure admiration.

I began shaking my head vehemently. It's surprising how the script of your life when seen from a linear, logical, and saner perspective, seems so fucking contrary to the kind of imagination you weave around it.

Zafar continued, 'And then before that, you had been a married man. You have a wife. And you ran away from her? Like you didn't feel even a pinch of shame in leaving your little wife? Your friend Zahed is too bad at keeping secrets. He just spilled everything. Well, let it be.'

'What is he doing these days?' I asked sorrowfully.

'The guy took up your path. Became a psychiatrist. Told me to tell you that he will visit you soon.'

'You mean,' I said, 'he knows I'm here?'

'Of course. But I'm assuming that you will be in jail soon. Or in Ward A.'

'Ward A, sir,' Dr Dean concurred. 'We can't let him go. He knows too much.'

'Well,' I said, 'I'm just glad that she will be gone tomorrow. That she will be free. It's fine if I die inside. It really is. I'm just glad that she will be gone for good.' Then I raised my head and looked at Staci, wondering if this had stirred something in her.

It hadn't.

'Well, Zafar boy, how did you break your funny nose?' I asked, looking at his spiteful face. 'You mind telling her? Who broke that nose of yours? Oh damn yes, I did,' I said, throwing my hands up and shaking my hips in my little victory dance. 'I did because they were giving you heroin, Staci. Even inside this asylum, they were never really treating you. They were running the morphine on you with the medicines. And of course, as I had previously pointed out, they were running the morphine on you with those injections. And they will keep running morphine on you, even if you are let go today. Even if you are discharged, just please don't go with this asshole Zafar. This guy will never keep you happy. He just wants to tame you.'

'That's fucking nonsense, you fucking small dogshit imposter,' Zafar barked.

Now, my dear, I have been a docile, faithful storyteller. I'm a humble man. As humble in real life as in this story. But that day when I saw tears roll down from those angelic eyes of my lover, I just couldn't hold it. I took off my shoes and threw them straight at the star of twenty-six films, and they landed right on his chest.

'Oh wow, so that's it from you, I guess,' Zafar said, 'You still want this looney, Staci?! Ha? Baby, answer me?'

'How dare you "baby" her, you cheap cocksucking hen-fucking son of a whore?' I said.

'I'm just so tired. So fucking done with all this mess. I don't want anybody really,' Staci whimpered. I think this was the first time we heard Staci as herself.

'That's fine with me,' I said.

'Were you really a married man?' Staci asked me. 'Why did you run away from your wife?'

'On the day I faked my death and walked away from my miserable wife,' I told Staci, 'I thought I was walking out of a won battle. I thought I had survived and endured life, and now that I didn't have anything to lose, I could live my life like a carefree maniac who looks at twisting falling leaves and claps thunderously because, after all, those are the small gifts of life. But my mightiest discovery had been…' But before I could finish, I heard a familiar irritating noise: this old knock, knock, knock,

knock, which sounded like the huge broken fan from the dining hall.

'But my mightiest discovery,' I told Staci, 'is that I learned that you truly begin to live on the day when you have actually lost everything. Life begins when death finishes.'

And then I told Staci everything. About Boston. About Tania. About Noel and her Nepal. About Bahubali. Fuck. I even told her about Santos.

Dr Dean and Zafar stood and heard me with uninterrupted attention. And then once I was done, Staci said in a softer tone, 'So if my calculations are right and if we were to totally believe in your narrative, then I'm assuming that you are still a virgin?'

'Why would you bring that up right now?'

'It's just funny. It all makes sense.'

'What makes sense?' I asked.

'That you are a scholarly virgin.'

'Well, all I can say,' I told her, 'is that my wife was so miserable that even street dogs and wild animals around my neighbourhood could easily find an outlet to let their sexual perversity out but not me.'

I was just glad that Staci was laughing again. It's funny sometimes that what you end up making the biggest deal of your life can sometimes be small enough to be laughed at.

'And honestly,' I said, 'I'm fucking scared to fall in love. I was actually just hoping you got out. I just want you to be out. It's fine if they kill me. Fuck even death is scary when somebody would miss you. There is nobody left in this world to miss me. But you, you should be out.'

'I love you,' she said faintly, mimicking it from her soft pink lips.

'Hell, Staci. I love you more, honey. I really do. I'm so sorry. I love you so much,' I said.

'But aren't you still married?' she asked.

'See Staci,' I explained, 'you are a British actress with a valid passport and a working visa for our motherland India. But the lady I married at that time, she didn't have citizenship for India. She was an illegal immigrant along with her entire family. Plus, we never registered the marriage. So she isn't and wasn't my wife at any point in time.'

'Ah,' Staci's face broke into a smile of relief.

'Hell, damn it, send both these bastards to Ward A,' Zafar groaned suddenly, looking at Dr Dean. 'Let them copulate and stink and die. Even this bitch isn't off heroin yet. I'm sure there should be no problem in, you know,' he said, 'notching up her treatment.'

'No problem at all,' Dr Dean said, 'We had already taken her samples today. The results should be coming to us anytime now. They would be sufficient to prove that she has been taking morphine even under the strictest of regimens. And, of course, there are cuts all over her hands and her legs, so we can safely ship them both to Ward A.'

I know it was an intimidating situation. Almost deadly. Almost fatal. But something about that entire arrangement was really wrong. Because the sound of that mighty exhaust from the dining was now very near me, and I felt that the dimensions had changed, and all of a sudden, I was practically in the dining hall from three days ago.

'The reports won't show shit,' I said. 'I changed her morphine with my pills weeks ago. I knew you were up to some shit right after I was done reading your stupid love letter, you stupid bastard.'

'What?' Dr Dean exclaimed.

'What the fuck!' Zafar yelled.

'No, sir. It's not possible. This bastard is lying. We at Clemency's ensure that our patients are taking all their medicines in their routine order.'

'Yes, sir,' I said. 'I have been taking that morphine for the last two weeks now. Quite a garden my life has become, I must say.' I looked at Staci, and her eyes were all tears.

'Send them off to Ward A, these cocksuckers,' Zafar screamed.

'Ward boy!' Dr Dean screamed, calling for the mighty ward boys just in case I planned to break Dr Dean's nose now.

'Code Red, ward boy!'

And the knock, knock, knock of the exhaust fan came to an excruciating intensity, and there he was—Harrison boy dressed in a proper ward boy's uniform with a mighty fan for a chainsaw in his butcher hands. Having blown away the mighty effects of functional fixedness, I reckoned how he used to cry and scream every day for the last five years whenever he crossed the dining hall because it was not really the knocking of the fan that harassed him. It's just that he deemed that to be a fit weapon for his plan of mass murder. And I remembered how he had asked Dr Dean to get that fan off from the kitchen as his birthday gift. And now here it was, his whirring fan attached to a small iron rod, and then I remembered how two weeks earlier he had volunteered to clean and wipe everybody's cars.

I remembered the tossing of Zafar's Maybach keys in the air that afternoon and then Harrison Brown removing the 100pr batteries from the Maybach, which he had hung on his classy Kolossal schoolbag to power his chainsaw. Amazed at the brilliant whirring of the fan and mightily scared of this boy, I tried looking for that glance of our mutual understanding and agreement in his eyes, but really all his eyes screamed was red murder.

He had planned to kill everyone at Clemency's. Then, right before my horrified eyes, even before Zafar could finish his sentence, Harrison Brown drove a fan straight into his stomach. Zafar only managed to get out the word 'Motherfucker' before the chainsaw ripped through his body. As Harrison pulled it free from Zafar's mutilated torso, a spray of blood splattered across Staci's face. She sat frozen on her bed, her eyes wide with shock and disgust. Dr Dean's life was taken with a grim sense of reverence, almost like it was an ode to some dark poetry. Harrison Brown swung hard, striking Dr Dean's sweat-glistening head. Then, without uttering a word, he paused and laughed. I glanced at Staci—her lips now tightly pressed together, hands covering her mouth. Her hair gently swayed in the breeze from the exhaust fan.

I thought Staci and I were next. But then Harrison Brown just stopped for a bit, and in his eyes, I caught a glimpse of guilt and helplessness. He was a child. Just a child. This was something he had to do. There was no other way towards his redemption. And somewhere I figured that in his eyes, there was still innocence. Vulnerability. A virtue I believe we both shared. A virtue I believe very few people share. I think that's why he let us live.

'Oh, I almost forgot,' I said.

'What?' Staci asked.

'Happy Birthday, Harrison boy. I forgot to wish you.' But Harrison Brown had already left, and the knock-knock of the fan was now playing in a separate block.

I looked at Staci. 'But I don't know what will happen to us tomorrow,' I said.

'That's true,' she said, still looking at me. Harrison's killing spree finally produced Clemency's first code red, and sirens were blazing across the asylum. Though our secret was now cut like a birthday cake, we still looked at each other in bafflement because tomorrow there would be a new doctor in the hospital, and I would be sent to a different hospital with a different ward. By the time I could go near Staci, the ward boys rushed in.

Dr Dean's skull had evacuated itself on the ground, and the boys looked at us in horror. Staci screamed and said, 'There. He has run into Ward B. Please save us.'

'Don't worry, madam,' one of the ward boys said, panting and still looking at the corpses in disbelief. The police are on the way. The new doctor has arrived. He was supposed to start work from tomorrow. But he is stepping in right away. I request you to kindly remain inside. Moron boy!' he said, looking at me, 'better look after her until we have the situation under control.' Before the boys could leave, a few more ward boys came in. And then the third event of the last night finally being set in motion, the new doctor had entered our room, and eyes were crossed and met, and behind his finally grown-up beard, I saw Dr Zahed finally looking at me with equal horror, as much as I was horrified upon knowing that the new doctor had come.

'That should be all, gentlemen,' Zahed said with his eyes still fixed on mine, 'Please control the situation in Ward B. Well, good evening, Ms Staci.' He greeted Staci, ignoring me completely until everybody else had left.

Zahed then looked at me and muttered, 'Five fucking years, young Moron.'

'Zahed,' I said with tears rolling down from my eyes.

'Five fucking years. I came as soon as I knew you were here, boy.'

'Wait, you both know each other?' Staci said.

And we looked at each other, recalling Staci's monochrome onyx eau de toilette ad from the dorm of our university.

'What is happening exactly over here?' he asked.

'Well, we are lovers, and I was about to let you know if,' I said, 'Mhmm ... if you could please leave us for some time.'

And then someone screamed from the outside, 'Bahubali has run away, sir. A patient from Ward A is missing.'

'Well,' Staci said laughing, 'Your Moron is still a virgin, and he shall remain to be until you ... you know, go and find that other patient.'

'Well, madam, there are a lot of cops outside. I lost this boy for five years. And looking at the situation right now, really, I am ready to lose him for another five, but I just hope you both will take good care of each other. You both must run away. I will erase your files. You both will be shown as discharged from Clemency's, and I'm hoping I will see you all in your home after things have quietened in here. Goodbye.'

I looked at this grown man, Zahed, fixing his medico coat, bidding his final goodbye as he left, shutting the door behind him.

'I'm wet,' she said.

'Even now? You are not even on morphine,' I said. *Patients on morphine withdrawal are susceptible to night-time sweats and extreme temperature fluctuations. With her, sometimes the sweating used to be so profuse that she needed to change her robe multiple times.*

She looked at me as if I were really a madman. 'I'm fucking wet. Loose your stupid virginity, you stupid Moron,' she said suddenly. And I reckoned that being from the world of dramatics if there was something that really could have aroused Staci, it would have been a true materialization of true murders and true reunions, which they otherwise are trained to fake in the cinema.

So I let life be. I held her warm, fudgy face and fixed her hair while she took off her top, revealing her perfect athletic body, and she took my hands and put them inside her knickers, and I felt what Bahubali had told me not long ago: 'A true pussy is a pussy which feels like home.'

So really ignoring the familiar whirring of a 35 mm camera (this distant noise that came from outside the window), I think all of us, finally, in the end—my Staci, Harrison Brown, even that escaped artist from Ward A, and I—found our solace.

6

A world of fantastic turbulence came crashing down behind us as Staci and I ran hand in hand through the storm of red sirens that filled the once-enchanted place I had entered two years ago with Bahubali. Outside, Zahed's car was parked in silence. It was the same old Sumo from the University. Our old dutiful sumo still shining as ever. And beside it, stood the figure I had forgotten long ago. The same old Santos. Seeing me running away with Ms Staci, I believe, he was so damn stunned that he could barely utter a word. He just stood there gaping at us in shock and disbelief. Once, I figure, when he had realized that the lady I was running with was not just any girl who just happened to resemble a megastar like Staci but Ms Staci herself, he gave me a sly friendly smile. Then he proceeded to touch his chest with both his hands and bow down in respect and honour. Still running, I waved at him from a distance. He waved back.

By the time we were nearing the main road, there was total silence in the backdrop. I think Harrison Brown would have likely come to a halt, and our Santos would have run to Zahed to inform him about the unfathomable sighting. Seeing him all awestruck again, dearly Zahed would have laughed and groaned because, after all, such were the affairs of our teenage sex-deprived, optimistic, pimple-ridden lives at one point in time.

We ran and ran for a few kilometres and then stopped suddenly and looked back and then at each other because, 'Really, why were we running? Was there any reason to run anymore? Was there any reason to run at all?'

A mighty shimmering truck sped past, leaving a cloud of dust in the ghostly streets. We stood there, unsure of what lay ahead—because what do you do when the journey has only ended? When death has come and gone, and life is just beginning?

'Have you seen my house?' I asked Staci.

'No silly. How can I?'

'Let me take you there.'

We had abandoned our homes long before life had started. Over the course of the next two days, we traversed incognito as shady backpackers. I think it was only on the second evening when we were in a secretive cab being driven to Delhi. She had a face mask on, but still, the poor old man driver of worldly wisdom couldn't help but stare at my angelic lover from the rear-view mirror (and not long ago there was another driver in another cab looking at my wife while she was nestling in her boss's arms). All of a sudden, thunder reverberated, and a bird learnt to fly from its nest that we were reminded, 'Eureka! We are rich!' Staci's money had been preserved carefully in some Swiss bank, the papers of which were kept safely in some locker in Delhi.

'How much do you think we have?

'About 250 million dollars,' she said a little too loudly. We were still in Agra, some three hours away from Delhi, but our driver ignored us like we were either on the way to the sanatorium or escaping from it. Though it did sound crazy, and we were still crazy, but then what had not been crazy? Insanity diffuses and sublimates but never leaves.

In the night when she was asleep, with her head resting on my shoulders, her pointy nails clawing at my t-shirt, she suddenly woke up in a haze. 'I think I'm going to quit acting. I want a family. I want to leave something worthwhile in this world.'

'I think, after one last film? Does that sound good?'

'But what would it be about?'

'About Clemency's and about Harrison Brown.'

'And the hills of Nepal and your unforgettable wife. About Dr Dean.'

'Haha! About Bahubali.' I faintly remembered that Bahubali had probably recorded us in the act. What else could have been a masterpiece, really? A twenty-four-year-old dead virgin copulating with the most prized damn beauty in the world. If that was the case, then I must retrieve his tape and destroy it.

After a day of travel, we realized that Zahed was going to delete our records anyway. As per the records of Clemency's, we were never brought there in the first place. We didn't exist in those files only. We were free. So why were we still hiding? Maybe it was just an old-time habit. I thought it would take a while for this habit to wear off. Though, by the time we reached Delhi, Staci was in her essence.

She dialled up some secretary of hers in Mumbai and asked for a jet to be sent to Delhi to fetch her. Sometimes, her existence overwhelmed me. For instance, when we were finally inside the Private Terminal of IGI, changing and fixing ourselves as if we were some enchanted rogues returning from a gruelling twenty-four-hour survival challenge in the Amazon. She emerged from her walk-in closet of our VIP suite room, wearing a white crop top, its straps curling around one shoulder while the other remained bare. Her perfectly round bosoms, once hailed as the National Treasure of our country, were a sight to behold, and I found myself mesmerized by the curves of her sleek abdomen in wild disbelief.

It was probably half past six when her private jet hit the tarmac against the endlessly glistening lights of Delhi's IGI terminal. The crowd at the terminal broke into pandemonium the moment a simple young fellow, who was drinking some fancy coffee had raised his head and spotted Staci. Here was the sudden discovery of a movie star, and of course, the first duty of a man is to announce and alert everyone to the presence of a celebrity. So he screamed, 'Oh that's Ms Staci!' Then, a schoolgirl screamed on seeing Staci and almost collapsed under a dizzy spell. Someone apparently broke away from the racks of the Relay Store (chips and chocolates scattered like ding ding Christmas night), and within five minutes, we were mobbed by hundreds of people, all screaming and clamouring. We wondered what on earth had gone wrong with the world.

I grew a little perplexed; I thought maybe they would pounce upon us right away. The world is no different from a mad house. Always a risk of getting pounced upon these days. But she held my hands and looked at me in such delight that I knew right then, in the most literal sense, what I had meant one day when I had told Zahed on our way to Phoebe's house party: that I was going to own this world in this white t-shirt.

Very soon, these pictures would end up on Noel's phone without me even thinking of sending them to her. I would be alive.

'I want to shift to Switzerland. It's so peaceful. It's so different. They have assisted suicide legal over there.'

'So?'

'So if I bother you much, you can always visit their counter.'

She was in love with me. I knew it because, as soon as she had said it, I saw an ache taking over her face. The turbulence over the flying zone was extreme, and we did have sex again; after all, we were all by ourselves in her twelve-seater Bombardier jet. But I think most of the excitement and neuroticism about the overall act was done two nights ago. Honestly, I didn't even want to fuck her or enact all my fantasies on her. I just wanted to listen to her. No matter if she was moaning ecstatically or joking loudly in her shrewd dark ways.

Sometimes people ask me what it took to endear a celebrity as great as Staci. I can't break away from my monologue to tell you some enchanted secret of which I had been made aware. But I can however tell you this. Behind those shimmering, glossy TV screens, behind the old Windows 98 monitor in Bahubali's house, Staci was real. Her dream of the Swiss Alps was real. The wars in Afghanistan and Iraq were real. Someday, in the summer, I want to go to Iraq and fire a few rounds from a semi-automatic, only to grasp that there exists a world beyond imagination where our dreams and fears are tangible.

Through all my suffering, these realities existed just a few kilometres away from my disoriented mind, which was so enmeshed in its own turmoil that it couldn't sense the truth beyond the confines of my hospital room.

When we landed at the Bodh Gaya Terminal, I asked, 'Was I a coward to run away from my life?'

To which Staci replied, 'It was outrageously fantastic to disappear. Most people only imagine and masturbate with those kinds of ideas. You did it. Ha!'

Faking death is not illegal or punishable under any jurisdiction.

At the Bodh Gaya airport, a matte black two-seater Merc AMG came rumbling and gurgling because well she was some star, wasn't she? She won't take a rickshaw home until of course, it's to raise a charity of some two million dollars. Even the saintly monks would have probably gotten a permanent spot on their conscience just by the mere sight of her walking towards that damned racing monster.

If you actually start living the way you dream, you would think of yourself as an imposter.

Four solid years of my absence had turned my home into wilderness. It hurts me to tell you how the changes were so drastic and belittling. Wild mosses had overgrown and had turned the lower parts of the wall green. Staci held my hands as we walked in as if she were imagining herself on a film set and there was a 300 mm Imax camera rolling around. She stared at my face with one of those reassuring looks that portray that the actress is totally and madly in love with the hero. But I don't think she was acting. In fact, Staci was not even Staci anymore. Hell, my home was not even home anymore. It had changed, and seeing it in this dreadful condition almost broke my heart. I had deserted so much to let life take over. Zahed. The university. My father's grave. I shook myself free and ran, and there it was, a grey stone over his tomb (I remembered how I had spent three days in choosing the grey tombstone), but that had not changed. I have come to learn that, unlike mine, death is the only permanence. Even Staci would evaporate someday. I hope that day is not sooner or earlier than my death. I would not want to leave another wife in this world for these crazy bastards to devour. A stray crow croaked and welcomed me.

'I think we can convert it into some fantastic old age home. Do you think you would want to come back here?'

'Would you stay here with me forever?'

'Yeah,' she said, a heartfelt smile breaking across her face. It was probably the most reassuring smile in the world. 'We can buy farms around. Raise chickens and have a few dogs.'

I know she wanted to move to Switzerland. But seeing her change her plan with such suddenness made me realize that probably she could do anything and everything for me. Hell, she did actually love me. That was all the reassurance I needed. It's not like I intended to stay here either.

A rickety armchair lay on the veranda, and the door of the house was shut with the same old lock Zahed had brought for the house. I thought I knew where Noel would have put the keys to the house. She always put it right beneath a marble meditating Buddha, but before I could go and fetch it, Staci—my rockstar—hit the lock with a rock so hard that the entire lock came cracking down. She winked at me—clearly, she loved this small mess she had created.

Inside there were debris and fragments of my haunted marriage. Noel had peaceably left the house as if she intended to return. When I inspected our own room (without intending to really know about Noel), I found a magnificent large painting of myself on the wall. The ones they use to commemorate the dead. And right beneath the painting, in the self-same model, there was a single pillow preserved along with a few well-tucked linen sheets (had she lived some saintly life after I had left, I wondered). Sometimes I wonder if the Cemetery House has brought more bad to me than good. The death of my father. A broken marriage. Things of that sort. But then I figure, had it not been for the Cemetery House and my horrible marriage, I would have never faked my death. I would have never become the pimp I was. I would have never ended up in Clemency's. I would have never met Staci. So then I realized that maybe Noel was not really a curse. I mean, she was a curse back then. But she was not a curse that was to last forever.

Being an actress has its own perks. No matter if the downfall can be dramatic. But when the trajectory is going upwards, there are a lot of impossible things that can be arranged overnight. For instance, a new life. That evening while we were sitting by my father's grave, Staci called her secretary again in Mumbai who then connected her to somebody from an embassy in New Delhi. After the call was concluded, she announced that a new passport and a new identity had been generated for me.

'Oh hell!' I said. 'What would be my new name?'

'We aren't changing names,' she said. 'Moron is good enough.'

Sometimes I sit on the porch of my house studio in Geneva and wonder if Noel was a bad person. Did she live happily after I left? But Staci tells me that it is my head's own way of making things more intimidating and threatening for me. So I have just left it to a final divine note: 'She just left. It just didn't work out.'

I still sometimes plan and even book tickets to the Gaya Airport because I intend to travel (sometimes even alone just to see my dead father). You can always put a bunch of fresh flowers on a grave. A correspondence with Zahed later on revealed that Noel had married some Nepali resort keeper from Namchi. Some scrawny guy with a responsible outlook towards life. I imagined that if she had subsisted in some marriage after my stupidity, she would even have had a baby by now. When I asked Zahed why he thought she never stayed in the Cemetery House, he told me quite simply that 'no man would readily live under the shadows of another man (except me)'.

In the winter, Lake Geneva presents a very candescent sight. It never freezes, but you can't put your mouth under a toppling water fountain and gulp on its humane water. Tourists swarm and buzz, and there are loud bakeries with molten Swiss chocolate and cheese. There was an incident only a few months ago when, by some rebuke of nature, there was a giant fire over the Alpine Hills of Switzerland. But the government was so pious that they arranged for an individual airlift for each and every Mooing Swiss Cattle, which was at risk of getting eschewed and barbequed in those mountains.

I have also come to learn surprisingly that after I had gotten everything in my hands, I find happiness and humour in the smaller things, like the Swiss cheese or the rescuing of cattle in distant mountains. Hell, I feel the tremors of an earthquake coming. I am Mason Moron, and my wife is telling me to end my story right here because she is sleepy as hell, and quite practically it is impossible for her to sleep until I hold her from behind and sleep with her. I could die happily now as her bigger spoon.

Epilogue

Dear Son,

It would as a matter of fact startle you to know that I had dreamt of you while I was a kid (virgin, loser, no pimples though, thanks to Jesus!) and I was serving my time in this dark sanatorium. I had to steal your mother from another man. Every decision you take will change the course of the future. Every time you decide to fall in love, it will probably be the genesis of an altogether different son in the future. For instance, had I ended up manufacturing you with my previous wife (Oh! I tried my best but thankfully the process only didn't happen, son). I loved that lady Noel deeply, but sometimes I imagine the horrible, detestable course in which I would have raised you with that wicked (bad word). I shrivel up, and then only a great sigh of relief leaves me when I finally see your actual mother at the dinner table.

I don't know if these rains would mesmerize you or whether you would despair someday because some girl from down the road would have crippled your little heart. But wherever and whenever that happens, I need you to understand that we all are living our lives for the first time, and therefore we are all doomed.

Anyway, I need you to understand that I will always love you, and your mother will always love you. Our love won't need the resplendent medium of a scenery or a song; our love would be with you irrespective of time and space.

Moron

Acknowledgements

I am grateful to Sherill, who taught me so much about life, childhood, loyalty, and love; you will always remain in my heart.

To my mom my dad for always believing in me.

To Avani, whose brother became a recluse but emerged stronger; I am sorry I couldn't be there for you. I can't believe you've grown so much! Damn, you are getting a job next year!

To Anamika, who made me believe in love, kindness, and humanity all over again.

To my maternal grandmother, Asha Jaiswal, whom I promised on her deathbed that I would touch people's heart someday.

To Praveen Tiwari, publishing director at BluOne Ink, who told me eight years ago that I could be a writer. He was the first person to see a spark in me. I am glad that you are my publisher. To Shreya Chakraborti, the copy editor, for bringing fresh insights into and tying loose ends in the narrative.

To Irshad Uncle for turning my dreams into reality. To Sumi Aunty for understanding the child in me.

To Neem Karoli Baba, who inspired me day and night and took my anxiety away.

To all my readers, thank you.

About the Author

Rithwik Aryan has the distinction of being one of the quickest dropouts of Harvard Extension School, Harvard University. He exited the hallowed institution within three months of starting his bachelor's degree in psychology to pursue a career in writing. It took him five years to meticulously craft his debut novel, *Out of Madness,* during which one-and-a-half years he spent inside two of India's most dangerous mental asylums—The Central Institute of Psychiatry and The Agra Mental Asylum—to bring to bear the hyper realistic elements of the setting in the narrative.